Property of Stone

Kings of Anarchy MC: Pennsylvania

Jeanne St. James

***

Credits:
Cover Artist: Gchelle Designs
Photographer: Emma Jane Photography
Cover Model: Josh Lamech
Editor: Encompass Press
Beta Readers: Author BJ Alpha, Lisa Figueroa, Nickiann Holt

***

www.jeannestjames.com

Sign up for my newsletter for insider information, author news, and new releases:
https://www.authorjeannestjames.com/

**Sign up for my newsletter for insider information, author news, and new releases:
https://www.authorjeannestjames.com/**

Anarchy - Where the Kings rule in chaos

Respect the Mother Chapter
Your loyalty stays with your patch
Brotherhood above all
Never touch another brother's ol' lady
Ride or die, no questions asked
Never back down from a fight
Never let a brother ride solo
Each chapter sets its own damn rules

Nobody fucks with the Kings

www.kingsofanarchymc.com

Glossary of Terms

Sled - biker slang for a motorcycle

Cage - bike slang for a vehicle with four wheels instead of two.

Strange/Randoms - sexual partners who are strangers/random people

Bid - Prison term

VIN - Vehicle Identification Number

CO - correctional officer/prison guard

MC Chapter - The National club with a National exec committee (President, VP, etc)

MC Charter - Each charter is run independently, does not answer to a mother charter or a national chapter

Sweet butt - A club girl. They hang around the MC and service the patched members in different ways

House mouse - normally a young woman who lives with a member for free in exchange for cleaning and keeping up his house

Chop shop - illegal garage that strips down stolen vehicles and sells the parts for profit

OEM - Original Equipment Manufacturer

Ol' lady - A woman considered property of a club member, similar to wife or girlfriend

PFA - Protection From Abuse order

STD - Sexually Transmitted Disease

Screw - Prison guard

Cuck - an insult meaning a weak or submissive man

Character List
Dead Man's Hollow, Pennsylvania Chapter:

<u>Officers:</u>
President - Ransom
VP - Stone
SAA/Enforcer - Ogre
Secretary - Lick
Treasurer - Outlaw
Road Captain - Wheels

<u>Other patched members mentioned:</u>
Chopper - runs the chop shop
Wrecker - runs the tow truck/steals cars
Bones - Former Army medic
Patch
Grim
Bolt
Devil Dog
Torch
Striker

Prospects mentioned:

Nut Sack

Gooch

Squid

Stinky

Shit stain

Sweet butts/club girls:

Juicy

Flaps

Swallow

Windy

Loosey

Slick - Head sweet butt

Prologue

Cast the First Stone

With his eyes scanning side to side, Stone strode through the parking lot of The Shoppes at Susquehanna Marketplace. A busy Saturday couldn't be a better time. But he sure as hell wasn't there to shop.

Fuck no.

The lot was packed with the types of cages Chopper needed. Since Stone happened to be down in Harrisburg earlier today to do a "collection," he figured he'd tool through some of the local malls to hunt for some rich fuckers' vehicles on his way back north.

The parts for luxury rides always brought in more scratch, but they also had more anti-theft shit, making them a fucking headache to pinch. But if the model was worth it, they found a way to steal it, since it would bring in a fuckload of scratch for their club's coffers.

Usually, Wrecker was stealth enough with either their self-loading Ford F-550, a plain, black, unmarked tow truck, or the Snatcher hydraulic setup installed in the bed of an unassuming F-350 pickup.

Either way, Wrecker was a pro on getting in, getting out, and getting the fuck going without getting pinched by the pigs or catching a bullet between the eyes from an overzealous owner. His club brother could steal a cage in under a minute, which was goddamn impressive.

Of course, all those rich motherfuckers had insurance and no doubt would be compensated fairly for their vehicle's permanent disappearance.

Stone ducked between two vehicles and spotted a Mercedes C-Class parked right fucking next to a BMW 3 Series, two of the easiest sedans to steal and always owned by douchebags.

How about that fucking luck?

He pursed his lips and slowly walked behind them both, keeping his cell phone low and inconspicuous as he snapped photos of their license plates.

Luckily, Devil Dog's ol' lady worked at the Department of Motor Vehicles and had access to run those registrations, making stealing cars even easier. She provided the home or business address of the vehicles they scouted and, *BOOM*, Wrecker stole it, giving Chopper more cages for him and his crew to strip down.

It only took them about an hour to dismantle a four-door douche-mobile. Those high and mighty assholes probably spent more time than that at the dealership when they bought the fucking thing.

Once the VINs were rendered illegible with a torch, the parts were sold to the highest bidder. That could be either on the black market, or to a local garage or body shop that didn't give a shit about where the part came from as long as it was untraceable. Local shops could charge their customers a premium for that OEM replacement part after buying it for a steal.

The Kings also recently hooked up with an individual with connections so they could sell high-dollar parts overseas. That had been a hell of a score for his club.

He sneered up at the sun. It was too ball-sweating hot today to be doing this kind of shit on foot. He dug into the front pocket of his jeans, pulled out a black elastic hair tie and secured his messy long hair into an equally messy knot at the back of his head.

That was better.

He scanned the parking lot again for either pigs or rent-a-pigs, AKA mall security. They were probably on a donut break. With his head back on a swivel, he worked his way down a few more rows, quickly snapping photos of potential targets as he went.

He never paused behind a vehicle for more than a second or two. He *never* wore his fucking cut. And when doing a collection job or other illegal shit, he always swapped out his sled's plate with one of the hundreds of fake ones they kept on hand. Luckily, some of his brothers had learned how to make plates in prison, a priceless skill learned while being *rehabilitated.*

Not him, though. Those CO cucks didn't trust him enough to allow him one of those jobs. He had no idea why.

A grin threatened to curve his lips.

Until he remembered how much being in the hole for bad behavior sucked. Being stuck in solitary confinement meant he had no one to fuck with, besides himself, or any *wet-behind-the-ears* screws.

Out of the corner of his eye, he spotted a pretty slit climbing out of a cage at the far end of the parking lot. Her ride wasn't worth stealing, that was for damn sure, but he wasn't interested in that. He was more focused on riding the woman now opening the back driver's side door on an old Honda Pilot.

Fuck yeah. He wouldn't mind one long, sweaty night with that piece. Her ass in those shorts was—

Oh, fuck no.

When she reached into the back seat, she helped a whole damn nut nugget out of the cage. He might be mini-sized baggage, but still baggage Stone didn't want to deal with. Even for one night.

Kids could create issues when he was wrecking some plump, juicy pussy. Assuming they weren't a damn cockblock in the first place.

He should know.

Fuck that shit.

He could find another cunt for his dick to fill. Because fuck if it would be that one.

He shook his head. *Damn shame.*

But that didn't mean he couldn't check out her sweet tits. Or enjoy an eyeful of the smooth bare legs he'd like sandwiching his face as she reached into the back seat again. She kept one hand locked on the kid while pulling out what looked like an overnight bag.

Then his goddamn view was blocked by some asshole who had parked right next to her and got out.

Weird that they were the only two vehicles in the farthest area of the lot. There was no reason for the dick to park right next to her with all the empty spots elsewhere. Unless...

Stone narrowed his eyes, took them in for a second, then headed toward his sled on the other side of the lot while still keeping them in his sights. The newcomer could be some trafficker wanting to snatch the kid or the woman, or, *fuck,* both. Despite the lot being busy, it was fucking stupid of her to park in an isolated area.

He hopped on his sled and after his girl roared to life, he began heading in that direction.

By the time he could see their vehicles again, he was still several rows away. He kept one eye on them and the other watching for cages backing out of spots and distracted pedestrians. Getting struck by a clueless driver or running over Sally Shopper was not on his list of things to do today.

But what he saw next made him forget everything else in that fucking parking lot. It also made him scowl.

And caused his blood pressure to spike.

The man was now in her damn face. They weren't having a civil conversation, either. Fuck no. The dickhead was yelling at her.

He couldn't hear what was being shouted, but that shit didn't matter. By her worried expression it, whatever it was, wasn't good.

She turned in what appeared to be an attempt to ignore him and leaned inside the Honda again. The asshole continued to crowd her and spew whatever bullshit he was spewing.

She had to know him. If a stranger approached any woman Stone knew shouting like that, the asshole's balls would find themselves deeply embedded in his body cavity. So deep that it would take surgical intervention to locate them again.

He had no fucking clue how she was keeping her shit together; he was on the verge of losing his and he wasn't even involved.

His eyes flicked down to the kid to see him now bawling.

Stone slipped his Harley into a spot with a clear view of the two vehicles and shut it down, but remained straddling his sled.

Since the man hadn't put his hands on the woman or kid

yet, it would be smart if Stone kept his distance and only observed. But his gut was screaming that something was way the fuck off here.

When she turned after finding whatever she'd been searching for in the Honda, she was gripping a light-blue stuffed elephant.

The moment she offered it to the kid, Stone saw her flinch right before the man backhanded her. Her head jerked violently from the impact and the elephant went flying through the air.

Goddamn, that had to fucking hurt.

Holding a hand to her cheek, she stared at the asshole with wide eyes and a gaping mouth.

Before Stone could even react, she grabbed her kid and was encouraging him to climb back into the Honda. Only, the man stopped her by grabbing her arm, whipping her around and punching her right in the fucking face, knocking her to the pavement.

What the actual fuck?

Stone ground his teeth and threw his leg over his sled. It was time to get involved.

He could no longer see her face. She had covered it with her hands trying to protect it from further blows, since the man still stood over her and continued to wail on her like he'd lost his goddamn mind.

As his legs quickly ate up the distance to where they were parked, a man to his left yelled, "Don't worry, I already called 9-1-1."

Don't fuckin' worry? "Motherfuckin' pussy," he growled.

Don't fucking worry, he'd handle it.

The asshole was now leaning over her, screaming and shaking a finger at her. That finger needed to be broken. Or severed. Or shoved up his fucking ass.

When the man straightened, Stone's pace went from urgent into crisis mode.

"Fuck you, asshole!" Stone yelled, trying to pull Asshole's attention when he didn't get there in time to stop him from kicking her ribs while she was still down.

Her body heaved and rocked from each impact.

For fuck's sake.

The motherfucker was so focused on the bleeding, injured woman, he was ignoring the kid and the fact that Stone was closing in on him with his fingers curled into tight fists, his jaw set, and his rage racing through every vein in his fucking body.

He had no idea who this fucker was to her, but that was a detail he couldn't give a shit about. What mattered was that he violently put his hands on a woman.

Ignoring the kid hiccup-sobbing for his mother, Stone remained laser-focused on the threat.

"Pick on someone your own goddamn size," he growled, coming in hot.

The blond-haired man spun to face Stone. "Who the fuck are—"

Before he could finish, Stone's fist said, *"Hello, howya doin'?"* to that big-ass nose and it exploded like an over-ripened tomato. Out loud, he answered, "Someone your own goddamn size."

Unfortunately, Asshole, now holding his crushed nose, was still upright. Something needed to be done about that, since that wasn't fucking acceptable.

Stone wiggled his fingers, trying to lure him out from between the vehicles and away from the woman and her son. But when Asshole didn't move, Stone grabbed his shirt and yanked him off balance before throwing him to the pavement behind the Pilot.

Now he had a better view of the woman and saw she had been knocked the fuck out.

Stone's narrowed gaze sliced back to Asshole and the world around him disappeared.

Once consumed by rage, he couldn't easily turn it back off, and this jackass deserved everything dished out to him.

Since Stone had no medical training, he couldn't help the woman, except in one way...revenge. And he'd be glad to dole it out.

He turned to see the man back on his feet and cursing him out, despite it being muffled due to his busted nose.

There was plenty more where that came from.

Stone stalked forward. "You feel like a goddamn man when you hit a woman?"

"She deserved it. She was trying to—"

"Don't give a fuck 'bout your reason. Whatever it is, it ain't fuckin' valid."

"Fuck you!"

One side of Stone's mouth pulled up. "Ain't gonna fuck you, but gonna fuck you up."

"You do and—"

He was tired of the bitch's whining.

Stone's fist automatically shot out and kissed Asshole's mouth this time, causing his legs to fold like an accordion when he crumpled to the ground.

"Guess you don't know how to duck and cover. Good for me, not good for you." Stone leaned down and tipped his ear forward. "Got nothin' to say now?"

A quick glance over at the still unconscious, bleeding woman and wailing kid brought a fresh wave of fury.

Grabbing Asshole's shirt, he hauled his ass back up. "Can't hit a man when he's fuckin' down, right?"

As Stone released his shirt, a right fist to the side of the head had the man hitting the pavement hard.

What a fuckin' pity.

But the fuck if he was done. This asshole needed a lesson he wouldn't soon forget.

Stone drop-kicked him in the ribs the same way he did the woman. Except Asshole hadn't been wearing heavy biker boots. His loafers didn't have quite the same impact.

His boots were great for stomping on roaches, too. And he'd never seen a bigger one than the one sprawled at his feet. So, he crushed it under the sole of his boot. Just to be safe, he did it again.

And one more for shits and giggles.

Once his rage lessened and reality began to return, he noticed the groaning man's head lolling back and forth. Asshole was bleeding from his nose, his mouth, even his ears.

Was he actually crying like a little bitch?

Now that was fucking embarrassing.

Bruises were already blooming on every inch of skin Stone could see not covered in blood. Asshole's eyes were swelling at a rapid rate. One cheek was split wide open from Stone's bulky rings and his lips wouldn't be yelling shit for a good while. He wouldn't be able to breathe through his nose anytime soon, either. The angle of his arm seemed to be a bit off, too.

Maybe Asshole was simply flexible.

Or maybe not.

"Hope you learned your fuckin' lesson," Stone growled and sucked a thick hocker from his nasal cavity into his mouth before spitting it on Asshole's face. "That's a little partin' gift from me to you."

Since Asshole was no longer an active threat, he didn't give him another glance. Instead, Stone approached the boy sitting on the ground next to his mother, clinging to her limp hand. "You okay, kid?"

With tears and snot covering his red face, the kid could only hiccup in answer. Once the high-pitched wails started again, Stone winced. *For fuck's sake.* He needed ear plugs. Or duct tape.

He squatted down and softly tapped the woman's unbruised cheek. "You in there?"

He brushed a lock of hair off her forehead and checked her pulse. It was strong. She was simply knocked out.

Stone had been there, done that, and woke up with a massive splitting headache. He had no doubt she'd experience the same. Luckily, he couldn't spot any broken bones. But that didn't mean she didn't have any.

"C'mon, wake the fuck up. Can't leave you here like this. Can't leave your kid alone." He sighed. He needed to get the fuck out of there before the pigs showed up. He tapped her cheek more firmly this time. "C'mon, woman. Don't got all fuckin' day. Wake the fuck up."

"M-m-mommy!" came another high-pitched wail.

At least her son could form words now. "Hey, kid, who's that mother—" *Fuck.* "Man?"

"He...he...he's my d-d-daddy." Another snot bubble expanded before popping like a damn overfilled balloon.

Jesus fucking Christ. How did that kid have any tears left? Or snot?

"Y-y-you hurt...him."

No shit. "Sorry, kid, but some lessons need to be learned the hard way." He tapped the mother's cheek again. "C'mon, woman, wake up." Why did women have to be so damn stubborn?

He *really* needed to get the fuck out of there.

Finally, her eyes fluttered open but remained unfocused. She was still out of it. Maybe even had a concussion.

He stood and offered his hand but every time she tried to grab it, she missed. So, he hauled her up and onto her feet, keeping a hold of her when she wobbled slightly. He propped her up against her Honda, making sure she didn't slide right back down into a heap.

"You okay?" He raked his gaze over her from top to toe. Blood soaked her blouse and her shorts. A sandal was missing and her sunglasses were gone.

She was going to have a hell of a shiner, a fat lip, and a couple of black eyes. Maybe even a few scars where her skin had split open. He was damn sure her ribs were at least bruised, if not broken.

She'd be hurting for a while. Most likely regretting her life choices. Like spitting out a nut nugget with a man who had no problem putting his hands on women. Especially the mother of his child. In front of the fucking kid, too. Couldn't be more of a piece of shit than that.

"Mommy!"

She winced when her boy squeezed in between them and hugged her thigh. Of course, still goddamn crying.

She placed a shaky hand on his head. "It's okay."

It wasn't. But if that was what the kid needed to hear to shut up, then whatever, lie to him. "Who's the piece of shit?"

Her already swelling eyes, one of them even had a blood spot developing, fell on the crumpled, unconscious asshole. "My ex."

"Why the fuck are you meetin' your asshole ex here with no one watchin' your fuckin' back?" Or packing heat.

"We meet here every Friday afternoon to exchange our son."

"Does it always go this fuckin' smoothly?"

She bared her teeth in a grimace. Yeah, he'd been there before. She had to be a fuckload of pain.

"I usually bring my mother. She's been sick and I couldn't find anyone else in time."

"You let that abusive cocksucker take your kid?"

Her head jerked back, then she winced. "I don't have a choice. It's court-ordered."

For fuck's sake. What fucking kangaroo court allowed that? Asshole shouldn't have visitations with a dead guppy that had been floating at the top of a fish bowl for the last thirty days, forget a living, breathing small human.

"You're bleeding," she whispered.

He glanced at his bloody knuckles. It was nothing. "Lot less than you." He pulled a bandana from his back pocket and shoved it at her. "Here. Press this against..." *Fuck.* Her eye, her nose, her mouth; she was bleeding in too many damn places. She could choose where to use it.

She took it and when she pressed it against her nose, she hissed in pain.

"You need to get yourself checked out. Gonna be hurtin' for a while. Now...it's been fuckin' fun but I gotta—"

That was when he heard it.

The goddamn sirens. The squealing tires.

Christ.

Then he saw it.

The flashing pig party lights.

The one party he tried to never attend.

Too fucking late.

The three little pigs barreled toward him like he was the big, bad wolf and was about to blow down their fucking house.

He ground out another curse as the three cruisers parked a half circle behind Honda and Asshole's cage.

As if on cue, all three driver's doors opened and pigs from the local PD crouched behind them, using them as shields. All with guns drawn.

Of fuckin' course. Fuck the tasers and go right for the kill shot.

"Turn around and lace your fingers behind your head!" shouted one uniformed oinker.

He set his jaw and contemplated his choices.

He *could* resist them, but that would only mean more time behind bars. Hard to help run a goddamn MC when you're stuck inside.

Add in the fact the blonde and her son had already dealt with enough trauma for the day; they really didn't need to see him get his ass kicked and dragged away.

For fuck's sake.

"Turn around and lace your fingers behind your head! Do it now!"

He was tempted to ask them, "Or what?" but he already knew. He'd been through this shit before. More times than he could count.

"I'm sorry." The woman's whisper shook as badly as her hands. She was probably going into shock. "Is there anything I can do?"

Not unless she wanted to be cuffed and stuffed, too. "Make sure you document what that motherfucker did and drag his ass back to court. Get a PFA for you and your kid." Not that the Protection From Abuse order was worth the paper it was printed on, but at least this bullshit with her ex would be documented.

With his bandana still pressed to her nose, she nodded. "I will. Again, I'm sorry you had to get involved."

"I'm not." It went against his grain to turn his back on the three pigs with their guns trained on him. But he did it—for her—then slowly lifted his arms and interlaced his fingers behind his head.

"Walk backwards toward the sound of my voice. Don't stop until I tell you."

Yeah, yeah, yeah. Same old fucking song and dance.

He could do this routine in his sleep.

They continued to annoy the fuck out of him by shouting more orders until they had him face-planted on a pig-mobile's hot hood and cuffed, searched, and divested of his knife, his keys, his chain wallet, his cell phone, and the remainder of the pre-rolled found stuffed deep in his front jeans pocket.

It was bullshit that any scratch made from the rides he took photos of today would now be used toward his defense fund.

He was damn sure that wouldn't go over well with Ransom. In fact, the prez might let him rot in prison this time.

And Stone wouldn't blame him one damn bit.

Chapter One

Thirteen months, two weeks, three days and six hours later

"Fuck me," Stone grumbled when he heard it.

"I am, baby. I'm fucking you *soooo* good."

Jesus fuckin' Christ.

He rolled his eyes to the ceiling for a second before dropping them to the ringing phone on the nightstand next to his bed in the clubhouse.

He had no idea who was calling, but it could be a good paying collection job and he could use the scratch. That left him no choice but to answer, even while one of their sweet butts rode his dick.

After thirteen months in the fucking slammer, he had a lot of catching up to do, so he'd been working his way through all of the Kings' club girls.

One at a time.

Two at a time.

Sometimes three at a time. It all depended on his mood and how much he wanted to drain his balls.

As soon as he tagged the phone, the ringing stopped. Two seconds later, it started again.

Of fuckin' course.

He set his jaw and glanced at Windy's huge tits as they flopped in time with her bouncing on his dick. "Give it a rest, woman. Need to take this."

"I'll go slower."

He closed his eyes and shook his head.

Windy earned her nickname honestly. There wasn't jack shit between her damn ears. But her pussy was tight and she could suck his nuts through his dick. Smarts weren't needed for that.

Bracing himself, he swiped his finger across the phone's screen and stuck it to his ear.

The computerized voice announced a collect call. That meant one thing...

"Fuckin' fuck." He reluctantly accepted the charge. "Better be good. In the middle of important business."

"Important business for you is fucking."

"Damn right it is. What d'you do?" He could guess. Sheena needed her ass bailed out.

Again.

If he didn't share a kid with the dumb cunt, he'd have bought her a one-way ticket to Siberia so he'd never have to see or hear from that mistake again.

Unfortunately, she *did* pop out his nut nugget so he was fucking stuck with her. At least for another eight years. After that, though, all fucking bets were off.

"Why do you assume I did anything?"

"'Cause you're callin' me collect from Dauphin County fuckin' Prison, that's why," he roared. "You sure ain't visitin'. What the fuck d'you do?"

He sat up abruptly, almost throwing Windy off. She dug

her long-ass nails into his thighs to keep her balance and to remain securely on his dick.

Goddamn pro right there.

"I cashed a few checks."

Translation: she *forged* a few checks. Probably more than a few. Enough to get busted and prosecuted. Again.

The annoyance rising up his throat left a bitter taste in his mouth. But then, to be fair, he'd been bitter ever since he found out Sheena was knocked up over ten years ago.

Best and worst day of his fucking life.

Loved his girl, but hated the cunt that held his baby hostage in her body for nine months.

"You needed more scratch for Sunny, shoulda reached the fuck out." He always made sure his girl had what she needed.

"First of all, dickhead, you've been *away* and I couldn't ask you for shit. But the money wasn't for Sunny."

"What the fuck you need scratch for, then?"

She didn't answer, and that was wasting fucking time. Prisons had a time limit on phone calls.

"What d'you need the scratch for, Sheena?"

When again she didn't answer, he figured it out.

God-fuckin'-damnit.

"Thought you were fuckin' clean!" he roared. He pulled the cell phone from his ear, dropped his head and shook it, trying to keep this shit together. Once he took a long breath through flared nostrils, he put the phone back to his ear. "Jesus fuckin' Christ, why you gotta be like that?"

"Fuck you, *Pebble.* You've got no room to talk. You just got out for doing something stupid yourself. That asshole move kept you from your daughter for over a damn year! Don't act like you're so high and mighty."

High would be a good state to be in right now to deal with her constant bullshit.

Since he wasn't, he gritted his teeth. Not because what she said hit home, but because she had called him Pebble. She only did it to get a rise out of him and he tried not to take the bait.

At least the cunt could've brought Sunny during visitation hours. Did she? Fuck no, no matter how many times he asked her.

"Listen, bitch. You know I ain't talkin' about you doin' another bid. Don't give a fuck about that. You like muff divin' in prison, that's on you, but you doin' meth around my girl is the last fuckin' straw." Sunny was never going back to her again. Her mother promised him she'd stay clean.

He should've known that was a lie. Sheena wouldn't know how to tell the truth if her life depended on it. That was why he had insisted on a DNA test when she announced she was knocked up and assumed it was his.

At first, he assumed it wasn't.

"Just try to keep her from me," came the empty threat.

It wasn't worth arguing. Sheena was now inside, he was now out. He currently held all the cards. "Wish I never stuck my dick in you."

"You're not the only one, asshole. You sucked in bed."

Bullshit. "That's why you chased my fuckin' dick?"

"I was high!"

"What's new?"

"And you didn't fight me off, *Pebble.*"

Because he'd been on a three-day bender himself, he couldn't remember half the pussy he fucked that Fourth of July long weekend. The only reason he remembered Sheena was because his swimmers decided to fuck him over hard by landing on her shore.

He should get snipped just to teach those cruel mother-fuckers a lesson.

"Are you going to pick up Sunny at Darla's or not?"

Goddamn Darla. She was as bad as Sheena. Maybe even worse. The woman sold her skanky cunt to get her mitts on drugs. She should call the Guinness Book of World Records because the cum dumpster probably had every STD known to man.

Maybe even some that haven't been identified yet.

He shuddered at the thought of sticking his dick in that woman's petri-dish pussy.

"Of fuckin' course I'm gonna get my baby girl. Sunny don't need to be around that whore." And this time she wasn't going back to Sheena after she got released. He might not be the best influence for his daughter, but he had to be a step up from her mother.

Or at least he fucking hoped so.

Goddamn it. Their girl's future was probably doomed between her two fucked-up parents. Poor Sunny had been born with a broken plastic spoon in her mouth instead of silver through no fault of her own.

"Darla still in Scumbag Estates?" If so, he'd have to pack extra heat. He might even have to bring along a few of his brothers.

"No, she's living in a pop-up camper in the RV park behind the trailer park."

For fuck's sake. That place was a haven for drug addicts. The news kept getting better by the second.

"Hey, Stone? Can you put money on my books?"

Was she serious? Now she wanted to act sweet? *Fuck that.*

"Why don't you ask *Pebble?*" Stone hung up and threw

his phone across the room before shoving Windy off his now-limp dick.

The sweet butt blinked at him wide-eyed. "You okay, Stone?"

"Fuck no. Gotta go rescue my daughter." Before Darla sold Sunny to the highest bidder to help fund her habit.

Guaranteed, if that happened, his next bid in prison would be permanent.

THE MEETING ROOM, like the rest of their clubhouse, might not be fancy, but it was theirs.

A massive mural of their Kings of Anarchy colors took up one wall. The rectangular table where they sat had the names of all past and present fully-patched members of the Pennsylvania chapter engraved in it.

Once they earned their colors, each member carved their own name into the long table's wood top themselves, using a buck or pocket knife, or any other blade they happened to have on hand. Some had even burned their names into the wood. The six founders of the Dead Man's Hollow, Pennsylvania chapter had started this tradition after establishing it back in the early eighties.

Out of habit, Stone rubbed his fingertip over a worn-down carving directly in front of his place at the table, where he sat to the right of their president, Ransom. The name belonged to the Kings' member who sponsored Stone.

Rubble.

His older brother. First by blood, then by club. Rubble was the one to convince Stone to slip on a prospect cut only a couple of days after his eighteenth birthday.

The only reason he didn't do it the day he turned old

enough was because he was too damn drunk and stoned. On top of the very important fact that he was also busy planting his dick in some bitch for those two days straight.

He found out later the woman had been forty-five.

He wouldn't have cared about her age, even if she told him up front, since she lured him to her fancy double-wide trailer with the promise of an endless supply of expensive whiskey and quality coke.

In those forty-eight hours, her massive fucking tits almost smothered him to death more times than he could count. He also discovered she could suck a knob off a door.

It was the best birthday in all of his eighteen years.

Until he sobered up.

Until she finally opened the shades in her bedroom and he saw her without all the heavy makeup. Without that tight-as-fuck shape-wear she squeezed herself into that he swore was invented solely to trick men. Until he saw her pussy flaps looked like a goddamn Arby's roast beef sandwich in the light of day.

His walk of shame turned into a sprint of horror and 'never agains.'

It was a hard lesson learned, but from then on out, his strict rule was to pick them only while he was still stone-cold sober.

Though, rules were meant to be broken. The whole reason he had a daughter.

But that horror story was also how he got his road name. When he told his brother what happened, and why he'd been missing for two days, Rubble started calling him Stones for having the damn stones to actually tell that story out loud. Stone dropped the extra S once he got his full set of patches a year later.

Now his road name could mean a shitload of things.

"Brother, why you got the sweet butts watchin' your girl?" he heard from his right.

"Don't got a fuckin' choice right now," he answered Lick. "Can't leave her alone."

"Get a house mouse."

Stone hooked an eyebrow at their club secretary. "Got one in mind?"

"Fuck no."

Stone shook his head. "Well, that's helpful, asshole."

"No, the asshole is you, lettin' those club whores watch your girl. I mean, what's Juicy gonna teach her? How to suck dick? She certainly ain't teachin' her math or spellin'."

"She learns that shit in school."

"They teach girls how to suck dick in school? Know a few that musta missed that fuckin' class."

"Lick—" Stone growled, but before he could finish, their treasurer, Outlaw, slammed his hand on the table.

"Where the fuck's Ogre?"

Stone glanced across the table to the empty spot on Ransom's right.

At the other end of the table, Wheels hooted loudly. "When the fuck is that bastard ever here on time?"

Stone could easily answer that. Not once in the eight years since Ogre was voted in as the chapter's sergeant at arms.

Ogre knew no one would say shit to his face about it. That was why he made a great club enforcer. To him, a fist could solve any problem. Or a knife. Or a gun. But anyone who knew Ogre, knew he didn't need a weapon. He'd put you six-feet under with a beatdown alone.

If you pulled a knife or gun on him? He'd fucking laugh. *If* Ogre actually laughed.

Stone wasn't sure if he'd ever heard it. For those that did, those motherfuckers' best bet was to run as fast and fucking far as their shaking legs would take them.

"You seriously got Juicy watchin' your kid?" Ransom asked beside him.

"Juicy, Slick, Windy, Loosey, Swallow...almost all of 'em," Lick answered for him.

Stone scowled at him.

"What the fuck, dude?" Ransom laughed. "You gotta be desperate."

"No shit," Stone grumbled. "Goddamn Sheena, man. The bitch promised me she'd stay clean this time."

"Hard to fix a junkie," Wheels began, "if they ain't willin' to fix themselves."

Their road captain should know. He lost his younger brother to a fentanyl overdose.

He should've known better than to fuck with fentanyl. Not much was prohibited from club property, but that shit was. Any member caught with it or doing it would be stripped of their colors.

"Yeah, well, I'm fuckin' done with that bullshit. Sunny ain't goin' back to Sheena after she gets out."

"Then you definitely need a house mouse," Ransom said.

How the fuck did the officer's meeting turn into a dissection of his life's choices?

His eyes flicked to the empty seat. Because goddamn Ogre was his normal late-ass self.

Motherfucker.

"Know one?" Stone asked his prez.

"Not off the top of my melon, no, but I'll ask around. Someone's gotta have a sister or cousin you can trust."

"You sayin' I can't trust our club girls?"

"Sure," Ransom answered, "you can trust them to suck and fuck the shit outta you. To help raise your kid? Fuck no."

"If you find one that's got big knockers and a tight cunt, even better, right?"

"Who?" Stone asked Wheels.

"The house mouse," he answered.

"Find one that can cook, too," Outlaw suggested, like it was that fucking easy.

"And doesn't bitch," Lick added.

Now they were weaving a fucking fairy tale.

He didn't need a house mouse who could suck and fuck him. He could get that anywhere. What he needed was someone stable in Sunny's life. Someone who wasn't a total fuck up and could take care of his daughter and his house when he wasn't there. Which was too often.

"Well, when you find one like that, send her my way," Stone told everyone at the table. "Now, can we get this fuckin' meetin' started?" He was done with this subject.

"Not without the big guy." Ransom tipped his head toward the still empty seat.

Goddamn Ogre.

A second later, they heard the heavy thump of boots right before the six-foot-four, three-hundred-pound monster shouldered his way through the door to the meeting room. On his heels, like always, was his one-hundred-fifty-pound brindle Presa Canario, Thor.

With a bite force of over five hundred pounds per square inch, the fucking dog's powerful jaws alone were deadly. So yeah, Ogre didn't need any weapons other than himself and his canine sidekick.

The sergeant at arms never went anywhere without his four-legged beast. He had even added a sidecar onto his Harley for him.

"'Bout fuckin' time, asshole!" Stone yelled as Ogre lumbered around the table to his spot at Ransom's left.

Ogre yanked out the chair and sank his weight into it, then he tipped his bearded chin down but lifted his dark, soulless eyes to stare across the table at Stone. "You say somethin'?"

Probably not the best idea to poke the grizzly bear. "Yeah, I was sayin' how much I've missed you." Stone puckered up and blew a kiss across the table.

Ogre rose from his seat, turned around, dropped his jeans to expose his ass, and pointed to one hairy bare cheek. "Kiss this, motherfucker."

"Prefer not to get pink eye, fuck you very much."

At the head of the table, Ransom howled with laughter and slammed his gavel down, then yelled, "Let's get this shit over with."

Best words Stone had heard since entering the room a half hour ago.

Chapter Two

It took a while to find him, but Taryn's determination finally paid off. It also helped that some of her past and current clients had connections with access to non-public records. It only took asking the right one. One who also didn't ask fifty questions on why she needed the info.

Or lecture her on searching for "trouble."

It was her opinion that day in the parking lot almost fourteen months ago, her savior had been nothing but "good trouble."

According to the info, James Conrad lived in Dead Man's Hollow. It was about an hour north of Harrisburg and only twenty minutes or so away from where she lived in Selinsgrove on the opposite side of the Susquehanna River.

Lifting her foot off the accelerator, she let her Honda Pilot slow enough so she could get a better view of her surroundings. She glanced at the map on her dashboard again. Was this right? The area seemed so remote, despite being only minutes from Sunbury.

"Make the next right onto Brush Valley Road," George, her monotone GPS voice, instructed.

Well, if George was telling her to take a right...

She followed his guidance and a minute later was surprised to find herself deep in a thickly wooded area.

"In a quarter mile, make a left onto Whiskey Springs Road."

"Okay, okay. But I'm not liking this." She wouldn't be surprised if the next road ended up being dirt.

Nobody was out here. At least she had cell phone coverage. It might not be strong but two bars was better than zero.

Her heart leapt into her throat.

Maybe this *was* a bad idea. But then again, so was marrying Victor.

She swore her life was one bad decision after another.

"Your destination is on your right," George announced.

"Are you sure, George? It sure looks like an old school to me." Maybe even an abandoned one.

Of course, George refused to answer her.

She pulled over and hunched down enough so she could get a better view of the sprawling two-story brick building at the top of a long, grassy slope. Surrounding the building and a majority of the property was a six-foot chain-link fence. Most likely installed to keep out vandals after the school was closed.

To the right of the school were double gates with one side wide open. The empty paved parking lot in front of those gates had seen better days.

From where Taryn sat, she could see the cracked and crumbling macadam also had some deep potholes wide enough to dent a rim, if not pop a tire, and the painted lines for the parking spots were barely visible, another sign that the lot hadn't been maintained in a long time.

George had to be mistaken. James Conrad could not be living at this address. He had to have provided a fake ID when he was arrested that day.

But why this property? He had to have some sort of ties to it.

Gnawing on her bottom lip, she contemplated her next steps. She could park in that lot and travel on foot through the gate. Or she could simply drive through it and straight up to the building.

However, the abundance of ominous "no trespassing" signs attached every few yards to the metal fence posts was a good indicator she needed to be cautious. She might not be welcome here, whether on foot or four wheels.

At least if she drove up, she could make a quick escape. That decided it.

She pulled through the gate.

When you get out, keep your door unlocked and your keys in your hand. Seconds might count.

Another huge parking lot at the top of the hill and much closer to the school had rusty signs stating the parking was for "staff only." Nobody was parked in that lot, either. However, she saw what appeared to be a few junk cars in the distance behind the school.

Once she parked, she could easily read a weather-stained concrete rectangle embedded in the brick above the entrance: Oaklyn Public School.

Public school. No indication whether it had been an elementary, junior high or middle school, or even a senior high.

No one made this type of school a home. Offices, maybe. A home, no.

It made no sense. This address *had* to be wrong. But since she was here, she might as well confirm it.

She glanced around one more time before climbing out. Once she did, she stood there for a few seconds, waiting to see if anyone would approach.

She didn't see a soul.

Once at the school's front entrance, she found the door handles chained together with a heavy-duty lock as well as two huge "no trespassing" signs.

She was sensing a theme here. A very unwelcoming one.

Since the door's dirty window panes were covered from the inside, she couldn't even get a peek inside.

Shit.

With a building this size, common sense said there was more than one way to get in. She only needed to find one that wasn't locked or blocked.

The landscaping around the exterior had probably been abandoned since the last time the school saw a student. What remained was dead and overgrown with weeds.

If someone did live here, they wanted it to look as uninviting as possible.

Goal achieved.

She headed back in the direction she had come from, but instead of returning to her car—what a sane person would do —she rounded the building and came across a metal basement door that was also locked.

Of course.

With a sigh, she continued on, heading around back. The school was bigger than at first glance. The placard by the front door stated it was built in 1927, but it looked like some major updates and additions had been done after that.

Obviously, none of them recent.

When she got to the rear of the property, her feet slowed to a stop and she blinked to make sure she was seeing all of it clearly. Either the place *was* occupied or it had been vandalized, she couldn't quite tell.

Or it could be a popular party spot for local teenagers.

She continued on her trek, taking it all in.

Rusty fifty-five-gallon drums, cut in half, had been used to make barbecue grills with the grates made out of stolen shopping carts. She hoped anyone eating off those were up to date on their tetanus shot.

She kept moving and spotted a burnt circle full of chunks of charcoal and piles of ashes. Stacked next to the huge fire pit was a mountain of wood pallets at least twelve feet high.

She next came across a covered pavilion built out of what appeared to be scrap wood and metal road signs. No surprise that it needed a fresh coat of paint. On the cracked concrete slab under the pavilion were six picnic tables and another half dozen were scattered around the rear schoolyard, some in the beaten-down grass and the rest in dirt.

Those weather-worn tables must've been used recently as they were not only covered in, but also surrounded by trash. Half-empty beer bottles full of cigarette butts. Smashed beer cans. Shards of broken bottles.

A few garbage cans also made from fifty-five-gallon drums dotted the area. No surprise, they were all overflowing. At least at one point, whoever had partied here made an effort to try to keep the area clean.

Apparently, that hadn't lasted long.

Not an ashtray could be found. But silly her, that was what the bottles and cans were for, right? Or maybe not, since she couldn't take one step without seeing crushed cigarette butts in the dirt under her feet.

About three hundred yards from the rear of the school and along the tree line, she spotted something that made the fine hairs on the back of her neck stand up.

A haphazard "shooting range." It included shredded paper targets of life-sized silhouettes as well as blown apart cans and bottles. A headless, armless mannequin had a massive hole blown through its torso, most likely made with a shotgun or a high-caliber handgun.

She was so out of her element.

She shouldn't have come here.

If Mr. Conrad truly lived at this address, it was screaming, "Leave me alone. Or else." He most likely didn't want her here looking for him. Even though she only wanted to thank him.

She should've mailed a damn postcard, or sent a "thanks for beating the crap out of my ex" greeting card.

"Hey, girly! You lost?"

She jumped out of her skin. Her heart skipped a beat or two and it took her a few seconds to find her breath so she could answer, "I...I'm not sure."

A bearded man with a beer belly so big he looked about to deliver triplets stood only yards away. His black leather vest couldn't be buttoned closed even if he tried. His worn jeans were dirty with brown and black stains. She didn't want to know from what.

She needed to pay better attention. This man approached her while she'd been distracted. She glanced around to make sure he was the only one and this wasn't an ambush.

He tipped his head and scratched at his long beard. "Huh. Pretty fuckin' sure you are. Best you get back in that cage of yours and skedaddle."

Cage? Skedaddle?

His scraggly salt and pepper beard was overdue to have a date with a weed whacker. It would take a day's work to find his lips in that mess.

Taryn would not volunteer to be on that search party.

His boots, similar to the ones James Conrad had been wearing, were covered in scuffs and dried mud. What gray-streaked hair remained on his head was pulled back into a thin ponytail. The man should stop fighting the good fight and shave it off.

He took a long drag on his cigarette, then flicked the still burning butt onto the ground.

This is why the "yard," or whatever it was called, looked the way it did.

"Like whatcha see, girly?" He yanked on his long beard again as if he was pointing out his best feature.

No, she was not interested in the man standing before her.

"I have business here." She squinted and read the patch on his vest, "Patch?"

"Business?" Patch chuckled. "You a whore?"

Her chin jerked into her neck. What kind of question was that? Besides a rude one. "No. Do I look like one?"

"No particular look for a whore. But if you ain't, then you don't belong here. Best you leave."

Just like that? "I'm looking for someone."

He planted a hand on his hip and shook his head. "Ain't we all?"

"His name is James Conrad."

Patch—even though he never confirmed that was his name, she might as well call him that—spat a stream of dark juice onto the ground, barely missing his own boot with the splatter. "James Conrad, huh? Nobody here by that name." He jerked his chin toward her Honda. "You tryin' to sell that ride?"

"What? No." She would need it to escape this paradise.

"Then, you got no business here."

That was his opinion. Taryn didn't agree. "I actually do."

"What?"

"What, what?" she asked.

He shook his head. "What fuckin' business you got here?"

"I need a word with Mr. Conrad."

"Mr. Conrad," he repeated in an amused mutter. "Jesus fuck."

"Does he not live here?"

"Like I said, girly, nobody here by that name."

Bullshit. "This came up as his address."

"That fuckin' so?"

"Yes, but if he doesn't live here then I'm sorry if I disturbed you." She wasn't. If he was going to lie, so was she.

One shaggy eyebrow rose. "He know you?"

What an odd question to ask if the man didn't live here. More proof he did. Or at least spent time here.

"Yes." Sort of.

She had no idea if James Conrad knew her name or if he would even remember her. The incident with Vic happened over a year ago. She did know James went to prison for his unfortunate part in it. As soon as she discovered he'd been freed, she began to search him out.

And here she was. But according to Patch, not at the right address.

"D'you even have any fuckin' clue where you're at?"

Another odd question. "A school?"

He chuckled. "Yeah, girly, what used to be a fuckin' school. Ain't that now."

"I figured it was no longer a school solely by the amount of empty beer and liquor bottles. Plus, I can't imagine a school cafeteria would serve up food from"—she flipped a hand toward the nearest halved steel drum—"one of those DIY grills."

"Ain't nothin' wrong with those grills." He rubbed the part of this gut that extended past the leather vest. "Makes some damn good eatin'."

"I'll take your word for it." She glanced to her left and eyed up the building. "So if it's not a school and not a residence, what is it?"

Patch turned around and hooked a thumb toward the back of his vest. "Know what these are?"

A large embroidered logo of a masked skull wearing a crooked crown was sandwiched between a downward curving top patch that screamed: KINGS OF ANARCHY and the lower upward curving patch that shouted: PENN-SYLVANIA. A smaller square patch with the letters "MC" to the right of the logo completed the look.

She might as well state the obvious. "Patches?"

"Know what they stand for?"

"No."

"Then you don't belong here." Patch made a shooing motion with his tattooed hand. "You best skedaddle." With that, he spun on his heel and headed back to the school.

"Wait!"

He did not wait, so Taryn ran after him.

That could be another bad decision in her lifetime long list of bad decisions, but her gut was telling her that, between Patch's actions and questions, James Conrad did live here.

"He had long dark brown or black hair, black facial hair, dark brown eyes. He's six foot or so and"—from the little she could see that day—"has tattoos."

A snort was heard from the man who continued to walk and did not slow down.

"Please! I only need a minute with him."

"He lasts longer than a minute."

What did that mean? Did she even want to know? "If you know that, then you know him!"

"Didn't say that," Patch threw over his shoulder, not slowing down.

She ran faster so she could catch him before he disappeared through a door she only just now noticed.

She got in front of him, then stopped, blocking his path. When he stepped to the right, so did she. When he moved to the left, she did the same. He shook his head. "Woman."

"Please. He helped me. I only want to thank him."

"Hire one of those planes that writes in the sky or somethin'."

She tipped her head to the side. "Would I tell them to fly it over this address?"

He dropped his gaze to his boots and muttered, "Fuck."

"Can you just tell him I'm here and only need a moment of his time? It would be greatly appreciated." She pointed to the ground. "I can wait out here."

"Might be waitin' a while."

"That's fine." It wasn't, but now she was determined to see him. The more Patch tried to get her to leave, the more she wanted to dig in her heels.

Patch kept his eyes locked with hers as he slowly leaned over and spat some more of that gross dark juice onto the ground.

Taryn quickly stepped back to avoid the splash.

Yuck.

When he straightened, he pulled a cell phone from the inside of his vest, jabbed at the screen, then put it to his ear. After a few seconds, he dropped it to his side. "He ain't answerin'."

"Try again, please."

With a long, aggravated sigh, he dialed again and put the phone back to his ear.

"No, ain't an emergency, brother. Some girly's here wantin' to see you." Patch eyed her up and down. "Possibly. Says she knows you. Maybe you fucked her before since she said she's here to thank you for your service."

Heat licked at her cheeks. "No, I—"

With a scowl, Patch turned his back on her. "Whatya wanna do? Want her to wait outside? Or you want me to send her up to join you?"

Join him? Doing what?

"Sure? She ain't half bad. Hard to see her tits under whatever the fuck she's wearin', though. Ass looks sweet enough."

When was he checking out her ass?

"Yep. You got it, brother." Patch stabbed at the screen to end the call, then tucked his phone away. He turned back to Taryn. "Come with me."

She quickly followed on his heels as he yanked open the door and went inside. Of course, not holding it for her. She caught it before it closed and quickly ducked through the doorway.

The school was definitely different on the inside, where a lot of updates had been done, versus the outside. The wide hallways remained but most of the doors to what might have once been classrooms were solid and without windows, making it impossible to see what was going on behind them.

The walls had been repainted and the floors were a polished concrete instead of tile or laminate.

She took as much in as she could as she tried to keep up with Patch. For an older, heavyset gentleman—and she was being *very* generous with that title—he was sure fast on his feet.

He stopped in an area that had the chained front doors to her left and a wide stairway to her right.

The huge design under her feet matched what was on the back of Patch's vest.

Interesting.

"Stay here. Stone said he'd be down when he's done."

"Done with what? And who is Stone?"

"More like done with who." Patch pointed at the floor. "Stay there. For your own good, best if you don't move."

Along the same vein as the no trespassing signs, his warning sounded ominous.

"Wait. I..."

Ignoring her, he continued across the foyer, if that was what it was called, and down the opposite hallway, eventually disappearing through a doorway on the right.

"Shit," she mumbled under her breath, then glanced up the stairway. She could only see as far as the first landing, where the stairs took a turn.

Wondering how long she'd have to wait, she slowly spun in a circle. The interior was really in much better shape than expected after seeing the unkempt and trashed exterior. Was it spotless? No. Garbage had accumulated in some corners but nothing like outside. Some graffiti-like writing also graced the walls.

She squinted, trying to make out some of it without moving from the spot she was assigned.

Grim was here was written in what could be a black marker.

Beware the Ogre was painted in large letters on another wall.

Grim? Ogre? Was this place turned into a haunted house

for Halloween? Because from what she saw so far, it would make a great one.

She twisted her head when she detected faint music at the far end of the hall. It took her a second to recognize Van Halen's *Hot for Teacher*.

Once again, she wondered about the purpose of the building and why James Conrad used it as his address. She glanced down at the design on the floor again.

Kings of Anarchy. Pennsylvania. MC.

MC...

She should know what MC stood for, shouldn't she? She hit the side button on her phone, lighting it up. Once she unlocked it, she immediately went to the browser to search for the letters "MC." She scanned what the search engine brought up.

McDonald's? No, it had nothing to do with the fast food chain.

Montgomery College? She glanced around and rolled her eyes. No.

Master of Ceremonies? *Sigh.*

Motorcycle club?

She blinked, then her fingers flew over the keyboard, typing: Kings of Anarchy MC.

Her eyes got wider with every word she read.

"Kings of Anarchy Motorcycle Club was established in the early 70s in southern California. They started patching over other clubs and expanding to more territories by the late 70s/early 80s. They now have established chapters in almost every state.

"Warning: This outlaw motorcycle club has created mayhem for decades. Their members are far from law-abiding and should be considered armed and dangerous. They've even adopted the motto: 'Nobody fucks with the Kings.'"

Her ears starting ringing and her pulse raced.

Holy shit. She needed to leave. Now.

Thump, thump, thump.

Shit. Someone was coming. She needed to go.

As she spun to head out the way she came in, she froze when she spotted him.

James Conrad.

Chapter Three

His unbrushed hair looked like he just rolled out of bed. He wore a white tank top under a black leather vest similar to Patch's. The difference between the two was that James could close his, if he chose. Which he probably didn't, since his jeans were unfastened and his hand was jammed down the front. Was he scratching his balls?

Her feet remained frozen in place while his brown eyes sliced past her like she was invisible.

Until he did a double-take.

His eyes now bore into her as he continued to descend the stairs. The closer he got, the more a recognizable smell filled her nostrils. Someone had been—or still was—so pickled that the alcohol was seeping through his pores.

He wasn't the only one descending the stairs. He was followed by two half-dressed women with just as messy hair. Though, calling them half-dressed was being charitable since one only wore a see-through panties and bra set and the other had on a tight mini-dress that barely covered her coochie and showed so much cleavage her nipples played peek-a-boo as she moved.

Now what Patch said made sense. *"More like done with who."*

When James stopped at the bottom of the steps, both women paused by his side and each planted a kiss on his cheeks at the same time.

"Later, baby," the brunette murmured.

"Repeat tonight?" the blonde purred, combing her long nails through his beard.

"Will let you know. Might got a job to do." His voice sounded as rough as he looked. He squeezed their asses before giving each one a stinging slap. "Get goin'. Got business to attend to."

The women's attention turned toward her. Taryn gave them an awkward wave, causing the blonde to roll her eyes. Both continued down the hallway in the direction of where she and Patch had entered the school.

Only, they didn't exit out that same door. Instead, they continued past it. She lost track of them when she heard a clearing of a throat and a grumbled, "Had a rough night."

She had no idea why he was giving her an excuse. She guessed it was best not to ask.

Not my circus, not my monkeys.

Say what you have to say and go. You are way out of your element here.

She awkwardly threw her hands up at her sides and grimaced. "Remember me?"

With pursed lips, his narrowed gaze slowly and thoroughly slid over her. "Since I ended up in a concrete box for over a year with no wet pussy and only my dry fuckin' fist, yeah. Hard to forget you."

She could safely assume he wasn't joking. "That's why I'm here."

"For what? Can't get that fuckin' time back."

Shit. Her apology would never fix that.

"I wanted to thank—" The look he shot her made her swallow the rest. She pressed her lips together and once again glanced down the hallway in the direction the women had disappeared. "Well, since you're busy..."

"Done bein' busy."

"I'm sure you have other things to...do," she finished weakly. "I'll give you your privacy. I only came here to thank you for intervening. And apologize for your arrest."

He snorted and shook his head.

Now that she did what she came to do, it was time to follow Patch's advice and *skedaddle.* "Well, it was...*uh*...nice... meeting you."

He snorted again. "Really?"

Taryn blinked. "Really, what?"

"Said was it nice meeting me. Why was it nice?"

Nobody had ever pressed her on that pleasantry before. She wasn't sure how to answer. "*Uh...*"

"Don't gotta feed me bullshit. Know you're only here 'cause of your guilt."

He nailed it. She felt horrible when he got arrested and ended up doing time on her behalf. She'd actually spent plenty of sleepless nights over it.

"Again, I only wanted to thank you for stepping in and stopping Vic from—"

"Beatin' the fuck outta you? Shoulda stepped in earlier."

"You didn't have to get involved at all, but you did. Unlike other witnesses."

"Buncha fuckin' pussies."

Okay, then. "Anyway, I said what I came here to say and now I need to go."

When Taryn turned to escape, he grabbed her wrist and stopped her. "Don't gotta leave."

Was he using the hand he just had down his pants? "I think I do. Patch was right when he said I don't belong here."

"Like a broken fuckin' clock, that fucker's right twice a damn day." He turned to face her. "Said you don't belong here. Where do you belong? With that asshole?"

"No." More like, *hell no.* If she didn't share a child with Vic, she'd never want to deal with him again.

He jerked his chin toward the hallway where she had come in. "Let's go."

If he planned on escorting her to the door, she'd gladly go with him.

As he set off down the long corridor, he groaned and pressed tattooed fingers to his temple.

"Hangover?" she asked as she followed behind him.

She'd take his simple grunt as a yes.

When he passed the exterior door she and Patch used earlier, she paused. This was where they parted ways.

He stopped abruptly, twisting his head to look over his shoulder.

"Well, thank you again."

"No."

No? "No, what?"

"Comin' with me."

Sure, sure. She'd get right on that because she had nothing better to do except hang out with an outlaw biker like they were besties. An everyday occurrence for her, right?

Wrong.

"Go with you where? Is there another exit that's closer to my car?" *Please say yes.*

"Need coffee."

That sounded like a personal problem and not one she needed to deal with. She already had her caffeine limit earlier. "I appreciate the invite, but I *really* need to get going."

"Came here to thank me, right?"

"Yes."

"Then, come with me."

Umm. How exactly did he want her to thank him? She already expressed her gratitude in words. She certainly wasn't going to do it a second time with action.

Going with him wherever he was headed would be a dumb idea. But then, so was coming to this place. Or insisting he meet with her. "I'm good. I don't need coffee."

"Stepped in to help you. Spent thirteen months in a cage like a fuckin' animal. A few more minutes of your time don't even compare."

Damn it. He was using her guilt against her.

What was one more bad decision?

He came closer, wrapped his long, tattooed fingers around the nape of her neck, gave it a gentle squeeze, then steered her down the hallway.

She took a last parting glance at what could've been her escape. "Just coffee, right?"

"Yeah," came his deep grumble.

"Are you hiding a Starbucks somewhere in this building?"

He snorted and kept moving. At the end of the hallway, he hooked a left and into what turned out to be the school's former cafeteria. Similar to outside, the garbage cans were overflowing, and trash, like cigarette butts, were strewn all over the floor and the old brown folding lunch tables with the attached round, red seats. Those were a flashback from her past. She remembered those dinosaurs from when she was in school.

"Juicy, get me some fuckin' coffee!" he shouted, then winced. "Gotta get the taste of your pussy outta my mouth."

Nice. "Mouthwash would work, too," Taryn mumbled under her breath.

"Don't forget to add the Jack," he ordered.

The brunette who had come down the stairs with him ducked into the kitchen behind the school's original serving line. Juicy was nothing like the lunch ladies Taryn remembered.

"Sit." James, or Stone, or whatever he was called, pointed at one of those round, uncomfortable seats she remembered turning her ass numb during lunchtime.

"Thank you but I'll pass since I'm not staying long."

With a shake of his head, he huffed out a breath. But before he could respond, Juicy came over and handed him a chipped Harley Davidson mug. "Here you go, baby."

Stone eyed the steaming coffee. "This shit fresh?"

"Windy made it about ten minutes ago."

Stone grimaced. "For fuck's sake. She's not allowed to make the fuckin' coffee."

Juicy shrugged, placated him by patting his chest, then went over to another man, also wearing a black leather vest, casually leaning back against the cafeteria wall.

Those vests seemed to be popular around here.

"I'm assuming that Juicy isn't the name she was born with."

In a flash, Juicy was on her knees at the biker's feet and his cock was filling her mouth.

Taryn's jaw threatened to drop but she somehow managed to keep her mouth shut. Probably because she was clenching her teeth.

Don't stare. Don't stare. Do not stare.

"Don't matter what name she was born with. That's the name we gave her." He took a long sip of the coffee, then pushed out a long sigh. "Guess it ain't gonna kill me."

Trying not to be too obvious, Taryn flipped a finger in Juicy's direction. "You just had sex with her, right?"

"Yeah?"

That "yeah" clearly meant, *"So? What about it?"*

Okay, then. She turned her back to the action along the wall. Otherwise, she'd lose the battle on not gawking. "So, you're a biker."

He chuckled and swallowed another mouthful of coffee. Of course he laughed. Her assumption was stupid because James Conrad was wearing the same type of vest that Patch had been. The same as the man getting head against the wall.

Don't look.

When he fingered her chef's jacket near her name embroidered over her heart, that pounding organ leapt into her throat. "Taryn."

That finger was too close for comfort. Especially when he rubbed that same finger directly over the letters while repeating her name in a low whisper.

Good lord. The way he said it sent a shiver shimmying down her spine and caused her nipples to pop like turkey timers.

That reaction wasn't due to nerves this time, but now was not the time to explore what caused it.

"Reminds me of a cut."

She took a step back, breaking the contact. She shook her head, not understanding what he meant.

"A cut, babe." He tugged on his leather vest. "Our colors. Who we are and what we represent. Our brotherhood."

He pointed to a rectangular embroidered patch with the

name Patch had called him. *STONE.* Below it, another similar patch said *VICE PRESIDENT.* The right side of his chest included another rectangular patch with DEAD MAN'S HOLLOW and right above it, a yellow diamond-shaped patch simply had "1%" embroidered on it.

Of course, she noticed on their way to the cafeteria that the back of his vest had the same large patches as Patch.

"Is Stone a nickname?"

"Road names are earned."

Semantics. She could say the same about nicknames. "How did you earn yours?"

He shook his head. "Story for another time, babe."

Taryn doubted she'd be staying for that story time. "What does that yellow diamond mean?"

"Means we live by our own damn rules."

That was no surprise. "I have to ask...is everyone here a biker?"

"You see anyone with a dick wearin' a cut like mine, then yeah. You see pussy wanderin' 'round wearin' a cut with rockers on the back statin' they're property of the Kings, then no. They're a club whore."

"Juicy isn't wearing a cut." She wasn't wearing much of anything.

"'Cause I just got done fuckin' her, babe. She tends to lose track of her shit."

"If you don't mind not calling me—"

"Babe."

"Yes, that."

One corner of his mouth pulled up. At least she could see his mouth, unlike Patch's.

He lifted a *wait-a-minute* finger and took his now-empty mug over to Juicy and the guy with his cock in her mouth. He handed it to Juicy. Did he want her to stop what she was doing so she could get him a refill?

"Case you need to spit. 'Cause Grim's cum's probably hard to swallow." He headed back in Taryn's direction. "Unlike mine," he added.

The creases at the corners of his eyes deepened with amusement and his grin totally changed his face. It made him look approachable and actually pleasant to look at. Unlike when he was scowling.

He pulled a pack of Marlboro's from inside his vest—*cut* —and tucked one between his lips. After putting away the pack, he patted his vest—*cut*—until he found a lighter. After a few flicks of the Zippo, the tip glowed red and he sucked the smoke deep into his lungs.

It escaped his mouth when he asked, "Why's it that color?"

"My chef's coat?"

"That what it is? Thought chefs wore white."

Today she had worn turquoise, but she had one in every color of the rainbow. "Some do. Some like a little more excitement in their life."

His brow dropped low. "How's wearin' that color excitin'?"

It wasn't to him, apparently. His excitement came from handing a mug to a woman on her knees while she gave head. "I guess I live a boring life." After comparing hers to Juicy's, she was perfectly fine with boring.

"Got a restaurant?"

"No."

His eyebrows pinned together. "Where you work, then?"

"I'm a personal chef. I cook in people's homes or at their events. Like for a family Thanksgiving, an anniversary, or birthday party. I travel to my clients. They don't travel to me.

I also teach cooking classes sometimes when asked. There's a coffee shop in Camp Hill that requests me a lot."

Teaching those classes gave her some much-needed extra cash since Vic was so far behind on his child support payments.

"Bet they make better coffee than Windy." He took another drag on his cigarette and shot the smoke out of his nostrils. "So...like...whaddya make?"

She frowned. "What do I make? Food." Was he dense? And why was he asking all of these questions? Did she have to tell him outright that she wasn't interested in being his bestie?

He huffed, "Yeah, no shit. Like what?"

She wanted to roll her eyes at him but wasn't sure if he'd get offended. "Do you want me to run down my full menu options?"

He blew another long stream of white smoke over her head. "Grilled cheese?"

"I can handle that."

"Mac and cheese?"

Was this guy for real? "I've pulled it off before."

"Some of those"—he waved around the hand holding the cigarette and his forehead creased—"deep fried cheese sticks?"

Was this a test? "Do you have a thing for cheese?"

"It's all right. But ain't for me."

"Are you having a party that needs catered?"

"No. My kid."

"Your kid is having a party that needs catered?" Could this man give her actual answers before she screamed? It was like pulling teeth.

"No, my kid needs food."

"Most do." She shook her head. "Just a hint here...when

your lips form words they should make sense to the person hearing them. I know English is a difficult language to learn but you're off to a good start. Keep practicing."

The hand holding the cigarette paused halfway to his mouth and he stared at her. Not amused, not angry, nothing.

The smoke bellowed out from his nostrils like an aggravated bull. "Someone's got a smart mouth."

She guessed he didn't like her smart answers to his dumb questions, but she kept that tidbit to herself. She didn't know this guy and she should be careful. He could very well have a temper like Vic.

Chapter Four

"Sorry. I find your questions odd."

"Got a reason for 'em."

When Taryn turned her face up towards him, he became distracted for a second by the shade of her blue eyes. They almost matched the color of her jacket.

He slowly took her in from head to toe, noticing that she had to be a good half foot shorter than his six foot.

That day last year in the parking lot, she looked damn good from a distance. At least before her ex fucked her up and rearranged her face. Luckily, the motherfucker didn't do any permanent damage. At least that he could see.

The coat she wore didn't show any cleavage and didn't do shit for her curves but it couldn't hide the fact she had plenty to spare. Just how he liked his women.

Don't give him twigs for arms and legs and two buttons for tits. He needed something solid to grab onto. Thick thighs to smother him when a woman rode his face or to cushion his hips while he was banging the shit out of her. Tits big enough to grab a handful. An ass that could take a pounding. Wide hips that naturally rocked and rolled when a woman walked.

Unlike Loosey's washed-out blonde, Taryn's hair was more on the golden side. It had been down that day in the parking lot. Today, the length was gathered on the top of her head with some loose strands framing her face.

He had no opinion either way on what he liked better, but if anyone asked, he preferred it to be spread over his pillow.

Taryn tipped her head to the side. "What's the reason?"

She didn't belong here and that could work to Sunny's advantage. His brothers gave him shit for letting the sweet butts watch his daughter when he couldn't, but he agreed. It wasn't a good long-term plan.

Last thing he wanted was for his nut nugget to end up like Juicy, taking dick from anyone wearing a cut. Fuck that shit. He wanted much better for her. Between his past, as well as her mother's, the girl needed some kind of steady.

The fuck if that would come from him or Sheena.

"Can't cook. Someone needs to feed my baby girl." He quickly slipped in, "And me."

She frowned. "You can't cook...at all?"

"Toast."

"Okay, well..."

"Boxed spaghetti with sauce in a jar and frozen meatballs." That meal was simple enough.

Her eyebrows popped up her forehead. "I'm impressed."

Yeah, she was a fucking smart ass. Good thing he didn't mind a challenge. But his first challenge would be to convince her to go along with the plan that popped into his melon only minutes ago.

"Can also make a mean pot of coffee," he added. Not that

he usually had to. If he stayed in his room at church, one of the sweet butts made more whenever a pot was empty.

"I don't think your daughter should be drinking coffee."

"Better than beer."

"Debatable. Who's been feeding her up until now?"

"Her mother, mostly."

"What changed?"

"The bitch did more stupid shit and ended up back inside."

Suddenly, he recalled the conversation he had with one of the screws that first day back in his "home away from home." It just so happened to be about the woman now standing before him.

"What happened to that motherfucker who fucked up that chick?" Stone asked the guard as the wannabe pig escorted him to his cell.

"He's not dead, if that's what you're worried about. It was close though. Would've upped your charge from ag assault to murder."

Like he gave a fuck. "Ain't why I'm askin'."

"You fucked him up enough that he's still in the hospital. But they charged him with domestic violence and ag assault, if you really want to know. But don't worry, I'm sure he'll be our guest as soon as he's capable of breathing, talking, and walking again on his own."

"Deserved more than a fuckin' beatdown."

The screw shrugged. "Can't say I disagree with you, Conrad. You aren't a man if you have to beat up women. But some random on the street can't take justice into his own hands. Or fists."

That "random" glanced down at his split knuckles still covered in dried blood.

Her next words pulled him free from the memory. "By inside, I assume you mean jail."

He sucked on his teeth. "More like prison."

"Speaking of...why didn't you have a trial?"

Was that guilt still eating at her? "Faster and cheaper to just plead guilty and take a deal. Go in, do my time, get out. Think I wanna pay our lawyer more than I gotta and have twelve jurors who think their asses are too good to be my peers judgin' me when we all know I did it?"

"You were protecting me, though."

"Comes a point where the protection ends and the fuck around and find out stage begins."

"Just so you know, I pleaded with the cops to let you go. I explained that you were only protecting me."

He already knew that. The club attorney had let him read her statement she provided to the pigs. She also told the assistant district attorney that same thing. But it didn't do jack since the ADA had a hard-on over him. In Stone's opinion, twelve months was a shit deal, but the club attorney strongly suggested he take it. With his record, a jury trial, or even a bench trial, might've given him more time than that.

Of course, that twelve months turned into thirteen when he had to teach his dickhead cellie a lesson.

"Think they gave a fuckin' shit why I did it?"

"Apparently not."

"They see my cut. See my tats. To them, don't matter why I beat the fuck outta that asshole." He glanced at his now-healed knuckles. He would love to have another round with him. "Your ex did some time 'cause of that, too, right?"

Her head twitched. "He did."

"He out now?"

"Not yet. But soon. I got a PFA against him in preparation, just like you suggested."

Stone snorted. "A PFA's useless. Just a fuckin' piece of paper. All that's gonna do is give him a fuckin' paper cut. It ain't gonna protect you."

She sighed softly. "I'm aware, but I had to do something."

"He still gets your boy?"

Her lips pressed together and her expression hardened. "Once he gets out I'm sure he'll fight to get supervised visitation."

What the fuck. "Think he'll get it?"

"Not if it's up to me."

"Good. Anyway..." He needed to get back on track before she decided to leave. "Ain't lookin' for a mother for my kid."

Her face quickly went from determined to confused. "Well, that's good since I wasn't applying."

"Only need someone to help me out. Can't find a house mouse."

She blinked up at him. "Come again?"

A grin spread across his face. "Would like to. You volunteerin'?"

"No...not..." She shook her head. "What's a house mouse?"

"Like a housewife without the naggin' wife part."

Her mouth twitched, drawing his attention. "So, like a housekeeper? Or a nanny?"

"Kinda," he murmured, distracted when her tongue darted across her lips.

She glanced around. "Does your daughter stay here when you have her?" She tipped her head toward the spot where Juicy and Grim had been only a minute ago. Grim must've shot his load and left in thirty seconds flat.

He probably got head to take the edge off. It helped him last longer when it came to fucking his ol' lady.

"Nah. Got a room here but also got my own place."

"Like a house?"

"Got a roof and some walls."

"So does a tent."

He pressed his lips together, dropped his head and shook it. When he lifted it, he continued. "Maybe we can make a deal."

Her brow furrowed. "What kind of deal?"

"I protect you. You take care of my girl."

Her mouth dropped open and hung there. He tucked a thumb under her chin and closed it for her.

"I'm sorry, but what?" she whispered.

"Makin' you a deal. One that'll benefit us both."

"You want me to take care of your daughter?"

Why did she look so damn shocked? "Yeah. I mean, she goes to school and shit so it wouldn't be full time."

"I'm—"

"You too fuckin' good for that?"

She plucked at her chef's coat. "Maybe you missed it, but I already have a job."

"Don't mean you still can't do it."

"Maybe you didn't notice him that day, but I also have a son." The sarcasm in her voice was thick.

"Of course I fuckin' noticed. He was bawlin' and blowin' snot bubbles. But you havin' a kid means you already know what the fuck you're doin'. Don't gotta train you."

"Don't have to train me?" she repeated slowly.

"Yeah. Already take care of one kid, what's another?"

She grimaced. "*Umm*. Well...thank you for thinking of me, but I'll have to pass."

"Can protect you better than that useless protection order."

"Maybe I don't need personal protection."

He grabbed her chin and tilted her head this way and

that, making it obvious he was inspecting her face. "How long were you in the hospital?"

Her mouth gaped open for a few seconds before she answered, "Two days."

"Two fuckin' days too many."

"I agree."

"Never should've been alone with him."

"I agree with that statement, too."

"Will make sure that never happens again."

Her blue eyes went wide. "Are you saying you'll be my bodyguard twenty-four-seven?"

He could practically taste her disbelief. "No."

She threw up a hand. "Then..."

"Got a whole fuckin' club behind me. If you're under my protection, you're under the protection of twenty-three of my brothers and eight prospects." And a Presa Canario that probably weighed as much as she did and had much bigger teeth.

"What's a prospect?"

This woman didn't know shit about MCs. Time would tell if that would work for him or against him. "Dog shit."

"How would dog shit protect me?"

He shook his head. "Woman. Stop takin' shit literally. They gotta prove they're worthy of wearin' our colors."

"How do they do that?"

"By doin' whatever we tell them to do."

"Murder?"

"Yeah, sure."

"*Yeah, sure?*" she echoed, then shook her head. "While I appreciate it, as of now, I'll need to process this *generous* offer."

Bullshit. "You ain't gonna think about it."

"I have to consider Wren, too."

"Wren?"

"My son."

"His name is Wren?" He fought to keep his expression locked down. He didn't want to piss her off before he could convince her to move in with some random biker. That random biker being him. "Like the fuckin' bird?"

"Yes, like the bird."

"Ain't short for nothin'?"

"No."

Don't react, asshole. No snort, no laugh, not even a fuckin' grin. "Then, gonna protect your baby bird, too."

She sighed. "Like I said, I'll give it some thought."

"Don't got time for that. Need someone to help with Sunny now."

"Then the answer is no," she said with a shrug.

"Don't like that answer."

"It's the only one you're getting."

"You got a place?"

Her eyebrows shot up. "Like a house?"

"Yeah, you know...the place where you fuckin' live."

"Yes, for now."

"What does that mean?"

"I got the house in the divorce but, unfortunately, the mortgage is more than I can handle right now. That's why I don't have time to be a nanny for your daughter. I can barely take care of my own child."

"Ain't gonna be a nanny."

"Sure sounds like that's what you're looking for."

"Can't make the payments?" If not, this could help him convince her.

"It's a struggle."

"Why?"

"Vic had stopped paying child support even before he

was arrested. He won't help keep a roof over his own son's head."

"Why not?" Besides the fact her ex was a complete asshole.

"He wants me to lose the house. If I'm homeless, he figures he can fight for custody by claiming I'm an unfit mother. He wants to say I can't give Wren a stable home. That I'm irresponsible and can't care for him properly."

"That true?"

Her blonde head twitched. "That I'm a bad mother?"

"No, that he can pull that shit when he's the motherfucker not payin' child support."

She shrugged. "He has the money to pay a good lawyer while I'm financially struggling and can't."

"How? He's doin' time for beatin' the fuck outta you."

"His brother has a very successful chain of car dealerships and has powerful connections. Vic began working for him after we split."

"Get the courts to garnish his fuckin' wages."

"He lied and told the courts he was unemployed and now, due to his prison sentence, he's unemployable. But I know he was getting cash under the table while working for his brother. By getting paid in cash—"

"They can't garnish his fuckin' wages." *Un-fuckin'-believable.*

"Yes. He claims I destroyed his life by divorcing him, fighting for sole custody of Wren, asking for child support, and for getting him arrested, like that was my fault. His list of grievances against me is long. He wanted to destroy me financially in retaliation and I'm sure that won't change when he gets out."

"Petty motherfucker."

"That's putting it mildly. The divorce brought out a mean streak I never knew he had."

"Babe, everyone's got a mean streak. The only difference is what it takes for it to come out."

"Well, I feel like a fool for not recognizing the signs. If I would've seen the red flags before I got pregnant..."

"Then you wouldn't have your boy. If I would've pulled the fuck out, I wouldn't have my girl. Sometimes mistakes are worth it."

She stared at him like she was finally *seeing* him. Was she actually considering his offer? If so, he needed to close the deal. As fast as fucking possible.

"So, got an easy solution for your house. Let it go."

She bugged out her blue eyes at him. "Let it go? Then where will we live?"

Did he fuck up what little strides he already made with her? "Offered you a place. All free. Free house, free food, free utilities. Your Honda needs work, got it covered. Got everythin' fuckin' covered."

"Hold on. You want me to *live* with you?"

"How else you gonna take care of Sunny? How else am I gonna protect you?"

If she shook her head any harder, she might get whiplash. "I'm not. You're not."

"Yeah, you are."

Chapter Five

"*YEAH, YOU ARE.*"

Unfortunately, he wasn't wrong.

Taryn feared this would end up being another bullet point on her list of decisions she regretted. This one might be written all in capitals and in bold. With a string of exclamation points.

Because she was currently taking steps to move into a house owned by a biker with her six-year-old son so she could help care for that same biker's ten-year-old daughter.

How the hell did she get here?

By vehicle, obviously.

She turned right onto Village Road and slowly drove her Honda through the village of Dead Man's Hollow. The fact it was even still called a village was laughable. It was more like an area that time forgot.

A few single-family homes, still in livable condition, were mixed in with the buildings gradually returning to the earth as they deteriorated from weather and a lack of maintenance.

The only business on that stretch of road was GetGo.

The gas station/garage/convenience store combo, with an attached tiny post office, sat on the corner at one of the four crossroads. GetGo apparently was a one-stop shop, but she imagined most village residents took the short drive to Sunbury for the majority of their needs.

"Warnin', my place ain't big. Only got two bedrooms. One for me and Sunny's got her own room."

Oh yes, here she was, in a situation she never thought she'd be in...with a big, bad biker sitting in the passenger seat of her Honda Pilot.

He looked and smelled so much better today than on Monday. Most likely because he was no longer hungover or exhausted from pleasuring two women.

At. The. Same. Time.

He could've mentioned the fact that his place only had two bedrooms every time they spoke in the last few days when they were making arrangements.

Of course he hadn't.

He wanted her to say yes to his offer and only having two bedrooms would've put another checkmark in her "hell no" column.

"Easy solution, have Sunny sleep with you. I'll sleep with Wren."

She didn't have to turn to see he was staring at her. His dark eyes were burning a hole in the side of her head. "Ain't happenin'."

"What do you mean? I thought you wanted me to help out with Sunny."

"You're gonna. But gonna be sleepin' in my room."

"I am?" He couldn't mean...

"Yeah."

No. She wasn't sharing a room with a stranger. A *male* stranger. "That wasn't part of the deal."

"Yeah, it was. In the small print."

"Even if I agreed to that"—she never would—"where would Wren sleep?"

"A bunk bed."

"Where?"

"In Sunny's room."

Her head jerked back. This man must be smoking some pretty potent pot. "You want my son to sleep in the same room as your daughter?"

"He a pervert?"

"What? No!" She flip-flopped on whether she should laugh or cry at that ridiculous question.

"Then, it'll work for now. They're fuckin' kids."

"Won't Sunny mind sharing her room?" Especially with a stranger.

"Ain't up to her."

"She might end up hating you for that decision."

"Won't be the first time," he muttered. "But she don't make the decisions, I do."

"For me to agree with this, you need to take the couch."

"Too late. Already agreed. Maybe I don't got a couch."

"First of all, I can revoke my bad decision at any time. Second, if you don't have a couch"—she shot him a *sure, buddy* look—"you can buy a cot and sleep on that. In the basement, in the attic. I don't care."

"Said the house is small. No basement or attic."

Now she knew he was lying. "I bet you could find a really nice tent to pitch in the backyard."

"Kids might like that."

"It was for you, not them."

He sucked on his teeth.

She couldn't believe only three days ago he talked her into this arrangement.

She still debated on whether to put her house up for sale. While she couldn't afford to keep it, she also couldn't afford to let it go into foreclosure. Something Stone had suggested at the time.

"If I let it go into foreclosure, it'll ruin my credit." Something he didn't care about because the man probably didn't have any. If she had to guess, he paid for everything in cash.

A really scary look came over his face. "What the fuck's more important? Your life or your fuckin' credit? Your credit gonna raise your son?"

No, it wasn't.

One of the positives to this deal was, if she took his offer, once Vic was released from prison, he wouldn't know where she lived. The house wouldn't be in her name and if he needed to get a hold of her because of their son, he could go through her attorney.

"Then sell it, 'cause you ain't goin' back there. No reason to keep it."

She didn't even know the guy and here he was trying to control her life. "What about my stuff?"

"Know a guy who's got a movin' company."

Of course he did. "You want strangers to pack my stuff? All my personal belongings?"

"Said you ain't goin' back there."

"You said that, not me." She couldn't deny it would be smart to unload the house. It was too big and too expensive for her and Wren alone. She needed a smaller place with a reasonable mortgage payment. She was tired of struggling to maintain her marital home. One that also held bad memories.

While she had done her best for years, it was time to admit defeat. *"Stone..."*

"Babe..." He pulled in a breath through flared nostrils, then he ground out, *"That asshole knows where you live. He*

might be gettin' out any fuckin' time now. You ain't goin' back there."

"But—"

"Will get a coupla prospects to supervise the movin' crew."

"Great," she said dryly. "Where am I storing all of my stuff?" She would need it for her next home since, if she took his offer, she'd only be watching his daughter until he found someone else to permanently take over.

Her involvement would only be temporary.

"Got a trailer out back at the clubhouse that we can empty and use to store your shit. This way, you need it? It's within reach. Better yet, ain't gonna cost you a damn thing."

"You have all the answers, don't you?"

"Yeah."

"Are those answers always right?"

"Yeah."

At the time, she had rolled her eyes at his cocky answer. Now, she rolled them at the memory.

But he was correct about one thing: Vic knew where she and Wren lived since he had also lived there previously. Of course, he didn't know where Stone lived, or that they would be temporarily staying with him.

That could work to her benefit. After what he did to her in front of his own damn son, Vic did not deserve to know where they relocated. Wren had been so traumatized, she had to take him to therapy for months, despite her money already being stretched thin. But it had been worth every pinched penny since Wren was almost back to his happy, little boy self.

Her only worry was how Wren would react when he came face-to-face with Vic again. Something they might not be able to avoid if her ex's supervised visitation was approved.

Her stomach churned.

As a mother, she wanted to protect Wren as best as she could. Even if it was from his own father.

They were almost at the end of the village when Stone said, "Last one on the right."

The house was definitely dated on the outside. She hoped it was a similar case like the former school and was much better on the inside.

"Pull up to the garage." The cracked macadam driveway ended at a detached two car garage behind the house but sat off to the right.

"Every time you come home, want you parkin' in the garage. Best to keep your cage out of view."

"I doubt Vic will be tooling through Dead Man's Hollow."

"Never know. He could hire someone to find you."

Well, that was terrifying.

She can't believe the man she married, the man she had loved, the man she chose to have a child with, turned out to be so unstable.

"I've been meaning to ask: why do you call cars a cage?"

"Bikers are only really fuckin' free when we're on two wheels. When we're outrunnin' the rain, got the wind in our face, and chasin' a sunset. To a true biker, bein' inside a vehicle with four wheels is like bein' locked up."

"Makes sense," she murmured, shutting off her Honda. "But being inside a car means you won't get rained on. You could open a window if you need air and sunsets can be chased in a variety of ways."

He sucked on his teeth. "Find yourself a biker and you'll get it."

She would not be finding herself a biker. The one she

was dealing with currently was more than enough. "Do you want me to pull into the garage now?"

"Ain't gonna be here long. Gotta pick up your baby bird."

Great. He reminded her of her next problem. She would have to find a way to explain to her mother why she and Wren were moving in with a man she only just met.

She couldn't wait for that conversation.

After unfolding himself from the car, he grabbed his cut from where he'd thrown it on the backseat and shrugged it on. "You took it off only for the ride here? Is it uncomfortable?"

"Fuck no. My cut's a parta me. As comfortable as a well-used pussy."

This was who her son would be around? She could still back out of this deal since she hadn't even moved in a toothbrush yet.

However, she wasn't doing any of this for Stone. She was doing it to help protect Wren. Her son would always be her priority.

She was also doing it for Sunny, even though she hadn't met Stone's daughter yet. With the poor girl's mother currently in prison, the thought of a woman like Juicy taking care of an impressionable young girl...

She turned and studied the back of the house. He was right. It might be small but it had a backyard surrounded by a chain-link fence. Even though the size of the fenced area was half-decent, most of the space was taken up by an above-ground pool and a play-set that included a tunnel slide, swings, and objects for the kids to climb. Wren would love that.

Attached to the rear of the house was a small deck that looked like it had been built in the last few years. On that deck was a grill, a small table, and a few folding chairs.

She could picture Stone kicking back on the deck with a beer in hand and eyes on his daughter while she swam.

"Let me show you inside so you know what you're gonna need to bring from your place."

Probably not much except for some personal items and clothes for her and Wren. And, of course, the stuff needed to do her job as a personal chef.

Being able to bank her earnings while living rent- or mortgage-free would also be a benefit of moving in with Stone temporarily.

She'd be able to afford more therapy for Wren, if it was needed, as well as not having to rush to find a new home. She could take her time and find the right place.

When he headed through the gate, she followed. "When did you buy this house?"

Stone held open the screen door with his boot while he unlocked the door leading into the house. "Few years ago. Bought it for my mother when she was sick. Wanted her close. And despite the house bein' old, it's got good bones. Thought about sellin' it after she died, but never thought I'd have Sunny full-time. Now I do, got no choice but to keep it unless I wanna buy a bigger place."

"I'm sorry about your loss," she murmured, crossing the threshold behind him.

The back door led into a tiny entryway. When they headed to their right, they entered the kitchen. Stone might be comfortable on a Harley, but she always felt at home in a kitchen.

Cooking was her passion. She was lucky she could turn it into a career.

Fortunately, the appliances had all been updated more recently. Despite that, the cabinets most likely hadn't been touched since the seventies, except maybe for adding another coat of lime-green paint. Neither had the curtains. Or the decor.

"The kitchen's bigger than I expected." It might not be as huge and modern as a newer home, but it was functional.

"Mom couldn't do the steps toward the end so I moved her into the livin' room. Blew out the fuckin' wall between the kitchen and dinin' room to make it bigger and added another full bathroom downstairs. Before that, the house only had one bathroom up on the second floor."

That made sense. It was also very practical to expand the kitchen, since most people—unless they had huge families—didn't use a dining room very often. It tended to be wasted space.

She stayed on his heels as he made his way through the kitchen and past the full bathroom located at the front of the house. He hooked a left toward the front door, where the staircase to the second story was.

If she was standing out on the covered front porch looking at the house, the kitchen and bathroom took up the left side and the living room took up the right. That meant that there were only three rooms on the main floor. That might be tight for four people.

He tipped his head toward the stairs. "Gonna show you the rooms, then we can decide the sleepin' arrangements."

"I already know I won't be sharing your bed."

With a snort, he shook his head and headed upstairs.

At the top of the steps, she realized there were only three rooms up there, too. To the right of the stairway was a bedroom easily recognizable as belonging to his daughter. Not only because of how it was appropriately decorated for a ten-year-old girl but because of the bunk beds.

"You weren't lying about the bunk beds. She already has one."

"Yeah. Hate 'em 'cause they remind me of whenever I'm in the joint, but got it in case one of her friends wants to spend the night."

Taryn stood in the center of the room, slowly turning in a circle to take it all in. It might be tight for two kids, but it could work temporarily. Sunny might hate sharing her room but Wren would probably love it. In the past, he had bugged her for a sibling. Maybe this would get it out of his system and he'd never ask again.

She could hope, anyway.

"Does that happen often?" If she had a lot of sleepovers, she'd need to find other accommodations for her son during those times. Taryn doubted the girls would want Wren to join them.

"Never."

She spun to face him, only to find him with one hand glued to his hip as he stared out the window. "She's never had friends over?"

He turned, his expression a blank mask. "Some of my brothers' nut nuggets will come swim but none of the asshole parents from her school will let their kids come over."

Nut nuggets? She never heard that crass term used for children. Rugrats, yes. Nut nuggets, no.

"Why not?"

He tugged on his cut.

Oh.

But wait... "Because you belong to a club?"

"Ain't just any club."

"Do you want to explain that? I thought it was a group of people who all owned motorcycles."

"Not people. Men. Not any fuckin' motorcycle, Harleys," he corrected.

"Okay, the members all ride Harleys." And, apparently, were all men.

"It's a brotherhood. Ridin' ain't a hobby, it's a lifestyle."

"It still doesn't explain why parents wouldn't want their children hanging out with yours." Alarm bells went off in her head. She was missing something here. Maybe something very important.

She stared at him. His countless tattoos. His leather cut. The way he beat down Vic. The women at their clubhouse. It was not a typical lifestyle but...

"How many of your club members have been arrested before?"

His nostrils flared as he considered her question. "Does it matter?"

"It could. How many?"

"All of 'em."

All of them? "Is that a requirement to join your brotherhood?"

"No."

Her eyes flicked to the yellow diamond patch on his cut.

"What does that yellow diamond mean?"

"Means we live by our own damn rules."

Chapter Six

TARYN PULLED out her cell phone and quickly did a search on what the one percent patch meant in this situation. She should've done this after their conversation on Monday.

Better late than never, right?

Shit. Wrong.

She read out loud from one of the *many* search results. "'The term one-percent originated in the 1940s when the American Motorcyclist Association stated that ninety-nine-percent of motorcyclists were law-abiding citizens, implying the remaining one-percent were outlaws.'"

When she leveled her gaze on him once more, he whispered, "Fuck."

"Do you follow *any* laws?"

He pursed his lips and shut down his expression again before answering, "A few."

A few. "I'm assuming that list is a lot shorter than the one with the laws you ignore." She didn't even wait for him to respond before posing another question she neglected to ask,

"What do you do for a living? I'm sure chasing sunsets on a motorcycle doesn't pay well."

"Got a few businesses."

Her eyebrows rose at that deflection. "The club or you?"

"I *am* the fuckin' club," he said with intensity while slapping his chest. "My brothers are the club. *We* are the fuckin' club."

"So, what businesses do the club own?" She had a feeling he wouldn't be forthcoming with his answer or, on the slim chance he was, she wouldn't like what he said.

"Got a garage and some tow trucks. We sell some parts. Also do some personal protection. A few collections here and there."

The blood drained from her face. "Protection and collections?" It sounded like the Mafia. Or a...gang.

She narrowed her eyes on him.

"Protection's exactly why you're fuckin' standin' here." He jabbed his finger toward the wood floor. "Offered it to you at no damn cost."

Taryn could argue the fact it wouldn't cost her. This decision could end up costing her a lot. Why was he getting so bent out of shape, anyway? "And the collection part?"

"People pay us to collect bad fuckin' debts, that's all."

She doubted that was all. "I think it's time for us to go."

"Gotta show you your room first."

"I don't think I'm going to need it. While I appreciate the generous offer, I'll have to pass. I'll take my chances once Vic is released."

His expression turned even harder and scarier. "The fuck you will. Fucker coulda killed you if I hadn't stepped in."

When she shook her head and turned to leave, he grabbed her arm and stopped her, then swung her around to face him. They now stood close enough she could see the dark gold flecks in his deep brown eyes.

"Don't care if your baby bird don't got a mother to raise him? You want that motherfucker raisin' him instead?"

"My mother would—"

"And how's she gonna protect your boy? She a good shot? Former fuckin' military? A pig? A damn black belt? What?"

A pig? She could figure that one out without Google.

Her mother was none of those things. She was a sixty-two-year-old grandmother.

Taryn closed her eyes and pulled in a deep, calming breath. Okay, he was right. As unstable as Vic was now, he could do something serious to her or even kidnap Wren. She also didn't want to put her mother at risk.

Shit. Shit. Shit.

It was clear that the man before her would not be afraid to do what needed to be done to protect them. He had stepped in that day without anyone asking. He went to prison for over a year for helping her.

Even after all of that, to this day, he was still willing to help.

She owed him.

She reminded herself that living here would only be temporary. Until she could find a better way to protect herself and her son. Until she could figure out a way to disappear by moving somewhere Vic would never find them.

Once Wren was eighteen, Taryn would let him decide whether he wanted a relationship with his biological father or not. Until then, it was up to her to protect him, too.

That was why she needed to take his offer. It might be the lesser of two evils.

She reminded herself it was only temporary.

A few months maybe.

That was it.

Since it sounded like Stone had connections with questionable people, maybe he could help her disappear. Finding a remote tropical island somewhere and becoming a private chef at some billionaire's fifth vacation home would be perfect.

Okay, before any of that could happen, she first had to get through today. And tomorrow. She needed to take one day at a time.

Everything didn't need to be decided this very minute. Including moving in with some outlaw biker who was most likely a career criminal.

"Let's finish this tour. I need to go pick up Wren from my mother's."

He grinned at that.

Grinned.

Because he knew he'd won and was being cocky about it.

Only, he shouldn't celebrate just yet.

Nothing was set in stone.

He tipped his head toward the bedroom door. "C'mon, gonna show you the rest of the house before you go."

After crossing the short hallway at the top of the stairs again, he pointed toward the full bathroom between the two bedrooms. She peeked her head in to see it had a tub she could use for Wren. It had also been updated in the last decade, luckily.

Was it perfectly clean? Not even close. But that was an easy fix.

"Besides watching Sunny when you're not here, what else would you expect from me?" *Please don't say sex. That was not going to happen.*

When a wicked smile spread across his face, Taryn shook her head. "Not that. You mentioned cooking the other day."

"Yeah."

That was easy enough. "Cleaning? Laundry?"

"If you want. Or can get one of the sweet butts to do it."

She followed him into the primary bedroom. "A what? Is that the name of a cleaning service?"

"Somethin' like that."

"How often do they come?"

The creases at the corner of his eyes deepened. "Daily."

She frowned as she glanced around his room. "Then they're slacking. It looks like this place hasn't been cleaned for a couple of weeks or more."

He dropped his head and scratched the back of his neck.

"You might want to fire them if this is the quality of their work."

His bedroom had clothes tossed into the corner. A boot here. A boot there. The bed hadn't been made. She wondered when the last time the sheets had been washed. Dust covered the furniture, too.

"Can't fire them," he said eventually.

She glanced his way. "Why? Do you have a contract with them?"

"Can't fire someone you don't pay."

Her brow dipped low. "Are you stiffing them?"

"Could say that."

"Then, no wonder the house looks like this."

"Know that little computer you got in your hand?"

"My phone?"

"Yeah, that. Might wanna do another search."

She stared at him. With pursed lips, she pulled up the search engine again and typed in... "Is it one word or two?"

"Don't fuckin' know or care."

Fine, then. She typed it out as two first and once again read the resulting definition out loud. "*Women who hang around the club and make themselves available for sex.*" Oh. "Those women..."

"Yeah."

"They're..."

"Yeah."

She quickly scanned the page further. She had to close her gaping mouth to ask, "They're *property* of your club?"

"Basically."

"Juicy?"

"Yeah."

"She and that blonde...did they have sex with you because they *had* to or because they wanted to."

"Nobody's forcin' any of our sweet butts to do shit," he grumbled.

"So, they can say no."

"Sweet butts don't say no."

"Are they the only two?"

"Fuck no."

"Just how many—" She lifted a hand and shook her head. "Don't tell me. I don't want to know how many women allow themselves to be used like that."

"Their choice. Again, no one's fuckin' forcin' them to be a club wh—" His head twitched. "Girl."

"A what?"

"No one's forcin' them to be a part of our club. It's a fuckin' volunteer position."

"Are all women property of the club or is it just these"—she waved her hand around—"sweet butts?"

"Any woman tied to our club's under our protection."

That answer had her narrowing her eyes on him.

Tonight she would do a much deeper dive on motorcycle clubs like the Kings of Anarchy. Whether what she found was good, bad, or ugly, she didn't want any more surprises.

Plus, his answers so far made her doubt he'd be one-hundred-percent truthful with her if she asked him any more. She'd do her own research.

Taryn turned her focus back on the room where she might be *potentially* sleeping within the next couple of days.

The dusty furniture in the room might be old but was solid. "That bed's big enough for both me and Wren to share. I'd rather he be in here with me than with Sunny."

"Gonna let him decide."

He would do what? "He's six and not capable of making good decisions. That's my job. And it should be yours, too, when it comes to your daughter."

He grunted.

Glancing one more time around the room located at the front of the house, she figured it would do for the short time she expected to stay here.

She pointed to a door in the corner of the room. "What's that door?"

"Stairs up to the attic."

Right. He had lied when he said the house didn't have one. "What's up there?"

"Storage. Maybe some bats, rats, and spiders, too."

She shuddered. "Got it. Don't go into the attic."

She followed him back downstairs and he took her into the only room they hadn't explored yet: the living room.

The room was full of dark, outdated paneling, but it had a brick fireplace with a stack of cut wood next to it. An insanely large TV hung on the wall above it and on the opposite side of the room was a couch.

Look at that. "That couch looks pretty comfy." *Hint. Hint.*

"Passed out on it plenty of nights, but not by choice."

"You said you keep a room at your clubhouse. You could always sleep there," she suggested.

"Who the fuck's gonna protect you at night, then?"

"An alarm system?"

Stone shook his head. "I'm the fuckin' alarm system."

All in all, the house was a two-story square box. The positives were that it didn't smell, it wouldn't take much to clean it, and she hadn't seen a mouse or roach yet, despite the warning he gave her when it came to the attic.

"Well, you gave me an option to consider. But like you said, it's small. Actually very small for four people. While a little outdated, it's well-maintained." Basically, it was livable.

The biggest obstacle would be the fact she'd be sharing it with a biker who thought he was above the law. One who, despite being rough around the edges, was pretty damn hot, too. Luckily, she'd have no problem resisting him since arrogant, pushy men were a turn-off for her.

Add in that scruffy facial hair, his long hair, and all of his tattoos...

Stone was definitely not her type.

But then, Vic had been and look what happened with that mistake.

"Yeah. Kept the house up for Mom, 'specially while she was sick."

Damn it.

Stone had bought a house for his sick mother. He wanted someone responsible to help take care of his daughter. He didn't turn his back when Vic was attacking her, when so many other "upstanding" citizens had. He offered his house for her and her son to stay in without asking for a dime.

All of that proved he wasn't a horrible human being, despite him being a criminal, right?

She sure as hell hoped so.

Because if he truly was a lawless monster, then moving in with him might end up being a bigger mistake than marrying her ex-husband.

Chapter Seven

When Stone pulled his sled into the driveway, he was relieved to see she had done what he said: parked her car in the garage, out of view.

While Taryn's asshole ex hadn't been sprung from the joint yet, that didn't mean he didn't have anyone on the outside keeping an eye on her.

Or his son.

Because if he was her ex, that was what he would do.

As soon as his daughter got off his sled, she dropped her backpack onto the driveway and began unbuckling the strap on her helmet.

"Wait there," he told Sunny.

She squinted suspiciously at him. "Why?"

Just like her fucking mother, his girl had to question every-goddamn-thing.

"'Cause I fuckin' said so."

He didn't bother to avoid cursing around her. Not when she spent plenty of time at the clubhouse. She'd been around her foul-mouthed, pot-smoking, beer-drinking, whiskey-shooting "uncles" since she was in diapers.

What might be shocking to some was simply everyday life to her.

Using the app on his cell phone, he opened the garage door and parked his sled between Taryn's Pilot and his prized '67 Ford F-100 Flareside. The restored vintage truck was a lot older than him. Since being repainted in that candy-apple red metallic paint, it was prettier than him, too.

Stepping back out of the garage and into the afternoon sun, he saw—*surprise fuckin' surprise*—Sunny actually remained where he told her. His daughter's life was about to change the second she walked through the back door and he wanted to be by her side when that happened.

Plus, even at ten, Sunny could be pretty fucking mouthy. Just like fucking Sheena. And he didn't want to scare Taryn off not even a couple of hours after the prospects got finished moving in her shit.

Stone needed Taryn because Sunny needed Taryn, even if his daughter didn't know it yet.

That meant he needed to keep the woman not only safe, but content.

It also meant he'd be sleeping on the fucking couch for a while. She refused to move in until he agreed with that. While that sucked, it would be another sacrifice he was willing to make when it came to his baby girl.

He took Sunny's backpack from her and flung one of the straps over his shoulder. "C'mon. Taryn's waitin' to meet you. You be nice, yeah?"

She rolled her eyes at him. Just like fucking Sheena.

He should've picked a better sperm receptacle for his kid. But then, he hadn't planned on any of his swimmers having a fucking playdate with her scrambled eggs.

Sunny wrinkled her nose. "Why does she need to move in with us?"

"She needs my help and I need hers, that's fuckin' why. Made a deal."

"But I like to hang out with Juicy and Loosey."

"That's the problem," he muttered under his breath.

Sunny peered up at him as they climbed the deck steps. "What help does she need?"

"Her ex is a bad man."

"That's what Mom says about you."

Stone ground his teeth. He struggled to not say bad shit about her mother. At least in front of her. All bets were off when Sunny wasn't in earshot.

"He hit her."

Sunny stopped at the door. "You said boys aren't supposed to hit girls."

"Damn right. Any ever touch you, you tell me and I'm gonna handle it." He unlocked the door—besides making her park in the garage, he insisted Taryn keep the doors locked when he wasn't around—and indicated that Sunny should precede him inside.

"So, she's not a patch who—"

Stone slapped a hand over her mouth before Taryn could hear the rest. He leveled a warning look at his baby girl.

She bugged her little brown eyes at him like she was innocent.

She was far from that.

He wasn't afraid of much, but one thing that scared the shit out of him was how Sunny would act once she was a teen. Or, *hell*, even a tween.

Her teenage years were going to kill him. Just dig a goddamn hole and preorder his headstone now. No autopsy needed.

Cause of death: Girl dad.

Any man who had one would nod and simply understand.

With a hand on his daughter's shoulder, he steered her into the kitchen. Taryn was fussing with something on the counter.

Whatever she was cooking made his fucking mouth water and the house smell the best it had ever smelled.

He had given Taryn a wad of cash yesterday and sent a prospect along with her to the supermarket in Sunbury to stock the kitchen however she wanted.

Apparently, that was scratch well spent.

He couldn't put the introduction off any longer. He squeezed Sunny's shoulder to remind her to behave.

When Taryn turned, her gaze skipped over him and landed right on his girl. "Hi!" The smile she wore wasn't forced but warm and welcoming.

"Hi," Sunny greeted, not as enthusiastically. She turned to glance up at Stone, "*Daaaad—*"

"No." He glanced over at Taryn to see that smile had slipped a little. *Fuck.* "Taryn, this is the fruit of my loins, Sunny. Sunny, this is Taryn."

Taryn straightened her smile and asked his girl, "Is Sunny a nickname?"

When Sunny didn't answer, he nudged her.

When she still didn't answer, Stone did it for her. "Sunflower."

"Oh! Sunflower is such a beautiful name."

"It's stupid," Sunny grumbled.

Of fuckin' course.

Taryn quickly recovered her surprise. Whether it was due to learning Sunny's full name or because of his daughter's attitude, Stone wasn't sure. "It's unique."

"Dumb," his daughter grumbled.

"For fuck's sake, be glad your mother didn't name you Nut Sack," he growled.

Taryn's mouth gaped for a second as she turned wide eyes toward him. "Nut Sack?"

"Prospect," he answered.

"Oh, I thought his name was Gooch."

"Sent Gooch with you yesterday, but he ain't the only prospect."

"Oh. Did he choose that nickname?"

"Fuck no."

Her eyes widened again when he cursed. This time he realized it was an unspoken message. He shrugged in answer. "So, anyway, now you two met."

"Are you hungry?" Taryn asked Sunny. "I made Million Dollar Pasta. Have you ever had it before?"

"No."

While he loved his baby girl and would do anything for her, Stone's patience was currently running thin.

Taryn's eyebrows pinched together. "No, you're not hungry or no, you haven't had it before?"

His daughter set her jaw and spouted, "Just no. No to you. No to this whole thing."

For fuck's sake. "All right, go up to your room and watch TV or somethin' before you get grounded."

"Grounded for what?" Sunny screeched.

Stone winced. "For whatever I want. Could start with that shitty attitude you got."

"I don't—"

He pointed toward the front of the house. "Upstairs. Will call you when we're ready to eat."

"But—"

"No. Upstairs. Now."

With a grumble, Sunny jerked her backpack out of his hand and stomped away.

With his eyes squeezed shut in an attempt to keep his shit together, he waited until he heard her bedroom door slam before turning back to Taryn.

She was now leaning back against the counter with her arms crossed over her chest, making her tits look bigger than they actually were. It also made him want to bury his face in her cleavage.

"She don't like change."

"Most people don't."

Stone's eyes rose from her tits. "Kid gets anythin' she needs, even shit she don't. No reason for that bullshit."

"She's a child. And on that note...do you always curse like that in front of her?"

"Hard to avoid it. Anyway, she's so used to hearin' it, ain't any big deal."

"Unless she uses them herself where she shouldn't. Like at school."

"She don't. Told her they're big persons' words and she ain't allowed to use them."

She leveled a skeptical look in his direction.

He shrugged. "Shit happens."

He expected her to give him more shit about it, but instead, she changed the subject. "You seem very dedicated to her."

"She's my only nut nugget."

She blinked a few times, then shook her head. If she stuck around long enough, she would get used to the shit he said and stop reacting.

"Were you there when she was born?"

"No."

"Why not?"

"Wasn't sure she was mine 'til I got the DNA results back."

"What?"

"Yeah. Sheena said she was mine, but that baby coulda been anybody's. If you knew the bitch, you'd know not to trust her. She bounced from dick to dick. She got me at a weak moment."

Taryn cocked an eyebrow. "Did that weak moment have to do with alcohol?"

"Could be."

"Does that mean you had no say in her name?"

Stone snorted. "Fuck no. As you heard, she fuckin' loves it, too."

"What would you have named her, then?"

"Durex."

Taryn blinked in confusion again.

"Wrap."

"I don't understand."

"A wrap. The thing you put on your dick so you don't plant a seed in a bitch garden." Maybe the woman didn't use them.

After knocking up Sheena while he was trashed, he decided he'd never be without at least two in his wallet. He made sure he kept a shitload next to his bed at both the club-house and the house.

If he ever wanted another kid, he wanted to choose the mother, not have her choose him without him knowing.

"Do you get along with your ex?"

"Ain't my ex. Just someone I nutted in durin' a weekend-long pig roast. Ended up bein' an expensive fuckin' load."

"I guess you didn't take precautions."

"Hard to do when you don't even remember the fuckin' part."

"Sounds like a hard lesson to learn."

"Sure as fuck was. It's one thing to party and wake up hungover. It's another to wake up with a goddamn bun in the oven. And a fuckin' broken oven at that."

When she turned back to stir whatever was in the pot plugged into the wall, he glanced around.

If there was a six-year-old boy in this house, he sure as fuck was quiet. The exact opposite of that day in the parking lot. "So, where's your baby bird?"

She covered the pot with a glass lid and turned. "At the playground with my mother. She'll drop him off in time for dinner. And please don't call him that in front of him."

Instead of agreeing, he asked, "She good with you movin' in with me?"

"I didn't move in with you, I..." She sighed. "I haven't actually told her yet. I planned on letting her know when she drops him off."

"She gonna freak?"

"Possibly. So, can you be on your best behavior?"

He ignored that, too. "Whataya makin'?"

Whatever it was smelled damn good. His stomach growled just getting a whiff of it.

A frown etched her face. "Million Dollar Pasta."

"Oh, thought you were jerkin' Sunny's chain."

"No, it's a real dish. I'm keeping the meal simple tonight since I'm tired from unpacking. Since it's a dish Wren loves and it's easy to throw together in the crockpot, I hoped Sunny might like it, too."

"When she ain't bein' a brat, she ain't a picky eater."

"Are you?"

"A brat? Sometimes. Picky? Nope. Like pussy, long as it ain't rotten or moldy, gonna eat it."

Taryn's cheeks expanded like a chipmunk before her

breath exploded from her. "Those are the types of comments you need to refrain from when my mother is here. Please."

His chin jerked back. "What was wrong with it?"

"If you don't know, then..." Taryn shook her head.

"Got it. Be on my best behavior when Momma Bird's momma is here."

Taryn groaned and a look of defeat filled her face.

Shit. He needed to do better. He needed someone to help with Sunny and doing stupid shit could scare Taryn away.

Problem was, he was being himself. He wasn't going to change his ways simply to appease her.

Fuck. Maybe he'd try for Sunny's sake.

He wasn't making any promises, though.

Chapter Eight

When her mother's text stated she'd arrive in the next few minutes, Taryn checked dinner one more time before heading outside to meet her.

She wanted to make sure her mother's initial shock of seeing her temporary home—and who she'd be sharing it with—didn't cause her to lock her car doors and speed away with Taryn's son in tow. All in the name of Wren's best interest.

On the outside, the situation might not seem ideal.

On the inside...*shit.* She had no idea how the situation would play out. Not yet, anyway. She'd only finished moving in this afternoon and hadn't even spent one night under Stone's roof yet.

Time would tell.

In the meantime, she had to make sure everything appeared hunky dory to her mother.

For Wren's sake.

Hers, too.

"Hi, Mommy!" Wren's Spiderman lunchbox bounced

against his hip as he ran to her. She squatted down, opened her arms, and grunted when he hit her full speed.

She pressed a kiss to his forehead and ruffled his hair. "How was school, little man?"

"Good," he answered in a sing-song voice. "Paulie tried to kiss Debbie when we were at recess."

"Oh no."

"Yeah, she didn't like it so she pushed him down and he cried."

Good. "Oh no," she repeated. "Did he apologize?"

Wren shook his head. "No. Mrs. Tuttle told Debbie to apologize to Paulie."

What?

"Debbie's mommy came and was *maaaaad*. She was all red in the face and shaking her finger at Mrs. Tuttle."

Good.

Taryn got to her feet but tipped his face up toward her. "Did you learn anything from that?"

Wren squinted up at her. "Not to kiss girls."

That would work.

"You must always, always, *always* ask permission to touch anyone first, and if someone doesn't want to be kissed, then you don't kiss them."

He swung his lunchbox around. "Okay." His eyes landed on the house behind her. "This where we're gonna live, Mommy?"

"Yes, for now. And, look! It's got a pool!"

He bounced on his toes. "Yay!"

She turned toward her mother. "Thanks for picking him up from school."

Her mother's worried green eyes shifted from inspecting the back of the house to her. "Of course. We had fun at the playground."

"Gramma said not to throw rocks at the squirrels."

"I agree with Grandma. How about you don't throw rocks at all?"

Wren pouted.

Suddenly, her mother's spine snapped straight when her attention was drawn to something beyond Taryn. *Shit. Shit. Shit.* Taryn guessed her mother wasn't looking at something, but more like *someone.*

"He's behind me, isn't he?" Taryn whispered.

"By he, do you mean a tall man full of tattoos with a scruffy beard and even messier long hair?"

"That would be him."

"Why, Taryn?"

"It's not like that. This is only a temporary pit stop in the rat race of my life."

Her mother pursed her lips as she inspected him head to toe.

"Remember me, kid?" Stone asked Wren when he stepped up beside her.

With her son's little hand shading his eyes from the sun, he peered up at the much taller man. "*Noooo.*"

That could be a good thing. He was still dealing with some PTSD from that day over a year ago, despite the therapy. Unfortunately, seeing his father, the only male figure in his life, beat the crap out of his mother would stick with him for a long time.

She'd also be working for a long time on fixing her mistake of meeting Vic to exchange Wren without anyone else accompanying her.

All due to that goddamn court order.

If she had canceled, Vic would've made her life a living hell. He looked for any excuse to take her back to court for custody. That meant she had no choice but to take the risk.

One that obviously hadn't paid off.

She didn't want Stone reminding Wren of that day all over again. She bugged her eyes out at the biker in an unspoken warning. "Of course he doesn't. You only met for a minute that *busy* day."

His dark eyes flicked to her before dropping to Wren. When he lifted his gaze back to her, he gave her a single nod in understanding.

Thankfully, the man could pick up on clues. She gave him a pointed smile. "Stone, can you take Wren inside, please? I'll be in in a minute."

He stared at her for a long minute before once again giving her a nod of understanding. "Ready for dinner, Baby Bird?"

Taryn closed her eyes and pushed a breath through her nose. Did he call Wren that on purpose after she asked him not to?

Men.

But she forgave him quickly when he offered his hand to her son and he guided Wren to the house.

"Did you call me a baby bird?" her son asked.

Taryn could only see the outline of his profile as the man glanced down at her six-year-old. "Ain't that your name?"

The sound of Wren's belly laugh warmed her heart. "*Nooooo!* My name is Wren."

"That's what I said."

"No, it isn't!"

"Must need your ears cleaned out, Baby Bird."

Taryn's smile disintegrated the second she turned back and saw her mother's expression locked down tight.

Great. Here comes a lecture in three...two...

"Taryn, have you thought this through?"

"Thought what through?"

Her mother flapped her hand around. "Whatever this is. I know you're struggling to take care of the house, but this..." She shook her head.

"He offered me a place to live with my son for free, Mom. In exchange, I only need to help with his daughter."

The things you have to do when you're desperate...

"He might not be charging you rent, but I'm sure it will cost you in other ways." She focused on the back door through which Wren and Stone disappeared. "How do you even know him?"

Shit. Her mother only knew a man stepped in to stop Vic that day, but because of the violence involved, she figured it was best not to tell her it had been Stone. Especially since Vic ended up in the hospital afterward for quite a while.

Knowing Stone had the potential to be that violent—even if only when pushed—would make her mother freak out and insist that Taryn not share the same roof.

Yes, his reaction had been a little over the top—even though she only saw the results afterward in light of her being knocked out—but at least he'd been brave enough to step in to help her.

"He was the one who stepped in to help me when Vic..."

Her mother lifted a hand. "Understood. But, Taryn, take it from me, you shouldn't rely on a man. And this feels a lot like that."

"Mom, I think I already learned that lesson." A few times over.

"Are you sure about this? I'm worried about you, Taryn. I'm worried about my grandson. He seems like the opposite of a good man."

Taryn sighed. "Are you going by facts or perception?"

"Well, he looks"—her mom flapped a hand around again—"unkempt."

Unkempt?

He looked more together today than that first day she sought him out at the old school. But then, he didn't have a hangover today and hadn't just shared a bed with two women.

In fact, he looked damn good today. A tight, black tank hugged his amazing physique. The man certainly did not have a typical biker body. At least according to what she saw on Google. She figured they'd all look more like Patch.

"He doesn't look respectable."

Because he wasn't. "Looking respectable and being respectable are two different things, Mom. You know who *looks* respectable but, in reality, isn't? *That's* who you should be worried about, not Stone."

"Stone," she huffed. "What kind of name is that?"

"A nickname. That's all."

"Well, I don't like it."

"Then, I won't call you that. Remember, this is only temporary."

"I can take Wren."

Taryn's heart skipped a beat. "No. I want him with me. And not only that, he'll have Sunny. She'll be the sister he never had." Or at least she hoped so. There was no telling with Sunny's attitude whether she would be kind to Wren or not.

Her mother clicked her tongue.

Taryn shook her head. "Please don't turn into Grandma."

Her mother squeezed Taryn's arm. "I know my apartment is small, but if this turns out to be not as you expected, don't hesitate to come stay with me. We'll figure it out. You didn't put the house up for sale yet, did you?"

"I'm meeting the agent this week."

Her mother sighed.

"It's for the best, Mom. The house is too much for me to handle, especially with only one income, and I'm worried Vic will show up at the door after he's released. He blames me for his conviction and incarceration."

"He deserves more time than what he got."

"I won't argue that."

"But he's a good example of some of the bad choices you make." She turned her eyes back to the house. "Please be careful."

"I will. Do you want to join us for dinner? I made Million Dollar Pasta."

"Another time. I'm meeting the girls to play Pinochle tonight."

She gave her mother a hug. "Well, have fun. Say hello to the ladies for me and thank you for dropping off Wren."

Her mother squeezed her so tightly Taryn could hardly take a breath. "Please be careful, Taryn. A mother worries."

"I know, Mom. I'm a mother, too."

THE GUT PUNCH from a tiny foot had Taryn's eyes popping open. For a second she had no idea where she was. Until it hit her...

This was not her house. Or her bedroom.

Or her normal life.

She twisted her head to see Wren sleeping sideways in his favorite Sonic the Hedgehog pajamas and taking up too much real estate in Stone's king-sized bed. How could a six year old, only weighing in at about fifty pounds, take up that much space?

After dislodging Wren's other foot from under her chin,

she unplugged her cell phone from the charger, glanced at the time, and groaned.

It was way too early.

However, she had a private dinner scheduled today so she might as well get up, plan breakfast, then start prepping the ingredients for her event later and loading whatever she'd need into the car.

She had no idea how Sunny prepared for school in the morning, other than maybe eating breakfast. Taryn needed to figure out her daily routine, too.

Stone's daughter had picked at the pasta last night, wrinkling her nose dramatically after every bite she pretended to force down.

Stone scarfed down the contents of his bowl in under a minute, then went back for seconds.

Wren watched him closely and tried to do the same. He failed, thankfully, since Taryn didn't want to be up all night with a boy with an upset stomach from eating too much.

However, seeing Wren mimick Stone worried her a little. Especially since her son was like a sponge who seemed to absorb all the wrong things.

But all through dinner, the kids hardly spoke two words to each other. Taryn hoped that would change and soon.

Maybe if she made waffles this morning, they could all sit down at the table together and make an effort to interact more than last night.

The second Sunny "finished" dinner, she'd left the table and went back up to her room, once again slamming the door. Stone ended up polishing off her bowl, too, totally ignoring his daughter's dramatic display.

She could understand him not feeding into her tantrum, but at the time, she was concerned he hadn't even addressed it. Later last night, she did hear his deep voice coming from her room, but had no idea what that "talk" was about.

Of course, blending families took time and patience. Bumps could be expected along the way. Taryn planned on giving Sunny time and space. Forcing the girl to accept Taryn and Wren might only make things worse and she could come to resent them.

If she didn't already.

Taryn certainly didn't miss the side-eye Sunny kept giving her father as he teased and talked to Wren. Her son had been thrilled with the attention. Sunny, not so much.

Taryn groaned softly as she rolled out of bed, made sure all her body parts were tucked away since she had slept in a tank top and pajama bottoms, then after a quick pit stop in the upstairs bathroom, padded barefooted downstairs.

The house was too quiet.

That could mean that Stone and Sunny were still asleep. When she reached the foot of the stairs, she could turn right into the expanded kitchen area or hook a left into the living room. Maybe she'd have a little discussion with Stone about Sunny's school morning routine before she tackled making waffles.

Her feet stuttered as she spotted Stone on the couch, completely knocked out and only wearing an unbuttoned pair of jeans with the zipper partially open and one hand shoved down his pants. His other arm dangled off the couch with his hand only a few inches from a half-empty beer bottle sitting on the floor nearby. It looked like he zonked out while reaching for that same beer.

She inched her way closer so she could get a good look at him without him knowing.

The man had so many tattoos. So, *so* many. They covered his arms, his hands, his chest, his stomach...

She wondered if more inked artwork covered his legs and back, too. The man must not be bothered by needles.

One tattoo in particular caught her eye. It was also the only one in color that she could see in a sea of black and gray.

While it made sense because of his daughter, the beautifully detailed and colorful Sunflower tattoo above his heart was unexpected for such a rough-and-tumble type of guy like Stone.

Despite only knowing him less than a week, she already knew how much he loved his daughter. After seeing what he did to Vic, she had no doubt he'd probably kill for Sunny.

She gasped when a hand flashed out, grabbing her wrist and jerking her off balance.

She didn't land on the soft couch, she landed on a very hard body.

"Mornin'."

That rough, sleepy greeting shouldn't cause flutters in her belly or lightning to race down her spine.

Neither should the hard-on pressing against her hip.

Or the hand cupping her ass.

Or those lips curled up in a knowing smile.

Or those dark, heated eyes locked with hers.

She swallowed so she could loosen her throat enough to speak. "Can you—"

"Mornin'," he repeated, cutting off her request.

The man was too damn confident for his own good.

When she went to climb off him, he kept her there. Pressed against his body. The steady beat of his heart thumping against the hand she had planted on his very warm chest. "Stone..."

A grin slowly spread across his face as he released his hold on her so she could scramble to her feet. She quickly checked to make sure one of her boobs didn't escape the side of her tank top in an attempt to wave hello.

"Mornin'," he repeated for a third time.

Taryn was sensing a theme. "Morning."

With a loud yawn, he sat up. "Way you were checkin' me out, figured you might be interested in a mornin' quickie." Clawing his fingers through his long, black hair did the exact opposite of taming that wild mane.

She wondered if he even owned a brush. She definitely didn't notice any hair products for men in the bathroom.

Hell, she wouldn't be surprised if his cologne was gasoline and his beard oil made from motor oil.

When he scratched his bare chest, her eyes focused on where his long fingers touched.

When he scrubbed them down his beard, she got sucked in watching that, too.

Her reaction was not good. Since he was not her type, it made no damn sense.

Yes, he was hot.

Yes, he was surprisingly sexy.

But she had never been into "bad boy" types, and if anyone fit that bill, it was the man sitting on the couch making her insides feel as warm as his skin had been.

Making her fingers itch to explore every tattoo.

You're here to do a job in exchange for a roof over your head and some protection. That's it. Don't let him distract you.

Right. Onto the business at hand. "Hungry?"

"Definitely could eat. How d'you want me to do that?" He added a cocky grin.

"The kitchen table's a good place."

"I'm good with that, too. We just gotta hurry before the kids wake up. How quiet can you be?"

Her traitor pussy twinged in response.

He seemed determined to throw her off her game. "Does Sunny like waffles?"

"Her father sure as fuck does. Long as they ain't blue."

What? "Blue waffles? Do you mean blueberry?"

One side of his mouth pulled up. "Know you like to look up shit on your cell phone, babe. Best if you skip that search."

She stared at him. "I'm going to take a wild guess here and say blue waffles have nothing to do with food."

"Yeah, ain't nothin' you'd wanna eat."

"Since you must've tried them, I'll take your word for it."

He chuckled, then stood and arched his back, stretching it. "Fuck, my back's killin' me." That movement caused her to visually explore his unexpectedly fit body. It was nothing like Patch's. Or Gooch's. Or, hell, most of the other bikers she had come into contact with already. "Why don't you sleep in the bunkbed in Sunny's room?"

"More space on the couch than in that fuckin' bunkbed."

"Would you rather Wren and I take the bunkbeds and you and Sunny share the bed in your room?" Then maybe she wouldn't wake up sore from being kicked.

One dark eyebrow raised. "Don't mind sharin' my bed, just not with my girl."

"Why?"

"Ain't obvious?"

"I wouldn't have asked if it was."

He grabbed his crotch, drawing her eyes back to his erection.

"Oh." *That.*

Damn.

She agreed that would get awkward, even if it was a completely normal function for a man.

"Yeah, *oh.* Wanna help me get rid of it before the nut nuggets roll downstairs for breakfast?"

"Sure. Stand right there." She pointed to the spot in front of her.

A sly grin curved his lips as he moved into place.

When his hands went to his already partially opened zipper, she stopped him with an extended palm. "No reason to remove your jeans."

Creases marred his forehead. "Then how you gonna suck me off?"

"I was planning on kneeing you in the nuts. I figured that would help with that issue."

"Not what I was thinkin'."

"Of course not. Also, can you refrain from calling the kids nut nuggets in front of them? I really don't need Wren going to school and proudly announcing that he's a nut nugget." Because her son would definitely do that. Especially with the way he seemed to worship Stone last night.

"Well, he is."

"Debatable. All right, if you think she'll eat them, I'll go make waffles."

"Want help?"

Her eyes went wide. "Are you offering?"

"Fuck no. Gonna go wake up Sunny. Good if she learns how to make her dad waffles. Girl needs to earn her damn keep."

Was he joking? Or was he only trying to pull a reaction from her?

"Before you do that, let's discuss her schedule and routine while I prepare the batter."

Chapter Nine

As Taryn eyed the mountain of dishes in the sink, she knew the mess had been worth it.

Sunny had scarfed down two big Belgian waffles drowning in syrup, along with two breakfast sausages.

Stone had eaten four waffles, six sausages, and chugged two mugs of java.

Wren barely made it through one waffle but managed to shovel in two sausages.

They were now out of maple syrup so she added it to her shopping list.

She needed to take Wren to school and start prepping for tonight's dinner. Both theirs and her client's.

Tonight might have to be another crockpot meal or a casserole that could be easily popped in the oven since she'd be working elsewhere at dinner time.

Stone never said what time dinner needed to be ready, but Taryn knew what hour Wren started asking what was for dinner. Or bombarding her with suggestions.

Like hot dog slices in baked beans. Or mac and cheese. Or a sugary cereal.

Normally, she tried to make him healthier options and only serve those "junk food" meals on an occasion.

Tonight might be one of those occasions. Without being too obvious, she tried to figure out some of Sunny's favorite foods, but Stone's daughter was too tightlipped. She ate, dumped her dish in the sink, then disappeared upstairs without even a thank you. Taryn assumed to get ready for school.

After Sunny left the table, Taryn and Stone continued their conversation about Sunny's morning routine so she could be on top of it. Since both kids were in elementary school, their schedules aligned, luckily. The only difference was where they attended school.

Boot steps behind her had her turning to see Stone striding into the room fully dressed for the day. Whatever that entailed.

Of course, his outfit was a carbon copy of how he dressed yesterday and the previous days. Worn jeans hugged his long legs, heavy black boots covered his feet, and he wore his MC cut.

The only change she noticed day to day was what he wore under that cut. Today it was a T-shirt that had seen better days, advertising a local Harley-Davidson dealership.

His black hair was pulled up high into a man-bun, most likely because he'd be hopping on his bike when he left. His beard looked a little neater this morning, as if he'd made an effort to tame it.

His dark espresso eyes were focused on her, doing the exact same thing: taking her in from head to toe, even though she hadn't showered or changed yet. She looked exactly the same as when she sat across from him at breakfast.

Still…his eyes taking a slow stroll over her from the top of her head, over her face, pausing on her pink ribbed tank top—where her nipples decided to stand up and shout "hello!"—and then racing quickly down her PJ-covered legs, finishing at her bare feet, made her feel some kind of way.

While neither disgust nor a feeling of being visually violated, it was still one she needed to ignore. Just like earlier when he pulled her down on top of him.

If she ignored the warmth pooling between her legs, maybe it would go away.

When their gazes locked, she did not like the grin he wore.

Or maybe she liked it too much.

Stop it! He's not for you. You are not *for him. Stop making horrible decisions that affect not only you, but Wren.*

To try to get past this weird, unexplainable attraction she had to this biker, she flipped a hand toward the sink. "I'll clean up the kitchen after I get back from dropping Wren off at school."

"Don't gotta do that."

"The food will dry on the—"

"Droppin' him off at school. Gotta take Sunny, so will drop him off, too. Will take my truck."

That would save her so much time but… "His school is across the river."

"Yep. And best if you switch him over to Sunny's school this week. Don't wanna go pick him up one afternoon to find your ex got him first. That would suck."

That certainly would suck. "I have to head over to a new client's house this afternoon and I won't be back until after dinner. I can still have something simple ready for you, though."

"Gonna grab pizza."

"I thought you wanted me to cook for—"

"Gonna grab pizza," he repeated in a tone that brooked no argument.

Okay, then.

"Who's watchin' Baby Bird when you're gone?"

Shit. She assumed he would. "Who's watching Sunny?"

Please don't say a sweet butt.

A muscle in his jaw jumped and he scraped a hand down his thick beard. "Guess I am."

She really wondered if him watching the kids was any better than a sweet butt. At least he had a personal stake in keeping one of them alive.

"I won't be home late." Why did that feel strange to say? "I don't leave until they finish dessert and the table's cleared."

"When's he done with school?"

"About 3:10, why?"

"Gonna get him from school, too."

"I can have my mo—"

"Gonna get him from school," Stone repeated more firmly.

Taryn threw up her palms in surrender. "Fine." Truth be told, that was a relief. She didn't want to put that burden on her mother if she could avoid it.

Sunny sauntered through the kitchen, not sparing her or Stone a glance since her head was tipped down as she did something on her cell phone.

Did a ten-year-old really need a cell phone? Taryn mentally sighed. She had no doubt Wren would be asking for one of those next.

The back door slammed as she went outside.

"Jesus fuck," Stone muttered under his breath and shook his head.

Taryn agreed with his assessment. The girl hadn't even

hit the moody teen years yet. If she was like this now... "Give her some time. Her mom just went to jail—"

"Nothin' new."

"And two strangers moved into her father's house," she finished. "Does Sunny need me to make her lunch?"

Stone shook his head. "She's got scratch."

Her brow pulled low. "Scratch?"

He rubbed the pads of his fingers together to indicate money.

If only there was a translation app dedicated to biker speak.

Smaller feet slapping on the floor came next and her little gremlin joined them in the kitchen. She grabbed his lunchbox off of the counter and held it out to him.

His little face turned up to her. "Mom, is the bus coming, or are you taking me to school?"

"The bus won't pick you up here, buddy, so Stone will drop you off this morning."

He squinted his eyes until they were almost slits and huffed. "Why won't the bus pick me up?"

"Because this house is in another school district. For now, someone will have to drop you off and pick you up. Stone said he'll come get you this afternoon, too, okay?"

His face lit up. "Yay!"

Great. She really didn't need him to be worshipping a man who belonged to a motorcycle club, cursed, smoked, and drank. Possibly even did drugs.

Ugh. She should've asked him about the drugs prior to moving in. If he did anything more than pot...even if he only smoked pot, she didn't want him to do it in front of her very impressionable son.

She would need to have that conversation with Stone but not in front of Wren. With his curious little mind, he'd be asking a boatload of questions she wouldn't want to answer. Not when he was only six.

She'd hold off on the sex, booze, and drug discussion with him until her first grader was a little older.

Stone ruffled Wren's hair. "Ready, Baby Bird?"

Taryn clenched her teeth in an effort not to scold the thirty-something-year-old biker.

"Tweet, tweet," her son chirped and flapped his elbows. "*Tweeeeeeet.*"

Oh, good lord.

"Let's roll," Stone urged with a cocky grin, heading outside.

Taryn followed him out but stopped at the top of the deck steps since she was still barefooted. "Grab the booster seat from my Honda and please drive carefully!" she called out to Stone.

He flicked a couple of fingers above his shoulder. At least that was some sort of acknowledgment that he heard her.

Her gaze dropped from the tall man to the much shorter boy.

Wren's short legs were scrambling to keep up with Stone's much longer ones. Once again, his lunchbox bounced wildly off his legs. She wouldn't be surprised if it was leaving bruises behind.

Sunny waited for her father just inside the open garage door, still busy fussing with her phone.

"Have a good day at school, okay? Please be good for your teacher." When she didn't get a response from her son, she called out to him again. "Did you hear me, Wren?"

Without stopping, but sounding annoyed, Wren yelled up to the sky, "Okay, Mommy!"

Her lungs seized when he almost tripped over his own

feet. He quickly caught himself and disappeared into the garage.

She blew out her held breath.

That could've been ugly. Him face-planting on the driveway might have ended up with them spending hours in the emergency room. Beyond her baby getting hurt, she couldn't afford a hospital visit right now.

Stone stopped in front of his daughter and when she didn't look up, he snagged the phone from her fingers as she was still typing. Sunny glared at him as he tucked the phone inside his cut and shook his head to whatever she was saying.

From the girl's posture, she was clearly giving her father some attitude. In return, he simply shrugged and disappeared inside the garage.

She waited on the deck just in case Stone had any problems installing the booster seat in his truck. More importantly, she wanted to make sure he actually used it.

Not even five minutes later, he reversed his old truck—old in age, not in looks—out of the garage, did an impressively smooth K-turn, then headed down the driveway.

As the restored Ford passed her, she could see Sunny pouting in the middle and Wren with his nose pushed up and smashed against the passenger window so he looked like a piglet.

Smearing snot on Stone's window wouldn't be a very nice thank you for the favor he was doing her by taking Wren to school.

Slapping a hand onto her forehead, she whispered, "How is this my life?"

How did she get to the point she had an instant family with an outlaw biker?

One who had no problem breaking the law and even beating up people to within an inch of their life. All this instant family needed was a broken, white picket fence, a rusty minivan, and a damn three-legged dog.

Vic. This was all because of Vic.

Proof that one bad decision could cause a rippling effect that created havoc in every other aspect of her life.

HER CELL PHONE lit up on the counter when it rang.

Shit. It was the school so she had no choice but to take it. She glanced around to make sure her client wasn't within earshot and answered it, covering her mouth to contain the sound. "Hello?"

"Mrs. Gentry?"

That reminded her: when she had some spare funds, she needed to change her last name back to her maiden name. She was tempted to change Wren's last name, too, but that might infuriate Vic even more.

"Yes?" she whispered. "Is something wrong with Wren?"

"Not quite. A teacher saw him heading toward a man on a motorcycle and stopped him. Do you know this person or should I call the police?"

Was it Stone? It had to be. "Did he say who he was?"

"We didn't ask. Only two other people besides yourself are on your authorized pickup list. Gail Howard..."

Her mother.

"And Victor Gentry."

Her blood ran cold. Did she forget to remove him? "Can you remove Mr. Gentry from the list?"

"You want Wren's father removed from the list?"

She ignored the mix of surprise and condemnation in the woman's question. "Yes. Can you do that for me?"

"No. Unfortunately, I'd need a court order for that."

Shit. "He's being released from prison soon and—"

"I'm sorry, Mrs. Gentry, but I can't stop a parent from picking up their child unless a court order is in place."

She pulled in a breath. She couldn't argue with a school official in her client's kitchen. "Then, can you add Stone for me?" She closed her eyes and shook her head. "Sorry, Stone is his nickname. His name is James Conrad."

"Is that who's waiting at the curb? Do you know he's wearing a vest that's tied to a local biker gang?"

Crap. Crap. Crap. "I have no idea if it's Mr. Conrad. It could be one of his associates." She grimaced. She should've used *friend* instead of *associate.* It made it sound like he *did* belong to a criminal organization.

"Well, if the person isn't on the authorized list..."

"Can you give me a moment, please, for me to check with him?"

"Sure," followed a long, impatient sigh.

Taryn quickly texted Stone: *Are you at Wren's school to pick him up?*

She only hoped he'd respond in a reasonable amount of time or she'd have to send her mother again. If she couldn't get a hold of her mother, she'd have to leave the dinner she was preparing. Doing so might cause the loss of that client's future business and maybe even a bad review. She couldn't afford to lose even one of her clients. She needed to increase her client base, not reduce it.

Thankfully, his response came quickly. Only, it wasn't the one she wanted to hear.

No.

Who is? Nobody can pick him up unless they're on a list. Being the father of a school-age child, shouldn't he know how it worked?

She slapped her own forehead. Of course, with all the recent big changes, she forgot that herself.

Another text followed quickly: *A prospect called Shit Stain. Put him on the list.*

That had to be a joke. His name couldn't be Shit Stain. And she certainly wasn't repeating that to the school admin.

Be serious. What's his real name? She tapped her nails impatiently on the counter, keeping an eye out for the homeowner.

No fuckn clue. Only know him as Shit Stain.

Her mouth dropped open. She quickly texted: *Find out his real name. I'm not giving that to the school administrator.*

Another minute went by. *Gimme sex. Gonna text him.*

"Gimme sex?" she whispered. Her fingers flew across the electronic keyboard. *Do you mean: give me a sec?*

She didn't get an answer.

The seconds ticked by as she waited.

Lee Carlin.

She put the phone back to her ear. "The man at the curb is Lee Carlin. I give you permission to release Wren into his custody."

Did she really, though?

She glanced around the kitchen and sighed. It wasn't like she could just up and leave to go get him. Even if she could get a hold of her mother, Wren might have to wait at the school for her to arrive and she was sure the staff wouldn't be happy about staying late.

Neither would Wren.

"Mrs. Gentry..."

Of course, the woman had to keep reminding Taryn of the damn mistake she made by marrying Vic. Her second mistake was taking his last name.

"You'll need to come in and sign the form for these new additions."

"If you'll let Wren go with him today, I promise I'll be in this week to do so." The administrator didn't need to know that was a lie since Stone was right, she needed to register him at Sunny's school instead. Right now, she only needed someone to get him home.

Apparently, that someone's name was Shit Stain.

She groaned.

"Don't forget to bring along the court order to remove your husband."

"Ex-husband," Taryn corrected. Actually, soon he'd be considered more than an ex-husband, he'd labeled an ex-con, too. "And thank you for making this exception."

"This will be the one and only time, Mrs. Gentry. I'd like to keep my job."

She wasn't the only one. She needed to get off the phone and get back to work. Word of mouth was everything in her business. Without recommendations from her current and former clients, she would no longer have a career.

And without it, she wouldn't even be able to afford a tent to live in.

After she hung up, she glanced around at the interrupted food prep, but her mind was still on what just went down.

Taryn needed to put transferring Wren's school at the top of her list this week. He wouldn't be able to attend that school district once she sold the house and moved elsewhere, anyway. If she never put Vic on the list at the new school in the first place, maybe she wouldn't need a court order to keep him off it. And if she did...

Suddenly, she realized there was a bigger issue than Shit Stain's name.

Her six-year-old would be riding on the back of a damn

motorcycle! Was that even legal? He wasn't even allowed to ride in a vehicle without a booster seat! What if he fell off? What if Shit Stain wrecked his bike?

Did Shit Stain even have a helmet for Wren?

Anxiety caused her heart to thump wildly. All kinds of disastrous images popped into her head.

Was she a bad mother for allowing a prospect from an "outlaw" MC to pick up her child?

Before she could text Stone all her concerns, her phone dinged again with an incoming text.

Stone had sent a photo.

In that photo was an excited Wren on the back of a prospect named Shit Stain's Harley. His smile was so big, it was blinding. The caption? *Badass biker in the makn.*

Great. But at least her son was wearing a helmet that actually fit him and the prospect's bike had what looked like a seat with a back to it so Wren wouldn't tumble off.

She'd take that small win.

Chapter Ten

"Have you seen Stone?"

The female voice echoing down the hallway made Stone jerk. What the fuck was she doing here?

She was supposed to text him what time she'd be home so he could get Wren back to the house before she got there.

For fuck's sake. He was about to get served a healthy helping of shit since he brought her son to The Castle. But he told Taryn he'd get the kids pizza for dinner and that was what he did. He just failed to mention it would be for their kids *and* his brothers. And that they'd be eating it at the Kings' clubhouse.

Apparently, time got away from him since making two dozen pies took the pizza shop a fuck of a lot longer than expected. Add in the amount of time it took to answer her boy's five fucking thousand questions about the Kings, the brotherhood, their clubhouse, and everything else he spied with his two little curious eyes.

"Yo, VP, a momma bear's here lookin' for you. Thinkin' that cub belongs to her," he heard next.

From where he was leaning against the wall right inside of the cafeteria's entryway, he could keep an eye on Wren while adding some much-needed nicotine to his bloodstream.

Smoke escaped his lungs when he twisted his head and told Grim, "Ain't a cub, he's a baby bird."

Grim appeared in his sight with Taryn quickly following. No surprise, she looked wired as fuck.

Yep, Momma Bird wasn't fucking happy that she had to track down her fledgling. "Thanks, brother, got it from here."

With a smirk, Grim gave him a chin lift and disappeared.

As soon as Taryn spotted Wren sitting at one of the cafeteria tables coloring, she visibly relaxed.

"Boy's fine."

She sighed. "I see that. I got home and the house was empty. I panicked thinking he ended up in the hospital after you sent me that picture of him on the back of a motorcycle."

"Sent a text askin' when you'd be home. Musta missed it."

She narrowed her baby blues on him. "I did, but why did you ask? So you could bring him home before I got there?"

Stone figured a grunt was the safest answer. Since it wasn't a truth or a lie, it couldn't be held against him either way.

When she plugged her hands on her hips, his gaze was drawn to those curves. "I didn't say you could bring him here."

He slowly lifted his gaze, taking in the rest of her. She was once again dressed in one of those shapeless chef uniforms with her name embroidered over her tit. He'd take how she was dressed this morning any day over that shit.

Especially since, this morning, she hadn't been wearing a bra. He hated those fucking things. They should be considered false advertising. One minute tits look perfectly perky, then once freed, they become deflated balloons.

"Didn't say I couldn't," he countered around the cigarette tucked between his lips.

"I figured that would be assumed."

"That was your first mistake." He took another long drag, inhaling the smoke deep into his lungs before blowing it up and away from her.

"One of many," she mumbled under her breath and turned back to take in the large room.

While she did so, Stone tried to see it through her eyes. Admittedly, the scene wasn't good.

Garbage overflowed onto the floor from the few trash cans they did have. Cigarette butts littered the room. Empty pizza boxes, beer bottles, and even bottles of booze covered the tables.

He made a mental note to make sure the cafeteria was on the sweet butts' cleaning rotation at the next officer's meeting.

But that mess wasn't even the half of it.

Some of his brothers sat at a table, stoned as fuck and still scarfing down cold pizza like it tasted better than prime pussy.

Only, that wasn't the worst of what she was seeing. Wren was happily chirping away a million miles a minute to the sweet butt sitting next to him also coloring with crayons.

Christ.

He didn't like the taste of shit but he was about to eat some.

"Holy shit," she whispered as she finished taking in the disaster left behind. "Was a pack of ravenous wolves invited to this pizza party?"

"Sweet butts gonna clean it up."

"You mean the one coloring next to Wren?"

Again, his safest answer was another grunt.

She sighed her disappointment again. This time a lot louder. "Where's Sunny?"

At least she wasn't hauling her kid out of there and moving back to the house she couldn't afford and needed to unload.

Thank fuck her house was now empty and all of her shit was being stored here on the property. Made it a little more difficult to just up and leave.

Unless she went running to her mother's.

"Said she'd be up in my room watchin' television." His daughter was still bent about him taking her phone this morning, but he had told her to put it away once and once should be all it took.

Now she wouldn't get it back until the morning. That made his girl cranky, but he was even crankier when she didn't listen to him. And fuck if he was repeating himself.

"Okay, well. I guess I'll take him...home."

Why did her face scrunch up like she was sucking on musty balls when she said "home?"

At least she had a fucking roof over her goddamn head for her and her kid. One where her asshole ex couldn't find her once he was no longer getting three hots and a cot.

"Are you staying? Do you want me to take Sunny?"

"Yeah. Just know she's bein' a total bitch right now 'cause I took her phone."

"Yes, well...if you haven't noticed, she normally isn't a little ray of sunshine towards me, Stone."

"Know it. That pissy attitude don't change, she's gonna lose her phone 'til it does. And if that ain't enough, she's gonna lose TV privileges, too."

All she'd be getting was one of those coloring books and a box of fucking crayons to keep her occupied.

"Let's go get her," he suggested.

Her jaw dropped open and her blue eyes went wide. "You want me to come with you? I can wait here with Wren."

"Yeah, wanna show you around since this is gonna be Baby Bird's nest away from home."

"*Uh. I—*"

Here came the shit. He cut off the flow by yelling out, "Swallow!"

The sweet butt sitting next to Wren lifted her bleach-blonde head.

"Keep an eye on the kid, yeah?"

"Anything for you, Stone."

That was what he always wanted to hear. He tipped his face down to Taryn. "That's Swallow."

"I heard. Do you call her Big Bird?"

"Her name ain't got nothin' to do with a bird." Stone cocked one eyebrow at her, smothering a grin. "Let's just say she got no gag reflexes."

"Oh." Taryn chewed on her bottom lip as she considered the woman across the room coloring with her son. "I'll assume you tested that out."

"Often." Stone tugged that plump bottom lip down with the pad of his thumb. "How 'bout you?"

She pulled her head back, freeing herself from his touch. "How about me, what?"

"Askin' 'bout your gag reflexes."

She blinked. And blinked again. "What does that have to do with taking care of your daughter?"

It didn't. It had to do with taking care of him.

The blood drained from her face. "You don't expect more than that, do you? Because if so—"

He grabbed her arm and turned her toward the propped-open double doors. "C'mon. Let's go make sure my bad atti-tude hasn't run away."

"Did she threaten that?"

Stone huffed, dropped the cigarette butt, and crushed it beneath his boot.

Her mouth gaped open. "You're just going to leave that there?"

"Like I said, sweet butts will get it. And yeah, she threatened to become a hobo and ride the rails so she no longer gotta listen to her dick of a dad."

"I could imagine her saying that."

"I don't need to since I fuckin' heard it with my own two ears."

They headed down the long hallway toward the stairs at the end of the hallway that led up to the second floor.

When he opened the fire door for her to enter the stairway, she said, "These aren't the stairs you came down the other day."

"Nope. The Castle's got three. One on each end and the main one in the center."

"The Castle? But this is a former school."

"Yeah, nickname for our clubhouse since we're Kings."

She stopped at the bottom of the steps. "Do you have a throne?"

"Yeah. At the head of the table."

"I don't know what any of that means."

He jerked his chin up, indicating she should head upstairs. She shot him a frown but began to hoof it up the steps.

Stone watched her hips and ass rock and roll with each step she took. "You will. More time you spend here, the more you're gonna learn." Only, he was a bit worried that the more she learned about his MC, the more she wasn't going to like it.

"But I don't plan on spending time here and I don't think Wren should, either. He's very impressionable and—"

"Woman, he's safer here than anywhere else." Her son now being under Stone's protection meant he was under his whole club's protection, too. They'd make sure anyone regretted fucking with the kid.

Including the asshole whose nuts he spawned from.

But for now, he'd keep that to himself. She needed to be gradually introduced to this lifestyle. If she got overwhelmed, she might haul ass and he'd have to find someone else to help with Sunny.

This morning, he liked waking up to her being in his house. Despite him being stuck on the couch. Hopefully, he could convince her to change that sleeping arrangement soon.

"While that might be true, it's not his safety I'm concerned about. Along that same vein, I don't want him on the back of a motorcycle. He's only six."

"He liked it."

"He also likes sour gummy worms for breakfast. That doesn't mean I'll let him eat them." She paused at the midway landing.

"Keep goin'," he urged.

"Shouldn't you be leading the way?"

Fuck no. Then he wouldn't get the view he was currently getting. "Ain't nowhere to go but up. Ain't gonna get lost."

At the top of the stairway, she paused in front of the steel door.

While he doubted she expected him to open the door for her, he did it anyway, pretending he was a gentleman when he was far from that.

As soon as the door slammed behind them, he spotted another club girl headed their way.

At least she was fucking dressed. By dressed, he meant her tits and cunt were covered.

Of course, as soon as Flaps reached them, she gave him a sly smile and went toe-to-toe with him to rake her nails through his beard. "Hey, baby. Were you coming to find me? Do you want me to come visit you later once Sunny's gone?"

Stone's eyes sliced to Taryn. Like the sweet butt, she was waiting for his answer. Only, a grunt wasn't going to cut it this time.

Fuck. "Ain't gonna be here later." He wasn't sure if that was true or not, but that was what he was going with for now.

Flaps's smile dipped downward. "Oh, too bad. I miss your beard tickling my—"

"'Nother time." Stone cut her off before she got into more specifics, grabbed Taryn's elbow, and put some distance between the two women. He waited until he heard the fire door slam shut behind them to say, "That's Flaps."

Taryn groaned. "Flaps. Do I want to know how she got that name?"

She probably didn't, but he'd tell her anyway. "Her lips flap. Both the ones on her face and the ones between her—"

"Got it!" Taryn shouted over him.

Stone smothered his smirk. "Got that nickname honestly."

"As did Swallow, right?"

"And Loosey, Windy, Juicy, and Slick."

Taryn groaned as they continued down the hallway. "I'm sensing a theme,"

"If the name fits...ain't that right?"

"Actually..." she started.

"Anyway, you need somethin', you tell them to get it for you."

"I thought they were only here for sex."

"Nope. They're here to serve and service us."

"Like slaves?"

"Ain't slaves."

"But why do they stay?"

"Why wouldn't they? They ain't bein' held against their fuckin' will. They wanna leave, they know where the fuckin' door is."

"Do they bring you your pipe, a robe, and a bourbon when you walk through the door?" she asked jokingly.

"If I tell 'em, they'll bring me my pipe and a damn whiskey. And they'll sit on my dick when I'm tokin' and drinkin', too."

Taryn's eyebrows almost hit her hairline. "How does one apply for this position?"

"Ain't for you."

"Oh, I wasn't asking for me. I prefer to live in the current century, thank you very much."

"Friend brings them to a party or somethin' and they stay 'cause they want the life." Or to try to get their claws in a brother so they can become an ol' lady.

"Do they live here?"

"Most, yeah." The old school had so many rooms that everyone in the club, whether a patched member, a prospect, or even a club whore, could have a place to stay if they wanted. However, the prospects had to double up. So did the sweet butts.

Except for Slick. She'd been around the longest and was responsible for the rest of them. Kind of like a house mother. She made sure the sweet butts weren't only sucking off the MC's tit. If one of the sweet butts had a problem, they went to her first rather than annoying any of the brothers.

The best rooms were given to club officers, like Stone. It was one of the perks of being voted in to sit at the table.

"Why do you keep a room here when you have a house close by?"

"Convenience." And for those times he partied so fucking hard he couldn't even swing a leg over his sled without hitting the dirt face-first. "Had all the classrooms turned into efficiencies and all twenty-eight are claimed."

"Does every member live here?"

"Depends if they got an ol' lady or a family. Most of them keep a room here but don't live here full time."

"An ol' lady...they're like a wife, right?"

"Kinda, yeah. When you see 'em they sometimes wear 'Property of' cuts."

Someone must have done some research. He could just imagine what her search history looked like ever since that day she first showed up at The Castle. Hopefully the feds didn't flag her account.

"Property of what?"

"Of their ol' man. Their cuts identify who they belong to and are leather like ours. The sweet butts cuts are denim and say 'Property of the Kings.'"

"Representation for an MC is important, huh?"

"Cuts are a symbol of our brotherhood and loyalty. Also makes a damn statement." So did the colors inked into their backs.

"What statement is that?"

"Nobody fucks with the Kings or what belongs to us. You do, you're gonna fuckin' regret it. Guaranteed."

Chapter Eleven

"It sounds like the Kings are serious about protecting what's theirs. But from what I'm hearing, the women are considered club property. Does that include the sweet butts?"

"Yeah. Kids, too." This woman asked a lot of damn questions, but at least it showed she was interested. Her questions so far were pretty generic so he could answer them, but if she started asking about actual club business, he might have to shut that shit down.

"Are there valid threats against the club?"

That question bordered on what she couldn't know so he answered that one carefully. "Threats can come out of nowhere, as you should know. When it comes to club property—ol' ladies, kids, sweet butts—we got their back if anyone fucks with 'em for any reason. Just like I got yours."

"Besides protection and getting the privilege to 'serve and service' you and your brothers, why else do these sweet butts stay?"

"Don't think our dicks are enough?"

"I'll take a highly educated guess and say no. Do they get any other benefits that don't have to do with sex or violence?"

Stone snorted. "Get loads of benefits if they follow the rules."

"What rules?"

"We give 'em scratch every month to get tested."

"I'm assuming you're not testing their IQ but for sexually transmitted diseases."

Even better, the woman had a sense of humor. He liked that. "Yeah. Gotta keep their shit clean." By shit, he meant slit.

"That's it?"

"They don't suck or fuck anyone but fully-patched members. No prospects. No hang-arounds. Nobody outside the club. They do, they're out."

"Okay, so your brotherhood can share them but nobody else. And?"

He kept waiting for one of his answers to send her into a feminist freakout. But so far, she'd been rolling with it all. "They're available at all fuckin' times."

"No exceptions?"

"Some exceptions. We ain't tyrants."

She rolled her blue eyes. "What else?"

"Can't be causin' drama all the fuckin' time."

"Is that common?"

"If we let it get outta control. That's why we got rules." Everybody had rules. Members, prospects, ol' ladies, and sweet butts. But they weren't all the same. The club's bylaws covered most of the rules, but not all.

"What would they cause drama about?"

"Woman, askin' too many fuckin' questions."

"I'm curious. I want to learn more about this lifestyle since it now touches me and Wren."

He had to give her that. She had a son to worry about. "Ol' ladies like to give the sweet butts shit if their ol' man's stickin' their dick in them."

"I'd imagine that *could* cause some drama."

"But we don't wanna hear it. Don't wanna see it. Ol' ladies and the club wh— girls know the deal. And if they don't, they learn real fuckin' fast if they wanna keep that cut on their back."

"It sounds like if they follow the rules and don't get into cat fights, they"—she lifted one finger—"get money to get tested for STDs and they"—she lifted a second finger—"can only have sex with club members." She dropped her hand and shook her head. "That doesn't sound like a fair deal."

"Ain't all they get. They get a wad of scratch every month for whatever the fuck they need. Food, clothes, for their kids, whatever. They need wheels, they get wheels. They need their wheels worked on, we take care of it. They get fed. They get a roof over their heads without payin' a fuckin' dime. No rent, no utilities, no nothin'."

"Basically, they get transportation, room and board," she summarized, "in exchange for *serving and servicing* your brotherhood."

His chin jerked back into his neck. "That ain't enough?"

Taryn shrugged. "I can't speak for them."

But she *could* speak for herself. "What about for you? You now got room and board, too, at no cost to you."

"I can't say there isn't a cost..."

"Ain't even takin' my dick." But that could easily be changed. All she had to do was say the word. He'd have his fucking jeans down around his ankles in a flash. He'd have no problem looking past that get-up she wore when she worked.

"We already negotiated a deal."

"Might need to renegotiate."

She made a noise that didn't sound like she agreed with him.

They stopped in front of one of the converted classrooms on the opposite side of the building from the cafeteria. The pane of glass in any of the old classroom doors that remained had been blacked-out for privacy, but he didn't need to see inside to know his girl was in there fuming. It was obvious from the blare of the television easily heard through the thick wood door.

Yeah, her teenage years were going to be a fucking blast. "This one's mine."

The door better not be locked. If it was, he was taking Sunny's phone out to the pavement and running it over with his fucking truck.

He was relieved when the knob turned easily. She must have learned her lesson the last time she locked him out during one of her preteen tantrums. He had grabbed his tools and removed her bedroom door.

Problem fucking solved.

She didn't get her door back for a month since, at the time, she had been only staying with him on the weekends.

The officers all got corner rooms since they had more windows. Unlike the other former classrooms, they had two stretches of windows instead of one. Having a shitload of windows allowed him to open them all up and air out his room when it started to smell too much like tobacco, pot, and pussy. Not to mention dirty clothes.

The view was pretty damn good, too.

But of course, Sunny had all of the blinds pulled shut and the room was dark as fuck. The only light came from the glow of the television. He swore the volume had to be up around level fifty.

He got no response from his girl when he grabbed the

remote off the couch cushion, shut off the TV, and tossed the remote out of reach.

He stopped in front of Sunny where she was curled up on the couch.

"Done mopin'?"

His girl frowned up at him. "Can I have my phone back?"

"Nope."

"Then nope."

He sighed. "Taryn's here to take you home."

"I don't want to go with her."

"Actin' like you got a choice. Here's a clue...you don't. When you're my age, you can have a say. 'Til then?" He shook his head.

Movement had him glancing up to see Taryn wandering around, checking out his room.

Like the cafeteria, he tried to see it through her eyes as he went over to the blinds and began to open them. At least enough that it wasn't as dark as a fucking coffin. Though it did kind of smell like a rotting corpse.

Yeah, he couldn't imagine she'd be impressed. The room worked for him, but probably not for her.

Clothes were in a pile on the floor next to the unmade bed. The couch Sunny tried to disappear into was old and had cigarette burns, tears, and scratches all over the fake black leather. He had a mini-fridge in one corner full of beer. Dirty dishes and empty beer bottles and overflowing ashtrays pretty much made up the decor.

Yeah, he'd have a talk with Slick. Showing Taryn around was making it painfully obvious that the sweet butts were slacking in their duties.

Taryn moved back to the center of the room and turned in a circle. "No bathroom?"

"Down the hall. Too much scratch to put plumbin' in every room."

"Showers?"

"Locker rooms off the old gymnasium. Stay here normally unless I got pissy pants over there." He tipped his head toward the couch.

"The house is nicer."

"Got two eyes in my own head. But when you're shit-faced, all you need's a bed and a place to piss."

She wrinkled her nose. "The way it smells in here makes me wonder if you even get out of bed to use the restroom."

He'd have to make it to his bed first.

"Get your shit and get ready to go," he told Sunny. His daughter grumbled something under her breath but he let it go. He needed to start picking his battles with her.

When Stone heard a sharp intake of breath, his gaze sliced from his daughter to her. Her face was pale as she read something on her phone.

Within three long strides he was next to her. "What's wrong?"

She handed him the phone without a word since she didn't need to say shit, her trembling fingers said it all.

He quickly scanned the email generated from the Victim Notification System.

For fuck's sake, looked like her asshole ex was getting his freedom soon.

AFTER THE KIDS went to bed, they went outside to discuss the shit with her ex. Stone was sprawled in one of the chairs with his knees bent and his boots spread wide, a cold beer next to his foot and a joint between his fingers while Taryn wore a path in the deck by pacing back and forth from one end to the other. She had one hand plastered to her forehead, the other planted on her hip.

He took another long drag on the joint, then held it deep before pushing the smoke out of his nostrils. The next time she passed him, he held it out to her. "Maybe some of this shit would help."

She paused to stare at what he was offering. She bugged her eyes out at him. "The kids are just upstairs."

"They ain't asleep?"

"Wren is. I'm not sure about Sunny. I didn't check in on her since I'm sure she has her room booby-trapped." She flapped her hand around. "Anyway, only one thing will help in this situation."

"What's that?"

She didn't answer but he already knew what it was. She just didn't want to say it out loud. He didn't blame her. Despite that fucker kicking her ass, she didn't want to off the father of her son.

Though, that would be the best solution to keep her safe.

He held out the joint again. "Sure you don't want a hit?"

She sighed and shook her head. "Someone needs to stay sober for the kids."

He shook his head and chuckled. "Think I can't function after smokin' a little dope?"

"I don't know, can you?"

"It's pot. Ain't heroin. One makes you chill, the other makes you useless. If anyone needs to fuckin' chill right now, it's you."

"I can't help it that I'm worried. The day I've been dreading is almost here."

He snagged his beer to wash away some of his cotton mouth. "Babe, he don't know where you are. Suggest movin' Baby Bird's school before the end of the month like we talked about. Get your house on the market ASAP. Sooner you dump that, the better." Then the only thing left of her life Vic the Dick knew about would be her business. The only good thing about that was she rarely cooked at the same location. The bad thing was that motherfucker could set her up with a fake booking as a trap.

For fuck's sake, that could be bad. "Think he'll seek you out?"

"He's not going to be happy when he can't find me or Wren. I already know he's pissed about the PFAs and the fact he'll never get even partial custody of our son again. Hell, he'll be lucky if he gets supervised visitation. He's not going to accept any of that and simply go away. He's had more than a year to stew about it."

Yeah, in the past he'd spent many a month in the joint planning on exacting revenge on whoever put him there. He hadn't been out for blood with this Gentry asshole, but now that the man's former family was living with Stone, he wouldn't hesitate to do what needed to be done. No intervention by the pigs would be needed.

"I'm meeting the real estate agent at the house this weekend. Luckily, she said the market is still hot so it'll sell fast. If I need to, I can take whatever equity is left, if any, and move somewhere he'll never find us."

Stone didn't like the sound of that. It had only been a couple of days since she'd moved in and now she was already planning on shipping out? That would leave him fucked when it came to Sunny. He'd be scrambling to find someone to watch her who wasn't a sweet butt. Until he had a lead for a possible house mouse, Taryn was his best option. "Court's gonna let you take your boy outta state?"

"I don't know. I don't see why not if Vic is a threat."

"He ain't a threat to Baby Bird. Just to you."

When that reality hit her, Taryn collapsed into the chair next to him, dropped her head, fisted her hair, and released a scream she tried but failed to muffle.

Hopefully, it didn't wake the damn kids. He didn't want them overhearing this line of conversation.

He took another hit of the joint before licking his fingertips and putting it out by pinching the end. He tucked the remainder into the tin he had put in the front pocket of his jeans since he'd left his cut inside. "Got you covered, babe. We agreed, you do for me, I do for you. Here's one thing I'm gonna do. Once he's out, gonna have me or one of my brothers shadowin' you at all times. If I ain't with you, one of them will be. You go nowhere without one of us."

She squeezed her eyes shut and groaned. "Stone..."

"Nope. Ain't a negotiation. It's a rule. One that ain't gonna be broken. Tell me you get me."

"I hear what—"

"No. That ain't it."

"Listen—"

"No."

"But—"

"No."

She growled.

He grinned.

"Fuck you."

His grin widened. "All right. Where you wanna do it? Right here on the deck?"

"That's not funny."

Or they could do it in his truck. Her Honda. A closet. He didn't fucking care. When he got back earlier, she had already changed into skin-tight leggings and one of those cotton tank tops. Only problem with that was, tonight she wore a sports bra under it that flattened out her tits.

That had to go. If it was up to him, he'd shred the fucking thing with his knife.

"Hear me laughin'? The deal is I protect you. Doin' my job."

"And I need to do *my* job. My clients aren't going to want a bearded, beer-bellied biker that smells like whiskey and weed in their kitchen. I'll lose business."

"They can sit in your cage while you work." He needed to consider getting her a different vehicle, too. Vic the Dick would probably recognize it. The club had plenty of vehicles to choose from. Parking lots full. All they had to do was choose one, snag it without getting caught, and swap out the VINs.

"Stone..."

Only, she'd probably shit a brick if she found out she was driving a stolen cage. But at least it would be better than the piece of shit she was driving now.

Beggars couldn't be fucking choosy.

"Woman. This ain't a negotiation but a fuckin' fact. Just accept it if you don't wanna end up in the hospital again. Or worse."

She deflated in the chair next to him. Like she lost all will and was giving up. "How the hell did I get here?"

She wasn't asking him but he answered anyway. "Married the wrong fuckin' guy. You ain't the first; ain't gonna be the last. Wanna say that most women learn after hookin' up with their first motherfucker but that ain't true. Some never fuckin' learn." Windy was one of them. Somehow she got knocked around by every dick she ever set her eyes on. She was a "motherfucker magnet." Becoming a sweet butt was the best thing for her. Nobody would fuck with her now. And if they did, they would quickly learn...

Nobody fucked with the Kings.

Chapter Twelve

Taryn really didn't need to be reminded of one of the worst choices she'd ever made in her life. And she'd made quite a few doozies. But it was too late to right that wrong, so now she had to minimize the damage as best as she could.

It really sucked that once Vic got out, her life would change *again*. Taryn's wish was to live in peace and raise her son to be a good man.

Not like his father.

"I understand we struck a deal, but please remember, I'm not working *for* you. You're not my boss." Stone could not give her orders and expect her to comply without question.

"Yep."

That didn't sound like he understood the assignment. "Yep? Consider me a volunteer. An *unpaid* volunteer."

"Babe, that's what a volunteer is...unpaid."

Of course, he purposely missed the point. "I own a business."

"Yep."

She sighed and raked fingers through her hair. "Again,

that means you're not my boss. Our deal doesn't mean you get to dictate everything in my life now."

"Yep."

She squeezed her eyes shut while gritting her teeth. It was important he was clear on that point. "You know what that means?"

"Yep."

Instead of dragging fingers through her hair again, she was about to yank it out in frustration. "Good," she somehow managed to say without shrieking. Barely.

He sat up and snagged his beer, but didn't take another drink. He let the bottle dangle from his fingers between his thighs. He was gearing up for something...

"Okay, once your ex gets out, this is how it's gonna be..."

She knew it.

"You ain't goin' back to teachin' classes at that place in Camp Hill. You keep one of the prospects with you at all your jobs. If not one of them, one of my brothers if I ain't available. I'm available, it'll be me. You wanna teach cookin' classes, there's a thing called the fuckin' internet. Set up a camera in the kitchen and cook." Then he downed what was left in the bottle before setting it back on the deck.

Her eyebrows shot up. "You must have the memory of a gnat. I just told you you're not my boss."

"Can't forget since it was just a minute ago." He tapped his temple with a finger. "Got a memory like a trap."

With all the pot he smoked, she doubted it. "Right. And that was why I had to remind you."

"Got it." He sat back in the chair and stretched his long legs out in front of him.

She wished she could be that relaxed right now. Only, the men in her life, both Stone and Vic, were making that difficult. "I'm not sure you do. While I appreciate your concern and offering your protection, I need you to stay out of my actual business." She was talking about her professional business, but that could apply to her personal life as well. She came here to help out with this daughter and to get out from under a house she couldn't afford, not to live with a dictator.

Her business was her only source of income.

He pursed his lips and drew a hand down his beard. "No."

"No, you won't?"

"Gonna treat you how I treat you. Either gonna like it or you ain't."

Say what? "And if I don't?"

"You'll get over it."

"Wow. No wonder you're single."

He cocked an eyebrow at her. "Ain't the only single one sittin' on this deck, babe. Anyway, bein' single's my choice."

"So is that attitude."

Stone's lips pressed together to smother either amusement or annoyance.

Taryn's guess? The first one.

Good God. Sunny got her attitude honestly. She was Stone in a much younger, female form. No DNA test needed.

"Wanna talk about attitude? You got a smart mouth." A grin slowly spread across his face as he stared at her there. "What else can you do with it?"

Of course, his focused attention made her lick her lips out of instinct. "My attitude?"

"Your mouth."

Damn. Him asking that crude question shouldn't make her pussy twinge and her nipples ache. Instead, she should be offended. Proof her brain was *not* attached to her lady parts.

Because if they were, they would not be betraying her with a bossy biker like Stone.

Maybe her unexpected reaction was due to the fact it had been a while since she'd experienced any kind of intimacy. The last time was with Vic. And that was...

Depressing.

She actually couldn't remember the last time she'd been touched intimately. Or even shared a simple kiss with an adult member of the opposite sex.

Since she'd been busting her ass trying to grow her business—and in turn, increase her income—along with raising her son, that didn't give her much time to date. Or, hell, even have a random, occasional hookup.

With pursed lips, she twisted her neck to stare back at him.

A dark eyebrow cocked. "What?"

She shook her head. *No, Taryn. No! You need to smack yourself on the nose with a rolled up newspaper. Get any thoughts of Stone, his tattoos and that freaking beard out of your head.*

His red flags were not waving; they were whipping around in hurricane-force winds.

"Still waitin' for an answer."

She shrugged like his words didn't affect her in any way. "Like most people, I use my mouth for communication and sustenance."

"Got a son. Had to use it for more than that."

"It had nothing to do with getting pregnant. If I had used my mouth instead, Wren wouldn't be here."

She couldn't say she wished she didn't have Wren since he was her world, but that didn't mean she couldn't wish he had a different father. Just like Stone wished Sunny had a different mother.

But both of them had to deal with what life had handed them.

Here she was, sitting on the back deck of a house she was temporarily living in with a non-law-abiding biker in her attempt at "dealing."

Life was crazy and unpredictable.

A year ago, Stone had come to her rescue. Now...

He had once again come to her rescue.

Shit. The man went to *prison* for her. Maybe not *for* her, but because of her. Stone lost over thirteen months of his freedom, thirteen months of being away from his daughter, for defending her.

She closed her eyes and blew out a breath. She owed him. "You're right."

"Usually am."

She ignored that. "I realize you're looking out for my best interests. I tracked you down to thank you for getting involved at the Shoppes at Susquehanna, but I need to thank you again for opening your home to not only me, but my son. For caring enough to be worried about our safety."

"We're both benefittin' here. Ain't all one-sided, Taryn." His head tipped to the side as he studied her. "Can think of somethin' else that can mutually benefit us both."

"What?" He was talking about sex, wasn't he?

She startled when he surged to his feet, spun, grabbed her wrist, and yanked her from her seat. When her mouth opened to ask him what he was doing, he took it.

He took her mouth without warning. Without asking.

Simply claimed it like it was his.

Holy shit.

She should be clawing his eyes out, not digging her nails into his shirt and clinging to him.

She should be shoving him away, not pulling him closer.

She should be biting his tongue, not allowing it to tangle so damn skillfully with hers.

She should be cursing at the gall of his actions, not groaning in encouragement.

What was wrong with her? Was it shock? Or awe?

He would *not* be her next bad decision. He. Would. Not.

She couldn't afford any more bad decisions. They had already cost her enough.

When he deepened the kiss and continued to plunder her mouth, her body whispered, *"What's one more mistake?"* and melted against him.

While his hands were fisted in the hair on both sides of her head, keeping her right where he wanted her, it wasn't necessary. She wasn't going anywhere. It would be impossible even if she tried, since she had not one functional bone left in her body. Not freaking one. They had all disintegrated into liquid. *He* was what was holding her up.

His strong hands, his hard chest, his hard...everything.

His words whispered across her lips. "Wanna make another deal with you."

"I know where this is going." She needed to resist.

"Want my bed back."

Oh, was that it? No deal needed. "I can take the couch."

"With you in it."

Her brain glitched, causing her to blink up at him while rubbing her face where his thick beard had tickled and scratched her skin. Maybe she imagined that last part. Maybe it was wishful thinking on her part.

Wait. No. That was *not* what she wanted!

"Did I...did you..."

It would be stupid to get involved with him—sexually or otherwise—beyond their initial deal.

He dipped his head down and locked gazes with her.

"You heard what I said. Gonna assume by your reaction to that kiss, you ain't totally against that deal."

Any euphoria still lingering from that toe-curling kiss was now completely gone and her spine had returned. "And you'd be wrong. That wouldn't be smart on my part. I need to do better for Wren. Sharing a bed with you just down the hall from our kids wouldn't be showing them a good example."

She needed to pull away, put space between him, but his grip on her hair kept her close.

Stone snorted. "Think Sunny don't know about sex?"

"You explained the birds and the bees to her already?" She was only ten!

His eyebrows pinched together. "Birds and bees? Fuck no. Her whole life she's been around people with no problem showin' their whole ass. Includin' her mother."

"You, too?"

"And me. She knows sex is a part of life. Don't mean she's allowed to have it 'til she's thirty, but she ain't dumb about it. No reason to keep her in the dark 'bout somethin' that's parta human nature."

She pushed a hand against his chest. "Can you release me?"

"I can, but we ain't fuckin' done here." His dark eyes traced every line of her face before dropping to her chest.

When one side of his mouth pulled up, she knew exactly why.

Once again, her body betrayed her. It tried to convince her that giving him what he wanted wouldn't be a bad thing. Her brain was screaming otherwise.

Her ex-husband not only broke her heart but tried to break her.

She had no doubt the man offering himself up to her was far, *far* more dangerous than Vic.

Taking care of his daughter was one thing. "Taking care" of Sunny's father was quite another.

"Ain't gotta be a big thing. Could simply be a mutual scratchin' of itches."

"If you have an itch, I'd suggest going to a doctor. It could be a contagious rash and you wouldn't want it to spread."

"I need to prove to you how much you want me?"

"No. I can simply tell you if you need to hear it." She was afraid if he kissed her again she'd self-combust.

"You lie a lot?"

He released her hair but before she had a chance to put space between them so she could think straight, he planted his hands on her ass and pulled her even closer. She swore the heat from his palms would leave scorch marks behind.

"Stone."

"Yeah, babe?" His soft words whispered over her lips.

She closed her eyes and whispered, "I can't do this."

"Sure you can. You're just worried you're gonna like it too much and want more."

Her eyes flashed open and she silently mouthed, "Wow." The arrogance!

He slowly thrust his hard cock against her belly. "Right? Pretty fuckin' impressive. That could be yours. Just say the word and I'll go up and move Baby Bird into Sunny's room."

That simple. She only had to tell him yes and he'd go up and move her sleeping son to his daughter's room.

Only, he wasn't taking into account the questions their children might ask about that change.

"Gonna get you in my bed one way or another."

"That sounds like a threat."

"Ain't a threat. It's a promise now I know I don't turn you off."

"Who said you didn't?"

"Your hard-as-fuck nipples, you suckin' on my tongue, the deep groan that made my balls ache, the way you ground yourself against my dick. Those were damn good signs. Bet if I checked, your panties are soaked, too."

"Ha. Jokes on you, I'm not wearing any." Her eyes widened and she slapped a hand over her mouth in horror. *Holy shit.* Did she actually reveal that?

One side of his mouth slowly lifted. "Want you spread wide on my bed as I eat your pussy. Want you face down ass up as I fuck you from behind. Want—"

"Okay!" she shouted over him. "I get it."

"Plan on gettin' it. Just gotta say the word."

His confidence was a turn-on; his pushiness was not. "I'll consider your generous offer. But at this point, I need to politely decline."

"You'll change your mind."

Why did she believe him? "Are you sure about that?"

"Yeah."

"Do you only want me because I'm convenient?"

"Not a goddamn thing to do with convenience. Can have sweet butts at the snap of my fingers. *That's* fuckin' convenient. See what I want and I go for it."

She did catch the fact "sweet butts" was plural. Like she witnessed that day earlier in the week.

Damn. How was this still the same week that she had tracked him down? It was crazy how fast life could change.

"I think it's time for me to go to bed. Alone." Of course, she wouldn't be alone since she was still sharing a bed with Wren. If she moved to the couch, her son would be forced to share Sunny's room. That might make Stone's daughter hate Taryn even more.

"Ain't gonna be alone."

"You're right. I'll be sleeping next to my son." Having

Wren sharing a bed with her was one way to prevent Stone from joining her without an invitation.

Because she was afraid of what she'd do if Wren wasn't with her and Stone came tapping on the door. Hell, he probably wouldn't even knock, he'd just walk right in.

She would not be doing the right thing by answering the door and inviting him in. Luckily, Wren made a great cock block.

"Sleep on it," he suggested.

"Your bed? I will."

He snorted and shook his head.

"Now, can you release me so I can go inside?"

With a deep sigh, he slowly removed his hands. "You know where to find me if you change your mind."

She took the opportunity to put some space between them before he changed his.

Or she did.

"By the way, you taste like beer and pot," she tossed over her shoulder as she opened the back door and stepped inside.

"Better than if I ate a shit sandwich."

"Debatable." The door shut behind her.

Chapter Thirteen

Taryn smothered her groan of frustration with a pillow. At least it wasn't a maniacal scream.

She twisted her head to the right to see it was only one in the morning.

One.

Only an hour after the last time she checked since she'd been trying to fall asleep since ten. She'd done nothing but toss and turn for the last three hours.

She glanced over to her left at her son. He slept like the dead, so most things didn't wake him up. Only, he was more like the walking dead with his constant kneeing and kicking as he slept.

Wren did not make a great bed partner. Especially since he was also like a compact space heater. Why was the male species so damn hot when they slept? They turned beds into ovens.

She sighed softly and went back to staring up at the dark ceiling. At this rate, she would never get any sleep.

Why? For one obvious reason.

Stone.

His body.

His lips.

That damn kiss.

She kept replaying it over and over in her mind. Every time she did, her pussy twinged, her breath caught, and her breasts ached.

All over a simple kiss!

She needed to think about other things. Like what finger foods she would need to prepare for a ladies' afternoon tea tomorrow.

She needed energy, not to be exhausted from a lack of sleep, because she'd be busy all morning doing prep work. She also needed to avoid being tired and cranky when dealing with a dozen demanding women. The monthly gathering of the Selinsgrove Society Group was a regular gig and she didn't want to lose their bookings.

The ladies might treat her as if she was invisible while there, but Taryn could live with that since their money was very real when it landed in her bank account.

Maybe she'd record her prep work later this morning as a test for the online cooking classes. She regretfully admitted that Stone's suggestion was a good idea and she wished she would've thought of it first. If she got enough people interested in her online cooking videos, it could be a nice additional source of income. And who couldn't use that?

She quickly needed to put a plan together and put it into motion before Vic was released. Because once he was, she had a feeling she'd be in some sort of lockdown herself. As soon as he got his freedom, she would lose hers.

Why did everything have to be a struggle?

Damn it, life wasn't fair. At what point did she actually

get to sit back and enjoy it? Would she still be busting her ass when she was seventy? Eighty?

When was the last time she'd done something for herself? Not for her son, not for her business, but simply for herself. She didn't pamper herself in any way because she couldn't afford it. No massages, no mani-pedis, no vacations, no new clothes or shoes.

Nothing.

She'd been all work and no play for too long now.

She was pretty damn certain if she went downstairs, Stone would be happy to "play" with her. He probably wouldn't care if she used him for sex and then immediately went back to bed. If she had to take an educated guess, he wasn't the cuddle in the afterglow type.

Like he mentioned, they could both benefit from a quick, meaningless bump and grind.

Sex might help her sleep.

Sex might relieve some of the tension. The worry.

Sex might...

Make her orgasm.

Sharing a bed with Wren made it so she couldn't even do a little self-help. And DIY was the only reason she'd had *any* orgasms at all for the past few years.

As soon as she shoved the bedding aside and her feet touched the wood floor, she knew...

She was about to add another entry to her long, long list of mistakes.

But did that stop her from sneaking out of the bedroom and heading downstairs before reality hit her and she changed her mind?

Of course it didn't.

BARE FEET CREEPING DOWN the steps pushed the blood from his wide-awake brain down to his formerly sleeping dick.

Could be she was only coming down for a glass of water.

Or a late night snack.

Even better would be if that snack was named Stone.

Since her coming downstairs in the middle of the night could go either way, he waited to see if Taryn turned right to head into the kitchen or left into the living room once she hit the bottom of the steps.

He drove his hand into his boxers and gave his balls a tug.

Make a fuckin' left.

He held his breath and forced himself to remain on the couch as she hesitated in the front entryway.

Make a goddamn left.

He freed his hand and closed his eyes, pretending he hadn't been restless since the moment she went inside after their little "talk" on the deck.

Her bare feet padding on the wood floor was easier to pick up the closer she got.

Oh yeah. He might be her late-night snack. Or a way to quench her thirst.

His dick twitched in anticipation.

Her breathing had a hitch to it. She was probably debating whether fucking him would be a mistake or not.

He could honestly say it would be.

Because once she had a piece of him, she'd never look at another man the same again.

He snorted.

Fuck. Busted.

He opened his eyes to see her standing only inches away, wearing the loose PJ bottoms and very tight tank top she normally wore to bed. No light was needed to see her diamond-hard nipples trying to punch a hole through the cotton.

As he opened his mouth to ask her what she wanted, Taryn jammed a finger against his lips and shook her head.

Hot damn. If she wanted to play it like that...

He was game.

She would get what she wanted. He'd get what he wanted. Both would be winners.

He smothered his grin.

He knew she'd eventually want a taste of his skills but hadn't expected it to be so soon. He figured he'd have to work for it, and he'd been willing to put in that work. Little did he know that the simple kiss earlier would do all the heavy lifting for him.

Her wanting him to stay silent confirmed she didn't come downstairs because of an emergency or to have a conversation. She wanted action, not words.

Only, they couldn't fuck right out in the open on the couch. Not with the kids upstairs. Despite Sunny witnessing a lot of shit she probably shouldn't whenever she was at The Castle, Stone made an effort for that shit not to include him.

Catching her father pounding pussy might scar her for life.

And as for Taryn's son...

No.

If Wren caught them, Taryn would never forgive him. Even though Stone wouldn't be the only one involved, he'd be blamed for her kid needing years of therapy.

But if he didn't find somewhere private to go, this wouldn't go far.

He considered their options.

A closet. That would be tight.

Her Honda or his truck, since they were parked in the

garage. That would be inconvenient. Plus, they wouldn't hear the kids if there was a problem.

Or...

She gasped softly as his hand shot out like a striking cobra and captured her wrist. Within seconds, he was on his feet, pulling her back through the front foyer to the other side of the house.

The downstairs bathroom might not be huge, but it had a lock and more space than any of the closets. The ability to watch himself in the mirror as he fucked her would also be a bonus.

Still without a word between them, he steered her into the bathroom and released her before closing and locking the door.

When he flicked on the lights and turned...

Fuck yeah.

A flush had worked up her slender throat, her nipples were screaming his name, her bottom lip was clamped between her teeth, and her eyes glittered like blue diamonds as they focused on his hard-as-fuck dick.

Since she didn't want them to speak, they'd need to show each other what they wanted instead. He'd go first.

Snagging her hand again, he wrapped her fingers around his hard length before moving it up and down. Once she took over, he grasped the back of her neck and pulled her into him, crushing their mouths together.

Her breath puffed raggedly as he dragged his tongue through her mouth, exploring every corner. Thumbing one of her tight nipples, he was annoyed that she still wore that tank.

Wanting no barriers but a wrap between them, he ended the kiss.

She didn't stop him when he ripped her top over her head, tossing it aside.

She didn't stop him when he shoved her PJ bottoms down, leaving her in only black panties.

She didn't stop him when he shoved his own boxers down far enough they fell to his feet on their own, freeing his erection.

She didn't stop him when he hooked his fingers in her panties and did the same with them.

Despite her compliance...the urge to rush clawed at his core. He was afraid once reality hit her, she'd change her mind and leave him holding his own dick.

This could be his one and only shot with her. Because he was pretty damn sure once the light of day was upon them, he'd be added to her list of mistakes right below Vic the Dick.

Stone wouldn't deny that he belonged there.

He was not a good guy. Laws didn't pertain to him and the only rules he respected had to do with the KOAMC.

His world was made up of two very important things: his daughter and his club. Without Sunny and his brotherhood, his heart had no reason to keep pumping. The Kings were in his blood and that same blood ran through Sunny's veins.

He lived for both and would die for them, too.

Wrapping her hot, little fingers around his dick again, she began to jerk him off, bringing him back to the room. His hips twitched, wanting to follow her rhythmic pumping, but if he started doing that, he might not be able to stop.

Again, this might be a once and done scenario, so he couldn't blow it. In more ways than one.

He regretfully peeled her fingers from around his throbbing length and went to the closet, digging around for a box of wraps. He kept a supply in both bathrooms as well as his bedroom and in the kitchen *just in case*. Since he never wanted to be caught with his pants down and no way to protect himself.

A hard, expensive lesson only needed to be learned once.

Condoms were definitely cheaper than diapers and everything else needed to raise a kid. More importantly, it stopped him from being attached to some crazy bitch for a minimum of eighteen years. One hell of a prison sentence.

If he ever had a kid again, he'd want to choose the mother, not the other way around. Getting pregnant wasn't a way to lock him down, it was a guaranteed way to alienate him.

As it was, one nut nugget was more than enough to deal with right now, fuck you very much. He was also damn sure the woman in the bathroom with him didn't want to get knocked up again anytime soon. They might not have a lot in common, but they had that.

Despite Taryn's desire for them to say nothing, Stone was finding it more difficult than expected to trap his thoughts inside his head. Whatever popped in there usually spewed from his mouth.

To keep from fucking up this opportunity, he tossed one of the wraps found in the closet onto the vanity. No reason to put it on yet. *Fuck that.* He had other plans first.

One had to do with his late-night munchies.

To keep his mouth busy so he didn't blow her unspoken rule of staying silent, he took her mouth again. Aside from the kiss they shared on the deck, he hadn't kissed a woman in a long fucking time. The only time he was interested in a woman's mouth was when she was sucking his dick or licking his balls. Or tickling his taint with her tongue.

He had no reason to swap spit with any female. He never kissed Sheena the night they made Sunny and he still wasn't sure if her pregnancy was an accident or the bitch had tried to trap him.

If so, the joke was on her. She had to carry his daughter for nine months, suffer through the pregnancy and everything that went along with that, and in the end, the plan backfired. She didn't get what she wanted. Sheena never got to be his backpack on his sled. Never got to sleep in his bed. She damn sure never wore his cut and never would.

She never got shit from him except for Sunny.

What the fuck was wrong with him? He currently had a woman he wanted at his fingertips and here he was thinking about a woman he didn't want, not even if she was the last slit remaining on Earth. He'd rather cut his fucking balls off, stuff them in a blender and...

What the actual fuck!

In an effort to shake those thoughts free, he squeezed Taryn's tit and swept his tongue through her mouth again. Rolling the hard tip between his thumb and forefinger, he drew a moan from her.

Fuck yeah. That was better.

Her fingers weaved their way into his loose hair before they curled and held fast. As long as she didn't leave a bald spot, he didn't give a shit how much she pulled on his scalp. And, *what d'ya know*, his dick approved of the slight sting.

Her tits fit perfectly in his palm. Just like her nipples would fit perfectly in his mouth, his dick perfectly in her pussy, a finger or two perfectly up her ass.

That list sounded like the perfect plan of attack.

He swallowed her gasp when he plucked her nipples. First one, then the other as he deepened the kiss, practically tickling her tonsils.

Kissing her was dick-hardening hot, but he kept in mind she could pull the plug on this bathroom action at any time. And fuck if he wanted to miss out on what was waiting for him: a slick pussy that would sheath him like a well-oiled baseball glove.

As much as he didn't want to rush, he also couldn't take

the time to explore every fucking inch of her. A bathroom sucked for that anyway. While it worked in a pinch, if he really wanted to do her right, he'd prefer to have her spread eagle on a bed where he had room to work and plenty of time to do so.

Without breaking the seal of their lips, he hooked his arms around her ass and lifted her until she was perched on the vanity.

After kneeing her legs open wider, he caught her hot, sweet scent of arousal.

Fuck yeah. If he touched her there...

Fuck that.

When he touched her there, he would find her soaked and ready for him.

Guaran-fucking-teed.

Chapter Fourteen

He was finding it goddamn difficult not to say shit. Stone was used to barking orders at whoever was on top of or under him, whether it was a sweet butt or some random snatch at The Castle for one of their parties.

After freeing her mouth, he dropped his to her tit, sucking one already hard-as-fuck nipple deep and making sure to scrape the tip with his teeth.

Her eyelids became heavy. Her mouth gaped. Her breathing sped up. Her nipples quickly became swollen and shiny from him sucking on them.

He was tempted to leave his mark in the rounded, soft flesh. *Oh yeah.* He wanted to mark her and mark her good. That way he could see a reminder of what they were about to do in this fucking room tomorrow and maybe even the next day.

Not that he'd need a reminder. He doubted he'd forget it any time soon. Taryn was not his usual pump and dump.

She was not a sweet butt or a hang-around. Or some drunk chick invited to one of their weekend-long blow-outs getting her thrills by hanging out with a bunch of outlaw bikers.

Taryn was a woman he had to live with for at least the next few months. If not longer. They'd have to face each other every day. They'd need to coordinate their kids' schedules.

He also needed to make sure everyone under his roof remained safe. For that reason, it was important he kept who the fuck she was and why she was living with him front and center. Especially if he wanted her to stay.

After seeing how Taryn interacted with and parented her son, he desperately wanted her to stay for his daughter. Sunny needed someone steady in her life. Someone to keep her from growing up to be a total degenerate.

That person was not Sheena. It certainly wasn't the sweet butts. And if he had to admit it, it might not even be him. He tried his best but sometimes—*fuck*, most of the time —his best wasn't good enough.

By arching her back, Taryn shoved her tit deeper into his mouth, giving him proof without any words of her approval of his actions.

He wasn't sure about her, but he had a few more things on his to-do list yet. It was time to get down to business.

Dropping his hand between her thighs, he swept a finger through her hot center, finding her slick as fuck.

Fuck yeah.

Two of his fingers easily slipped inside while he ground his thumb against her swollen clit. Rocking against his fingers, she drove them even deeper at the same time he scored the hard tip of a nipple with his teeth.

Her hips popped up off the counter and a soft cry hit his ears.

For fuck's sake, this woman's responses—even as restrained as they were—might be his undoing.

Normally, he concentrated on driving his dick home until he came. He kept it simple: in, out, over.

Not tonight. Fuck no. Tonight he wanted to make sure Taryn enjoyed the ride. While he wanted to believe it was because he didn't want to scare her away, that might not be it at all. It had to be because he wanted her to come back for more.

Since she was living in his house and was right at his fingertips, he didn't want this to be only a once and done thing. They could be doing this on a regular basis.

That would make this whole agreement even sweeter. At least for him. Especially if he could talk her into sharing his bed. How convenient would it be to roll over and be able to fuck her in the morning, at night, in the middle of the night, at the ass crack of dawn, or in the middle of the damn day when the kids were at school?

Fuck. Maybe if he gave her multiple orgasms, Stone might be able to convince her to move Wren out of his bed and allow him to slide back in.

Of course, he couldn't ask her that fucking question because he had to keep his goddamn trap shut. That was harder than his damn dick.

But at least he now had a goal other than him simply busting a nut.

He continued to thrust his fingers in and out of her pussy, occasionally curling them enough to find the spot that drove women wild. When he cared enough to do so. Taryn would be the exception since he normally didn't. He expected the women in his life to take care of his needs, not the other way around.

Throwing her head back, she stiffened seconds before she

exploded around his fingers with a muffled cry. Did she hold back her response due to the kids being right upstairs or because of her own no talking rule?

Either way, it was loud enough to pull a grin from him.

He slowly continued to glide his fingers in and out until her pussy no longer pulsed around him.

Damn, he was good, if he said so himself.

One orgasm down...

Now he needed to make her come with his mouth, then his dick. Hopefully three would be the lucky number to make her see the benefit of them sharing a bed.

Slipping his slick fingers from her, he sucked on them for a little appetizer before he chowed down.

Her chest still heaved and her pupils had expanded as she focused on him. He kept their gazes locked as pushed her knees farther apart so he'd have room to work his magic with his tongue.

He rarely went down on a woman. Not because he didn't like it, he certainly fucking did, but because he wasn't eating leftovers. He had no fucking clue which—or how many—of his brothers had been there before him.

As for the randoms showing up at parties, he had no idea who they were or where they came from. Using a wrap to protect himself was one thing, tonguing their questionable cunts was another.

Her head dropped forward to watch him as he sank to his knees on the damn hard tile floor and separated her with his thumbs to stare at her juicy pink center. But only for a second before he dove right in face first.

Damn. He should've pulled his hair up and out of the way. At moments like these, his long hair became annoying.

Christ, did he really give a shit about getting messy?

When he inhaled deeply, pulling her sweet scent deep into his lungs, his answer was *fuck no.*

He sucked one plump fold into his mouth, then the other, before driving his tongue inside her. But it was when he shifted to the smooth pearl hidden within her clam that her hips bucked against his face, smearing the result of his work into his beard and hair.

She tasted a fuck of a lot better than any of the meals she'd cooked so far. And they'd been the best he'd had in a while. If not ever.

He flicked her clit with his tongue before sucking on it roughly, causing her hips to jump. He really should finger fuck her again but he was determined to make her come this time solely using his mouth. And, of course, his magical tongue.

He tugged and teased, causing the thighs now clamped around his ears to tremble and shake.

He was no longer able to see or hear. Exactly how he preferred it when he fell face first into pussy.

But, for fuck's sake, he needed for her to come soon. He was ready for the main event. Switching his tongue into turbo mode, he didn't give even a second of mercy to her clit or cunt.

He didn't even let up when her thighs sandwiched his head so tightly, he thought she might pop it like a balloon. That could be a sign that she was about to come again, only she was no longer giving him room to work.

When her hips surged up once more, her pussy smashed his nose. Pulling back to take a breath, he could clearly see she was riding out another orgasm.

Hell yeah. Orgasm number two.

Her unrestrained reactions went right to his dick. It was hard as fuck and aching, pissed at him for holding off for so long. The crown was slick and a string of precum swung precariously from the tip in anticipation of finally filling her.

Time to kick this ride into third gear.

Before she even stopped shuddering, he grabbed a fistful of her hair and pulled her head back, exposing the long, delicate line of her throat. He slowly slid his nose along her heated skin with his fingers following before wrapping around her neck like a collar. He flexed his fingers and dug the tips deeper, feeling her pulse beat as fast as a hummingbird's wings under his palm.

As soon as he released her hair, he crushed his lips against hers, claiming her mouth again just like he was about to claim her pussy.

Keeping a hand on her throat, he used the other to tuck the foil package between his teeth to rip it open, letting the wrapper drop to the floor as he managed to roll the condom on single-handedly. He lined himself up by tucking the tip of his dick at the center of his target. He held her steady by gripping the soft flesh covering her hips.

Despite the urge to quickly bang one out, he gritted his teeth and took his time entering her, inch by inch, until his dick was encased in her velvety heat all the way to the root. Until he hit the end of her.

She was tight compared to the sweet butts, making him wonder how long it had been since she'd had anyone inside her. Then it hit him like a baseball bat to the head. Whatever that answer was, he didn't fucking care.

It was his pussy now.

All right, maybe not for forever, but for the next ten minutes. When she squeezed and stretched around his length, it became clear that it might be more like two minutes. And that was being generous.

Whatever.

While it might be impossible to go any deeper, he wanted to. Fuck did he want to. Apparently, so did she.

It certainly didn't fucking help his endurance when her nails drilled into his ass, trying to pull him even deeper. That was going to leave a mark. But he didn't give a fuck about any battle wounds. He'd wear them proudly.

Her breath hissed out of her as he held her tightly, flexed his knees, and drove himself up and into her over and over.

This didn't have to take long, it only needed to be fucking great. A taste of what he could do to her in hopes she'd want to do it again. He fucking *needed* to do this again.

No fake noises. No goddamn agenda. No bullshit.

It was about one simple result: pleasure.

Pumping in and out of her, slowly at first, he found a pace that worked for them both. Attempting to draw out her next orgasm. If he achieved it, it would be her third. And her last.

Because he was close to being done.

Especially once she wrapped her legs around his hips, digging her heels into the back of his thighs, and met him thrust for thrust.

He teetered dangerously when she ground her clit against him and her pussy clamped tightly around his dick.

Then her face softened, her eyelids slid shut, and her mouth went slack.

A second later, she shattered around him.

Thank fuck. Now it was his turn.

Gritting his teeth and not even waiting for her orgasm to end, he began to piston his hips. His breath pumped from his lungs with each forceful thrust he made in an attempt to screw her right into the vanity. Each drive upward was deeper and quicker than the last, until there was nowhere left for him to go.

She dug her nails into his ass even deeper to prevent herself from slamming into the mirror, possibly shattering it.

That would suck.

Not because he'd need to replace it, because she might get cut and the noise might wake up the kids. Sunny was too damn smart to believe the bathroom mirror exploded on its own. In the middle of the night.

When they were all supposed to be sleeping.

With a grunt he swore came all the way from his toes, he slammed her one more time, planting himself deep. He closed his eyes as his dick pulsed and his balls emptied.

The second he could think semi-straight, he dropped his forehead to her shoulder and sucked in oxygen to slow both his pounding heart and his breathing.

She came three fucking times. A record for him because he normally didn't give a shit after a woman came once. And he was being generous with that. He wasn't fucking them for their pleasure but for his own.

This was the first time since he'd been inexperienced that he cared if the woman was satisfied when he was finished.

Despite that, he was not expecting her to quickly release his ass, plant her hands against his chest, and push.

He reluctantly opened his eyes to see hers wide and her face pale.

What the fuck? That was not the reaction he expected after all the effort he had put into this.

Was that a look of regret she was wearing?

Goddamn it. That didn't bode well for him convincing her to let him back in his own bed.

Collaring the wrap at the base of his dick, he slipped from her and stepped back, giving her space. "What's wrong?"

Fuck her no talking rule. That was now officially over.

She set her jaw and shook her head, still not saying a damn word.

"I hurt you?"

No answer.

"It suck?"

Again, no answer as she scrambled to get dressed.

"Made you come three fuckin' times," he announced like she wasn't aware of that fact.

Unless she'd been faking it?

No, she'd have no reason to fake it. What he heard and felt was far from fake, unlike some of the shit that came out of a sweet butt's mouth.

He stood watching her finish pull on her PJ bottoms and her tank back over her head. "Babe."

Fuck, he needed to know where this went wrong.

"Taryn."

She paused with her hand on the door knob and didn't even bother to turn around when she said, "We don't speak about this ever again."

Then she was gone.

Chapter Fifteen

THE MAN GAVE her three intense orgasms last night. Or more like early this morning.

Taryn was lucky to have even one with Vic. Stone went above and beyond when he didn't stop until she'd had *three.* That might have been a record for her.

Later, while lying in the man's bed without him, she went over how she reacted afterward. He seemed to be getting pissed as she ignored his questions.

Truthfully, she didn't have any answers. He possibly thought from how she responded that he had sucked. That was far from the truth.

And *that* was the problem. Not the fact they had sex.

The sex had been great. Soul satisfying. Even toe-curling. Definitely orgasm inducing. Better than she would've ever expected from a *rough-around-the-edges* biker.

Only, having sex with him should have flushed him from her system.

It did the exact opposite.

But as good as it had been and as tempted as she was to

knock boots with him again, after he came, reality had crept in.

No, not crept in. Hit her like a two-by-four across the forehead.

She had given in to her impulse and regretted it immediately afterward. Again, not because he sucked, but because she hardly knew him. And what she did know...

She blew out a breath.

He was an ex-con. He belonged to a motorcycle club and certainly wasn't an upstanding citizen of society.

Add in the fact that they had to live together and both had young children living under the same roof. Impressionable children who should be looking up to them as examples and not hypocrites.

Since she couldn't fall asleep after going back upstairs and she didn't want to wake Wren with her restlessness, she decided she might as well get up and get a jump on the day.

She had finger foods to make for the tea party later.

On her way to the kitchen, she purposely didn't peek into the living room to see if Stone was awake or asleep. Once there, she pulled out all the ingredients she had purchased yesterday, along with the kitchen equipment she had moved in to fill his mostly empty kitchen cabinets. Important items she'd need to keep making a living.

Once she had everything set out in an organized fashion, along with a written copy of the ladies' requested menu, she decided this morning's prep would be a great time to test out doing videos. Especially since the kids were still in bed and weren't expected to wake up for at least another half an hour.

She could get a lot done in thirty minutes if she wasn't interrupted.

Yesterday, she had set up a dedicated YouTube channel for this new endeavor, but now she needed content and subscribers. Actually, a shitload of subscribers so her videos could be monetized. She planned to start out on the popular free video site and see how comfortable she was in front of a camera, plus how successful her videos were before switching over to a virtual teaching site. One that would cost her money and eat into her earnings.

After setting up her cell phone, she adjusted it until everything important was included in the shot.

Then she took a deep breath to settle her nerves, despite the fact that, one, it was really early in the morning and her intended audience might be sleeping, and two, she had zero subscribers. That meant the number of watchers might be small, if she even had any at all.

For now, that could be a good thing. This way if she screwed up, less people would witness it. And technically, if it was embarrassingly bad, she could delete it.

She was okay with public speaking, but not great. The only reason she was half decent was due to the classes she'd been teaching in Camp Hill for the past few years. Only, those classes were usually made up of a dozen or less people.

If this new venture took off, she could potentially be teaching thousands. Her stomach churned at that thought.

You can do this, Taryn! Just pretend no one's watching and you're in the kitchen alone doing what you love...cooking.

This could turn out to be easy money if she put out the right content. She even spent a couple of hours watching other cooking videos last night before attempting to sleep. She made notes on what she liked, what she wanted to avoid, and which videos seemed to draw a larger audience.

It also gave her ideas on the type of content she wanted to make to fill her YouTube channel. She wanted to provide helpful cooking techniques that were *real* and tested, unlike all the videos all over social media that were only made for shock value or even outrage.

Some of those actually made her want to puke.

Worse, some videos weren't even real, they were created with artificial intelligence. After seeing that, she vowed she would hand make everything. Nothing would be fake.

She also wanted to come off as genuine and down-to-Earth and not superficial like some of the other social influencers she'd come across.

Unlike some of the videos she came across, if she screwed up, she would explain her mistake and how to fix it. Not just edit it out.

Taryn shook her head at her crazy fantasy of possibly being the next Julia Child and, before hitting the record button, downed the rest of the coffee in her mug. Caffeine was sorely needed since her ass was already dragging from the lack of sleep. Maybe she'd take a quick nap once the kids were off to school, Stone was off to do whatever the hell he did, and before heading over to the ladies' monthly tea.

Those ladies alone could be wearisome. But they were regular paying customers and tended to tip well, despite her telling them that tips were unnecessary.

"Okay, you can do this," she whispered. "Nobody will be watching. It's good practice."

Giving herself a nod, she pushed the button to go live and began her demo. After briefly introducing herself, she explained slowly and clearly everything as she did it and the reasons why. As the minutes ticked by, she occasionally glanced at the number of watchers and tried not to show her shock.

Or her panic.

Holy shit! She already had fifty subscribers and over seventy-five people watching!

Don't hyperventilate.

Be professional. Don't rush. Be thorough. Slip in a few tasteful jokes. Keep it fun. Nobody wants a stiff, awkward robot.

What she wasn't expecting was the real-time comments. No surprise, some were downright rude. Asking her to take off her top. Telling her that her techniques were wrong. Even adding puking emojis because of the recipe she was making.

But she expected that from a social media site full of keyboard warriors. She doubted any of them would come to her in-person classes and be brave enough to say those same things to her face. She needed to learn to ignore the bad and concentrate on all the good. The compliments. The questions. The watchers who quickly subscribed to her channel.

This might actually work!

She'd have to thank Stone for the idea. She should thank him for the orgasms, too, but she didn't want to ever speak of it again.

It could be a mistake easily forgotten. A once and done thing. Because she surely didn't want to have sex with him again. Of course not. That would be foolish. And make things messy.

They had to coexist in this house. Work together for a common goal: taking care of the kids and keeping them safe.

"Spread the cream cheese evenly over the cucumber rounds and top with a small piece of salmon. Then sprinkle with dill or any of your favorite seasonings. And don't forget the basics: salt and pepper!"

She did it! She got through the first dish. Yes, it was simple, and no, it wasn't a cooked dish, but it had gone better than expected.

With a smile, she quickly scanned the comments to see if

she needed to answer any more questions or clarify any of the steps before she logged off.

Looks delicious!

"Yes, I promise you this combo *is* delicious! And the recipe is so simple and refreshing. It's the perfect finger food for any gathering. Especially in the summer."

Drooling!

I'd do that in a hot second!

Her smile widened. "I'm glad I could motivate you to make these!"

Yummy!

Give me a bite of that perfect peach.

Peach? This dish didn't include peaches. It was cucumber, smoked salmon and—

A noise made her spin around to see Stone sauntering through the kitchen wearing nothing but his very, *very* snug boxer briefs.

Oh. My. God.

All his tattoos are on full display, as was his undeniable bulge.

No wonder her audience was going nuts. They weren't making comments about her food, they were lusting over Stone in his damn underwear!

Suddenly, the temperature in the kitchen became as hot as if she'd been baking all day. Her cheeks were on fire.

Then she spotted something she had missed. *Holy shit.* He had the same patches on the back of his cut *inked into his back!* He never told her he was marked like that and last night...this morning...in the bathroom, she hadn't seen it. Just his...

A breath slipped from between her parted lips.

His MC affiliation was the last thing she wanted her

audience to see. Even more concerning was the fact that those very easy to read tats could identify him—who he was and what he represented—as well as identify her and possibly where she was currently living.

Her heart tumbled in her now-tight chest.

That identifiable information could be dangerous. Especially since her YouTube channel was public. And those videos could be easily shared. Even go viral.

She quickly untied the apron she donned earlier, ripped it over her head and dropped it over his. At least that would cover what looked like what was left of his deflating morning wood.

He seriously had the nerve to look offended?

Now truly in a panic, she mouthed, "Get out," while her back was to the camera.

His eyebrows stitched together as he tugged with confusion at the apron. "Why?"

Trying not to make too much of a scene, she stage whispered, "Get out! They can see you!" Keeping her hand below the counter, she jabbed a finger toward her phone.

When he lifted his head, the creases in his forehead were deeper. "Who?" He pulled the apron back over his head and tossed it on the counter.

Since being subtle wasn't working, she pointed to her phone propped on the counter, hoping her body was blocking the audience's view.

His confusion cleared. "You on a video call?"

"No! I'm in the middle of a live cooking demonstration," she hissed.

Nudging her out of the way, he leaned closer to the phone until his face filled the screen. "People are watchin' live?"

Oh, good God!

"See those comments rolling up the screen?" Or emojis. Since now it was full of fire emojis, shocked face emojis, drooling emojis, even eggplant emojis, as well as some puking emojis. This time she didn't think those last ones were meant for the recipe.

When he squinted his eyes and leaned even closer to the screen, another flurry of comments scrolled up at a furious pace. There were so many she couldn't even catch what any of them said.

With a grin, he smoothed out his beard, combed fingers through his messy bedhead, and stepped back. But of course, wearing a smirk, he immediately shoved his hand down his boxer briefs and scratched his balls.

"Stone," she groaned. The Earth could open up and swallow her at any time now.

He had the gall to shrug. "Babe. Need coffee." That was the moment he spotted the full pot she had made and headed over there.

Now her audience had not only a great view of his ass, but all of that ink on his back.

Shit. "Your back."

He muttered a, "Fuck," swiped the coffee pot and a mug before stepping out of the camera's view.

Only, it was too late. Everyone had a good view of what his tats represented.

She needed to wrap up the video with a quickness.

She plastered on a smile she hoped didn't come off as forced and spoke quickly, "Okay, so the rest of the menu for today's luncheon will include deviled eggs with crumbled bacon topping, a classic rotini pasta salad, low-carb lettuce wraps, and two different types of tea sandwiches. I'll record the rest and upload to my channel later today. However, this wraps up today's live demonstration on making cucumber salmon bites. Make sure to subscribe to my channel so you don't miss any of my future recipes or live demos. Thank you for joining me and tell your friends!" She quickly turned off the video feed and blew out a frustrated breath.

She was afraid to look at all the comments. Luckily, she could delete any that didn't have to do with the food. She had a feeling that would take a while. Since she didn't want to delete the video, she might also have to find a way to edit him out. Or at least blur his MC tattoos.

Note to self: find a free video editing program and learn how to use it.

Taryn heard, "That why you didn't wanna talk earlier? You were savin' up all your words for this?"

While she recognized the amusement in his tone, she wasn't finding his little "show" humorous.

An ache in her fingers made her realize she was holding on to the counter with a death grip. Releasing it, she turned, crossed her arms over her chest, and studied the man now leaning back against the counter only a couple of feet away, wearing a sly grin.

When he lifted the mug of coffee to his lips and guzzled some down, it hit her that he wasn't stressing about showing off his bulge or his identifiable tats.

"You don't care that everyone saw the colors on your back?"

"Nope. Wear 'em on my back when I wear my cut."

"You're not worried about anyone figuring out where you —we—live and coming here?"

"Let 'em try."

She was afraid someone just might. Someone like Vic.

With a sigh, she waved her hand in front of his mostly naked body. Proof that: "This kitchen isn't going to work for my live videos." Between Stone and the kids, she might have a lot of interruptions.

"Thought you were gonna record them, not do 'em live."

"I plan to record more and post them to my YouTube account, but to monetize it, I need to reach a certain amount of subscribers first. My research showed that going live is the fastest way to get them. Right now, that may be my best marketing tool since I'm only starting out and it costs me nothing but time. But I can't have you or the kids crashing my videos." Especially Stone in tight boxer briefs that emphasized his assets.

"Do it when the house is empty."

She rolled her eyes. "Now why didn't I think of that? Anyway, that's easier said than done. It's not like you have an actual day job and are gone set hours. In fact, I don't even know how you make money." She frowned. "How *do* you make money?"

The man owned a vintage truck, a Harley Davidson, a house...

He had to pay for all of that somehow.

Certainly not with his "assets."

"Same as anybody else. Fuckin' work for it."

"By doing what?"

"Like you, the club's got our own businesses. We all got a hand in 'em 'cause we all benefit."

That still didn't answer her question. "What kind of businesses?"

He downed the rest of his coffee, then went over to refill his mug. While he did so, she struggled to keep her eyes from his ass. *Perfect peach* was right.

He shook his head. "Told you all this shit already. We got

a coupla tow trucks. Also work on vehicles. Offer protection. Collect bad debts."

Now she remembered that list. So much had happened this week alone that she was overwhelmed and couldn't remember all the small details.

Not that those details would be considered small, but they hadn't been her priority at the time.

"You have a repair shop that's open to the public?"

"Never said it was public."

Maybe the first two businesses weren't so legit after all. The only private garages she knew of serviced their own fleet. She doubted the Kings had a fleet of work vehicles.

Something didn't smell right. "Where's it located?"

"At The Castle."

"I don't remember seeing anything that looked like a garage."

"Weren't lookin' hard enough."

Of course. "You also mentioned protection and collections." Activities normally tied to organized crime.

"Yeah."

That was his answer? Just *yeah?* "Are you saying the club runs a legitimate security agency as well as a collection agency?"

He snorted. *Well,* there was her answer. The Kings were probably no better than the Mob.

"Are *any* of these businesses legal?"

"Depends on who you're askin'."

She knew Stone had no problem with breaking the law. She didn't try to convince herself otherwise. But was his criminal activity a lot worse than what she thought?

"First of all, I'm asking *you*. Second, the legality of a business isn't an opinion. If you weren't aware, pesky things exist called laws. Either the club businesses follow those laws or they don't." She tilted her head to the side.. "Which one is it?"

"First of all," he echoed, "club business ain't anyone's business 'cept members. Second, that don't include *you*."

"Tell me, if my Honda needs work, where am I taking it?"

"You give it to me and it'll get done."

With that answer, she had to assume that none of their businesses were legal. It sounded like they didn't even have legitimate-looking "fronts" typically used to launder illegally obtained money. That also meant the majority, if not all, of the money the club—and their members—earned was dirty.

Were they so arrogant that they didn't think they'd get caught?

Probably not, since Taryn could take an educated guess that none of these "businesses" were new.

That also meant the house where she and Wren were staying was purchased with money earned by doing crimes. The truck that Wren had rode in was probably restored with the same dirty money.

All of that should bother her. She'd never been one to break the law. Now she was living in the middle of a crime ring.

Could she be considered guilty by association?

Worse, what kind of mother was she by not removing Wren from the situation?

But was Vic any better? The man beat the crap out of her *in front* of their son. The man Wren was *supposed* to look up to, to learn his morals from, was the last person Taryn now wanted to have access to him.

It was a dilemma that made her brain ache.

Yes, Vic was a bad man. But so was Stone.

The difference: Stone wanted to protect her. Vic was out for blood.

The choice might not be easy, but it was clear...

Wren's well-being came before anything.

She could easily use the Kings as examples to teach him the difference between right and wrong.

But not if she was dead.

Chapter Sixteen

Yesterday, Stone brought Taryn over to inspect the old cafeteria's kitchen to see if it would work better for her video classes. Or demos. Or whatever the fuck she called what she was doing online.

That cucumber bullshit she made the other morning didn't look good at all. Or filling. If she served that to his brothers, they'd probably look at her sideways before spitting it at her.

Most of the kitchen might still be original but the commercial-quality appliances had been updated a few years back. Better yet, the kitchen area was a lot bigger than the one at the house, giving her more room to work. She'd have more burners, ovens, fridge and freezer storage, a huge stock room, and all the rest of the shit she had gone nuts over when she saw it.

With her eyes lit up, she *ooo*'d and *aah*'d over shit he'd never think twice about.

She was also excited about having a fuckton of storage for some of her chef equipment, unlike back at the house. At least the shit she wouldn't need to keep there to make them meals at home. A requirement of their agreement.

Since she'd be coming over to The Castle on a regular basis, he had given her a key to the gate. When he handed it to her, she had stared at it in surprise.

"Every time I've been here, the gate hasn't been locked."

"'Cause there wasn't a threat. Now there is." Or would be soon as soon as that motherfucking ex of hers got sprung. *"Gonna be locked twenty-four-seven 'til that threat's been eliminated."*

Her brow furrowed. "Eliminated?"

Fuck. *Maybe he should've picked a better word. Neutralized? Dispatched? Silenced? Buried six feet under? Floating down the Susquehanna River? "No longer a threat."*

"He's not even out yet."

"Stupid to get caught with our asses hangin' out."

He had told all his brothers, as well as the prospects and sweet butts, that they needed to stay vigilant and always keep the gates locked. If they saw anyone suspicious, they needed to let him or Ogre know.

Since security cameras had been installed around the exterior of the former school years ago, he had Nut Sack check all the feeds to make sure they were all functioning since they hardly ever checked them unless they had a reason.

It had been a long fucking time since they'd had a reason. Usually no one fucked with the Kings.

Not even the pigs.

He and his brothers were all fucking pros when it came to getting in and out of a situation without getting caught. On the slim fucking chance anyone was nabbed, then they knew better than to tie the crime to the club.

If they did...

Yeah, no one fucking did. They all knew the consequences after that prison or jail door opened again. If they even made it out still breathing.

A lot of his brothers, including Stone, still had connections on the inside in various facilities around the state. Prison was also a great place to recruit new prospects since some ex-cons didn't have a place to land after doing their bid. The Kings gave them one in exchange for their loyalty. And that loyalty meant keeping their fucking traps shut whenever they found themselves sporting metal bracelets.

First rule of getting pinched: Don't say shit except to demand an attorney.

Second rule: Don't say shit until the club attorney—kept on retainer for good reason—arrived at the location they were being detained.

Even then, don't say shit. The attorney was paid a goddamn fortune to flap his gums.

They drilled that into every new prospect's gray matter.

Once the prospects moved everything Taryn would need into the kitchen—even some of her shit from the storage trailer—he asked her what else she'd need and she happily gave him a long list.

But what mattered to Taryn wasn't what mattered to him. To Stone, the main benefit of having her recording at The Castle was that someone would always be around to keep an eye on her.

After a couple of the club girls had done the grocery shopping for Taryn, she cooked a huge meal for everyone last night.

While scarfing down the food, Stone swore his brothers all shot loads in their pants. No one had ever cooked anything that good in the club's kitchen before. The pasta with homemade fucking meatballs was shoveled into their pie holes like they hadn't eaten in a goddamn week.

While Stone agreed the food *was* good, in truth, most of them were probably stoned as fuck and had the munchies.

Today, she was back in the kitchen with a list of recipes she wanted to record to add content to her channel. The smell alone made Stone's mouth water. No fucking surprise, his brothers were circling like a pack of starving dogs, just waiting for her to toss them scraps.

Yeah, he doubted she'd ever be alone while doing her thing here at the clubhouse. That peace of mind also meant Stone could go make some scratch later. He had two collection jobs to do today down in Lancaster County for a loan shark they worked with on the regular.

Bottom line: borrow money from a sketchy motherfucker and not pay it back? Better have that cash in your fucking pocket when Stone or one of his brothers showed up to collect what was owed and you hadn't bothered to pay back.

They got the money? They might only get a few broken fingers as a late fee.

They don't?

Yeah, a few broken fingers would be the least of their worries. They might be missing those fingers. Or some teeth. Even a whole hand. It all depended on the amount owed and what the loan shark wanted in "interest."

Doing collections was one of his favorite things to do. Assholes desperate enough to borrow money from an "illegal banker" never went to the cops. No matter how many broken bones or severed digits they earned for not making their loan payments in a timely manner.

Excuses didn't work for loan sharks. They didn't give a fuck what the issue was, they just wanted their fucking money. Of course with an inflated amount of interest. It pissed the lender off even more when they had to lose a cut of that scratch to the Kings.

Stone's MC occasionally did a little loan sharking of their own, but only with people they knew could make payments. Charging an insane amount of interest was easy scratch for the club.

He needed to leave soon to get those jobs done but he had to wait on Taryn to finish putting her shit away after recording the last video on her list. They had come directly to the clubhouse in her Honda after dropping the kids off at school this morning. Tomorrow, he'd let her drive herself so he could go do his thing while she did hers.

But that was tomorrow. Today, he wanted to be close enough to keep an eye on her, but not up her ass. So he leaned back just inside the propped-open cafeteria doors with a knee bent and a boot planted on the wall. Taking a long drag on his cigarette, he caught glimpses of her behind the school's former serving line, cleaning up and putting shit away.

By the time he finished his smoke and had crushed it under his boot, she appeared from the kitchen and headed in his direction with a smile filling her face and a spring to her step.

Cooking made the woman happy.

Stuffing their pie holes made his brothers happy.

A match made in fucking Heaven.

But her trek to him came to a complete stop when someone stepped into her path.

Stone's eyes narrowed on one of their newer prospects.

What the fuck was Gooch doing?

When Taryn tried to skirt around him, he once again blocked her, reaching for the strand of hair that had escaped her bun and twisting it around his finger.

Fuck that shit. Stone's teeth clenched and he pushed off the wall.

Gooch playing with her hair was a control move the shit-for-brains was trying to pass off as flirty. Stone saw right through that bullshit.

So did Taryn.

With her previous smile now upside down, she jerked her head back, trying to free herself.

As much as Stone wanted to rush over to them, he waited to see if Gooch found his smarts.

Or caught a knee to his nuts since Taryn was not happy.

She wasn't the only fucking one.

Whatever hissed warning came out of her mouth made it look as though she was spitting venom. Then Gooch prevented her from skirting around him with a tighter grip on her hair. A hold no longer playful, but forceful.

The prospect must've missed the memo about Taryn being off-limits, since, apparently, Gooch's fucking pea brain had dropped from his head to his dick. Stone would be happy to help him put it back into place.

It was time to step in and school the motherfucker on what level a prospect was in their MC...

Rock bottom.

From the corner of his eye, he saw one side of Ogre's mouth hike up as he sat back to watch the upcoming lesson.

Stone was there in a few long and determined strides. "Let her fuckin' go."

Not waiting for the answer, he grabbed a wide-eyed Gooch's wrist and twisted with enough force to break more than just his grip. With a satisfying *snap, crackle, pop,* the prospect's knees buckled and he shouted in pain.

But he damn well released the woman he never should

have laid a hand on. The same hand now jacked in a way it shouldn't be.

Damn shame.

"She look like fuckin' club property?" Stone growled.

"She's...here...ain't...she?" Gooch blew out a breath between each word. Most likely an attempt not to cry like the little bitch he was.

"Don't ever fuckin' touch shit you know's off-limits. Thought I made myself fuckin' clear about Taryn. Guess not. Since she's livin' under my roof, that means she's off... fuckin'...limits." His volume might have increased a cunt hair for those last three words.

At least enough to make Gooch wince.

Stone shot a glance toward Ogre where he sat at one of the cafeteria tables with Thor by his side. He had returned to finishing off a plate of whatever Taryn had made for one of her videos.

While the club's enforcer had watched the whole exchange, he'd wait on Stone to decide the next step. And whether or not the enforcer should step in and take over.

Since they had somewhere to go and he didn't want Taryn to witness the rest of the hard lesson about to be taught, Stone jerked his chin toward the injured prospect. Ogre dipped his head just enough to acknowledge the silent order. The sergeant at arms would take it from there.

"No, man! I didn't know!" Gooch yelled. "Didn't mean to step on your toes, brother."

Stone sucked on his teeth. "You ain't my brother. Ain't nothin' but dog shit. No more, no less. Guess you need a reminder of that."

The panicked prospect insisted, "It won't happen again! I fuckin' swear!"

"Damn right it won't."

It would only take a flick of the sergeant at arms' wrist for Thor to take down Gooch and rip out his throat. Stone had seen it before but not on one of their own. While impressive, it was goddamn gruesome.

"Let's go," he barked at Taryn, grabbing her elbow and steering her out of the cafeteria and toward the exit. "Time to pick up the kids."

Once out in the hallway, she asked, "Are you mad at me?"

With a frown, he stopped and spun on her. "I look mad at you?" He thought he was controlling his temper pretty fucking well, all things considered.

"You look furious."

With a shake of his head and once again taking long strides, he pulled her along with him. She glanced back over her shoulder toward the cafeteria.

Stone didn't need to do the same since he knew what was about to happen. And he didn't give a fucking shit. He trusted Ogre to do his job. He didn't need to supervise it.

"What's going to happen to him? What will Ogre—"

"Don't fuckin' ask questions you don't wanna know the answers to. Promise, you don't wanna know."

"But—"

Stone jerked to another stop. "Just said to let it go, yeah? You like him touchin' you?"

With a set jaw, she plugged her hands on her hips. "Of course not. But that doesn't mean I want him to be hurt."

"How we deal with club business is just that...club business, so let it fuckin' go, woman."

"Listen, I don't give a crap if you boss your brothers around, but you do *not* get to boss me around. We had this discussion before. I don't work for you. I'm only helping you out temporarily."

Damn. Despite fighting a grin—since he preferred not to

have his nuts permanently implanted in his body cavity by her knee—one side of his mouth pulled up.

"You think that's funny?"

Yeah, he certainly liked the fire in her. His dick agreed. "Think it's pretty fuckin' hot when you snap back." He grabbed her arm again and urged her forward. "C'mon, let's go before Sunny starts textin' me every five fuckin' seconds askin' where the fuck I am." If she did, he'd lose his shit for real.

"You took her phone away," she reminded him.

Fuck, that was right. "Don't Baby Bird got a phone?" He wouldn't put it past his girl to use someone else's to harass her father.

"Of course not. He's too young."

Was she trying to make a point that Sunny shouldn't have one, either?

Stone shoved the back door open and jerked his chin to indicate that she should go through first. Like the fucking gentleman he was, of course.

He snorted softly and followed her outside. "Probably should get him one so he can get a holda you in case your asshole ex tries to snatch him."

Her cheeks lost all color and she bugged her eyes out at him. "Don't say that! Vic's not on the list at the new school."

He hated to tell her that her ex could snatch him anywhere, not only at a public school. But again, Stone planned on handling that threat. Hopefully before anything like that happened.

"Anyway, Wren needs to concentrate in class, not be playing on his phone. Because that's what he'd do: play video games."

"Ain't allowed to have it out in class."

"And I'm sure they all follow that rule," she said dryly.

When they reached her Honda in the paved lot, she paused. "I was thinking…"

He grunted. *This should be good.*

"The guys swarmed around when I was cooking. They wanted to eat whatever I was making."

And water was fucking wet. "Why the club decided to cover some of the expenses. You think if the club don't benefit, we were gonna agree to pay for a goddamn top-of-the-fuckin'-line mixer?" The officers had a quick informal meeting yesterday to get approval for her to use the kitchen for her business and to help fund some of the shit she needed. Luckily, everyone sitting at the table saw how having a chef onsite would benefit them.

The only thing better than empty balls were full guts.

Her mouth twisted. "That wasn't top of the line."

"Are you shittin' me? That contraption cost a shit-ton of scratch."

"It's good, but it isn't the best. Now the best—"

Stone lifted a palm and stopped her right there. "Don't give a shit."

He shrugged out of his cut, flipped it inside out, and slipped it back on before climbing behind the wheel of her Pilot.

That had been another argument. Because of her insurance, she didn't think he should be driving her cage. *For fuck's sake*, if it was up to him, he wouldn't be, either. It was a piece of shit, but his truck wasn't big enough for two adults and two kids.

Anyway, the fuck if he was letting a woman drive him around if he could help it. He might as well chop off his balls and jam them into Taryn's new mixer.

Luckily, she didn't argue this afternoon, unlike this morning. She got right into the passenger side without a complaint.

Thank fuck.

After driving the Honda through the gate, he locked it behind them. Once he slid back behind the wheel and shoved the shifter into Drive, he heard, "Seatbelt."

He shot her a look.

"My car. My insurance. Follow the laws."

He continued to stare at her, pulling in an irritated breath.

She smiled and shrugged. "Or I'll have to drive."

"For fuck's sake," he grumbled, strapping himself in. "Happy?"

"You will be if you get in an accident and it saved you from eating the windshield."

He turned onto Whiskey Springs Road. "Probably eat the airbag, not the glass."

"Do you want that pretty mug of yours all messed up?"

He tugged on his chin hairs and shot her a grin. "You sayin' I'm pretty?"

She stared straight ahead and grumbled, "You're not half bad." His grin flattened out when she said, "I have another idea..."

Chapter Seventeen

"I HAVE ANOTHER IDEA..."

Muffling his groan at that announcement, he steered the Honda in the direction of the elementary school. He was damn sure their kids were getting impatient. "Never finished the first one."

"Oh. I was going to ask if I can put any of them to work since they're circling like—"

"A pack of starving wild dogs? Yeah, long as they don't got somethin' to do for the club. The club always comes first. Them stuffin' their traps don't. Any of 'em get' handsy or if one of the prospects or sweet butts don't listen when you tell them to do somethin', lemme or Ogre know. We'll handle it."

"I hope we can avoid that."

She wasn't the only one. Stone thought everyone understood what he told them the other day. He had been pretty fucking clear about what Taryn was and what she wasn't.

When she didn't move on to the next subject immediately, he glanced over at her again but she was now staring out of the passenger-side window. "What other shit's on your mind?"

He might regret asking, since he wasn't sure he really wanted to know what was on any woman's mind. Women were goddamn confusing and he wasn't sure if he'd ever understand them.

"While filming today, it came to me that—if it's acceptable with your club, of course—I could use the kitchen to make premade meals. The Castle has enough cooler space for me to store or freeze them until they're delivered. A lot of people too busy to cook, or who simply want portion control, like to buy premade meals a week at a time. I never had a prep or storage area big enough to offer that service before."

And now she did. The woman was definitely hustling to make ends meet. Add that to the list of ways she impressed him. "How they gonna get these meals?"

"I guess I'll have to deliver them since I'm sure you don't want them picking them up at the clubhouse."

"Fuck no. We don't need people wanderin' around our grounds or seein' shit they don't need to see." And that could be a shitload of different things.

No one needed to know how the Kings made their scratch. Or what went on at the former school grounds. And they sure as fuck didn't need to know a hell of a busy chop shop was hidden beyond the tree line. They'd even gone as far as putting camouflage netting over whatever they could so it wouldn't be as noticeable from the air.

Having some random discover one of their illegal sources of scratch—especially the most profitable one—could draw unnecessary heat. Enough that it could burn the damn club to the ground. All because Taryn wanted to sell a goddamn frozen pasta dish to a lazy fuck who couldn't cook their own shit. Or didn't want to order takeout.

Her, "That's what I figured," brought him back to the conversation.

He had to admit, her idea was a solid one. There was only one problem. "You ain't deliverin' them. We'll get a prospect to deliver them for you." The fuck if she was delivering shit to some random fuck's house. Especially with her ex about to be on the loose.

Her mouth dropped open. "So, my customers will get beef Bolognese with a side of badass biker?"

An amused smile curled his lips. "You think bikers are badass?"

"Well, aren't you?"

"Fuck yeah we are. Will make sure they don't wear their cuts while bein' your delivery boys."

"It's not only wearing a cut that's a problem. What if the customer asks questions?"

"Answers are free."

She sighed. "They'll be the face of my business, Stone."

"Will tell 'em to plaster on a fuckin' smile and be as sweet as that chocolate pie you made the other day for the kids, too." He managed to hoover three pieces himself.

"And will they?"

"They want patched in? They're gonna kiss your fuckin' ass. You can teach 'em how you want 'em to be with customers."

This new venture could actually be another benefit to their MC. Especially if it made decent scratch.

"But, just so you know, club's gonna take a cut for this delivery service."

"What?"

Did she really think she'd get free labor and put all the scratch in her own pocket? They were the Kings, not some fucking pussy-ass jokers. "Long as you're cookin' in the kitchen, the members get to eat what you make, so no one's gonna mind takin' scratch from the club coffers to cover what's needed. But tyin' up a prospect with shit other than club business is gonna cost. Tellin' you now, it's the only way it's gonna happen."

"How much will this service cost me?"

"Will have a sit-down with the other officers and figure it out."

"Well, whatever it is, I'll have to work that cost into the price of the meals, so let's not get crazy with it, *yeah?*" She had deepened her voice for the added "yeah."

He pressed his lips together to smother his amusement. The woman had a bit of an attitude today. He might have to knock the bottom out of her along with that attitude later. Once the kids were asleep. "Yeah, got it. But it ain't all my decision. Gotta vote on this kinda shit."

"Like a democracy. How soon can you find that out so I can come up with a business plan?"

"Gotta ask Ransom to schedule a meetin'. So, don't know. Soon." He'd shoot the prez a text after they picked up the kids.

"Do you think it's a good idea?"

He glanced over at her, not bothering to hide his surprise. "You care what I think?"

She jerked up a shoulder in a half-assed shrug. "Sure. Why not?"

Damn. She trusted his opinion.

He sliced his eyes back to the road and didn't smother his grin this time. "Think it's a great fuckin' idea. Puts more scratch in your pocket and more in the club coffers. Sounds like a win-fuckin'-win to me."

If it kept her ass at The Castle instead of going to those damn personal chef bookings where he couldn't keep an eye on her, even better. Once Vic the Dick was dealt with, she could go back to doing all the shit she was doing before.

Or she could keep finding alternate ways to line her pockets. He wouldn't give a fuck either way, as long as she was safe.

"I appreciate you helping me pivot my business."

"Got a deal, remember? I keep you and Baby Bird safe, you take care of me and my mini-monster." For Stone, that "taking care of" part needed more sex, though. However, he wasn't going to bring that up in an enclosed space. An escape plan was always needed when bringing up any topic that might piss off a woman.

He wasn't fucking stupid.

Depending on who was asked.

"'Til I tell you different, this is how it's gonna go. You drop the kids off at school on the way to The Castle. Do your thing. When I can't get the kids from school, will get someone else to pick them up and drop them off there. Once you're done for the day, then you bring them home with you."

She *hmm*'d. "I know I just told you not to boss me around, but I can live with this plan."

He huffed, "Thank fuck for that. But even if you couldn't, you ain't got a choice."

"I always have a choice."

"Not when it comes to your safety. Remember, I'm in charge of that."

Luckily, whatever response she was about to spew evaporated due to him pulling up to the curb outside of the school. Of course, her kid was sitting on the curb, reading a book like a civilized nut nugget, while his was shooting daggers at the Honda with her narrowed eyes.

Most likely at the occupants, too.

As soon as the Honda rolled to a stop, the rear driver-side

door was flung open and his girl climbed in with a very audible huff followed by a loud announcement of, "You're late." Like her old man couldn't tell fucking time.

"Better late than never," he muttered, his eyes locked on Taryn's ass as she climbed out of the cage to help her kid get in.

"Never would mean I'd go into foster care. Maybe my new family would let me have my phone."

"Doubt it."

"Should we test that theory?"

Why did he get served generous helpings of shit from his spawn while Taryn got hugs from hers? Maybe he needed to trade in his decade-old model for a new one. "Sure. You wanna go into foster care? Live with some strangers that got a shitload of other nut nuggets? Gonna hafta share a room. Wear hand-me-downs. Will get no fuckin' allowance and loads of fuckin' rules. Gonna learn quickly that poutin' won't get you what you want."

"I don't get what I want now."

He glanced at his mouthy daughter in the rearview mirror as she strapped in without being told, unlike her old man. "Yeah? What shit don't you got? Ain't sufferin' for nothin'."

"I don't have my phone."

"Then get a fuckin' job and buy one."

"You get a job!" Sunny snapped back just as Taryn finished getting Wren settled in his booster seat.

Some days he regretted sticking his dick in Sheena more than others. Today was one of those days. "Baby Bird don't got a phone."

"Because he's a baby!"

Stone winced at her high-pitched shriek. Good thing

Taryn had her door open as she climbed back in, otherwise his eardrums might have ruptured.

"I'm not a baby!" Wren yelled back.

For fuck's sake. Who the fuck became a parent willingly and chose to deal with this kind of shit?

He should have gotten neutered the second he was capable of getting a hard-on.

Sunny rolled her brown eyes. "If you're not a baby, then why did you cry at lunch?"

What the fuck?

Both he and Taryn spun in their seats. "You cried at lunch? Why?"

Wren lowered his eyes, pulled in a big breath and pushed out his bottom lip.

When he didn't answer his mother right away, Stone repeated the question. He wanted some damn answers. "Why'd you cry at lunch, Baby Bird?"

"A kid took my lunchbox."

He expected Taryn to get bent out of shape about Wren answering Stone instead of her, but then she shouted, "What?"

"What the fuck?" Stone barked. "Which kid?"

"Dunno his name." Wren held up a hand over his head. "Big kid. Much bigger than me."

"Everyone's bigger than you," Sunny muttered.

Wren pounded his fist on his thigh. "That's not true!"

For fuck's sake, his girl was a pro at pissing people off.

"Did you tell your teacher?" Taryn asked a little more quietly, but Stone could see her anger simmering right beneath the surface.

No doubt she had better control over her temper than he did.

"No. He told me if I snitched, I'd get stitches."

With her mouth hanging open, she glanced at Stone. Then with a shake of her head, Taryn asked Sunny, "Is bullying typical at your school?"

Sunny shrugged. "How would I know? Nobody fucks with the Kings."

A snort shot out of Stone's nose before he could stop it.

"That's not funny," Taryn muttered under her breath.

"Yeah, but true." Stone once again addressed his daughter, "Sunny, you make it clear to everyone in that school that he's under the Kings' protection too, yeah?"

She wrinkled her nose. "Do I have to?"

His eyebrows shot up his forehead. "Did those fuckin' words come outta my mouth?"

Sunny's mouth twisted. "Yes."

"Then there's your answer."

She crossed her arms over her chest and turned to stare out of her window, a clear sign she was done with this conversation.

Only Stone was not. "You make it known, Sunny. Then, Baby Bird, if they still fuck with you, you let me know. Gonna handle it."

A groan could be heard from the passenger seat. "As his mother, I would handle it, not you."

"Sunny, do what I said. It don't work, Momma Bird's gonna handle it."

Taryn sighed.

"What? Am I wrong, Momma Bird?"

She simply shook her head. He needed to head off any further discussion of this shit when they were alone. No doubt it would go sideways and get heated.

He hoped to get sex from her later, not an argument.

"Here's the deal...you gotta go into that school 'cause

some asshole kid needs a reckonin', then my ass is gonna be right by your side."

"I said I can handle it."

"Yeah, you're gonna handle it and I'm gonna make sure it's handled. You get your lunchbox back?" The last was directed at the annoyed woman's son.

"No."

"You tell that little bastard he don't give it back, I'm gonna break all his fuckin' fingers."

"No! Don't you dare say that, Wren. You might get kicked out of school and you just got enrolled there. I'll call the principal in the morning."

Stone met Wren's gaze in the rearview mirror, and as soon as the kid gave him a small smile, Stone smothered his own and began heading home.

Chapter Eighteen

STONE SCOOPED up the sleeping boy, careful not to wake him. Taryn had mentioned the other morning how Baby Bird slept like the dead. He sure as fuck hoped that was true. He didn't need her son waking in the middle of Stone's plan and fucking it up.

A plan he had come up with while he once again stared restlessly at the ceiling from the goddamn couch.

Why couldn't he sleep? Because of the temptation on the second floor. The one in *his* bed.

Seeing the prospect trying to get a piece of her today proved he wasn't the only one she tempted. Of course, she hadn't done it on purpose. She hadn't been flirting or even toying with any of the club members—not even him—while at The Castle, but even without that, something about her drew men.

It could be she wasn't even aware of it.

But he was.

It was refreshing to have a woman in their midst whose

goal wasn't to collar one of them. Or be worried more about the way she looked.

Taryn was simply trying to get by in life and make a damn living. Trying to raise her son right. Trying not to get beat to fuck by her dickhead ex.

However, he needed to get this plan rolling before Taryn woke up, too. He thought it was a damn good one. Of fucking course, she might not agree and put a stop to it.

When he had headed into his bedroom, he had nudged the door wider with his foot so he could carry Wren back through it without knocking the kid silly. Bonking his head against the door frame might wake up the whole household, including his own cranky crotch fruit.

After creeping up the steps and on his way to his bedroom, he had opened Sunny's bedroom door to peek inside to make sure she was crashed, too. The proof was the soft snoring coming from under the covers pulled over her head. His girl liked to burrow deep when she slept.

Come winter, she'd be wrapped up like a fucking burrito.

He carefully carried Baby Bird into her room, keeping an eye on the sleeping boy. His eyes were still closed, his mouth hanging open wide enough to catch flies, and every muscle soft like jelly.

Good.

After gently placing the kid on the top bunk, Stone covered him up before quietly slipping back out of the room and securing the door behind him. Both kids would be surprised come morning, but they needed to get used to sharing the room since Stone planned on reclaiming his bed.

With Taryn in it.

He avoided the squeaky floorboard on his way back to his room, closed the door with a soft click, then twisted the lock so their nut nuggets didn't barge in without warning.

He'd prefer to avoid that cockblock. He'd also prefer that Wren didn't catch Stone's ass railing his mother. That could cause all kinds of emotional damage for both Taryn and her son.

He shucked his boxers, leaving them where they dropped. While fisting his dick, he approached the bed and paused to study an out-cold Taryn.

She had to be worn out from spending the day shooting content for her new YouTube channel. How filming videos about cooking were so damn tiring, he had no fucking clue.

But he was happy to see that she took his suggestion seriously. He had no doubt she'd be successful at it. The more money she made from teaching online classes—maybe even doing that meal prep shit—the less she'd have to go into a stranger's home.

Which could be a dangerous fucking undertaking on a good day.

While those videos would keep her busy in the daylight, tonight, no videos would be made. *Hell no*, tonight would be all live action.

He grinned.

As long as she didn't shut him down.

His grin flattened at that possibility.

All he needed to do was play his cards right and convince her that what they did in the bathroom should be done on a regular basis.

A bonus to their original agreement.

Another win-fucking-win.

Sitting on the edge of the bed, the sheet whispered along her smooth skin as he slid it down and exposed her tempting flesh. He quickly discovered she no longer wore the PJ bottoms she had on earlier, but only a pair of underwear that looked similar to his boxers. He was pretty fucking sure his daughter called them something like boy shorts.

Didn't fucking matter.

He settled more than just his ass on the mattress, doing his best not to shake it too much since he wasn't ready for her to wake up. Not yet, anyway. He wanted to take this time to explore her when she wasn't in motion. When she was completely unaware and relaxed.

When he could appreciate her fully without any interruptions.

With her lying on her stomach, one arm tucked under the pillow, he studied every inch he could see. From the dark strands of hair covering her face to the feminine curves of her shoulders, the arch of her spine, the dip found at the small of her back, the rise of her fuckable ass cheeks in that snug red cotton.

He curled his fingers tightly into his palms to fight the urge to smack them. To watch them jiggle from the impact. Possibly explore an area he doubted anyone had touched yet.

He'd volunteer to be the first.

His gaze followed the descending slope of her ass—he was tempted to sink his teeth there—to her soft thighs. He visually traced her calves before ending with her bare feet.

He noticed days ago how cute her toes were. The nails were painted a light pink, the same as the short nails on her hands. She probably had to keep them trimmed due to working with food.

In the little over a week he'd known her, he'd seen zero evidence of this woman being high maintenance. She didn't wear heavy makeup or a bunch of flashy jewelry. No fake hair, fake lashes or even fake nails. The bathroom wasn't overflowing with a bunch of bullshit to make her look good and fake out a man.

He swore some women had a product for each part of her damn body. A few times he'd woken up in a woman's bed and went to take a piss only to find the counter covered in expensive bullshit used to make them look better than they were in reality.

He preferred women who didn't give him a jump scare when he woke up next to them after their makeup had worn off. Of course, when his buzz was, too.

When Taryn wasn't wearing her chef uniform, she just wore casual clothes. Jeans, T-shirts, shit like that. He hadn't seen her in a dress or heels yet.

Stone couldn't say he'd hate it, though. With her banging body and natural beauty, he bet she'd look smoking hot dressed up. She'd look even hotter when he bent her over, flipped that dress up and fucked her from behind.

Fuck yeah.

He pumped his fist faster.

It was time to stop fantasizing and time to start touching something other than his own dick. Licking, nipping, and biting was also on his to-do list. Maybe even leave behind a mark or two before he was through.

Fucking her in his bed would be a hell of a lot better than the quick fuck downstairs on the vanity in that cramped bathroom, despite having no complaints about it. Here, he could get comfortable and take his time appreciating her.

Instead of a midnight snack, he would enjoy a full-course meal.

For fuck's sake, he needed to stop imagining it and start doing it.

With a single finger, he swept her hair over her bare shoulder, then softly pressed his lips where her neck and hairline met.

Her hair smelled damn good. Fruity. Nothing with a heavy scent.

For better access, he settled over her on his hands and knees, caging her in but careful to keep his weight off her. He wanted to avoid startling her awake and scaring the shit out of her.

Using the tip of his tongue, he drew a line down her neck, only stopping when he reached the neckline of one of the ribbed tank tops she liked to sleep in. Tonight's was white and he was damn sure if he rolled her over, he'd be able to make out her pink nipples through the fabric.

He'd get to them soon enough.

Again, as long as she didn't wake up swinging and clobber the shit out of him. If she told him to fuck off, he would. He wanted her to want this as much as he did.

If he gave her good dick tonight, she'd be more open to him giving it to her every night. On top of getting a piece of Taryn, his other goal was to stop sleeping on the fucking couch. His aching back hated him.

After lightly skimming his lips over her shoulders, he skipped everywhere still covered with clothes and concentrated on her luscious legs. He continued on his path, brushing his lips over the warm, smooth skin of her thighs, the back of her knees on his way down to her toes.

At mid-calf, she jerked awake, but didn't move even an inch until he finished. She didn't need to announce she was no longer sleeping. The goosebumps now decorating her flesh did that.

She cleared the sleep from her throat. "You're not Wren."

"Sure as fuck hope not," he murmured against her warm skin. He was going to continue with his plan until she said otherwise.

"What are you doing in here?"

Damn, her husky whisper hit him right in the dick. "Remember the birds and the bees talk you mentioned the other day? I need to have it with you?"

"Not funny."

"Ain't tryin' to make you laugh. Prefer to make you come."

She stretched like one of the stray cats hanging around The Castle and released a long moan.

At least she didn't scream at him to fuck off. Or shove him off. Or punch him in the nuts. He took those as good signs his ass wasn't going to get kicked out of her bed. *His* bed.

"Where's Wren?"

"Asleep on the top bunk in Sunny's room."

"When he wakes up, he's not going to know where he is."

"Kid's smart enough to figure it out."

"I'm not sure I want him sleeping in there."

"Damn sure I don't want him sleepin' in here." He'd normally inform her that it was his bed and that meant his rules. One of those rules being no kids sharing his bed. But he'd keep that shit to himself for now since he didn't want to risk Taryn kicking his ass out of his own bed.

He straddled her hips once she rolled over, her blue eyes blinking up at him. He grinned down at her when she checked out his hard-to-miss erection.

Her eyes went from sleepy to heated in an instant. "You could poke an eye out with that."

"Gonna take that as you sayin' I'm huge."

"That's not what I said."

"That's what I heard." Squeezing the tip, he milked a bead of precum as proof of the effect she had on him. "This is all for you."

"Does it come with a return receipt?"

He snorted. "Final sale. No returns."

"I don't even get to test it before I buy?"

"Got to test drive my cock the other night."

"Did I? I don't remember." Even though her expression remained the same, the corners of her eyes wrinkled.

He played along. "Damn! You sayin' fuckin' me is forgettable? Guess I gotta change up some things and tweak my performance."

"How will you do that?"

"Ain't gonna tell you, just gonna show you." It was time to get serious. "I want you naked."

"I'd say the same if you already hadn't taken it upon yourself to do so," she countered with her eyes flashing. Hunger and determination filled them.

"Guess you wanna get lucky tonight." No luck needed.

"I figured it was *you* getting lucky."

He couldn't argue that so he didn't. Instead, he climbed off her and offered her a hand. "Sit up."

Once she clasped it, he pulled her upright. He then peeled off her tank top, exposing her tits and hard-as-fuck nipples, and tossed it over his shoulder, not giving a shit where it landed. He shimmied her underwear down her legs, tossing them somewhere behind him, too.

No need for those.

Now all of her smooth skin and every damn curve was exposed, calling to him. Including the dark-blonde patch of hair at the top of her cunt. He wanted to jam his nose deep and simply inhale her scent.

He'd get there soon enough since he'd much rather smell a sweet pussy than some overpowering perfume in an overpriced bottle. But first, he wanted to finish exploring the woman since he didn't get a chance to do that last time.

He wasn't getting short changed from that tonight.

Fuck no.

All they had to do was limit the noise so they didn't wake up the kids. Having them pounding on the door while he was pounding Taryn would suck.

Now that he'd rid her of those boy shorts, he could continue with proving to her that sharing a bed with him would be nothing but a great opportunity and not a drawback.

For the both of them.

With one last peek at her sexy-as-fuck toes, he worked his way back up, kissing and licking along the way. He skipped over her pussy—he would concentrate on that soon enough—and sucked one dark-pink nipple deep into his mouth, tugging on it with his lips and flicking the rock-hard tip with his tongue.

Her soft groan and the slight arching of her back encouraged him to do the same with the other one. He could spend a shitload of time on her tits alone, they were that enticing, but there was no way he had the patience for that.

He continued to tease her tits with his mouth and tongue until he regretfully had to move on. With a wet pop, he released her now swollen, shiny nipple and shifted until they were face to face.

As soon as their gazes locked, he snagged her hair, fisted it tightly, and took her mouth for his very fucking own.

To claim it. Make it his. The same as he planned to do with her pussy.

He couldn't wait to dive in for a midnight snack. One she didn't have to cook.

His dick was getting impatient, too.

Soon.

For fuck's sake, Taryn was living under his damn roof and helping with his kid. He couldn't treat her simply like a hole to be filled. Instead, he once again had to make sure she was thoroughly fucking satisfied.

Otherwise, he'd be living on the couch indefinitely.

But he wanted this for more than only getting back in his own bed. That was simply a bonus. If he had to admit it, he really wanted *her* for as long as he could have her. Whether it was for the next few weeks or the next few months.

This was not normal for him. Not at fucking all.

When a groan rose from deep within her, he caught it and gave it back to her after combining it with his own.

He normally didn't give a shit about kissing—but, again, this situation was far from fucking normal—and her lips were so damn soft and addicting. It also helped that he knew those lips hadn't been wrapped around any of his brothers' dicks.

Even fucking better, she hadn't been shared in any way with any of his brothers. Not one fucking way.

Fuck yeah.

That was rare in his world.

Breaking off the kiss and on his way south to chow down, he paused once again on her tits since they were as tempting as her mouth.

Goddamn perfection.

They might not smother him to death but they fit his palm perfectly and had a good weight to them. She'd probably be pissed if she could read his thoughts and knew he was judging her tits like fruit in the produce department.

He kneaded one, then the other, as he alternated sucking them.

But he didn't stay there long since he was getting impatient and so was his demanding dick. It was screaming at him for some relief.

Soon.

He licked a path from her right nipple down her belly,

across the faded scar he assumed came from a C-section, skimmed his mouth over her golden pubes, then using his shoulders, nudged her thighs wider so he had room to settle between them.

He separated her with his fingers and stared at her shiny pink center.

Damn.

He was pretty fucking sure the sweet, tempting scent of her arousal was the closest he'd ever get to Heaven.

He was dying for another taste. "Feet on my shoulders. Keep yourself open to me. Want you to enjoy this as much as I'm gonna."

Chapter Nineteen

As soon as Taryn's feet were planted on his shoulders, Stone pushed forward, shoving her knees closer to her tits.

She was now right where he wanted her. On her back, with her pussy only inches away from his mouth. He quickly closed that gap, smashing his face between her legs, and immediately went to town.

The noise she made at the back of her throat caused him to raise his eyes and his dick to flex. With her eyelids pinned shut, she twisted the sheet within her fingers while pants softly escaped her gaped lips.

Yeah, she was into it and not complaining. And he planned to do shit to her that guaranteed not one complaint would be lodged.

Not a damn one.

As he continued his onslaught on her already juicy pussy, her hips danced and thighs quivered. A long, soft sigh escaped her and her eyes squeezed shut even tighter while he worked his magic. His lips sucked, his tongue flicked and plunged, his teeth scraped along the tender flesh.

She curled up enough to dig her fingers into the back of his head before shoving his face into her pussy to the point he struggled to take a breath.

If it took him suffocating to get her to come with his mouth, then so fucking be it.

She could ride his face until he turned blue since making her come all over his beard was a fuck of a lot more important than breathing. To him, good pussy was just as important as oxygen.

It would be at the top of his list if oxygen wasn't needed for him to live.

Unfortunately, it was.

With her head thrown back, she released a long groan as he pulled out all his time-tested techniques. If it was up to him, he'd leave nothing on her untouched tonight. Except for one spot he was damn sure Taryn wouldn't be open to him exploring.

Not yet, anyway. He had time to work on that. Just not tonight.

"Make me come," she repeated in a moaned chant. "Make me come. Please, make me come."

He guessed words were allowed tonight. He took that as a step closer to him both returning to his own bed and her accepting her fate. That being, she'd be joining him in that bed.

He hoped to fuck he wasn't wrong.

After circling her clit with the tip of his tongue, he sucked it hard, causing her to bow off the bed and smash her pussy into his nose. Only, breaking his nose wasn't going to stop him either.

She had to be fucking close...

It became obvious when she grabbed a pillow and stuffed it over her own face to smother her cry.

Fuck yeah.

His initial plan was to continue to lick, suck and nibble until she begged him to stop. Until she couldn't take anymore.

But the truth was, Stone was the fucking weak one. He was the one who couldn't take any more. He needed to move on before his plans ended up in the damn shitter. With how intensely his dick was throbbing, it felt about to blow.

And that would suck.

If he shot his load too early, she might not let him wait it out in his own damn bed until he was ready to go again. Once she got hers, she might not give a fuck about his.

So, yeah, he needed to keep his shit packed tight and stuffing his face with her pie wasn't helping his goddamn dilemma.

He lifted his head to see the result of his work: her head thrown back, her eyes closed and her mouth lax.

But he wasn't done.

Not even fucking close.

After dislodging himself from between her thighs, he reached for his main stash of wraps kept in the nightstand drawer.

One unplanned nut nugget was more than enough for now. In fact, some days his mini-monster's attitude was enough for him to slice off his own balls. Fuck making an appointment for a vasectomy.

While he loved his girl to death, "death" was the right term when it came to her since she might be the fucking death of him. She loved to push his patience. It didn't help that he didn't have a lot to begin with.

Yeah, the fuck if he was barebacking it with any woman. Even if she told him she was on birth control. He trusted that assurance about as much as he trusted the fucking pigs—the badge wearing kind, not the slab of bacon kind—which was zero.

Her eyes blinked open once he returned to settle on his knees between her legs. He held up the foil wrapper. "Good with this, right?"

Best to ask first than be accused later. A lesson he'd learned the hard way.

If a woman was joining him in his room at the clubhouse, she no doubt wanted to be there. The last time he fucked Taryn, it was clear she wanted it because *she* came to *him*. But since he invited himself to his own damn bed, he wanted to be crystal fucking clear.

It would really suck for Sunny if both parents were doing a bid behind bars at the same time.

So, no shit, it didn't hurt to make sure. He lifted an eyebrow at her slow response. "Yeah?"

Maybe she lost her ability to think and speak from the intense orgasm he gave her with only his mouth. He fought his grin.

Finally, her answer was a soft smile and the cocking of her knees to give him full access.

No taking that the wrong way.

She wanted it.

She wanted him.

She was going to get what she wanted.

He quickly tore open the wrap and rolled it on, his dick pounding with its own heartbeat the whole time in anticipation.

He then settled his hips between her thighs but before he planted himself deep, he latched his lips on the curve of one tit. When he slowly sank his teeth in, Taryn jammed her pelvis up and into him, encouraging him to fuck her without having to say a damn word. Once he released her, he swirled his tongue over her pebbled flesh.

He and his dick were more than ready, willing and able to take this to the next level.

Her hips shot up when the thick crown bumped against her sensitive, slick flesh. Fisting himself, he used his cock to nudge her open, then slid the head through her slick folds until it caught. Right where he needed to be. Right where she wanted him.

His goal tonight—besides getting off that crappy couch—was to claim that pussy as his for as long as she lived under his roof, as long as she needed protection. As long as she needed him.

Stone selfishly considered letting Vic the Dick live longer than originally planned. Of course, that would be a dick move since wanting her for himself was not more important than her safety.

But then, his brain had dropped into his balls. This was not a good time for making real plans or any deep thinking.

It was more about driving himself deep.

So, that was what he did.

With a sharp thrust, he planted himself to the root, drawing a gasp-turned-moan from her as he filled her and her wet heat surrounding him like a snug velvet glove.

A perfect damn fit, as if they had been made for each other.

With her already soaked, he easily glided in and out of her and was able to take full smooth strokes rim to root.

Christ, she felt so damn good.

This right here was why he had been unable to sleep on that damn couch. Knowing he could be on the second floor doing this and not stuck fucking his own fist. Or having to find a sweet butt tomorrow to relieve his balls.

It had been a while since he fucked anyone who wasn't a sweet butt or a willing hang-around. The difference between a fuck who only did it to get something out of it versus doing it for pleasure and orgasms was night and fucking day. The woman currently wrapped around him had not faked shit yet. Every reaction he'd experienced so far was one hundred percent genuine.

How aroused she was. Her moans. Her groans. Her gasps.

Everything that was quickly driving him to the edge.

Taryn was no sweet butt. No chick hanging out at a Kings' party trying to get her claws into him or one of his brothers.

Fuck no.

She didn't insult him with the over-the-top squeals or the screamed *"yes, yes, yes!"* like from some of the sweet butts. Every time they "acted" during sex, he stopped and threatened to find a way to shut them the fuck up. Including cutting off their air supply.

While the sweet butts were convenient and more than willing to do whatever he or his brothers asked, sometimes—*fuck*, a lot of times—they got on his fucking nerves.

Taryn was a hell of a nice change.

Sometimes change was good. Or needed.

Because truthfully, he was getting bored with his limited sexual selection. And he really didn't want to go out and track down some strange. That usually took too much effort for not enough reward.

Wrapping her legs around his hips and digging her heels into the backs of his thighs, she jammed her pelvis up and into him to not only drive him even deeper, but so he'd hit all the right spots.

With a groan, she continued to lift her hips to meet each

of his thrusts with one of her own. Her short fingernails drilled into his ass in an effort to pull him even deeper.

If he could, he would.

When her nails scraped up his back, he shuddered while he imagined her leaving claw marks behind. A souvenir that he could look at in the mirror later and remember.

Though, he doubted he'd forget this any time soon. Because he certainly couldn't stop reliving their little "get-together" in the downstairs bathroom.

Usually when he was supposed to be concentrating on something else.

Like right fucking now.

Get with the goddamn program, asshole. You're dick deep in pussy and you're not even present.

His hips surged and stuttered, then he began to power up into her more frantically.

All he wanted to do was pump fast and hard and just explode inside her.

For fuck's sake. He needed to slow down, to draw this out as long as possible. But he was finding it fucking impossible.

He needed to fucking wait.

He wanted her to come.

To save himself, he claimed her mouth again. Their tongues twisting and tangling together. But only seconds later, he broke his mouth free and twisted his head to the side, closing his eyes, and panted.

It was never like this when he fucked other women. But then, he also didn't give a fuck what any other woman thought about his performance.

Unlike with Taryn.

He needed to pull out all the stops and get her to come soon.

Jamming his hand between him, he pinched her clit hard.

But when she bucked against him, she had no idea how dangerous that was.

For fuck's sake, he was trying to get *her* to come, not lose his own shit.

Needing another distraction, he once again sank his teeth into her tit, not as gently this time, then dragged his tongue over the mark left behind.

She didn't tell him to stop. *Fuck no.* Her pussy squeezed him even tighter. He slipped that in his sexual toolbox for next time.

But that move didn't distract him, it only made him teeter dangerously.

Planting his knees deeper into the mattress, he began to piston his hips and power up and into her until he couldn't drive himself any deeper into her molten heat. She took everything he gave her and gave it back to him, thrust for fucking thrust.

Spearing herself on his cock.

Grinding against him.

Driving him out of his fucking mind.

Her sharp gasp turned into a low moan. And he had to clench his teeth as her core rippled around him. Since he was already standing dangerously to the edge, she was about to knock his ass over.

Hold out. Just a little damn longer. She's almost there.

Thank fuck he was right.

With a low wail, she tensed and exploded around him. Not only could he feel the wave after wave of her orgasm trying to sabotage him, but he swore she gushed all over him. This was one damn time he wished he hadn't worn a wrap.

When her climax faded away, she sank bonelessly into the mattress.

Soft. Pliant. Satisfied.

Fuck yeah.

It was go time.

Unfortunately, "go" only meant three more pumps before his balls screamed, "Enough!" With one last tilt of his hips, he sank himself to the root, closed his eyes and shot his load with a groaned, "Fuck."

She continued to cling to him as he waited for reality to return.

He met her eyes as soon as he opened his. "You good?"

Goddamn! Was he a victim of body snatchers? When the fuck had he ever asked that?

The corners of her lips curled up slightly. "Do you really need me to answer that?"

Fuck no he didn't, but it didn't hurt to ask. Especially since, for once in his life, he was trying to make an impression.

If not body snatchers, it had to be old age creeping up on him.

With another groan, he rolled off her and flopped onto his back, his lungs still starved for oxygen and his heart still trying to knock a hole in his chest. But at least his empty balls were happy as shit.

Hell, so was he.

Of course she'd want to share his bed with him now. By nailing her as good as he did, he nailed this "interview."

He slipped off the wrap, careful not to spill it all over the damn bed, tied it off, and set it aside.

"I've never done that before," she whispered up to the ceiling.

He tucked an arm under his head and turned it just enough to let his eyes trace her profile.

"Came the last time we fucked." No way did she fake any

of her orgasms. He was a damn pro at telling the difference. Sometimes he cared, most times he didn't give a shit.

But tonight wasn't most times.

"No, not that. That rush of fluid."

Well, damn. One side of his mouth pulled up. "Yeah, woman, I made you squirt."

She turned her own head to give him wide blue eyes. "Really? I thought that was a myth."

"Ain't no myth. Most men don't know how to make a woman do it." Obviously, Vic the Dick never got the job done. But the fuck if he was asking her if that was true and unintentionally inviting that fucker to join them in this bed.

"And you do?"

He tried not to grin like a cocky asshole. It was a struggle. "Just proved it, didn't I?"

She stretched with a groan. "I think I might need to see if it happens again. It could've been a fluke."

She might be fucking with him, but what she said sounded damn good to his ears. Not the *fluke* part but the *again* part.

They could disprove that myth as much as she wanted. Even again tonight.

"Takin' that as you invitin' me to stay? Or are you banishin' me back to the couch?"

When she stared at him, he could see the wheels turning. She wanted him—what just happened proved that—but he could also see her worried about getting too deeply involved in what he represented.

She didn't want to be tied to a motorcycle club, whether for business or personal reasons.

He got it. That life wasn't for everyone.

Only, she might not realize it was too late. Her life was now entwined with his. She was living in his house. Helping with his kid. She'll be running a big chunk of her business from The Castle.

Whether she liked it or not, she was under his protection and that also meant the club's. And the Kings only protected what belonged to them.

But fuck if he was telling her that. That was a discussion for another day. If they had to have it at all.

It took way too fucking long for her to finally answer, even though it should've been a simple yes. "I don't want the kids seeing us sleeping in the same bed."

For fuck's sake.

That didn't go as planned.

Sunny wouldn't give a shit they were in the same bed. She was already having a tantrum about Taryn living with them, where he "slept" wasn't going to change that. At ten going on *ten*-acious, she thought she could be left home alone.

Fuck that.

Stone was not only worried about what trouble Sunny would get into being by herself, but with him being a part of the Kings, other dangers existed. Maybe not direct threats like a rival MC—they hadn't dealt with anything like that in a while, for good reason—but it only took one pissed off Porsche owner to find out it was the Kings who pinched his overpriced sports car, or someone they roughed up while doing a collection, to come looking for revenge.

Danger always lurked around the next corner.

Snagging one of the Kings' kids—or even an ol' lady—would be a quick way to bring the club to its knees. At least temporarily. Because once they could rise again, those motherfuckers would regret it.

Because nobody fucked with the Kings.

Taryn's worry didn't center around threats. She was probably worried that if Sunny found out her father was sleeping with a woman she wasn't happy with, then his girl's attitude would only get worse.

She most likely also thought it would be a bad example for Wren.

Truth was, Stone simply living his life—who he was, what he did and how he did it—was more of a bad example than the two of them sharing a damn bed.

He would need to put in more work on assuring her that if the only roadblock to him joining her every night was the kids, that could be easily overcome.

"Gonna give you that now. But promise it's gonna change. If we gotta have a conversation with the kids, we have a conversation with the kids. Sunny ain't gonna give a shit so that leaves dealin' with Baby Bird."

Taryn sighed and rubbed a hand over her eyes. "It's late, Stone. Now is not the time to make a decision like this."

"Like I said, gonna give you that for now. But tellin' you, I ain't sleepin' too much longer on that fuckin' couch."

"I offered to take the bunk beds with Wren. We can still do that and then you can have your bed back."

It wasn't only about where he was sleeping. "Would rather share my bed with you than Sunny. Don't gotta tell you why."

With that, he rolled off the bed and onto his feet. After snagging his boxers from the floor, he didn't bother to pull them on since he still needed to clean up. He'd do that downstairs and then try to get in a few ZZZ's before the kids got up.

Tomorrow, he'd come up with a way to tell them.

Chapter Twenty

Taryn hurried down the stairs, following her nose. Before heading down, she had peeked into Sunny's room and saw both kids still knocked out.

While she felt bad for kicking Stone out of his own bed last night, she didn't want to make any rash decisions when it came to him. Or their situation, really.

She also didn't want Wren thinking that this was a permanent move. It wasn't. Staying with Stone was only temporary.

They weren't a "thing." They weren't even dating.

How did she explain that to Wren? And if she did, at six, would he even understand?

Convenience did not take precedence over common sense.

Yes, she was a woman with needs and yes, Stone knew how to take care of that particular need, but she was also a mother first and foremost.

Wren was the most important person in her life. Almost everything she did, she did for him, including hustling to make a living. Like with the new YouTube channel and the meal prep, now that her channel had enough subscribers to be monetized.

She hoped to keep building her audience for her online demos and free classes to the point she could use a subscription-based site to start charging. She could even do different mini-courses. Like one for one-dish meals. Another for—

Her thoughts disintegrated when she turned the corner to head into the kitchen.

That was the enticing scent filling her nostrils.

Breakfast. Only, she was supposed to be making it, not Stone.

She blinked at the sight that greeted her.

Stone looked out of place standing at the stove. Next to him, the counter was covered with ingredients. Eggs. An empty package of bacon. An open loaf of bread. Butter. Not to mention all the scattered utensils, mixing bowls, and more.

The kitchen was a mess. Obviously, Stone was not an organized cook.

It was the thought that counted, right? Sure, but she'd be the one cleaning up the disaster once he was done.

The tattoo on his bare, broad back was hard to miss since it was pointed in her direction. Once again, reminding her what type of man she'd paired up with.

Was Stone a better one than Vic? That remained to be seen.

She was damn sure Stone had done plenty of bad things in his life and probably would do a lot more. In the short time she'd known him, she'd already learned he and his brothers didn't respect any laws or the people who enforced those laws. They also did not follow society's norms. They proudly lived by their own rules.

Luckily, none of that had touched her personally.

Yet.

Unlike Vic beating the crap out of her in front of their son. That left a lasting mark on both her and Wren.

That was another reason why she hesitated to share a bed with Stone. What Wren witnessed that day from his own father was a horrible example of a man. She wasn't convinced Stone was any better.

The Kings' vice president could be her next huge mistake, if not her final one, if things went badly.

While his morals might be questionable, on the outside—despite the massive amount of tattoos—he was one fine physical specimen.

Worse, he knew it, too.

This morning the man in question only wore loose jeans clinging precariously to his narrow hips, exposing two delicious dimples above his ass and the black elastic waistband of his boxer briefs.

Since her presence was given away when her stomach growled loudly, she finished entering the kitchen. "You said you couldn't cook, but that smells good."

Not bothering to turn or even look at her, he announced, "Not as good as your pussy."

All the oxygen rushed from her lungs and that same pussy clenched when her brain was suddenly flooded with last night's memory. Especially when it came to his skills with his tongue.

It was *chef's kiss*. Of course, being both a chef and the recipient of that spectacular pleasure, she had it on good authority.

Taryn fought the urge to immediately start cleaning up the disaster on the counter and instead, joined him at the stove. "I beg to differ." She checked out the pans on the burners. "Nothing smells as good as crispy bacon." Was he using the bacon grease to cook the eggs?

Smart.

"You'd be wrong."

"Well, if you thought my pussy smelled better than bacon, you'd be eating that right now."

She slapped a hand over her mouth and her eyes went wide the second she realized what had come out of her mouth. *Holy shit.* When had she ever talked like that? Was his crudeness rubbing off on her? One of her worries when it came to Wren spending a bunch of time with the Kings.

Stone glanced over at her in time to catch the heat burning her cheeks. Of course.

One side of his mouth hiked up. "Figured we could eat breakfast together before the kids get up and have a little discussion on how to handle me movin' back upstairs."

The man was certainly determined. "I told you that I can move—"

He cut her off with a growled, "That ain't it."

Taryn sighed at his perseverance. "Stone, I don't want—"

"That ain't the answer, either."

"Maybe not your preferred answer, no, but, news flash, it's not an actual conversation unless it involves at least two people. Anything less than that is simply a dictatorship. An actual discussion also means we both have opinions, whether they're the same or not."

"Not all opinions are valid." He pointed the spatula used to stir the scrambled eggs toward the table. Her mouth dropped open as she watched small bits of cooked egg get flung onto the previously clean floor. "Go sit. Gonna bring your plate over."

"Oh, I get service with breakfast." She might not be looking forward to this particular talk but she was looking forward to tasting the meal he prepared. She hoped it was good enough to be worth the mess he created at least.

"If that's what you want, sure thing. Get naked, climb on the table, and spread your legs. Gonna be there in a sec to service you." He followed that up with a blinding smile.

Which actually distracted her for a second.

Or two.

Maybe even three.

Damn it. "I meant—"

He shook his head. "Know what you meant. Go sit."

"Can I grab a cup of coffee first? I'll need caffeine in preparation for this newest negotiation."

He tipped his head toward the coffeemaker and she headed in that direction while he placed the full plates on the table and took a seat.

Once she had her first sip of the much-needed fuel, she settled into the chair across from him. "I'm surprised you're not using some of that bacon fat to grease me up for this discussion."

He shoveled a small mountain of scrambled eggs into his mouth. Of course he was still chewing when he stated, "Won't need it."

"Why's that?"

"The only discussin' we're havin' is comin' up with what to tell the kids. Ain't a debate whether I'm moving back into my own bed."

He shot her a look when she opened her mouth. She shut it and took another sip of her coffee. Clearly, she'd *not* had enough caffeine to deal with this yet.

"My own bed with you in it."

Like she needed that clarification.

"Shoulda put that in the initial agreement."

"If you had, I wouldn't have agreed to move in." It was

bad enough she'd moved into the house of a man she didn't know, but to immediately share his bed with him?

That would be even crazier.

His steaming mug of coffee hovered near his mouth as he eyed her over the rim. "But now you got to try out the goods."

"Contrary to what you believe, you're not irresistible." Taryn tasted a forkful of the eggs. They had a surprising kick to them. "What did you put in these?"

"Shot of hot sauce." He shoved a whole slice of bacon into his mouth at once.

"Any milk?" She nibbled on a slice herself. The bacon was perfectly crisp. Had he been lying about not being able to cook?

"A touch. Like how I flicked the tip of my tongue against your clit last night."

Her mouthful of bacon almost went down the wrong pipe. She cleared her throat and studied the shirtless biker sitting across the table.

While eggs, bacon, and toast was a simple breakfast to make, a bad cook could even screw that up in so many ways. By under- or over-cooking the ingredients, or over- or under-seasoning it, burning the bacon, not cooking it enough...the list was endless.

But even the bread had been toasted to a perfect brown.

"You lied."

He cocked a dark eyebrow at her. "About?"

"Not being able to cook." She swept her fork over her plate. "You made cooking a hot breakfast seem easy."

He shrugged. "Can handle that, but not much else."

Baring his straight, white teeth, he sank them into the crunchy, buttered toast. Just like he sank them into her breasts last night. She fought her shudder at the memory, but lost.

Good thing Stone didn't notice her reaction. "Made this for dinner shitloads of times for Sunny. Didn't want her eatin' cereal for breakfast *and* dinner."

"I'm sure she wouldn't care." Kids usually loved cereal.

"Maybe not. Didn't need Sheena up my ass about it."

"Her mother cares about her diet?" From the little Taryn had heard about her from both Stone and his biker brothers, that would be surprising.

Stone snorted and stabbed at his eggs with more force than necessary. "Fuck no. But the bitch is always lookin' for ammo to use against me. Anyway, let's get this over with before the nut nuggets roll downstairs."

Taryn groaned. "Calling Wren a nut nugget is worse than Baby Bird."

Of course that went ignored. "When they sit down for breakfast, gonna tell them the news."

"Stone..."

He tipped his head and lifted a hand with his palm out. "Know your concern. Think I'm a bad influence for your kid."

That was a given. It was one of the quandaries she'd had to work through before agreeing to move in. "You can't deny that none of you Kings are upstanding citizens. That's a fact, not a criticism. However, that ship has already set sail and disappeared over the horizon. This is more about him thinking we're together and going to stay that way." Like a normal couple.

Nothing about this agreement was normal.

Nothing in her *life* was normal right now.

She had to face the fact she might be failing as a mother.

Would a good mother move her six-year-old in with an outlaw biker?

Would a good mother allow that six-year-old to hang out at that biker's clubhouse?

None with a lick of common sense.

Even so, her decision had mostly boiled down to self-preservation.

Between her lingering trauma from what Vic had done, plus her worry about what her ex could do—take a mother away from her son in a very violent way—held more weight than whatever Wren witnessed while they lived with Stone.

That could fade and be forgotten. The death of a parent could not.

She sure hoped she was right this time because her batting average was horrible.

Stone hadn't been offended when she said he was a bad influence. But then, she wasn't offended when anyone pointed out her mistakes. The truth might be hard to swallow but that was what it was. The truth.

She had to remember that to learn from mistakes, one had to make them first.

"You do know we've only known each other for a little over a week, right?" she reminded him.

"Fucked women after only knowin' them for two minutes. Got a point?" He popped the last of his toast into his mouth and chewed.

She groaned under her breath. He seemed the type of guy to relentlessly pursue what he wanted until he got it.

A frustrating combination of being both stubborn and persistent.

She already knew she was going to lose this battle and the couch would be empty tonight. "So tell me, you had to put some thought into this, right? How do we explain the sleeping situation to our children?"

"Easy. Couch is killin' my back. That's a fuckin' fact.

Gonna tell them while you're here, the adults are gonna share one room, the kids the other. That's it. We don't gotta tell 'em that I'm divin' face first into your pussy every night. Or that you're ridin' my dick. Ain't their business. What we do behind a locked door is ours."

A breath had hissed from her at the thought of him eating her out every night. That plan didn't exactly sound horrible. "But beyond the sex."

"Outside of the bedroom, we act like roommates. Inside, then..." He grinned and shrugged.

He made it sound so damn simple when it really wasn't.

"This won't be an issue once my house is sold. Once it is, I plan on moving somewhere Vic won't find us." Hopefully. Though, that might mean moving to Antarctica. "In the meantime, if I allow this, I'll have to continually remind Wren that our stay here is only for a short time."

With a shake of his head, his snort sounded suspiciously like "allow." He shoved his chair back, grabbed their mugs, and headed over to top both off with more coffee.

Taryn hadn't even realized she had paused her fork halfway to her mouth to watch that whole production.

Like a damn porno. *Bow chicka wow wow.*

When he turned to come back to the table, she quickly stuck the fork in her mouth to hide the fact it had been gaped open. At least she hadn't been drooling.

Why the hell did he have to be so damn hot and not some ugly troll? It would make resisting him easier.

After setting the full mugs on the table, Stone settled back into his chair with a grunt. "What's goin' on with your house?"

"The agent's having the first open house this weekend."

"You gotta be there?"

She could already see his thoughts churning about

sending protection along with her if she had to be in attendance. "No. The only thing I need to do is let her do her thing. Once it's sold, I'll have to show up to sign the papers at closing."

She couldn't find a new place without being free of that debt. Being self-employed didn't help, either. Without a steady paycheck, it made getting a mortgage on her own even more difficult.

In reality, the longer she stayed with Stone, the more she could save. However, that agreement with him was also a debt, just of a different nature.

"Think it's gonna sell fast?"

Taryn sighed. "I sure hope so. The mortgage and monthly expenses are sucking the funds from my account faster than I can earn them."

"Shit's hangin' around your neck."

Like a damn albatross. "It is. And it's dragging me down. I need to get out from under it as soon as possible."

"It insured?"

"Of course. It's required when you have a mortgage."

A smile slowly crossed his sinfully handsome face.

It was both breath-taking and worrisome. "I don't like that smile."

He shrugged and chugged more coffee. "Insurance money would pay off your mortgage and any other debt hangin' over your head, right?"

He sure liked to simplify complex issues. But that wasn't always possible.

"What I would get would go toward paying off the damn mortgage, Stone. That debt doesn't simply disappear when the house does."

He frowned. "You owe more than the house is worth?"

"No, but since Vic had taken out a second mortgage, any

of the equity we had built up disappeared." And she also had no idea what happened to that money. Since she got the house in the divorce, she somehow got stuck with that extra debt.

The divorce attorney she picked was also on her long lists of mistakes. While she'd learned from that one, she hoped she never had to go through a divorce again.

"Fuck," he groaned.

"I second that. But please don't get it in your head to burn down my house or anything. I don't need to be charged with insurance fraud."

"For arson?"

Her eyebrows rose. "For a *planned* arson."

"You ain't no fun," he muttered, leaning back in his chair and extending his long legs under the table until they brushed against hers.

She rolled her eyes. "You're right. I don't find going to jail fun. How about you?"

Before he could answer, small feet were heard heading down the stairway.

It was time to end this conversation and begin making the kids breakfast. Then hope Stone's "conversation" with them went off without a hitch.

When it came to Sunny, Taryn might as well don some armor instead of an apron.

Chapter Twenty-One

Taryn really needed to invest in some good video editing software. The four videos she'd shot while prepping food in The Castle's kitchen were far from perfect.

The bloopers ended up being out of control. Add in the copious amount of cursing from the bikers in the background and hardly any of the raw footage had turned out usable. At least she hadn't been doing another "live" and the videos would be fine once cleaned up and certain words bleeped out.

She had a long list of recipes she wanted to make and record. However, right now she was concentrating on two weeks' worth of dinners for one of her long-time clients. She'd freeze the packaged home-cooked meals overnight and have them delivered to his residence tomorrow.

As she portioned the food into containers, a deep, "What's all that?" right behind her made her startle.

Stone somehow snuck up on her. She needed to be more aware of her surroundings. While she trusted Stone for the most part, she wasn't sure about the rest of his brothers yet.

The only reason she was getting to know them at all was because they were stalking her in the cafeteria hoping she'd offer them anything extra.

Of course, she didn't mind sharing anything leftover since the club was covering the cost of the ingredients. What benefited her also benefited them.

She tried to put aside enough every day for their own dinner, if it wasn't all hoovered down by the Kings brotherhood in under thirty seconds flat.

She glanced over her shoulder at the sexy biker not scrounging for food. "It's part of the meal prep side business. The other day, I sent out an email to all my current clients and told them I'd be branching out. I got a lot more interest than I expected." Hopefully, that part of the business would grow organically strictly due to word of mouth, which was the best kind of advertising since it was free. "I need to deliver these tomorrow."

His head jerked back and his jaw popped. "Talked about that shit."

Oh, brother. Here we go! Vic hadn't even been released yet and Stone already had her on lockdown. "Well, then I have fourteen frozen meals to be delivered to a client tomorrow. Who do you want to do that?"

She also needed to go to the restaurant supply store down in Harrisburg to buy to-go containers in bulk. It wouldn't look professional to deliver them in cheap, upcycled cold cut containers.

She really needed customized labels for the containers, too. So much to do!

"Told you, gonna get one of the prospects."

"Do you have any who sport a semi clean-cut look or do they all look like obvious bikers?" Men most of her clients wouldn't answer the door for if they stood on their front stoop.

"You see anyone lookin' like they can get away with wearin' fuckin' polo shirts?"

"No, but..." *Damn*, a simple uniform would be great. He kept coming up with good ideas, whether he meant to or not.

Off-brand polo shirts weren't super expensive and they could wear them with jeans, especially since the prospect would only be delivering the meals, not serving them.

"Thanks for that idea. I'll have some polo shirts made up with my logo. I'll just need to know which prospect will be assigned to me so I can find out his size."

Stone only stared at her.

She shrugged. "If you don't want me delivering the meals, then whoever is will be representing my business. *Talked about that shit*," she echoed in a gruff voice.

At his deep chuckle, an electrical current shot all the way from the center of her chest to the tips of her toes. Of course it also lit up one particular area on her.

She couldn't understand why a biker with a man-bun turned her on so much. Maybe she should simply admit she wasn't the best judge of character.

A good excuse for why she married Vic.

When was she going to learn? Her body answered for her: apparently, not today.

"Will see if any of em's willin' to do it."

"Can you do that like...soon?"

"Yeah."

"And if no one volunteers?"

"Gonna handle it."

He was *gonna handle it*. Proof that prospects didn't have a choice when a patched member ordered them to do something.

Well, that wasn't exactly true. Stone explained that they had to comply if they wanted to keep their prospect cut. If they didn't, then they lost the opportunity to patch in and they were told to hit the road. But they were limited to those two choices.

It was the same with sweet butts.

It had quickly become clear to Taryn that the Kings lived in their own world. They lived by their MC rules. To them, the club's rules were more important than any federal or state laws. Either a patched or prospective member abided by them or...else.

She really didn't want to know what that "or else" meant. She could safely assume it wasn't a handshake and a parting gift. Especially after what she had witnessed with Gooch.

In fact, she hadn't seen that prospect since that day. In fact, she should—

"Don't fuckin' ask questions you don't wanna know the answers to."

She assumed what happened to him was "club business" and not hers.

Yikes. In less than two weeks she had learned way more about motorcycle clubs than she ever wanted to know and she had only scratched the surface.

"Did you figure out what percentage the club will be taking for this exclusive white-glove service?"

His eyebrows shot almost to his hairline. "Want them to wear gloves?"

"Well, of course. These are well-off clients and..." Her laughter burst from her when she couldn't hold it back any longer. "I'm only messing with you."

Stone didn't even crack a smile. In fact, he looked distracted.

The heat reflected in his eyes made her pussy clench.

He stepped closer and caged her in by placing his hands on the counter on both sides of her. He leaned in until his mouth was a hairsbreadth from her ear and whispered, "Like what I did to you last night?"

She pulled in a shuddered breath. The man had a knack of turning her from a solid to a liquid in only seconds.

She certainly had enjoyed his actions last night. She had no complaints when it came to sex with Stone, despite him being rough around the edges. Really, more than only the edges. The man was rough all the way to his core and he made no apologies about that.

Okay, she had one complaint. He wanted sex constantly. If it wasn't for the kids, she had a feeling she wouldn't be able to walk. Or she'd be doing a bow-legged shuffle like a seventy-five-year-old cowboy. The man was insatiable.

But then, if it wasn't for the kids, she wouldn't be in her current living situation. She wouldn't have needed to move in with him and would not have had sex with him in the first place.

Again, before Stone, she'd known squat about bikers. By their appearance alone she would've assumed their skills between the sheets would be lacking. Even selfish.

It could be that Stone was an anomaly since he never left her wanting more. He always made sure she had at least two orgasms and was well-satisfied afterward.

Such a contrast to her past lovers. A couple had been good, a couple okay, and then she had a couple of selfish ones.

She originally thought Vic was decent. Until Stone. The biker blew her ex out of the water.

That also meant she would now use him as her gauge for future sexual partners. That could be good or it could be bad if no one else ever lived up to him.

But she wasn't telling him any of that.

Right now, with his proximity, her nipples were puckered and aching and her breath had become shallow.

She was surprised to find that she couldn't wait until tonight and their "private time behind the locked door."

His warm breath tickled her ear. "Kids are out there, so gonna keep my hands to myself. But later, all bets will be off and I'm gonna be very hands-on."

Right. Even though they'd been sharing a bed for a week now, they were simply "roommates" to the kids and nothing more. That meant no intimacy or physical contact when their children were around.

It was a good compromise and made her feel better about her decision to share his bed.

It turned out, the conversation with the kids a week ago hadn't been much of anything. Neither cared that they were sleeping in the same bed. They thought Stone and Taryn were simply laying their heads down next to each other every night.

Of course, the biggest issue that came up was from Sunny complaining about sharing her room with a six-year-old boy. She was not happy about having a "baby" sleeping in her room.

Stone flat out told her to "suck it up."

No surprise, that only made his daughter more cranky about the situation. Which, in turn, made him more cranky.

Luckily, Wren considered sharing Sunny's room more of a fun adventure since he'd always wanted a sibling.

Taryn tried to stay out of that whole conversation that morning since she felt bad that Sunny wasn't happy about the situation. But with only two bedrooms in the house, their options were limited.

Good thing the living situation wouldn't last forever.

"Whatcha doin' Sunday?"

"I thought about taking the day off. I could use a break." The last two weeks had been a whirlwind with moving out of her house, putting it up for sale, moving in with Stone, and having to pivot with her business.

"Agreed. You been kickin' ass. Got the perfect break for you."

"What's that?" She expected him to say that they would spend the day in bed. Even though, in reality, that would be impossible with the kids around.

"Goin' for a run. Want you to come with."

Her brow dropped low. "You run? Do you even own a pair of sneakers?"

He shot her a look which clearly said, *what-the-fuck?* "Not that kinda run. On my sled."

"Why?"

"Why the fuck not? It's somethin' the club does on a regular basis when the weather's good."

"Will it be the whole club?"

"For the most part. No prospects or sweet butts. But any patched members available."

Taryn wondered what made any of them unavailable. A lot of them lived at The Castle and seemed to not have to leave for actual jobs. In fact, it didn't seem like Stone or his brothers followed any kind of schedule at all.

They had managed to turn a hobby into a complete lifestyle.

The few times she'd been on the back of his bike, it had been for the quick trip between The Castle and his house. Even in that short amount of time, she could see the appeal of "having the wind in my face and my knees in the breeze" as Stone explained on more than one occasion.

So, yes, she'd love to go for a longer ride with him. Only

one thing—more like two small things—stopped her from immediately agreeing. "What about the kids?"

"Can get someone to stay with them for the time we'd be gone."

She groaned. "A sweet butt?" Their whole living arrangement was questionable enough, she really didn't want a woman used by the club for sex to be babysitting. She had to draw a line somewhere. Even if that line was a bit wonky.

She shook her head. "I can ask my mother to come stay at the house." At least her mother wouldn't be wearing a skirt short enough to show off her butt cheeks.

"Guessin' that's a yes."

"As long as she's free."

"If she ain't and you don't want a sweet butt hangin' at the house, can get one of the prospects."

As if that was any better. But life had been so crazy lately, she could really use the break. Going for a motorcycle ride might clear her head. It also might stave off the impending dread of Vic's upcoming release, at least for a little while. "How long are these runs?"

"A few hours, dependin' on the route our road captain takes. We try to stick to back roads."

"To avoid law enforcement?"

"To avoid dickheads who can't drive."

"That's a good reason, too," she murmured as she glanced out past the former serving line to see what her son was up to. He hadn't bugged her in at least a half hour.

What she found wasn't surprising. Wren loved animals, so whenever he saw one, he was drawn to it like a moth to a flame.

He currently sat on the cafeteria floor—*dirty* floor, she noted—using Thor, Ogre's scary looking dog, as a backrest. Her son was mindlessly petting the canine and rubbing his ears while reading out loud from a book Taryn made him bring along to keep him occupied.

The huge dog's eyes were nothing more than slits because he was eating up the attention. At least the hundred and fifty pound dog wasn't eating Wren.

"I'm glad Thor's tolerant to Wren's attention and his long-winded story time. He reminds me of some of you bikers. Intimidating on the outside and..." She was going to say mushy on the inside, but that wouldn't be correct. "Never mind," she muttered.

Stone grunted. "Dog's well trained. Can do some damage if ordered. Despite that, Thor's a good babysitter."

Taryn said, "The dog can't watch our children, Stone," before he got that idea in his head. "Plus, I'm pretty sure that's...illegal. Oh wait..." She rolled her eyes. The Kings certainly didn't give a crap about what was legal and what wasn't.

"Ain't sayin' the dog's gonna babysit on Sunday since Thor rides shotgun with Ogre."

"Really?"

"Yeah, got a sidecar for him. That beast ain't ever far from him. But ain't sayin' the dog won't keep an eye on the kids when he's near them. He's known Sunny since she was a tiny nut nugget."

She swallowed down the frustration from him constantly using that term. To stay sane, she needed to learn to laugh at it instead. "Anyway, if my mom has plans, I'll just stay behind with the kids."

"Ain't gonna happen."

"It's not up to you."

"Sure as fuck is."

Since he still had her caged in with his arms, when she turned to face him, they were only inches apart. With a tilt of her head, she locked eyes with him. "I thought it was an invitation, not a demand."

"It is."

"Which one?"

"Both."

She sighed. "Are all bikers as bossy as you?"

"Haven't met them all, but if I hadta guess, yeah."

"Must be in the genes."

"Got somethin' in my jeans." He grabbed his crotch and shook it.

She rolled her eyes. "Genes with a G."

He snorted. "Huh. Musta spelled it wrong my whole fuckin' life."

"I'll ask my mother about Sunday and let you know. By the way, you never did answer me about the percentage the club wants, and I also need to know who's going to do the delivery tomorrow. I'll need to give him some pointers before he goes."

His eyes dropped to her chest, even though it was covered by an apron.

He straightened, took a step back to put some space between them, and curled his fingers into his palms. "Tempted to touch you right now. Maybe the kids can take Thor for a walk."

"They are not taking that beast for a walk. And we agreed to keep it behind closed, *locked* doors."

"Regrettin' that agreement," he muttered.

"You still haven't answered my question."

"What question?"

She sighed. "Really?"

His cocky grin should be a total turn-off, not the exact opposite.

Goddamn it! Why did he have this effect on her?

"We debated chargin' a percentage or a flat fee per delivery. The officers agreed to take a percentage of your sales when it comes to the delivered shit. This way the club can continue to pay for the ingredients for you."

Sometimes talking to him was like pulling teeth. "And what's the percentage?"

She braced herself, worried that it would be some outrageous amount. Having them buy the ingredients was a huge help but she still needed to make a profit. She wasn't going to do all the work for free.

His answering grimace made her stomach flip. "What?"

"Started to discuss it and the meetin' got off track."

She closed her eyes and shook her head.

"How 'bout this? Won't charge you for the stuff delivered tomorrow. Will corner Ransom soon and get a number for you."

"Can you convince him to keep that number low?" Very low, if it was up to her.

His answering smile blinded her. "Might be easier to convince him if you suck my dick tonight."

"Why does everything have to be a negotiation?"

Stone shrugged. "Okay, then I'm just gonna tell you... suck my cock tonight."

"Stone..."

"We ain't gonna fuck you." He leaned in closer again with a look in his dark eyes that made her lose her breath. "The Kings won't, but I sure as fuck will."

Chapter Twenty-Two

Stone twisted the throttle to make sure he didn't drop too far back and out of formation.

Despite being vice president, Stone usually took tail with Ogre. Once voted in, the sergeant at arms began to ride in the back of the lineup where it was easier to keep an eye on everyone. He hated to keep looking behind him to make sure everyone was okay.

Instead, Wheels, their road captain, led the pack taking the VP's normal spot and Ransom, the president, rode to his left.

The formation was long this afternoon. Since the weather was perfect—a rare occurrence in Pennsylvania—almost everyone had joined the run.

Because Taryn was able to convince her mother to watch the kids—*thank fuck*—her pussy was currently smashed against his ass, her tits into his back, her arms wrapped tightly around his waist, and her hands planted firmly on his gut under his cut.

For some damn reason, having her on the back of his sled

just felt right. And that spot wasn't normally filled unless he brought along Sunny.

Not even twenty minutes into the run, Stone curled a possessive hand around her knee. Because, again, it felt natural. Of fucking course, that got some looks of surprise from his nosy-assed brothers.

Thank fuck he didn't give a shit about what they thought.

The same way he didn't give a fuck about the smart-ass grins he got when he originally pulled up to the formation with Taryn as his backpack.

He had no damn reason to keep the fact that she was sharing his bed from his brothers. When it came down to it, he didn't give a shit about their opinion on it.

Never did, never would.

But including her on the run also cemented the fact that, during the time Taryn was under the Kings' protection, his brothers needed to remain hands off. They were welcome to eat her food but fuck if they were getting their mouths anywhere near her pussy. That was reserved for Stone.

Anybody else would get their tongue cut out.

Maybe even a few fingers broken, if not plugged in the forehead with a forty-five caliber round from his Smith & Wesson.

At the two breaks they made along the route, Taryn would stretch her legs and try to strike up a conversation with some of the ol' ladies along for the ride.

While it pissed Stone the fuck off that most of the women side-eyed her, their reaction was to be expected. It usually took a while for the Kings' sisterhood to warm up to someone new since most women who came around the club didn't stick around long.

Most for not more than a night.

Some women glorified the MC life in their head and

thought they could handle a "bad boy," but in reality, found it was far from what they expected. The lifestyle wasn't for everyone. Fact was, it could be brutal.

No fucking lie, getting involved with a biker could be rough on a good day. The ol' ladies had to grow thick-as-fuck skin and figure out ways to wrangle their stubborn men without them being aware of it.

Out of necessity, they became damn good at it.

Watching the members of the sisterhood skillfully manipulate Stone's brothers could be more entertaining than watching a bad-ass action flick. He always had a chuckle when his biker brother finally figured it out. Usually after it was too late.

A grin grew under the bandana covering the lower half of his face. The one he used so he wouldn't have to pick bugs from between his teeth later.

Taryn chose not to wear a helmet either and, instead, had borrowed a skull cap from him to keep her long hair from becoming a tangled fucking knot. She had no need to cover her face, besides wearing sunglasses, since Stone made the perfect bug and debris shield.

His fingers automatically flexed around her knee when the memory of the other morning popped into his head. Stone had watched Taryn attempting to train Shit Stain, the one ordered to do her deliveries since no one else stepped up. The prospect grumbled when he found out he was the "chosen" one and wore a grumpy puss as Taryn went about explaining how to do the deliveries and deal with her clients. Stone risked busting a nut with how hard he laughed at the whole damn thing.

Dealing with Shit Stain was proof that Taryn had the patience of a fucking saint. And explained why she could deal with Sunny and her larger-than-life attitude.

Once she finished teaching Shit Stain what to say and how to act during the deliveries—and made him practice a few times—Stone warned him that if she lost any clients due to something he said or did, consequences would follow.

The prospect took that warning seriously and stopped his grumbling. At least in front of Stone. He also told Taryn loudly in front of Shit Stain that if the prospect caused her any problems to let him know and he'd handle it.

That made Taryn chew on her bottom lip since she was getting a clue as to how Stone "handled" things. It sure as fuck wasn't with an employee review.

While watching the circus, Ransom had stepped up next to Stone and bumped their shoulders together. "What the fuck, brother? She's tryin' to teach that stupid motherfucker how to be polite?"

"Yeah. Had doubts that the fuckin' idiot was even teachable."

The Kings' president smirked. "He's provin' you wrong."

"Ain't so sure about that. At least it's been entertainin'. Let's see how far she fuckin' gets before askin' for someone with a half a brain to replace him."

"Then I guess you won't be doin' them, either," he said on a chuckle. "Hell, after dealin' with his dumb ass, she might end up sneakin' out to do her own damn deliveries."

"Better fuckin' not," he growled.

Ransom barked out a laugh and slapped him on the back. "Have her make up a buncha prepackaged meals for us. Would be nice to be able to eat some decent food when she ain't here."

"She already planned on doin' that since the club's coverin' the groceries, remember? But we never decided what our cut's gonna be for usin' Shit for Brains."

Ransom pursed his lips and scraped a hand down his

bearded cheek. "For fuck's sake. We began to discuss it at the meetin' but got off track."

"Like fuckin' normal. So, whataya think? She wants to know since she's gonna have to figure that into what she charges these rich cucks."

"Thinkin' at least ten."

That was the number Stone already had in his head. He figured it was more than fair. "Ten's a good number. Can't imagine she'll bitch at that." Though, most women found any reason to bitch. As did a certain ten-year-old girl child.

Ransom cocked an eyebrow. "And if she does?"

"Gonna tell her ten and that's that."

The prez hooted softly. "That's that? Good fuckin' luck with that, brother. You know that ain't always how it works with goddamn women. Can tell you ain't never dealt with pussy longer than it takes to shoot your load. If you think your baby girl's attitude sucks ass when she ain't happy, wait 'til you deal with that same shit from a full-grown woman."

"Forgettin' that it's 'cause of that same baby girl I gotta deal with that kinda shit from the cunt she came outta. Only fucked Sheena once and now gotta deal with nasty attitude for at least another eight goddamn years. Worst prison fuckin' sentence I ever served." Thinking about Sunny's mother always made his damn blood pressure rise. "Anyway, already told Taryn the club's takin' a cut."

"Just 'cause you told her don't mean she listened."

"She heard me," Stone muttered. "Gonna tell her ten percent."

"And *that's that.*" With a shake of his head, Ransom disappeared. Stone could hear him chuckling all the way down the hallway.

Stone turned his attention back toward Taryn and Shit Stain. Not only did the prospect still look miserable as fuck, but now so did Taryn. Despite that, she was still managing to cling to whatever patience she had left.

The fact she made the prospect wear the button-down cook's shirt she bought the night before might have something to do with him looking so fucking miserable. They had taken the kids along with them down to Harrisburg to pick up needed supplies at Restaurant Depot, then headed to the Cracker Barrel for dinner.

Stone had to admit the restaurant chain's food was crap. He used to think it was decent until he compared it to Taryn's.

The woman was certainly spoiling them with some damn good cooking. It was really going to suck once she moved out and he was back to take-out and microwaving frozen meals.

Even Sunny scarfed down every homemade meal, no matter how bent she still was about Taryn and Wren living with them. She might wrinkle her nose and pinch her face like she didn't like it, but the proof she did was her clean plate.

Stone had hoped Sunny would accept Taryn and Wren faster than she was, but then, his daughter was stubborn like her old man. He could say she got it honestly.

Three hours into the run, Wheels gave the signal that they were heading back to the clubhouse. That warned his brothers that others could and would break out of formation if they had other shit to do.

The only thing Stone had to do was Taryn. His plan was to finish the run at The Castle and do her good in his room there since her mother was watching the kids. He couldn't let that golden opportunity go to waste. He wasn't sure if Taryn would agree, but his dick sure fucking did.

Since they avoided main roads whenever possible, they

took the road that went through Trevorton, a tiny town south of Dead Man's Hollow.

When their chapter was first established, they claimed a ten-mile radius around the former school as the Kings' territory. Trevorton was located in that area, along with the diner just east of it, which was a regular stop for them, especially since it was a place where they didn't get harassed.

So no one, not fucking one of them, expected to see four Harleys not belonging to any of the Kings lined up right out in front of the diner.

That had Ransom quickly slowing down the formation as they rode by. In unison, every damn head turned to check out the possible trespassers.

Stone had no idea who the sleds belonged to, whether they were only hobby riders or if they belonged to another MC. If it was the latter, that would be a major fucking problem.

Not only for the Kings but for those unknown MC members.

But first, they needed to verify who the fuck those Harleys belonged to. Could be a bunch of nobodies. Could be another club scouting their territory. Since the Kings have ruled their area since the late 70s, not one damn club in most of Pennsylvania didn't know that fact.

Whether they had to learn it the hard way or not.

If a lesson needed to be taught today, he and his brothers would certainly take them to school.

It was Ransom, not Wheels, giving the signal to pull off ahead. Less than three miles later, they found an area large enough for all of them to get off the road.

Stone immediately heeled his kickstand down and swung a leg over his sled. Once his boots were planted solidly on the ground, he yanked his bandana down to tell Taryn, "Stay here. Don't get off my sled."

"What's going on? Is there a problem?"

He scratched the back of his neck. "Yeah, might be a problem. Gonna discuss how to handle it."

Her eyes might be hidden behind her dark sunglasses, but Stone couldn't miss her deeply furrowed brow. "Should I be worried?"

"Nope." With that, he took long strides to the front of the pack where most of his brothers were gathering around Ransom and Ogre. Since he was VP, he elbowed his way to the center just in time to hear their sergeant at arms say, "No damn clubs reached out to me. Did any reach out to you about bein' in the area today?"

With his expression holding a hell of a lot of unhappy, Ransom shook his head. "Fuck no. Woulda said somethin' if they had."

"Wanna head back to The Castle and drop the ol' ladies off before we deal with this bullshit?"

Again, Ransom shook his head. "No goddamn time for that. If another club's encroachin', the ol' ladies all know what needs to be done."

Ogre glanced at Stone. "'Cept yours."

"Maybe 'cause she ain't my ol' lady." Taryn was the only female on the run who wasn't.

The sergeant at arms huffed, "Not yet, anyway."

"Ain't lookin' for that. You know it's only temporary. She ain't lookin' for permanent and I ain't, either."

A muscle in Ransom's cheek popped. "Now ain't a time for this shit."

"What do we wanna do?" Chopper, appearing a bit wired, asked what everyone wanted to know.

In truth, they all got a bit wired when another MC was in the area. They looked at any club that wasn't a Kings chapter as a possible rival unless the other club was an already established ally. Those were few and far between since they were careful who they aligned with.

Ransom answered Chopper, "If they ain't from a club, don't fuckin' matter. But if they're wearin' colors, it's an issue we gotta deal with."

Ogre bobbed his massive bald head. "Thinkin' we should wait here while sendin' a coupla us back. No point in the whole formation turnin' around. Don't wanna make a big deal outta it 'til we know who the fuck it is. Could also be a trap. What better way to get most of us in one spot than while on a fuckin' run? We all go back to investigate, next thing we fuckin' know is we're bein' surrounded by another goddamn club. Need to avoid that clusterfuck. We need the upper hand."

"Agreed. Best to step carefully so we don't step in deep shit. We'll send two."

"I'll go," Devil Dog volunteered, stepping forward.

Grim spoke up next from behind Stone. "Gonna go with him."

With a nod, Ransom ordered, "See who it is but stay outta sight. If it's just some weekend warriors, let 'em go. No harm, no foul. If they ain't and they go east, stick with 'em and keep me updated on your location. They ride west, let us know they're comin' our way so we can give them a proper Kings welcome. Keep your distance and try not to get spotted right away. Havin' to chase 'em will suck."

While Stone agreed with that plan, it was difficult to go undetected when you rode Harleys with straight-pipe exhausts. That was another good reason to only send a couple of brothers back to the diner. A group of two dozen bikers would catch attention quicker than only two.

After Devil and Grim jumped on their sleds and sped off, Stone glanced back to see Taryn now standing next to his own sled. At least she hadn't tried to approach him while they were having their little roadside meeting.

He should go back to her because, even from where he stood, her worry was obvious. But until he knew what they were doing next, she would only bombard him with questions he couldn't answer.

The longer they stood around with their fucking thumbs up their asses, the more restless he and his brothers got. He hoped to fuck the four Harleys belonged to some random riders so Taryn wouldn't witness how they'd be dealt with if they weren't.

He could take her back to The Castle and not wait around but that would be a dick move. It would make life easier for him but not for his brothers. And being VP, he needed to help Ransom lead, even if it was for a beat-down.

A few minutes later, the prez glanced at his phone when it dinged. He read the text out loud. "Twisted Souls."

"Those goddamn motherfuckers?" Ogre bellowed. "They got some balls on 'em." His chest expanded, probably trying to hold in all his fury.

For fuck's sake. That goddamn club. Members of the Twisted Souls MC were in their fucking area. Worse, without a fucking heads up. They had no reason to be in the Kings' territory unless they were scouting to expand their own.

That meant his brotherhood had no choice but to deliver a message. If they didn't, other clubs might see them as weak and try the same shit.

Fuck that, this needed to be dealt with here and now.

Since they gave the Kings no warning, the Kings wouldn't give them one in return.

It was one thing when a club was only riding through on a highway. Highways and interstates were considered neutral territory for the most part. But the minute patched members jumped off and onto a road running through another club's territory, it became an issue.

Especially since these fuckers weren't that far from the Kings' clubhouse.

That was fucked up. And soon, they'd be the same way.

"Where they headed?" Ogre asked.

Ransom glanced up from reading the latest text. "This way." Circling his hand above his head, he yelled, "Mount up. They're gonna be here in a few." He stabbed at his phone, then put it to his ear. "Squid. Gather up all the prospects you can find. Put them in the van and head toward Trevorton Road. And hurry the fuck up. Will update you if we change course. No draggin' your goddamn feet, either. Not if you want your rockers."

Once Ransom hung up, no other words needed to be said. The rest of their brothers all knew what needed to be done. It was time to not only school those motherfuckers, but confiscate their sleds. A tax they charged any club for entering their territory without permission.

Stone ate up the distance between him and Taryn.

"Now what?" she asked when he reached her.

"Gotta deliver a message."

"To whoever owns those four bikes? What kind of message?"

"Yeah. A fuckin' clear one."

"That says?"

"This is our territory. We fuckin' rule it. No one steps on our patch without our approval. No one."

"Maybe they didn't know it was your territory."

"Guess they're gonna fuckin' learn." It was a lesson about to be learned the hard way. "Hurry and get back on. Hold on fuckin' tight 'cause shit's about to go sideways."

Chapter Twenty-Three

Normally, from Trevorton they'd take Route 890 north to return to the clubhouse. The four bikers wearing Twisted Souls cuts— a dumb as fuck decision—continued west on Route 225, probably trying to find the nearest highway.

The way they shot past the Kings like their asses were on fire made it clear they realized they were caught in the wrong area. The only question was, were they here on purpose or by accident?

While it didn't matter either way when it came to how the Kings would handle the potential threat, it would be smart to find out if they had been scouting or not. If so, it would quickly land the Twisted Souls on the Kings' enemies list.

And that was not a good list to be on. That meant if they were spotted out in the wild—at any time or at any place— they most likely would never be heading back to their own territory again.

Since Devil Dog and Grim were trailing a distance

behind the four intruders, they quickly fell back into formation when the rest of the Kings pulled out.

"Hang on tight!" Stone warned Taryn again. "Shit might get wild."

Her fingers dug painfully into his gut. Unlike earlier when she was relaxed and enjoying the ride, she was now so damn stiff, he swore she turned into a concrete statue.

What was about to happen wasn't anything he wanted her to witness, especially since she was still considered an "outsider," but fuck if he was peeling off from the pack and leaving his brothers to deal with the problem without him.

He was the goddamn VP. He needed to act like it.

At the back of his mind, he thought this could be a good test for Taryn. And satisfy his curiosity on whether she could deal with the outlaw biker life and not be a damn snitch by tipping off the pigs. So far, she had rolled with the punches, but what was about to happen would be nothing like she'd experienced so far.

Ransom was right. None of what they were about to do would shock any of the ol' ladies. They knew the life, and what to expect, before they accepted their "property of" cuts.

To Taryn, this was all new and not a life she chose. She wasn't out to become an ol' lady and didn't plan on sticking around. The only reason she got involved with him at all was for protection from her abusive ex.

Only, what she was about to see with her very own fucking eyes might cause her to leave before the ex was even freed. She was about to find out that dealing with a single asshole like Vic the Dick was nothing compared to twenty-four. Thirty-two if he counted the prospects.

Since no main highway was easily accessible from where they were, it gave the Kings enough time to catch up to the small group before they could escape, despite the fact those motherfuckers were twisting their throttles hard and pushing their sleds to their limits. Stone wouldn't be surprised if one of them skidded out, kissed the pavement, and caught a bad case of road rash.

Hell, road rash would feel like a goddamn tickle compared to what his brothers were about to do to them: make them wish they never stepped foot in Kings' territory.

Ogre was no longer at the back of the pack with Stone. Instead, he had swapped spots with Wheels since he had a weapon none of the rest of them had. A hundred-and-fifty pound loyal beast with wickedly sharp teeth.

Since Chopper and Torch had the fastest sleds, Ransom gave them a hand signal to get out in front of the Twisted Souls while the rest of them caged the fuckers in.

Despite the four bikers trying to swerve around Stone's brothers, it only took a minute to surround them completely. As soon as Ransom rode to the front to join Chopper and Torch, they began to force the group to slow down.

Only, the Souls kept maneuvering in an effort to escape the cage. One almost took out Patch by sharply swerving at him. Another stiff-armed Bolt, trying to knock him off his Harley.

Thank fuck none of their evasive moves were successful and they were slowly forced off the road by tightening up the circle. As soon as they were all off road completely and at a stop, everyone was off their sleds and on their feet in a goddamn instant.

Stone shook his head when a TSMC member jumped from his sled and began to sprint toward the woods.

Chicken shit.

Little did that motherfucker know how much of a fucking mistake that was. But he would. In three…

Two…

"Get 'em, Thor!" Ogre bellowed.

That command alone was enough to make Stone's asshole pucker. He knew the damage Thor could inflict. The canine could rip out a fucker's throat within thirty seconds.

The nightmares he'd had after seeing that shit took a while to fade.

With a ferocious bark, the mastiff-type dog launched himself from the sidecar and tore after the biker on the run. While the biker was cooking, the massive dog was faster. That motherfucker could move when he wanted to, but most of the time, he preferred to lie around like a rug.

His brothers had already surrounded the remaining three and, while dodging flying fists, yanked them off their bikes. Despite that, they all paused to watch Thor do his thing.

When Thor launched himself this time, all his weight hit the fleeing biker, knocking him down. Hard.

Stone winced. That had to fucking hurt.

Ogre yelled, "Thor, hold!"

The Presa Canario clamped his teeth around the screaming biker's throat and held fast. The dog's training was damn impressive. Stone was happy as fuck it wasn't his neck with teeth clamped around it.

While Ogre kept his attention on Thor and the downed biker, the rest of them concentrated on the other three now forced to sit on their asses.

With over twenty Kings circling them, no one was going anywhere.

Hopefully, Taryn couldn't see past the wall of bodies.

With a quick glance at their patches, it looked like none of the Souls were officers for their club, unless the runner Thor had in his grip was one. If not, it made him wonder if their prez actually knew where they were.

Didn't matter, they would pay for their mistake either way.

Ransom got right into the face of the one with the name patch identifying him as Zero. "What the fuck you doin' here?"

Stone pushed through the wall of his brothers so he could hear the answer.

The biker had his hands up and palms out in surrender. "Just ridin' through, brother. Didn't realize we stepped on Kings' toes."

"First off, that's fuckin' bullshit, and second, you ain't my brother." He pointed to his own president patch. "See that? Your prez didn't bother to reach out to me. Not only is that fuckin' disrespectful, but a damn good way to make enemies."

"Your prez know you're just ridin' through?" Stone asked.

"No," Zero answered.

"Another bullshit answer," Ransom said. "When's the last time your club went for a joy ride in this area?"

None of them said shit.

"Fuck around and find out," Stone mumbled under his breath.

Just then, a large van pulled up behind them and five of their eight prospects spilled out.

This situation would be a good test for them, too. Because like the ol' ladies, this had to be a life they wanted to live before accepting their patches. And if they weren't willing to do what needed to be done, then they'd never earn those sacred rockers.

They were Kings not pussies.

"You want them doin' this or takin' the sleds back to the shop?" Stone asked Ransom.

"They can get the sleds outta here seein' as we're sittin'

ducks on the side of a road. Might not be a busy one, but still, someone might come the fuck along."

Damn.

Stone would've liked to see the recruits pull their damn weight. But the prez was right, the fewer witnesses the better. No damn witnesses would be Stone's preference.

The reality was, they couldn't take their time dealing with these assholes. It was too risky.

"You hear that?" Stone asked the prospects. A chorus of *yeahs* rose up. "Squid, don't fuckin' leave 'til we tell you. The rest of you, pick a sled and head back. You know where to take them."

With a smile, Chopper, who was in charge of the Kings' chop shop, hooted and rubbed his hands together. "We can have those fuckers broken down by midnight and a lot of those parts sold by mornin'. This will be a damn good haul."

Stone grunted.

"You can't take our rides!" the Twisted Soul with the road name Cruiser yelled.

Stone cocked an eyebrow. "Fuckin' stop us, then."

"That ain't all we're gonna take." Ogre's deep voice came from outside the circle. "Make a fuckin' hole!" The circle opened up and Ogre marched the biker with puncture wounds decorating his neck into the center and shoved him to the ground with the other three. His blood-splattered name patch claimed his road name was Reno.

"Watch 'em," Ogre ordered Thor. "Next time you try to run, ain't gonna call him off. Last thing you're gonna fuckin' see is his big-ass teeth snappin' at your ass. You hear me?"

Thor didn't leave the sergeant at arms' side, but he did keep an eye on all the stupid fucks on the ground.

So much for convincing Taryn that Thor wouldn't hurt

Baby Bird. He had a feeling the woman wouldn't want her son around the dog after this.

Hell, she might not want to be around any of them after this.

Ogre barked, "Were you assholes up here scoutin'?"

Bandit answered, "Just ridin' through. Askin' for a pass this time. Won't happen again."

"Damn right it won't happen again," the sergeant at arms growled. "But ain't takin' your fuckin' word for it. You all scoutin'?"

"No," came from Cruiser.

Ogre used his size fourteen boot to slam him in the chest, knocking him over. "Bullshit."

The fallen biker scrambled to sit back up but before he could, Lick muttered, "Think they're lyin'," and drop-kicked the guy in the head.

Cruiser would not be cruising anywhere for a while since he was now knocked out cold.

"Take their fuckin' cuts," Ransom ordered Squid.

"What the fuck?" Reno shouted.

When he tried to jump to his feet, Lick yanked him back down to the ground using the guy's pony tail. "Nobody fuckin' told you to get up. Sit the fuck down."

"You can't take our cuts," he insisted, his face red.

"The fuck we can't. Take 'em," Ransom ordered the prospect again. "Take them back to The Castle, throw 'em in one of the burn barrels and light 'em the fuck on fire."

Damn, that was cold. Stone would rather take a beatdown than have his colors reduced to ashes. Cuts were goddamn sacred. So much so, rules on how to wear them and how to handle them when they weren't on their backs had to be followed.

Having your cut stripped or stolen was worse than losing your fucking ride.

A few of Stone's brothers ripped the cuts off the Souls and handed them to Squid. The three still-conscious bikers yelled and fought to hold onto them the whole time.

That got them introduced to a few more boots.

Using all his weight, Ogre ground his on Zero's hand, causing the biker to scream and attempt to scramble away.

He didn't get far. But he did get a crushed throttle hand. He probably wouldn't be riding again any time soon.

But they weren't done yet.

"None of you fuckers gonna admit you were scoutin' Kings' territory?" Stone asked, circling the four intruders. He stopped in front of Zero, who still clutched his hand to his chest with a pained expression. "No? Since you ain't answerin', guessin' you don't need use of your mouth." Zero quickly forgot about his hand when Stone booted him right in the face.

Blood splattered and a few teeth went flying. Now he wouldn't only need the bones in his hand set, he'd need some new choppers.

Zero was now rolling on the ground, groaning in pain.

Shame, that.

Stone stopped in front of Reno next. "Since you still got your teeth, you can fuckin' answer."

With a quick glance at his brother, Zero, the wide-eyed Reno shook his head. "Ain't scoutin'. Just on a run."

"Just the four of you? Bullshit. Try again."

Reno braced, waiting for the kick to the face, but it didn't come. Instead, Outlaw, the Kings' treasurer, slipped up behind him, grabbed the Soul's bearded chin, ripped his head back and sliced his throat.

That trip to Reno was canceled lickety-fucking-split, all except for the gurgling.

"Too fuckin' easy," Ogre complained. A few grumbles of agreement circled the Kings.

Ransom shook his head in disappointment. "Outlaw, drag his ass into the goddamn woods and out of sight. Might as well start a damn pile."

Stone stopped in front of Bandit next. "Why you in the area?"

"The weather—"

Stone made a buzzing sound. "Wrong answer. Thanks for fuckin' playin'." He glanced around. "Who wants this one?"

"C'mon, man! It's the—"

Bones stepped forward and clocked Bandit in the face, busting the biker's nose and splitting his lip. "Shut the fuck up," he yelled with a grimace while shaking out his hand. "Fuck!"

Ogre barked out a laugh. "Stupid ass. That's why we wear steel-tips. To stomp on shit. Now you gone and fucked up your jerk-off hand."

"Actin' like a baby biker just makin' his way in the world," Lick said on a laugh. "Guess you learned the hard way, Bones, just like these other fuckers will soon enough."

"All right, seems like they're gonna deny the truth about why they were in our territory. Territory they fuckin' know is ours. Time to finish sendin' our message before some concerned citizen decides to call the pigs." Ransom scanned the circle and ordered, "Get it done," then stepped out the way to light a cigarette.

As the circle closed in on the surrounded bikers, Stone also stepped back next to Ransom and looked around. Squid had finally left with the van and the cuts, but this crowd of bikers and their rides would still catch plenty of attention. Even if they couldn't see the bloody heaps in the center of that crowd.

Now they needed to get their message delivered to the other MC's president and get the fuck out of there.

Once Stone's own cigarette was lit, he glanced over to his parked sled to find it surrounded by the ol' ladies. Were they giving Taryn shit or supporting her? It could go either way with them, since some of them could be pretty fucking catty.

He ground his teeth. None of them better say a goddamn bad word to her. Not a fucking one.

Even from where he stood he could see her face was white and her eyes wider than normal as she watched what was going on. Luckily, she couldn't get a clear view.

Fuck.

He turned back. "Let's wrap this shit up. Someone grab one of their cell phones. Then drag the fuckers into the woods where the other one is and tie 'em up. Use their own belts if you gotta."

Patch broke free from the group and offered a bloody cell phone to Ransom, who stared at it. "Couldn't wipe it the fuck off first?"

"With what? Everything's now bloody on them. Also had to use the asshole's finger to unlock it."

"For fuck's sake," the prez grumbled, carefully taking the phone. He began scrolling through it. "Anyone know the name of their fuckin' prez?"

The crowd parted again and Torch pointed to the Twisted Soul crumpled in a heap at his bloody boot. "Ask this stupid motherfucker. Pretty sure his jaw's still workin'. For now, anyway." Torch leaned over and asked, "Who's in charge of you stupid fucks?"

All Stone heard was a gurgled answer.

Ransom squinted at Torch. "What the fuck did he say?"

"Think he said Pit Bull. That right?" Torch asked Zero.

Or, who Stone thought was Zero. Without their cuts and with the way their faces were mangled, it was now hard to tell them apart.

Fuckin' shame.

When Torch didn't get an answer, he kicked the Souls' member so hard the guy's head flopped back.

He was knocked the fuck out.

Ransom continued to scroll as he mumbled, "Gonna send a message to this Pit Bull on where to find them. Along with a warnin'."

"That won't be the only warnin'. Got one of my own," Stone told him.

"Found Pit Bull. Hopefully he's their fuckin' prez." In the middle of typing a text, Ransom announced, "Drag those fuckers into the woods and make sure you got them secured. Don't want them wakin' up and runnin' around, squawkin' like a fuckin' chicken with their fuckin' head cut off. That'll draw attention."

It certainly would. But it would at least be entertaining. However, the Kings would be long gone before those fuckers woke up from their naps. Though, one of them wasn't going to be waking up at all.

Stone sucked on this teeth. Again, *a fuckin' shame.*

Ransom finished with, "Soon as that's done, get ready to mount up so we can get the fuck outta here."

Stone followed his brothers dragging the bodies into the woods and once they were left in a circle in the dead leaves and dirt, he slipped his knife from its sheath.

Bones stepped next to him. "What message you leavin'?"

"What d'you think?"

Bones gave him a toothy grin.

Stone quickly carved the message he wanted delivered to their president. Hell, to every damn Twisted Souls member.

He divided up the message between the four bikers. When he was done, he stepped back and took in his damn fine handiwork.

Blood now covered their faces and the skin was separated enough Stone swore he could see bone...but it was one way to make sure the message was clear. Each forehead held a part of the message:

NOBODY

FUCKS

WITH

THE KINGS

Stone had no clue if they were even still breathing. Didn't matter. Their own club could check on them when they came to collect them.

Ransom joined them and gave Stone a nod of approval at what he saw.

"What'd you say?"

Ransom handed him the cell phone and Stone read the text message.

Some of your Souls got lost. Don't worry, we found them. You can find them in the woods west of Trevorton. Got the next 6 hours. Any of you fuckers caught in Kings territory after that time limit, gonna suffer the same fate.

"Let's get the fuck outta here!" Ransom glanced around. "You know what to do next!"

They all throw their heads back and, with fists raised, yelled, "Nobody fucks with the Kings!"

Boots stomping, chest beating, and ear-splitting hoots filled the air.

It was enough to give Stone a damn chill.

It definitely made him smile.

The smile quickly died as he headed back to his sled and a waiting Taryn.

273

Chapter Twenty-Four

Three fucking days.

For three fucking days Taryn gave him the silent treatment.

Not only that, her kid was back to sharing Stone's bed. Without Stone in it. He was back to sleeping on the goddamn couch.

It could've been worse. She could've taken Baby Bird and bolted, leaving him scrambling to find someone else to help with Sunny. At least she was keeping her end of the bargain. As much as she probably didn't want to.

When he returned to his sled that day after dealing with the Twisted Souls, Taryn refused to meet his eyes and Bolt's ol' lady gave him a "good luck" look.

Once he swung his leg over his sled and started it, he told her to hang on and waited for her to do so.

She didn't.

With his patience close to snapping, he finally grabbed her arms and wrapped them around him. "Hang the fuck on."

Not only was she non-responsive, he detected a slight

tremble. Setting his jaw, he took off, but not before wondering if Taryn was now afraid of him after seeing what he and his brothers were capable of.

He knew by not taking her back to The Castle and letting his brothers handle the situation, it was a risk. He also didn't want to hide who the Kings were.

Her reaction also proved it was for the best that she wasn't sticking around long-term. She wouldn't be able to handle their lifestyle.

They weren't fucking choir boys. Or Boy Scouts. They were goddamn one-percenters. They were not a club trying to go legit. They liked their lifestyle and wanted to keep it that way. They made good scratch, they had each other's backs, and lived life however the fuck they wanted.

It was as perfect as it could fucking get.

Later that night, when she locked him out of his own damn room, all she said through the bedroom door was that she needed time to process what the Kings did to those other bikers.

He got it. For her, what happened had to be eye-opening.

For the Kings, it was everyday life.

They protected what was theirs. Period. If they didn't, they risked losing it all.

Guaranteed that was never going to fucking happen. Every last damn King would need to be wiped off the Earth first.

Despite her being bent out of shape over the incident, she had no problem continuing to use their commercial kitchen to record videos, do live streams, and meal prep. She had Shit Stain running all over fucking creation delivering them.

Apparently, the email Taryn had sent out to her client base announcing the new venture had been effective. She had a hard time keeping up with orders since they were rolling in at a rapid rate.

Stone had a feeling that business would end up bringing in more scratch than her being a private chef. Hell, she even found someone to create a website for customers to order and customize meals. Stone took that as a sign she might be sticking in the area, despite her ex soon being on the loose.

With what her side business was already bringing in, Outlaw, their treasurer, was as happy as a pig in shit, even with that "measly" ten percent cut. It was another easy source of income to help keep the club's coffers full. Stone couldn't forget it also kept their guts full. Not only for him and his daughter, but all his brothers, too.

That cut of her business was their only legit income source. Not that they were letting Uncle fucking Sam know about that one, either.

Tonight, Stone was done with Wren hogging his side of the bed. He was reclaiming it. If Taryn couldn't deal with it, then her son could go back to sleeping on the top bunk in Sunny's room and she could take the damn couch.

But it wasn't only the bed situation bothering him. It was the fucking silence. He never knew it could cut so damn deep.

Worse, according to the call she got from her attorney, Vic the Dick was to be released in only two days. Once he was, Stone wanted to stick as close as fucking possible to Taryn until that fucker was dealt with.

If she didn't like the way they dealt with the Twisted Souls, she'd probably hate the way he dealt with her ex even more.

Maybe it would be better if the fucker simply had an "accident."

A wet nose nudged his hand, but Thor didn't wait for

Stone's attention. Instead, the dog immediately laid down nearby with a groan and a loud yawn.

If Thor was in the vicinity, that meant so was his owner.

"Dickhead," Ogre greeted.

"Cocksucker," Stone greeted back. He pointed at Thor. "Dog acts like he got it fuckin' rough. Why's he yawnin' when he ain't done shit today 'cept sleep and take those massive shits?"

"Takin' a massive shit's hard fuckin' work. Also probably tired from pissin' on your sled tire," Ogre said with all seriousness.

"Gonna grab your favorite Sturgis shirt to clean it off, then."

"Ain't gonna be the first time one of my shirts got pissed on. Also ain't gonna be the last."

With a soft snort, Stone shook his head.

Ogre glanced across the cafeteria to the kitchen. "Still ain't talkin' to you?"

"Fuck no," Stone grumbled.

"Normally would say that's a fuckin' blessin' since it's hard to get some of these bitches to shut the fuck up. But seems like it's botherin' you."

Stone wasn't stupid enough to confirm or deny that fact. To Ogre or any of his brothers. He quickly changed the subject. "Got a favor."

Ogre grunted.

"Keep an eye on her when I ain't here, will ya?"

His brother cocked an eyebrow. "Ain't a babysitter. 'Specially for a piece of ass that I ain't gettin' a piece of." He grunted. "But then, right now you ain't either."

"Ain't askin' you to babysit, but when you and Thor are in here beggin' for scraps, just keep a fuckin' eye on her."

"Right. Lookin' more and more like she ain't just your

kid's babysitter. 'Specially when you brought her on the run Sunday."

"Made a deal. Just keepin' my end of it."

"Her cookin's damn good, but bet that sweet as fuck pie is way fuckin' better. No wonder you're pissed about her freezin' you out."

Stone sighed. He wasn't pissed. He was more annoyed.

"Also noticed since she moved in with you a few weeks ago you been sleepin' at home every damn night."

"'Cause I got my nut nugget full time now. Only reason."

"Thought her takin' care of your baby girl was why you made that deal with her." He jerked his chin toward the kitchen. "Also, should know I ain't the only one noticin' your lack of bustin' a nut with the sweet butts."

"Nobody should give a fuck where I'm stickin' my dick. Anyway, how the fuck am I supposed to protect her and the kids if I ain't at the house?" Why the fuck did he feel the need to defend his actions? He shouldn't.

"Didn't think her ol' man was out yet."

"Ex," Stone corrected. "He ain't. Two more days."

If he had a connection inside at the prison where fucker was taking his concrete block staycation, he'd make sure the fucker never walked free again. He'd be ending his bid by leaving with a toe tag, not his personal belongings.

"Then what?"

"Then I'm gonna deal with him."

Ogre pursed his lips as his gaze flicked back and forth between Stone and the kitchen. "She know you're gonna eighty-six him?"

To the Kings, *eighty-six* meant to take someone eight miles out and bury them six feet under. When he heard Taryn use it one day he almost broke his fucking neck doing a damn double-take. Wondering if she had some deep, dark secrets, he asked why she used that term. She explained it was common in the culinary industry when an item was removed from the menu due to running out of the ingredients to make it.

On one hand, he was relieved. On the other, also kind of disappointed she wasn't some badass Ninja chef.

"No," he answered the club enforcer.

"How d'you think she's gonna react to you dealin' with her boy's daddy when it bothered the fuck outta her with how we dealt with those Twisted motherfuckers?"

Of course, that would be a fucking issue unless... "She don't gotta know it was me."

Ogre lifted an eyebrow at him. "Want me to handle it?"

"Appreciate the offer, brother, but fuck no. This ain't a club issue, it's personal."

"I gotta remind you you're out on probation?"

"Who ain't?"

Ogre grunted again. "Ain't that the fuckin' truth. Think her ex is so whacked he's gonna come lookin' for her?"

"She's got his kid, so gonna assume so, yeah. Also expect him to be pissed about her movin' outta the house and puttin' it up for sale."

"What d'ya know about him?"

"Not much. Only got to know him up close and personal the day that motherfucker got handsy with her."

"And you got handsy with him."

"Couldn't let him continue to beat the fuck outta her like that. Worse, in front of their goddamn kid."

"Betcha that left a mark on him."

"Sure did leave a mark on that fucker. Why I spent that long thirteen months on an unplanned vacation."

"Meant the kid."

"Him, too. She admitted she hadta get him help 'cause of it." Stone tapped his temple.

"Damn," Ogre murmured, stroking his short beard.

"Wanna get him dealt with before he tries to snag Baby Bird or fuck up Taryn again." Just thinking about that shit made his fingers curl into fists.

If that happened, Stone would lose his fucking shit. Worse than that day in the parking lot. Taryn had been a stranger then, she was far from that now.

So yeah, dealing with Vic the Dick was now personal.

"Since when the fuck you become some kinda white fuckin' knight?"

"Since the second I saw that motherfucker poundin' Taryn into the ground with the kid watchin' it all and cryin' so damn hard he was gettin' sick. As much as I hate that cunt Sheena, I'd never do that shit to her. Especially in front of Sunny. She might be a shitty fuckin' parent, but she's still my girl's mother." He had to remind himself of that all the time. Because if it was up to him, he'd help Sheena disappear, too. And he wasn't talking about a temporary stay in prison.

Once again, he had to remind himself he was far from a perfect parent himself. In fact, he probably shouldn't be one at all. But the kid was still breathing so that was a good sign. Maybe. She sure used a lot of the air she breathed in to dish out unnecessary bullshit.

Hopefully she'd grow out of the terrible tens soon. Really fucking soon.

"Since Gentry's gonna be released in a coupla days, askin' for you to do me a solid by keepin' an eye on Taryn and her kid if she's here and I ain't."

This time Ogre didn't hesitate. "You got it, brother. Thor and I will keep an eye on her when we're around. But only 'cause she makes damn good grub."

Relieved, Stone clapped him on the back. "Thanks, brother."

Ogre was about to move on but stopped as soon as Shit Stain walked into the cafeteria wearing the cook shirt Taryn required for deliveries. As he began to pass them, his feet stuttered to a stop and he turned back.

"You fuckin' up?" Stone asked when the prospect came to stand in front of them, looking wired and like he had a damn secret to spill.

Shit Stain lips thinned out. "Has she complained?"

"Ain't askin' her. Askin' you."

"Been doin' everythin' she wants me to do. Ain't gonna risk not gettin' those rockers."

"Good," Stone murmured.

Shit Stain shuffled from foot to foot. "Hey, VP, figured you'd wanna know...these deliveries could be more of an opportunity than only makin' that ten percent."

"How's that?" the sergeant at arms asked before Stone could.

His eyes flicked from Ogre back to Stone. "You know all her clients got a shit-ton of scratch?"

No fucking shit. "Figured nobody livin' in your mom's pop-up camper can afford Taryn's meals."

Shit Stain's eyebrows pinched together. "What does that fuckin' mean?"

Stone shook his head since his insult flew right over the prospect's head. "Never fuckin' mind. Yeah, know you ain't deliverin' to the local trailer park, dipshit. What about her clients?"

"Thinkin' whenever I spot a luxury ride at these places, I can get the info and we can go back later to snag 'em for the chop shop." He added a huge shit-eating grin, like he thought his idea was fucking genius.

Stone wanted to wipe that grin off his fucking face. "Apparently, you weren't fuckin' thinkin', you stupid fuck." He took a quick glance toward the kitchen to make sure Taryn was still out of hearing distance. He lowered his voice anyway. "You start scoutin' at her clients house, pigs might put together a pattern that'll come back on her."

"They ain't gonna pin it on her."

"Sure as fuck will. It won't be marked up as coincidence if cages keep gettin' pinched from the same goddamn houses where you delivered. And if that comes to fuckin' light, it'll destroy everythin' she's workin' for and she might even catch a charge." He leaned in until they were almost nose-to-nose and growled, "Don't fuckin' do it. You don't shit where you eat."

One side of Shit Stain's mouth pulled up. "Got a thing for her, huh?"

Did that fuck for brains prospect really ask him that? "Think I answer your stupid fuckin' questions?"

Taryn would never forgive him if she got caught up in their chop shop business. Hell, she didn't even know it existed. He'd like to keep it that way.

But if he looked deep down, he realized his concern wasn't losing someone to help with Sunny, it was losing her in general. If she even caught wind of them fucking over her clients, she'd be in that same wind.

And for some fucking reason, despite knowing this arrangement was only supposed to be temporary, that shit bugged him.

It shouldn't since he knew better than to hook up with someone who couldn't handle the life. And this damn silent treatment was proving she might not be able to handle it.

Next to him, Ogre was shaking his head. "Stupid is as stupid does. The road name Shit for Brains does fit him a fuck of a lot better than Shit Stain. Maybe us officers need to vote on changin' it at the next meetin'."

"Bet that vote will be unanimous." Stone turned back to the prospect. "You do what you're told, that's fuckin' it. She tells you to jump, you fuckin' jump. I tell you to lick my fuckin' boots, you drop to your knees and tongue my goddamn dirty boots. Ogre wants you to pick up Thor's shit, then you pick it up with your bare fuckin' hands."

"I thought—"

"That's the fuckin' problem. You're a goddamn prospect. You ain't supposed to think," Ogre growled.

"Got it." Though, Shit Stain didn't look happy about that fact.

Stone cocked an eyebrow at him. "Sure?"

"Yeah," the prospect grumbled.

"Now, go do what you were told to do and get the fuck outta our faces. And keep your thinkin' to a minimum before you hurt yourself."

Stone and Ogre exchanged amused glances as Shit Stain hurried back to the kitchen for his next delivery.

"Goddamn prospects," Stone muttered with a shake of his head.

"Necessary evil. Can't forget we were all wet behind the fuckin' ears once."

"Don't think we were that fuckin' stupid."

"Problem is, stupid people don't realize they're fuckin' stupid."

Wasn't that the fucking truth?

Chapter Twenty-Five

Taryn needed to decide what she was going to do next. The million dollar question was: should she stay or should she go?

If she stayed, could she live with what the Kings—and Stone—did to those other bikers?

If she left, could she live with herself if something happened to her that would take her away from her son, leaving him motherless? Or could she live with Vic kidnapping Wren and taking him somewhere Taryn couldn't find them?

When it boiled down to it, the reality was she was in more danger from Vic than sticking around with Stone and his brothers. Vic had a personal vendetta against her. While the Kings, despite how dangerous they might be, had her back.

Her moral dilemma was likened to friending someone because they'd always been kind to her, then finding out they were a serial killer.

However, her only other option would be for her and her son to disappear to somewhere no one could ever find them.

Unfortunately, that would take a lot of planning and money. It also meant they'd be leaving her mother, Wren's only remaining grandparent, behind. And maybe never see her again.

Not only would they have to change their identities, she would need to find a new source of income. Not an easy thing to do. Plus, it would tank the career she'd worked so hard and spent so many years building.

Right now, her business was the only thing holding her life together. She couldn't afford to give it up. While she wished she had enough equity in the house to be able to do that, the reality was, she didn't.

She also didn't want her and Wren to be forced into hiding or on the run like fugitives for the next few years, if not even longer. To always be looking over their shoulders.

Such an abrupt change in his life wouldn't be fair to him, either. It would affect his education, his healthcare, his... everything.

She slapped a hand over her forehead and sighed. It was all too much but the reality was, Vic would be freed in less than forty-eight hours.

She was trying not to panic.

She was trying not to worry.

But the truth was, when Vic was released, he would be out for blood.

She knew that because he had said so at his trial. That threat in front of the judge was one reason he got more time than Stone for practically the same offense.

While he wouldn't know where she and Wren were currently living at first, it might not take long for him to find out. If her ex was determined to find them, he'd pull out all the stops to do so.

He might want to steal Wren simply for revenge since

doing it legally might now be out of his reach with his aggravated assault conviction. Especially since he was violent in front of his own son.

Even so, she did not trust the legal system to protect them. She couldn't count on the useless Protection From Abuse order. She also couldn't risk the judge handing even partial custody back to Vic. In the end, she had to rely on her own decisions to protect both of them.

That meant she needed to do *whatever* was needed to keep them both safe. Right now, that meant staying where she was. Even if it wasn't the most ideal situation.

Damn it.

She was stuck between a rock and a hard place. That "rock" being Stone.

She liked him. She really, *really* did. More than she ever thought she would. If she didn't, she wouldn't have been sharing more than the same roof.

That said, she didn't like some of the things he did. What she knew of, anyway. Guaranteed, she didn't know even a fraction of it.

He also wasn't a great role model for Wren, even though that was supposed to be Vic's job, not Stone's. One that her ex failed miserably at.

Bottom line, if she was staying, she needed to accept the way Stone lived his life. The Kings clearly lived by a code, even though it might not be one she agreed with. The bikers were loyal, protective, and treated each other like family. Proof that some shiny spots could be found on that tarnished lifestyle if you looked closely enough.

In addition, she needed to appreciate everything he had done for her, when he didn't have to, and stop freezing him out.

And if she had to admit it, she missed him sleeping next to her.

She missed the intimacy. Missed the way he curled around her at night, making her feel secure. And wanted. Something that had been missing in her life for the last few years.

She also missed the way he'd shoot her a random smile when she least expected it.

Since Sunday, their shared meals had been uncomfortable. Every time they sat down to eat, Taryn had concentrated on her food. In contrast, Stone stared across the table, focusing on her, even as he ate.

Of course, Sunny's eyeballs were permanently glued to the cell phone Stone returned to her a few days ago, ignoring everyone else at the table, while Wren chatted away about everything and also nothing, clueless to the uncomfortable undertones at the table.

Tonight's "family" dinner hadn't been any different.

As she pushed away from the table to start clearing the dirty dishes, Sunny was out of her seat and ready to bolt.

Stone's words stopped her dead in her tracks. "Clear the table before you go anywhere."

"Dad," she grumped, her expression holding a whole lot of unhappy.

"She made dinner, you ate it, you help clean up."

She stared daggers at her father. "You first."

Taryn pinned her lips together to keep her mouth from gaping open. Even though she worried about Stone and his brothers being a bad influence, maybe she should worry about his daughter, too. She didn't want that bad attitude rubbing off on her normally happy boy.

A muscle ticked in Stone's jaw. "Planned on it, but now you're gonna do it all."

Taryn stood in an attempt to defuse the situation. "It's fine, I can—"

Stone cut Taryn off. "Sit down. Let her clear the table."

"It's—"

"Nope. Sit down. Sunny's gonna clear the table, scrape the plates, rinse them good, and stick 'em all in the dishwasher." He addressed his daughter next. "Just be glad you ain't handwashin' them in a fuckin' river."

Taryn mentally groaned.

"Dad," his daughter started again.

He closed his eyes and released a sharp breath. "Don't got the patience for this bullshit tonight, Sunny. Taryn made you a damn good meal and you practically licked your plate. Least you can do is help clean up."

Okay, he wasn't a completely horrible role model. He had *some* good points. But it would be better if he used a softer tone and didn't liberally sprinkle his words with cursing.

She understood the whole "tough love" thing, but—

"Why would anyone wash their dishes in a river, Mommy?" Wren whispered to her.

Taryn leaned closer and murmured, "That's what they did before homes had running water. You had to go down to a creek or river and wash your things there, like dishes and clothes."

His little eyebrows knitted together. "Why didn't they have a dishwasher?"

"They hadn't been invented yet."

No surprise his next question didn't have anything to do with the current topic. "Can I go play outside?"

Having him do that would be a great idea right now. He didn't need to watch father and daughter butting heads. "Did Mrs. Landers give you any homework?"

"*Nooooo,*" he answered in a sing-song voice.

"Then yes. Just don't leave the backyard."

Stone added, "Stay away from the pool and make sure to stay where your mom can see you from the window, kid."

"Okay!" he shouted with excitement. He quickly shoved his chair away from the table and raced outside. She grimaced when he let the screen door slam behind him.

She pulled in a deep breath and reluctantly turned her attention back to the current conflict.

Stone now sat back with his tattooed arms crossed over his chest while keeping a bead on his daughter. With her expression pinched like she was sucking on a lemon, Sunny carried a stack of dirty dishes over to the sink.

"Make sure to scrape 'em first, daughter of mine, before rinsin'. If I gotta hire a plumber due to clogged pipes, gonna take it outta your allowance."

Taryn stayed in her seat and downed the rest of her wine, then stared longingly at the bottom of the empty glass. She wasn't a big drinker but now she regretted not buying another bottle.

"Sunny, you can leave the pots and pans. I'll take care of those." Especially since they were her top of the line set. As expensive as they were, Taryn took good care of them so they'd last since she couldn't afford to replace them any time soon.

But telling her that didn't stop Sunny from bashing the dishes around as she scraped and rinsed them before stacking them in the dishwasher.

Taryn figured it was best to stay out of it and let those two work it out. *Riiiiight.*

As soon as Sunny was done, she turned to her father. "Can I go now?"

"Yep. Thank you for helpin'."

"Thank you, Sunny," Taryn quickly added, plastering on a smile.

Sunny rolled her eyes and in a flash, disappeared. Seconds later, they could hear her feet stomping up the stairs with each step louder than the next.

While that conflict was over, she waited for the next battle since it was now only the two of them in the kitchen. And she'd been avoiding him as much as possible.

With the way he had stared at her over his food, she had a suspicion that would be coming to an end within the next few minutes.

Taryn carried her empty glass over to the sink to finish cleaning up. After rinsing it out and putting it in the dishwasher, she grabbed the nearest pot to start scrubbing.

But before she could do that, she found herself caged in by two thick, tattooed arms. Stone's heat seared her back and so did his breath against her ear when he growled, "Had enough of this bullshit. It ends tonight."

Maybe she shouldn't have wasted time over the dilemma to stay or go. Apparently, Stone decided for her. Even though she had nowhere else to go right now, she and Wren wouldn't stay where they weren't wanted. "I'll pack our things and—"

"That ain't what I meant."

With his hands planted on either side of her to prevent her escape, when she turned, they stood only inches apart.

Her stomach fluttered and her pulse began to race.

Not because she was afraid of him—even though she should be after what she witnessed—but, *for shit's sake,* because she missed his touch. She missed that time spent together in the dark, just the two of them. Cementing the fact that once again, she was the queen of bad decisions.

Maybe she fit in with the Kings better than she'd like to admit.

"Said you had to process shit. Gave you three fuckin' days to do that. Now I'm done. Now *you're* done. The processin' plant is now fuckin' closed."

She hadn't been lying to Stone when she said she needed to process what she'd seen. She did. She came up with the conclusion: she either had to accept the MC life as it was or reject it completely.

If she rejected it, she needed to reject Stone, too, since he was a King and a biker at his very core.

If she rejected Stone, she really needed to leave.

But she already convinced herself to stay. For Wren's sake. If she didn't have him, it would be easier to disappear. Easier to start over. She would only have herself to worry about.

However, she did have Wren and she wouldn't give him up for the world. Especially to her ex who decided using fists was more effective than words.

She would do whatever she had to do to protect her son. Unfortunately, she had limited options on how to do that.

She couldn't deny Stone had stepped up.

She couldn't deny she was attracted to him.

She couldn't deny she was developing feelings for him, too. And, of course, that discovery was eye-opening and a bit worrisome.

Of course their little patchwork "family" had rips and tears. It was far from perfect. But with a little work, they could turn something holey into something whole.

She mentally groaned. Maybe she shouldn't have drank that damn glass of wine. Any sense she had apparently fled like a bank robber after the alarm was pulled.

"I'm back in my bed. So are you. You need to process more shit, you do it with me next to you. You need to talk shit out, willin' to listen. But what I won't do is change. Not for you. Not for anyone. This is my fuckin' life and I like it the way it is. Is it perfect? Fuck no. Will it ever be? Fuck no."

At least he didn't try to sugar coat his lifestyle. He was who he was and wasn't afraid to admit it. "Stone—"

"Got a girl I'm tryin' to raise. I say tryin' 'cause no one knows better than me that I'm failin'. Don't mean I'm gonna give up. But by makin' that deal with you, thought I was doin' better for her. Still fuckin' believe that." He lightly brushed the back of his knuckle down her cheek. "You're a good momma bird."

Why did that low tone of his send lightning down her spine?

"She doesn't like me," Taryn whispered.

"She does. She just don't wanna admit she was wrong. She's fuckin' pigheaded like that."

A chip off the ol' stone. "Like you, you mean."

His brown eyes softened and so did his tight mouth. "Yeah, like me," he breathed. "Unfortunately for her, she got the worst of us. Need to dig deep to find the good and help coax that out."

"And you think I can help with that."

"Yeah, I do. She ain't blind. She ain't deaf. She sees and hears how you interact with Baby Bird. She's never seen that shit before. With Sheena, she's only seen the bad. Wish it hadn't taken her mother gettin' pinched for me to get her full-time, but if you wanna know the truth, glad it did."

His daughter definitely needed a fighting chance. It was easy to see Sunny was afraid to be happy. Or at least show it. Maybe because her happiness kept getting ripped away.

Taryn didn't know the reason, or even the answer to how to help her. Taryn wasn't a therapist, she was a mother. Unfortunately, she often questioned if she was a good one herself.

She could only do her best and hope it was good enough. Stone needed to do the same.

She had to remember if she gave up on Stone, she'd be giving up on Sunny, too. Despite her attitude, Taryn had no doubt Sunny was either a hurt or scared little girl deep inside.

Damn him for tugging on her heartstrings. For using his daughter as an excuse to keep her there. But he was right, not only should she stay for Wren's sake, but for Sunny's as well. His daughter needed a better female influence. One who wasn't a sweet butt or a woman in prison, even if that woman gave birth to her.

"So, about the bed situation…"

"No discussion needed. Already decided."

"I didn't have a say."

He put his lips to her ears. "Sayin' you don't want me slippin' between your thighs later?"

A ribbon of heat wove its way through her, landing between her legs.

"Don't want my tongue flickin' your clit?"

Her eyes slid shut with that memory. She squeezed her thighs together to stem the ache his words caused.

"Don't want me makin' you come so fuckin' hard you claw my back and scream my name?"

The only time she screamed out his name was when the kids weren't asleep down the short hallway. When they were, she contained it in her head. Too many times to count.

"Pussy got your tongue?"

Her eyes opened when she rolled them.

Was she going to let him back in the bed? Did she really want to continue a relationship with someone like him? Because them sleeping together, having those intimate moments, *was* a relationship. It might not be a serious one, but was one none-the-less.

She could deny it.

Stone could deny it.

But they'd both be lying.

Another worry was: if she stayed, she'd only fall harder.

Did that scare her? *Hell yes.*

She pushed at him hard enough to give her enough space to escape. But before she could slip out of his reach, he clamped a hand on her arm, stopping her.

She stared at his hand but he didn't remove it. Instead, he spun her to face him again. "Had enough time to get the fuck over it, Taryn."

"You killed one of those men. And badly hurt the others." She was having a hard time wiping the gaping throat of one of the Twisted Souls from her mind. He lost his life just for being on the wrong patch of Earth.

"I didn't kill the fucker."

Semantics.

She lifted a palm. "You had a part in it. You also didn't do anything to stop it."

Chapter Twenty-Six

"No shit. There's a reason for that."

"Yes, you explained it to me already. I don't think what they did deserved a death sentence."

With a shifting jaw, he straightened, then stiffly strode over to the window and looked out into the backyard, most likely checking on Wren.

On his way back to her, he began talking. "Gonna explain somethin' to you, Taryn, so maybe you'll get where the Kings are comin' from. Hell, where *I'm* comin' from when it comes to other clubs and why we don't tolerate other bikers violatin' our fuckin' boundaries. Don't usually talk about this shit but figured you needed to hear it so you can finish *processin'* it."

Her gut told her this wouldn't be some feel-good story. "Should I sit down for this?"

"Up to you."

She took that as a yes.

He leaned back against the counter next to the sink and waited until she was once again settled in her seat at the table before explaining, "My blood brother, Rubble, was a King.

He encouraged me to become one, too, and sponsored me as a prospect. He showed me all the good that could be found in an MC but he also became a victim of the bad side of this life."

Taryn wasn't sure she wanted to hear this story. Not with how Stone was acting and he'd only just begun.

White-knuckling the counter behind him, he dropped his head and took a couple of slow, deep breaths before carrying on. "Rubble was killed by a nomad club called the Shadow Warriors. They loved to fuckin' trespass in other clubs' territories and create havoc wherever the fuck they went. Now, my brother had some huge fuckin' balls. Too big for his own damn good. He confronted six Warriors by himself when he came across them in our territory." Stone shook his head. "Not sure what the fuck he was thinkin' since he was outnumbered. Like I said, balls too goddamn big for his own good." He pulled in another deep breath. "Those motherfuckers beat the fuck outta him, sliced off the colors tattooed on his back, and when they were done with him, dumped him on The Castle's front lawn. If it wasn't for the ripped off name patch they threw on top of his body, might not've even fuckin' known it was him right away."

Taryn swallowed her gasp. Telling this tale had to be painful for him.

"Good thing the Warriors were really dumb motherfuckers and dumped him there 'stead of some random spot or the Kings would've had no fuckin' clue who offed him. One of our brothers saw them takin' off, raised the alarm, and we fuckin' chased their asses."

He paused and stared off to the side as if reliving a memory. After a few seconds, his dark brown eyes turned back to her.

"We made sure that night those six motherfuckin'

Warriors would never be seen again. Occasionally, we'd spot some of those nomads afterward, but never in our territory. After a while, their numbers mysteriously seemed to thin. Then they stopped showin' up to rallies and poker runs, to the big bike weeks, like Sturgis and Daytona. Eventually, they just fuckin' vanished. Nobody knew what the fuck happened to them. Figured those assholes finally stepped on the wrong toes. Not sure whose, but if I knew, woulda wanted in on that farewell party. Unfortunately, didn't get an invite. If I ever find out who wiped those fuckers off the Earth, gonna buy 'em a fuckin' beer. Hell, a keg. Or even a whole hijacked beer truck. But that's one reason we don't tolerate other clubs disrespectin' our territory. Handlin' that shit with a quickness makes a fuckin' statement. You don't respect us, we certainly ain't gonna respect you. You fuck with us, we're gonna fuck you a lot harder. 'Cause one lesson we always teach is nobody...absolutely *nobody* fucks with the Kings."

Holy shit. That was a lot for her to take in. While her heart ached for his loss, that didn't make accepting how the Kings handled Twisted Souls any easier. "I'm sorry about what happened to your brother, but I can't begin to comprehend why people have to hate each other. Be violent with each other. *Hurt* each other. For what? It's all so senseless. Someone hates another simply because of a patch of ground. Or the color of their skin. Or religious beliefs. Or sexual orientation. Or the cut they wear on their back." Or because their wife divorced them, filed for full custody and, apparently, unreasonably expected a father to help support his own child.

"Human nature, babe. Comes down to a reaction to an action. Like that day your motherfuckin' ex beatin' the snot outta you. No way to stop him 'cept by doin' the same to him.

That's fuckin' reality. He wasn't gonna stop if I asked him nicely, even if added a goddamn 'pretty please' to that request. The man was seein' red. You were the target and he was the high-capacity bullet."

Of course, she missed everything that happened while she was knocked out cold, but she did see the results once she came to. Not to mention, during Vic's trial, the very graphic photos of what he looked like afterward. Clearly, her ex-husband wasn't the only one seeing red that day.

No, Stone had lost his temper as badly as Vic.

The bottom line was, Stone didn't get arrested for helping her. He got arrested for taking it past the point where Vic was no longer a threat. If he had stopped "beating the snot" out of Vic once Taryn was safe, then he most likely would've been able to walk away and not have been stuck in prison for thirteen months.

Despite that, she was grateful for what Stone did that day. Vic might have killed her. Might have permanently taken Wren's mother away from him. Then in the end, when Vic was arrested for murder, their son would've ended up an orphan. Or, at best, raised by Taryn's mother.

That possibility churned her stomach. She followed her instinct to head over to the window to check on Wren. She watched her six-year-old son smiling and laughing without a care in the world as he climbed all over the playset.

He had no idea what danger loomed.

But then, neither did Taryn.

Would Vic get out and leave them alone? Or would he be gunning for her, ready to repeat what happened at the Shoppes of Susquehanna? To "teach" her a lesson.

She closed her eyes and hugged her own waist.

Her life was a damn mess right now and she wasn't sure

how to clean it up. Any decision she made could make it even messier.

Taryn groaned when a nursery rhyme popped into her head. Part of one anyway. One she used to sing to Wren while wiggling his fingers and toes when he was a baby.

Eeny, meeny, miny, moe...

Should I stay or should I go?

The answer was clear. She had already decided to stay and just make the most of it by surviving.

Staying at least gave her a fighting chance. Or so she hoped.

Right now she was her son's sole provider. She needed to focus on her business so she could continue to keep Wren safe, happy, and healthy.

But that didn't mean she wouldn't worry.

With a last glance at her son, she headed back to the sink to finish cleaning up the kitchen.

When she got close to Stone, he snagged the waistband of her pants and jerked her hard enough that she slammed into him, the impact causing all the oxygen to flee her lungs.

He dipped his head down to her. "Need to know what you're thinkin', babe."

She tipped her eyes up to his. "I need to thank you again. For saving me that day. In turn, saving Wren from watching his mother be murdered right in front of his eyes. And saving us again when I needed to get out from under the financial burden of that house." Where they would've been sitting ducks if they had stayed. "I also appreciate the fact you explained about your brother despite it being difficult for you."

"That explanation help you process?"

"Yes, but that still doesn't mean I can dismiss the violence easily." She never would, no matter the reason.

"Fair enough." He tucked his thumb under her chin and dropped his head until his lips hovered over hers.

How could she miss his mouth this much after only three days? Prior to Stone, she went for a few years without sex. Now with him, she couldn't get enough.

"So, guessin' that yes also means Baby Bird's gonna be back sleepin' in his nest tonight?"

"It wasn't a no." A slow, cocky grin spread over his annoyingly handsome face. She grabbed the damp sponge sitting next to the sink and shoved it into his gut. "But first, practice what you preach. Wipe down the counters and table."

"Asshole's gettin' out tomorrow mornin'," Stone grumbled, with one arm tucked under his head.

Their chests still pumped rapidly and they both had a sheen of sweat covering their naked bodies.

"You don't need to remind me. My stomach has been in knots." Unfortunately, every time Stone mentioned it, it caused those knots to tighten.

"Figured the best sex in your fuckin' life helped take your mind off that shit."

There were too many other hours in the day for the worry to eat at her. "It did. For the thirty seconds it lasted."

Stone barked out a laugh. "Know that's a damn lie. Get it right. Best forty seconds of your life." He quickly sobered. "You talk to your attorney?"

"Yes. He warned Vic's attorney that he needs to abide by the PFA or he'll end up back in prison." Unfortunately, a Protection From Abuse order wasn't going to stop her ex from killing her. She'd be dead long before the cops could arrive to arrest him for a PFA violation.

"Was he always like that?" Stone rolled to his side and Taryn could feel his eyes drilling into the side of her face. "Was he a wife beater?"

She turned her head to face him. The intense look in Stone's brown eyes made her breath catch. "No."

"Then why the fuck did he do that shit? What the fuck changed?"

It was crazy that this man—a man she'd only known for a short time—cared more about her and Wren than the man she used to love and be married to. "Because he thought he could simply walk away from his family scot-free. He got pissed when I didn't let him slink away like the snake he turned out to be."

"Where was he slinkin' to?"

"His best friend's house."

Stone jerked his chin into his neck. "He gay?"

"No, but his best friend has a wife. Or *had* a wife. Neither has a spouse now and Vic no longer has a best friend."

"Chasin' pussy can fuck up a man's life."

"I'm assuming you're speaking from experience." She sighed. "Of course, when I went after child support, I got it. Obviously, Vic wasn't happy about that. He blamed me, just like when he was arrested. Despite that arrest being a consequence of his own actions."

"Him bein' inside means you ain't gettin' shit right now. Guess that was one way to avoid payin'."

"He mistakenly thought he could simply leave his family and never have to deal with me again. I wouldn't let him do that. I was holding him to his responsibilities. And that's what pissed him off."

"Thought he wanted custody of Baby Bird?"

"Only so he could avoid paying child support. Since he

wasn't paying at all, I filed for full custody instead of partial and that's why he confronted me in the parking lot. He knew if I got it, what he owed would've increased." Meaning he'd owe even more back child support if he ever got a job that didn't pay him under the table like his brother did.

"Guess he thought usin' his fists would get you to change your mind."

"It didn't work. I was granted full custody after he went to prison." Thankfully.

"As someone who pays support, gonna say that it can be cheaper than raisin' the kid yourself."

"It's also more work to do the actual child raising, as I'm sure you're learning now that Sunny's living here full-time. It doesn't take much of an effort to write a monthly check. Or have it automatically deducted from your pay. How did the court know what your monthly payment should be when you don't have a job on record?" Getting cash under the table was one way deadbeat dads got out of paying child support.

"No courts needed. We negotiated. I threw out a fair amount, Sheena countered with some fuckin' crazy amount and, surprised the fuck outta me, somehow we met in the middle. Probably the only time we agreed on anything. No matter what the amount ended up bein', planned on makin' sure my girl didn't go without. Whether she's with me or her mother."

"Do you think Sheena will fight to get Sunny back once she's released?"

"She can fight all the fuck she wants. Sunny ain't ever goin' back. Already told Sheena that."

Just because that was what he believed didn't mean it would pan out that way. "What if she takes you to court?" With no income on record, that would be a negative checkmark for his case.

Stone snorted. "She ain't takin' me to court 'cause she ain't payin' for no attorney. She also don't got any real job. When it comes down to it, she's a greedy bitch, so all I gotta do is throw some scratch at her and that'll be that."

"Until she needs more money."

"Drug addicts always do."

"Since she's a drug addict, weren't you concerned about Sunny not being taken care of properly?"

"Yeah, but like you said, don't got a job on record, so never woulda got custody in the first place if I took her to court. Got no proof how I can financially afford to take care of my girl. Did the only thing I could fuckin' do by checkin' in with Sunny daily when she wasn't with me to make sure she was good. Got clothes. Was fed. Got to school. Any issue, I stepped in. No longer gotta worry about that shit. Now just gotta deal with her miserable attitude twenty-four-seven." His mouth twisted.

"I wish she was happier."

Stone sighed and shook his head. "Yeah, me too."

"Is it because she misses her mom?"

"Doubt it. She don't like the fact I'm stricter than Sheena. She let her get away with too much fuckin' shit. Bottom line, don't want her endin' up like her mother. Anyway, back to Vic the Dick. Motherfucker's gettin' out so I need to go over those rules again."

Taryn mentally groaned. The man was like a broken record.

"Don't want you goin' anywhere without me knowin'. Not you. Not Baby Bird. You gotta go somewhere, I'm gonna be with you or one of the prospects will. If a prospect can do the errand you need done, then we're gonna keep shit simple and send one of them instead."

"What about school? I'm worried Vic will find out where Wren's attending and snatch him from there."

"Hope to have him handled before that ever happens."

Taryn blinked at that response. He had mentioned something along that vein before, but he never explained how he planned on doing that. That worried her. "How are you going to *handle* him? And will whatever that entails land you behind bars again? If you get caught doing something you shouldn't be, Sunny will have lost both parents to the prison system."

Stone rolled onto his back and pulled in a breath. "Yeah. Ain't gonna do shit that puts Sunny in foster care."

That was a relief.

She rolled toward him and traced one of his chest tattoos with her fingertip. He had so damn many, she swore it would take her a week to trace them all.

Bikers sure liked their tattoos.

And leather.

And badass-ery.

She was surprised when he grabbed her hand and interlocked their fingers together. They had never shared that kind of "intimacy" before. Yes, they had sex plenty of times so far, but holding hands was on a different level.

It was far from a "friends with benefits" scenario. That was how she looked at her sharing his bed. She never expected anything more.

She never expected *him* to want anything more.

Maybe he still didn't, but Stone didn't seem the type of guy to hold hands with women.

But him holding her hand actually felt...nice. Even normal. Not a word she'd associate with the whole situation up to that point.

Maybe he only did it to distract her. He certainly skirted around her question about what he planned on doing to Vic.

"You're more violent than he ever was."

"Yeah."

"That's your response? You're not even going to disagree?"

Stone shrugged. "No reason. It's the fuckin' truth."

Well, at least he owned it. But still... "That's not reassuring."

"Ain't meant to be. Sometimes the truth can't be ignored."

"I'm asking you, Stone, please, don't kill him. Or even have him killed. He's still my son's father. Despite what he did to me, I don't think he'd ever hurt Wren."

She was torn. Stone "handling" Vic would mean she and Wren could live the rest of their lives safe from her ex.

However, if she didn't let Stone do what he wanted to do, would she always be looking over her shoulder? Worried Vic would be waiting around the corner?

While she didn't want to continue living in fear, death was final. That wasn't a decision she should make. For anyone.

Time would tell if asking for leniency was a stupid decision. With her batting record, this could end up being a huge mistake.

His jaw turned to concrete and his fingers squeezed hers. "What about you? You think he won't do it again to teach you a lesson?"

"You already know that answer."

"He might not hurt Baby Bird, but that don't mean he won't use your son as a pawn. If your ex snags him, bet you'll do whatever he wants you to fuckin' do to get your boy back."

That was true. She would sacrifice herself if it meant

saving Wren. "That doesn't mean I want him dead. Maybe he learned his lesson inside." She could only hope.

Stone snorted. "You mean the same fuckin' way I did every fuckin' time? Can tell you most people inside don't change when they get out. Who they are at their core is who the fuck they are. Gonna take a major life alterin' moment to really change."

"Prison is a life altering moment."

"Yeah, right. Your worry stems from him blamin' you for all the bad shit in his life. And you have every fuckin' right to be worried. He ain't a reasonable motherfucker. Tellin' you now, he takes Baby Bird, he comes within ten miles of you, all fuckin' bets are off."

"I can live with that." Those words came out of her mouth, but could she? "But don't forget, my request is not only about Wren and me, it's also about keeping you from being arrested."

She didn't want Stone going to prison again because of her.

Not today. Not tomorrow. Not ever.

In a perfect world, Vic would move on and go about his life, leaving her and Wren alone. If he did and caught up on the mountain of back child support, she might eventually consent to supervised visits.

But this world was far from perfect.

She stared at the man lying next to her. The one she just had awesome sex with. The one who had gone above and beyond for her despite being an outlaw biker. Despite hardly knowing her.

A man assumed by society to have no morals because of who and what he was versus a man assumed to have plenty for the same reason.

As the saying went, looks could be deceiving.

One man she felt safe with. One she did not.

One she trusted. One she did not.

At the surface, Stone should be the one she was afraid of, the one to distrust. But it was the man who looked "normal" on the outside who was now completely unhinged on the inside.

Crazy how upside down life could be.

But she was done talking about Vic. It was only making her more anxious about his release. Especially since she was questioning her decision.

"By the way, my viewers are still asking about you. They're persistent." In fact, some of her followers were more interested in Stone than her recipes.

"What're they askin'?"

"You gave them an eyeful that morning a few weeks ago and they want more. A lot of them are still leaving comments demanding another glimpse. So I came up with an idea..."

One that might increase her subscribers, if he was willing...

Stone's lips flattened. "This idea involves me, don't it?"

"Well, we're talking about you."

He groaned. "What's the idea?"

"I'm considering recording a video series on my YouTube channel where I teach you how to cook. I would teach you different techniques and meals. Maybe even how to meal prep. Not only would that drive up my viewer count but it'll also prepare you for when you're dealin' with Sunny on your own again. No more cereal and pizza for dinner. Wouldn't you like to learn how to cook her a good meal?"

"Don't want to tie you to my club, babe. Could make it easy for your ex to find you."

"Don't wear your colors, or any identifiable clothing that ties you to the Kings. You could go shirtless and show off those tats," she suggested with a grin. "You'd wear an apron, of course, and we'd make sure that you don't show off the tattoo on your back. We can give you a fake name. I can even come up with a catchy title for the video series."

Using their clasped hands, he tugged her on top of him. Of course, she went willingly. He cocked an eyebrow as he stared up at her. "Gotta be shirtless?"

"Of course. I can't be hogging all this tattooed goodness. That would be selfish."

"You sayin' you don't mind sharin'?"

It was one thing for him to be on camera, another to be sleeping with a sweet butt or any other women at the same time they shared a home and a bed.

She couldn't expect him to be exclusive during this arrangement and wouldn't ask him to be, but she had a feeling he wasn't having sex with anyone else. She heard the whispers of the sweet butts and side comments from his club brothers.

No matter what he did during the day, no matter where he disappeared to, he always came home. He seemed to be the type of man that if he wanted to be loyal, he was loyal to the extreme.

"I don't consider you appearing in my videos or live streams as sharing. I consider that dishing up some eye candy. So, are you willing?"

Digging his hands into her hair, he smiled up at her. "Whatever you want, babe."

Whatever you want, babe.

She kind of liked the sound of that.

It also made that butterfly in her stomach flap its wings even faster.

Chapter Twenty-Seven

OF FUCKING COURSE the motherfucker had to be housed at SCI Dallas, an hour and a half northeast from The Castle.

And of fucking course the morning of his release, it had to be pouring rain.

While the first was a pain in his ass, the second might work in Stone's favor.

If it was up to him, he would've taken the easy route, snagged the fucker right off the street, and taken care of business. Then Vic the Dick would no longer be a threat to Taryn.

But, *fuck him*, that wasn't what she wanted. She simply wanted her ex to leave her and Baby Bird alone.

Stone didn't think that was going to work. Shit was never that easy. He knew plenty of assholes like Gentry and prison didn't help them turn over a new leaf.

When he really thought about it, letting Gentry continue to breathe could actually work in his favor by keeping Taryn under his roof longer. He'd admit it was a selfish take on his part, but he was liking their arrangement more than he ever thought he would.

If Stone took Gentry out—his initial plan—against Taryn's wishes, she might never forgive him and could potentially leave since she'd no longer have a threat hanging over her head.

And the fuck if he was ready for that.

He needed her to stay for Sunny's sake.

For fuck's sake.

The reality was, he needed her to stay for him, too.

Unfortunately, he assured her he'd handle it the way she wanted it handled. For Baby Bird. While he agreed not to take the fucker out, he never agreed not to have a face-to-face with him.

So, here the fuck he was, *willingly* sitting out in front of a place he hated the most.

A goddamn prison.

Stupid fuck. Lettin' a woman convince you to go against your goddamn instincts.

He hoped to hell her decision didn't turn around and bite him in the damn ass.

Stone glanced at the time on the vehicle's dashboard. Gentry should be walking free any moment now.

The cage Stone was currently driving was a nondescript, four-door Chevy sedan that one of his brothers pinched a few months ago. The parts weren't worth shit, so instead of stripping the vehicle down, they had swapped out the vehicle identification numbers with fake ones they made in-house, for both their own use and to sell for profit. They had also slapped on a coat of cheap paint and now kept it as a spare vehicle behind the garage to use for just this kind of shit.

Anonymity.

With a quick glance in the rearview mirror, he made sure

all of his long, black hair was still hidden under the baseball cap he'd pulled on as part of his disguise.

Despite it being ball-sweating weather, he also wore a long-sleeved T-shirt to hide as much of his ink as possible. Dark sunglasses covered his eyes and fingerless driving gloves covered his tattooed hands. The only thing he couldn't hide was his facial hair.

And his murderous scowl.

He really hated the idea of letting this abusive motherfucker live.

Really fucking hated it.

Because if it backfired…

Stone pushed out an irritated breath. His gut was screaming that he shouldn't follow Taryn's wishes.

She was aware of the risk.

Only, so was Stone.

His eyes narrowed on the gate as it opened and a man walked free. Stone had made that walk too many times.

Some prisons let you walk out. Others bussed you out and dropped you off in town.

Thank fuck Gentry wasn't being bussed. The screws didn't like when you tailed their transport vehicle. It made the assholes with guns twitchy for some fucking reason.

When Gentry reached the section of the parking lot where family members parked and waited, he glanced around, looking for the ride that would never show up.

Luckily, Stone would help him out.

He pulled in a breath through his nostrils in an attempt to cool his rage at seeing this fucker again. Then pulled out of the parking spot and stopped in front of Gentry, resisting the urge to plow him the fuck over.

Stone had to remind himself that running Taryn's ex down in front of a prison wouldn't go over too fucking well. If he did it in front of the guards and cameras, it would be him sitting inside that concrete box instead of outside, where he preferred.

He tipped the bill of his cap lower and powered down the Chevy's passenger window. "You Victor Gentry?"

Gentry's brow furrowed. "Yes?"

Stone jerked his head toward the rear passenger door. "Get in. I'm your ride. Sit on the passenger side. It'll balance out the vehicle's weight and help it ride better."

He wouldn't want any enemy sitting directly behind him. Since Gentry was fresh out of the joint from catching assault charges, the motherfucker most likely didn't have any weapons on him, but that didn't mean he couldn't do damage.

If Stone needed to take someone out and didn't have a gun or knife on him, he still had other tools. Like his hands or belt. He didn't need much to hurt or kill someone. A useful skill he'd picked up in one of his early prison bids.

"My brother's picking me up."

"He had an emergency. Booked my car instead."

The man's wet hair was now plastered to his head. Rain dripped down his face and his shirt was becoming soaked. "What emergency?"

"Didn't ask because it's not my business. My business is to transport you from point A to point B safely." He had to speak slowly so he had time to carefully choose his words. If he started talking in his normal sloppy, *don't-give-a-fuck* English, he was afraid Vic the Dick might realize it was a trap.

Because bottom line, it *was* a fucking trap. And that trap was about to snap shut.

"C'mon, man. If you don't get in now, when you do, you're gonna soak my back seat."

Gentry's head swiveled around one more time as if making sure his brother wasn't waiting for him.

Stone had made sure he wasn't.

Torch and Bolt carjacked him, threw Gentry's brother right out on the street, and took off in his fancy Audi. The bonus was, those parts would bring in a sweet amount of scratch.

"You wanna stand in the rain or you wanna go home? The ride's already paid for and isn't refundable. So, no skin off my back either way."

After grumbling something Stone couldn't make out, Gentry finally opened the door and slid inside, looking like a wet fucking dog.

Stone kept his eyes on him using the rearview mirror. "Buckle up."

Chopper had rigged the seat belt so it would lock and not release. The fucker would need to be cut free. They also had set the child-safety locks.

"Aren't you supposed to have some sort of ride share license posted or something?"

Or something. "Got it in the glovebox. Had a problem with people trying to steal it. So, where you headed, friend?"

Gentry glanced over at the prison and sighed as he buckled up. "Anywhere has to be better than here."

"I hear that." Stone glanced once again in the rearview. "But still need an address. Can't start drivin' 'til I know where I'm goin'."

Gentry rattled off an address and Stone plugged it into the car's GPS. Now he had the man's address in case the fucker tried any shit.

With one side of his mouth hiked up, he pulled out of the lot and headed south. But about a half hour into the long-ass trip, he altered the route.

Of course, Gentry noticed. "Hey, you're headed the wrong way."

No shit. "Know a shortcut."

"So do I and this isn't it."

"Gotta detour around some road construction. You know how those fu—those state workers love to inconvenience us taxpayers. Just sit back, relax, and enjoy your newfound freedom. I'll get you home safely," Stone lied.

Sitting back, Gentry murmured, "I miss driving."

"Sure you missed a lot of stuff. What did you do to get locked up?"

There was a long hesitation before he answered, "My ex-wife was trying to use my son as an excuse to drain me dry financially."

Bullshit. "Bitches, am I right? And using your kid against you like that? That's pretty low." Stone shook his head.

Gentry's eyes met his for a split second in the rearview. His reaction reminded Stone to keep his English as squeaky clean as possible. But, *damn*, was it work.

"So, how'd that land you inside if she was the one stealing from you?"

"I tried to convince her to change her mind."

Stone gripped the steering wheel hard so he wouldn't reach back and throat punch the fucker. "And that landed you at Dallas?"

"Yes. Unfortunately, some jackass intervened and the police showed up."

The "jackass" turned his head enough so Gentry could see his smile. "Think you convinced her?"

"I guess I'll see."

"And if she wasn't?"

Gentry stared out of the rain-streaked window.

Stone didn't like the fact he didn't answer.

Of course, if Stone had been asked that same sort of question, he wouldn't incriminate himself either. Especially to some stranger in a supposed ride share.

"Are you sure you know where we're going? This isn't the way to my condo. I think you're lost."

"Got it covered. Don't worry. It's either drive out of the way a little bit or sit in stopped construction traffic for an hour."

Five minutes later, Gentry was starting to get antsy. "Can you drop me off at the nearest gas station? I'll get someone to pick me up from there. You don't need to take me all the way home."

Stone's eyes flicked back up to the mirror. "The ride's paid for."

"I don't care."

"Sure. Let me find a safe place to drop you." Only, it wouldn't be a gas station or any public area. And it definitely wouldn't be safe. At least for Vic the Dick.

Stone continued heading farther away from civilization.

Gentry slammed the front passenger seat with this palm. "I want out of this vehicle!"

It was a damn shame that Taryn's ex was getting pissed.

Not that Stone gave a fuck. "Gonna give you what you want. Gotta find somewhere to drop you."

"But there's nothing around here. We're out in the boonies!"

No shit.

He turned onto a dirt service lane that led up to high-voltage power lines. Despite it being rough as fuck, he went far enough off the road that they wouldn't be spotted on the off-chance someone drove by.

Gentry better hope someone eventually came along,

otherwise, he would have a long fucking walk. *If* he was capable of walking after Stone was done with him.

Stone glanced at his cell phone. No coverage.

Perfect.

"This isn't a gas station!" The fucker yelled loud enough to make Stone wince.

"None 'round here."

"There isn't even a place to wait. Turn this car around and take me somewhere else!"

"Sound like a whiny bitch, Gentry."

"What?"

"What fuckin' part of that didn't you understand?"

Gentry huffed, "That guarantees you won't be getting a five-star rating."

"Oh fuckin' well," he muttered as he finally stopped about a quarter mile from the paved road.

Despite the fact they were now out in the woods with nothing around, Gentry immediately tried to get out. "The seatbelt is jammed!"

Another quick glance in the rearview showed that Gentry was yanking on the seatbelt in a panic.

That wasn't even the reason he should be panicking. But he'd find that out soon enough. "It can be funny like that. Need to get that fixed. Hold on, gonna help you."

"What kind of piece of shit is this? The door's stuck, too." He was shoving at it with all his might.

If he kept yanking on the door handle like that, it would break the fuck off. Then Stone was going to shove it up the man's ass. "Said I'm gonna help you. Give me a second."

Stone pulled the keys from the ignition and buried them deep in his front pocket, then shoved open the driver's door, got out, and rounded the vehicle. He pulled open the passenger door. From all dickhead's yanking, the seatbelt had tightened even more, pinning him to the back seat.

What a fuckin' shame.

"Got a message for you from the jackass..." He yanked off his hat and glasses and tossed them inside the car. Stone pulled up his sleeves to expose his tats and smiled. "Remember me, motherfucker?"

Gentry's eyes went wide, then he immediately scrambled for his cell phone. "You! I'm calling the fucking cops."

Besides no cell coverage where they were, Stone knew from experience that the man's phone was dead. It sat for almost a year and a half with the rest of his personal belongings and the fuck if those asshole screws were going to charge it for him.

No coverage and a dead cell phone battery was great for Stone, not so great for Vic the Dick.

"No you ain't." Stone took the heel of his palm and slammed it right into Gentry's nose. It crumpled and began to gush like a stomped grape.

"Hey, you asshole!" he screamed, cupping his hand over his nose.

His smile widened at the satisfaction that brought.

But he wasn't done yet. Not even close.

"Guess asshole's an upgrade from jackass." Stone plucked the useless phone from Gentry's fingers, dropped it on a large rock, and stomped on it with his boot.

"Hey!" came the muffled shout.

Stone picked up the busted phone and whipped it into the tree line for good measure. With it dead, the location couldn't even be pinged. The last known location would come up where the battery died. At SCI Dallas.

Stone loved it when a plan came together.

Slipping a knife from his pocket, he flipped it open and

began slicing through the seatbelt, freeing the fucker. "Do somethin' stupid and you're gonna regret it."

Blood continued to stream from Gentry's broken nose as Stone fisted the man's shirt and yanked him out of the car, flinging him to the ground.

Before Gentry could recover, Stone had his boot jammed on the man's neck.

Wouldn't take much to crush it.

And *damn*, was he tempted.

Pulling in a breath, Stone then pushed it out along with that urge.

He promised Taryn and he always tried to keep promises, whether they were good or bad.

"Gonna tell you this fuckin' once and it would be damn smart of you to heed my fuckin' words. Whatever you're plannin' to do to Taryn...warnin' you now, just forget it. Forget she exists. Forget your son exists. Did your fuckin' time, you can go on about your life. Stop fuckin' with hers."

Gentry wrapped the hand not cupping his broken nose above Stone's boot, trying to prevent his windpipe from being crushed. "It was because of her I ended up in prison."

Stone put a little more weight on that leg. "The fuck it was. Coulda exchanged your son without issue, then spent time with him as planned. 'Stead you decided you needed a vacation in the hospital, then an extended one in prison."

"Because of you!"

"All 'cause of you. You beat the fuck outta your ex, then I beat the fuck outta you. Only fair, right?"

"She was trying to get full custody of my son."

"I don't fuckin' blame her. And after what you did to her in that parking lot, she'll never hand over her boy to an unhinged motherfucker like you."

"You're the unhinged one!"

"Imagine thinkin' two things can't be true at once, you dumb fuck." He kept his boot on Gentry's throat to the point that if he fought back, he'd no longer be able to breathe or swallow.

Gentry continued to claw at Stone's leg. "Help! Somebody help me!"

"A squirrel ain't gonna be able to do jack shit besides shove an acorn in your pie hole. Your screamin' is annoyin' the fuck outta me. Sure it's annoyin' them, too."

"Help!"

Stone leaned down and growled, "Shut the fuck up."

"Help! Someone! Anyone!"

Stone was done with this bullshit. He needed to deliver his message and get the fuck out of there.

Peeling Gentry's hand off his jeans, Stone twisted the man's fingers until they bent in a direction they shouldn't.

"What the fuck!" Gentry's scream echoed through the woods.

Christ, his fingers itched to slice that fucker's throat to shut him the fuck up.

The asshole moaned as he clutched his mangled hand to his chest. "You're going to pay for this."

"Don't even think about callin' the pigs 'bout this. Promise you, you do, a whole fuckin' army's gonna hunt your ass down." Another promise he intended to keep. "We know your name. Where you work. Who your family is. Know where you live now, too. You fuck with Taryn or her son, that'll be the last thing you do. Today was child's play. You hear me?" Stone roared in his face.

"Fuck you," Gentry groaned. "Fuck you!"

Stone popped him in the mouth, then stared at the man writhing in pain on the ground. "I'll be the one teachin' your son how to kick a soccer ball since it won't be you. Lemme show you my skills." With that he hauled off and kicked Gentry in the ribs, hearing a satisfying crack.

Still not good enough.

Gentry, now curled in a ball on his side, exposed Stone's next target. This time he aimed for the man's kidney.

Oh yeah, that would leave a mark.

But Stone still wasn't satisfied that the man had learned his lesson, so he delivered one last blow.

A boot to the temple put Taryn's ex into a temporary time-out.

Stone - 2. Vic the Dick - 0.

For a final parting gift, he unzipped his jeans, yanked out his dick, and pissed on Gentry's busted up face.

That was going to sting.

Too bad he didn't need to take a shit, too.

Chapter Twenty-Eight

STONE TOOK it as a good sign that a whole month later they hadn't heard a fucking peep from Vic the Dick. The warning that Taryn still didn't know about—nor did she need to—must have been effective.

Using Gentry's release as an excuse, he had convinced her to stay with him a while longer—for her and Wren's safety, of fucking course—and continue playing house with their little patchwork family.

Crazy enough, that was what it had turned into. An actual family.

One Stone found he didn't mind coming home to.

No invisible collar choked his neck like it had when Sheena told him she was pregnant. He'd hardly been able to breathe for a fucking week.

At the time, he thought the life he loved was over. It turned out he was wrong. He didn't need to take Sheena as part of the deal when it came to his daughter.

Was she a thorn in his side? Damn right she was. But he didn't need to share a home or bed with her.

Maybe it was different with Taryn because he knew this wasn't long term and this arrangement would end eventually.

Right?

Damn.

That thought shouldn't fucking bother him as much as it did. Since he wasn't in the market for an ol' lady, her *staying* should bother him, not the idea of her leaving.

At what point did his goddamn brain shift?

Was it too much pot, beer, and whiskey softening his gray matter?

Or was it because the sex between him and Taryn was fucking awesome?

He couldn't get enough of sliding between her thighs, eating her pussy, or her lips on his dick. Despite fucking her every night and every damn morning, when he wasn't with her, he had an insane urge to hunt her down and fuck her where she stood.

Once they got off, they continued going about their day.

Thank fuck she never said no and wanted it as much as he did. Even better was when she was the initiator instead of him. Sometimes if he was nearby, she'd finish filming her content for the day, then would grab his hand and they'd head up to his room at The Castle. There, they could be as loud as they wanted since the kids were at school. And hearing a woman orgasming echoing down the hallway wasn't new to his brothers.

Or could his change of mindset be because of his girl slowly coming around to the fact that Momma and Baby Bird weren't flying the coop anytime soon? His girl was finally getting a fucking clue that Taryn was there *for* her; more caring and concerned about raising her right than Sunny's biological mother.

Fuckin' Sheena.

Sticking his dick in her was the biggest mistake in his life. Next to letting Taryn convince him not to kill Gentry.

But maybe he was wrong and Taryn would never have to deal with her abusive ex again.

For fuck's sake.

That motherfucker better not pop up once they all dropped their guard.

It was the potential of Gentry lying in wait for the perfect time to strike that had Taryn staying put. Because he doubted the woman would've agreed to stay under his roof simply because Stone wanted her to.

While it normally took his bristly daughter a while to warm up to strangers, Stone was floored the other night when he poked his head into her bedroom and the kids were talking to each other. An actual civilized *conversation.*

It blew his mind that not only was Sunny actively listening, she was responding to the six-year-old's constant chatter. And it wasn't to tell the boy to shut the hell up.

Yeah, he was proud of his girl for turning a corner. He only hoped she continued on that path.

Taryn had been a fucking saint when it came to dealing with his hostile child. She instinctively knew when to give Sunny space and only ever had kind words for his girl, no matter what Sunny spewed at her in return.

Yeah, her having the patience of a fucking saint was paying off.

Good thing Taryn had more than him, despite Sunny being his nut nugget.

Since it was late, Stone finished working his way up the stairs as quietly as possible.

He had a collection job all the fucking way down in Carlisle tonight. While he hadn't been excited about having to travel that far, that loan shark was a regular customer and gave them a hell of a nice percentage so it had been worth the long ride.

He glanced at his knuckles. And a little bit of pain.

After scrubbing away the blood, he found that they weren't busted up too badly. Most of the blood hadn't been his, but the dumb fuck's who had borrowed a hundred grand from a seedy loan shark, then expected leniency when he wasn't paying it back.

Tonight's "job" had received the memo Stone delivered loud and fucking clear. After a little convincing, he promised to pay it back, along with the interest, by the end of the month. If not, Stone would be giving him another visit. If a stronger statement was needed, he'd also bring one of his brothers along next time.

Stone liked to share the fun.

When he reached the second floor landing, he glanced toward Sunny's room. The door was open a few inches and from what he could see, the room was pitch dark.

The kids were most likely crashed.

Taryn tried to stay up and wait for him if he had a late job, but if she was asleep, he had plenty of time-tested techniques to wake her. His dick got harder with each stride he took toward his bedroom, knowing Taryn was behind his closed door.

Preferably naked.

Better yet, with her pussy dripping wet from playing with herself.

He grinned at his fantasy, adjusted his hard-on, then slipped silently through the door.

Damn. She might not be naked but she wore the next best thing. One of his T-shirts. She looked damn good in it, too, especially with it being from a local Harley dealership.

She might still not be a full-blown biker bitch yet, but she was slowly integrating into the MC lifestyle.

With her lips curved upward, she glanced up from whatever she was reading on her tablet.

"You watchin' porn?" he asked, like he always did when he caught her reading.

Her husky chuckle made his dick kick in his jeans. "I'm reading a romance novel."

"One with some those hot-as-fuck sex scenes?"

Sometimes she would get all worked up when reading and tackle him. He was glad she stuck to reading those types of books since he doubted he'd get the same reaction if she began reading thrillers.

She wiggled her eyebrows. "They're not bad."

That meant they were damn good. "Make you wet?"

"Hearing you coming up the steps did that for me."

Fuck.

As soon as he closed in on where she was sitting up against the headboard, she grabbed his hand and yanked on it. But before he could join her in bed, she froze and inspected his slightly busted knuckles.

"Holy shit! What happened to your hand?" She glanced up at his face, suspicion clear in her narrowed eyes.

He wouldn't lie to her but he also wouldn't tell her the truth.

Stone slipped his hand from hers and went over to his dresser. "Told you before, don't ask questions you don't wanna know the answers to. Had a job to do and that's all you gotta know."

"But—"

"Those fuckin' jobs pay for the roof over our heads, the food in our kids' guts, the gas to take them where they need to go."

"A legit job would do the same."

He shot her an annoyed look over his shoulder.

She sighed.

"Gotta do this dance again, Taryn? This is my fuckin' life. You might not like it but gotta accept it if you're gonna live in my world. Ain't changin' for anyone."

"Even for Sunny?"

"Everythin' I fuckin' do ends up benefittin' her." His kid wanted for nothing. If Sunny needed something, he got it for her. Being a part of the Kings made that happen.

He unhooked the chain from his wallet, slipped it from his back pocket, and set it on top of his dresser.

Behind him, he heard Taryn put her tablet aside and the bed shift. Seconds later, she hugged her arms tightly around his waist and pressed a kiss to his back. "Not if you lose your freedom."

He finished sliding his belt out of the loops, set that on the dresser too, and turned within her arms. He dropped his head and captured her gaze. "Would you be upset if I did?"

"Of course, I would."

"'Cause you'd be stuck with the kids?"

"I can handle the kids. Especially now that Sunny is warming up to both me and Wren. But that's not why."

"Then what would it be?" When her teeth clamped down on her bottom lip and her eyes flicked to the side, one side of his mouth pulled up. Just what he thought. "You'd miss me."

Her blue eyes flicked back to him. "Okay, I'll admit it. I would miss you."

His grin expanded into a smile. "Like hearin' that."

"I don't want to miss you."

"I like fuckin' you a lot, too."

"This has nothing to do with—" She pulled in a breath and blinked.

"What's it gotta do with?" Stone already knew the answer, even if she didn't want to say it.

He knew because he might be experiencing the same shit. Only, he tried not to think about it because he didn't go into this agreement with her in an attempt to change his life.

And, for fuck's sake, because of her, it *was* slowly changing.

The change wasn't a bad thing, it was just fucking unexpected.

If he claimed Taryn at the table as his ol' lady, he'd be stuck with the same pussy for the rest of his life. Could he live with being tied down? Or would he get so damn restless that he'd start searching for pussy elsewhere?

A couple of the Kings' ol' ladies were raised in the club. They didn't give a shit where their ol' man stuck his dick as long as he wrapped it tight, he came home at night, she maintained her position in the club, and he provided enough scratch for their family.

Taryn wouldn't be one of those. To her, that shit wouldn't be normal. She'd leave his ass the same way she left Gentry's.

If he fucked around, he'd "find out" the hard way.

No matter what, he wasn't rushing to hand her a "property of" cut. *Hell*, he wasn't sure if she'd even accept it.

He'd only known her a couple of months. That wasn't long enough to make a life-changing decision, despite the fact he liked her in his house, liked her in his bed, loved fucking her, liked her working in The Castle's kitchen where he could keep tabs on her, and she was great with his kid.

Damn.

That was too many positives to deny. He tried to think of any negatives.

The only one he could come up with immediately was the fact that if they ended up permanently together, he'd either have to buy another house or spend a fortune adding an addition onto his current one.

The reality was, they couldn't keep letting Wren and Sunny share a room. It wasn't fair to Sunny. As a girl child, she needed her privacy. And as a boy child who would soon be dealing with uncontrollable hormones, Baby Bird needed his, too. Maybe not now, but soon.

For Stone, jacking off as a teen had become a professional sport. If he only had a fucking dime for every time he pulled one off, he'd be a fucking millionaire.

But right now, sharing a room with Taryn's boy was a good lesson for Sunny when it came to dealing with shit she didn't like. She had to learn that she wasn't always going to get her way.

"It has to do with this." Taryn cupped the back of his head, rose up on her bare toes, and planted her lips on his.

Fuck yeah.

But he was pretty damn sure that sex wasn't the only reason why she would miss him.

When her tongue swept through his mouth, he held back to see how this would play out.

Pretty fucking well.

He loved a woman who took the initiative.

He loved a woman who didn't hide her body or her flaws. Taryn owned that shit.

He loved a woman...

His brain glitched.

Fuck.

No fucking way. That couldn't be right. Since when did he become some stupid cuck simping over some woman because she gave him a taste of her pussy?

But the woman kissing him and making his dick ache wasn't just "some woman." She was Taryn.

He knew damn well the only agenda she had when originally agreeing to their arrangement was wanting to keep Wren safe and out of her asshole ex's hands.

She certainly didn't do it to trap him.

Goddamn it.

She'd burrowed her way into his soul without even fucking trying.

And his stupid ass let it happen.

She was a woman who liked to fuck, cooked the best fucking meals, and could help raise Sunny to become a decent human being.

He couldn't ask for more than that. Especially since he loved to fuck, loved to eat her meals, and he wasn't sure he could raise Sunny to become a decent human.

He mentally shook that shit out of his head.

Now what?

Easy. Fuck her, go to bed, and worry about that shit tomorrow. Maybe because he had just burned a fatty right before coming in the house, he wasn't in the right state of mind.

That had to be it.

As she continued to control the kiss, he pushed the T-shirt up, snagged one of her nipples between his fingers, and rolled it. Her roaming tongue paused and her groan filled his mouth.

That groan needed to be in his ear, that tongue on his dick.

As soon as he twisted the other nipple, she ground against his hard-on.

Wedging her hand between them, she hurried to yank open the button on his jeans and slide down his zipper. As soon as she did, she dug her hand into his boxer briefs and grabbed the throbbing, solid length of him. Her thumb swirled a drop of precum around the head.

When she began jacking his dick, she was stepping in dangerous territory.

He stepped back, freeing himself from any impending disaster. "T-shirt off."

Her cheeks were flushed and heat filled her eyes as she grabbed the hem of his Harley tee and slowly lifted it over her head.

She learned a few weeks ago to not bother wearing panties to bed unless she wanted to have to replace them. He had zero fucking patience when he wanted to dive face first into her cunt.

"Pinch your nipples."

The color in her cheeks deepened as she did what he ordered. While he watched her twist her own nipples, he yanked his own T-shirt over his head and tossed it on top of his belt. He shoved his jeans and boxer briefs down next and easily stepped out of them since he had left his boots, socks, and cut downstairs.

As soon as he was naked, she fisted his dick again and began to pump away.

Grabbing her hips, he pulled her against him. He dragged his nose up her throat, then used his tongue on the way back down as she continued to jack him off. With a groan, he thrusted into her soft, warm palm.

They needed to move this along.

She must have thought the same thing, because without releasing him, she sank to her knees and she pulled him deep into her hot, wet mouth.

Holy fuck.

His eyes slid shut and his hips jerked in time with her

movement. When her teeth lightly scraped over the crown, he moved to stop her.

He was hanging by a fucking thread. Sometimes he let her finish him off, then took his time eating her out until he was hard again. While she was a fucking awesome cook, his favorite meal was between her thighs, but not tonight.

Tonight he didn't have the patience to wait to be inside her. He'd have to make it up to her tomorrow.

"Babe," he pushed out from between clenched teeth and grabbed her elbows to lift her to her feet. Seeing her lips shiny made his already aching dick flex. "Get on the bed."

When she turned, he slapped her ass hard enough that she jerked forward and barely smothered her squeal.

He took over pumping his own dick. "Hurry up, woman. My patience is gone."

"So is mine," she answered as she climbed on the bed. "You took too long to come home."

Home. That single word coming from her mouth made his heart swell and fill his chest.

Yeah, his home was now hers. She belonged here.

Tomorrow. Think about this fuckin' shit tomorrow when your brain ain't down in your dick.

Chapter Twenty-Nine

With Taryn's hands planted on his chest, she slowly slid up and down his hard-as-fuck dick. Her slick cunt swallowed it whole, then slowly revealed its length. Over and fucking over again.

When she began to take her sweet fucking time rocking and rolling her hips, it just about drove him out of his goddamn mind. On the other hand, if she rode him like a wild woman, he'd be in deep shit.

When he fingered her clit, she ground her pussy against him, driving him even deeper.

It was like Taryn was trying to sabotage him with how she moved, how soaked she was. Dripping down his length and onto his balls. Tempting him to blow his load before he was ready.

Fuck that. It was too soon.

He watched her tits bounce a few times before raising his gaze to see her head thrown back, her mouth gaping open and rapid puffs of breaths coming from her like an old steam engine.

For fuck's sake, seeing her like that almost backfired on him.

With his teeth gritted, he took a long, deep breath of his own and thought of...

Puppies.

Goldfish.

The fact his sled needed a good wash and shine.

The time he slammed some motherfucker's head into a cement block wall and watched him slowly slide to the ground, leaving a trail of blood behind.

Yeah, that did the trick to push him away from that edge.

Digging his fingers into her hips, he prepared to take over soon. He needed to quickly bring this across the finish line before he went past the point of no return.

With a twist, he rolled until she was under him and he was nestled between her soft, slick thighs.

"*Fuuuuuuuuuck,*" he groaned as he slid balls deep.

Her pussy was a warm, wet glove, pulsing around his hard-on.

He didn't know if she had ever been this responsive with any other men she'd been with before him, but he preferred to think she hadn't. That the two of them had some special sexual chemistry that made it so damn good.

He didn't care why it was, it just was.

Mine.

What the fuck? He pushed that random thought out of his brain and continued to thrust.

She's fuckin' mine.

A sharp pain shot through his chest. What the fuck was wrong with him? Was he having a damn heart attack? Was he going to die the way he always hoped, in the middle of fucking?

Damn, he wasn't ready for that yet. He had to finish

raising Sunny first before dropping dead from doing his favorite activity.

No other man better try touchin' her.

Why the fuck was his brain glitching? Not once had he ever had those kinds of thoughts with any other woman.

Only Taryn.

Not lettin' her go.

His brain had to be fucking broken.

Yeah, that had to be it. Too much pot or something.

Or...

Maybe he needed to stop ignoring the voice in his head and listen to it.

Damn it.

He dropped his mouth to her ear. "Babe..."

Her blue eyes flashed opened and he swore she could see straight into his soul and could hear his crazy thoughts.

Her soft smile was the last nail in his coffin.

His old life was about to be dead and buried. Worse, he was the one holding the damn shovel.

Did he keep digging, or did he break the shovel in half and save himself?

He tried to picture a day without Taryn in it.

It was fucking impossible. Worse, he didn't want to.

He didn't want to wake up in the mornings to an empty bed. He didn't want to go to bed at night without her next to him.

For fuck's sake.

The voice in his head was right.

Now what?

He pushed out a breath.

Now, he needed to convince her to stay.

. . .

His murmured *"Babe..."* had her opening her eyes—and smiling because she loved when he called her that—only to notice his face a bit paler than normal.

Had he seen a ghost? Did his life flash before his eyes?

Her smile fell. "What's wrong?"

He squeezed his eyes shut and his mouth opened to answer. It suddenly snapped shut and he shook his head. "Nothin'. All good."

She wasn't sure she believed that. But now wasn't the time to have a deep conversation when something else was currently deeply buried.

After wrapping her legs more securely around his hips, she tilted up her pelvis so he could hit that perfect spot.

This man was a rare find. He knew exactly where to find both her clit *and* her G-spot. When it came to her previous partners, it was one or the other, or worse, neither. This *rough-around-the-edges* biker was more skilled than any of the polished men she'd ever been with. Stone put them all to shame.

Was it fate he'd been in that parking lot a year and a half ago?

Was it fate she ended up living under his roof?

Was all of this meant to be?

No. Impossible. To think that was ludicrous.

Fate was a fickle bitch. It had to be a coincidence. Nothing more.

As soon as they could be assured Vic wouldn't rear his ugly head again, they'd go their separate ways. She'd go back to working as a personal chef, building her online presence and, of course, raising Wren.

He'd go back to his brothers and the club's sweet butts.

But who would help with Sunny?

The girl needed a responsible woman to look up to, not

sweet butts. Even a woman who tended to make mistakes like Taryn.

However, it wasn't only Sunny she worried about leaving behind.

It was Stone.

Her heart ached unbearably whenever she even considered moving on. That was why when he expressed concern about Vic's release, she'd decided to stay. She figured with her ex's volatile temper, if he planned on striking out at her, he would do it right away. Not wait.

Plus, it would give her more time to figure out how she really felt about Stone. And whether he felt the same.

She also needed to keep Wren in mind. His safety and well-being came above her own relationships.

The continuous roll of his hips as he surged up and into her, burying himself to the hilt with every thrust, brought her back to the bed. She'd worry about all of the other noise later. Right now, she should simply enjoy this time with Stone.

He pulled one nipple deep into his mouth, gently scissoring his teeth over the very tip. It was the perfect amount of pressure to cause her back to arch, her pussy to slam into him, and her nails to rake down his tattooed back.

He speared her harder and deeper, hitting the end of her every time.

In the past couple of months, he had learned what made her simmer, what made her boil, and what made her explode like a pressure cooker.

While they had also gotten pretty good about staying as quiet as possible during sex, sometimes it just couldn't be done.

Now was one of those times. She usually shoved her face into a pillow, but tonight she pulled his head down to hers and melded their lips together instead.

Another very hot option.

Her whimper was caught and contained by his mouth and her hips shot up as she tumbled head over heels. She swore her orgasm started all the way down in her toes and swept through her like a raging river.

She dug her nails in deeper and made sure their lips remained sealed together as a cry rose from her very center as wave after wave rushed through her.

And when her intense climax began to wane, he continued to pump through the aftershocks.

It was no surprise when his hips stuttered. She expected him to quickly follow her orgasm with his own. She was proven right when he grunted into her mouth during the next thrust and stayed buried deep.

After a final shudder rocked him, he released her mouth and continued to slowly glide in and out of her.

Her chest continued to pump as she caught her breath and her head fell back, exposing her throat. He slowly slid his nose up it, tickling her skin with that scratchy beard, then gently sank his teeth into her flesh before kissing the same spot.

She had never enjoyed sex this much before. Why did it take a bad boy biker with amazing skills to show her how it was supposed to be?

Stone rose up onto his elbows, combed her hair away from her face with his long fingers, and locked gazes with her. "Never realized I was so fuckin' bored with sex 'til you."

She blinked and her mouth gaped open at that unexpected confession. Did she misunderstand? "What?"

"Said was gettin' tired of sweet butts and randoms. Didn't realize it 'til you."

"Is that a compliment?"

"Sure ain't an insult."

Well, that was a relief. For a second, she thought she might be boring in bed and that was why Vic cheated. "Well, I thought men were clueless when it came to pleasing a woman. You proved otherwise." She wiggled her eyebrows.

With a low chuckle, he pressed a quick kiss to her lips. "Thank fuck I could help."

"You set the bar high."

"No one else should be tryin' to jump that fuckin' bar."

A ribbon of warmth weaved its way through her. "I won't be here forever. This was a temporary arrangement, right?"

He grunted but didn't deny it. Instead, he secured the condom at his root, slipped free, and rolled off the bed to dispose of it in the trash can they now kept by the bed for that purpose. They also now stocked baby wipes and towels in his room, too. She preferred the kids didn't find full condoms in the bathroom garbage and start asking questions.

Taryn wasn't ready to explain "the birds and the bees" to her six-year-old son. Of course, Sunny had learned about sex by hanging out at The Castle since she was a baby. It was unavoidable there.

Luckily, whenever Wren was hanging out in the cafeteria while she worked, the club members took it elsewhere. Stone must have said something to them.

He settled in next to her and tucked his bent arm under his head. "Now that your house is sold, you got thoughts on where you go next?"

Just as she thought, he didn't want her to stay. For him, this was strictly an arrangement. Any concern over her moving had to do with Sunny, not him.

That was no longer true for her and she'd hoped he had felt the same. Clearly, she was wrong. She was simply another woman in his bed. The only difference was that she had been a steady presence for the last couple of months.

Convenient and close.

"No, not yet. I've been too busy building my online business. You suggested I stay for a few more months and I figured it would help you out when it came to Sunny. Speaking of, have you looked for someone else to take my place when it comes to her?"

"Like you, been too busy."

The man didn't have any official employment. He occasionally was busy with a "job." He had plenty of time to start putting out feelers.

It was weird that he hadn't.

"Do you need help with that?"

"Nope."

"Well, I only have a few more months here." Staying longer would help her financially settle elsewhere. It might help her with a down payment on another home since it turned out she had zero equity from the sale of the house last month. She was just glad to have that monkey off her back.

"Stay as long as you need, babe. Know that you bein' here benefits you as well as me. Ain't kickin' your ass to the curb."

"I'm both relieved but also worried that I haven't heard from Vic at all. Not even to argue over getting Wren for visitation."

"Maybe it was never 'bout the kid in the first place and more 'bout the scratch."

Of course it was and that made her heart hurt for Wren. Her son still loved his father, despite what he'd witnessed. "My concern is he's quietly planning something with his lawyer."

"He ain't gonna get custody. Not with what he did to you."

She wished that were true. But the justice system wasn't always just. "I don't know. With the right lawyer..."

"Judge'll see it differently."

She chewed on her bottom lip as she considered his words. "I hope so."

Unfortunately, she couldn't afford another legal battle. It would wipe out the little bit of savings she had accumulated.

She didn't mind staying longer, especially now that the kids were getting along a lot better, but she was afraid she might continue down a slippery slope of wanting a different kind of arrangement with Stone.

One that didn't have anything to do with financial stability or with her safety.

It was finally her turn in line. If Stone couldn't pick the kids up from school, then Taryn paused whatever she was working on to do so since the school wasn't far from The Castle.

After putting her Honda in Park, she watched a herd of children race out the front doors and either head toward the school buses or toward a vehicle waiting in line to pick them up.

She scanned the flow of kids.

Sunny was usually impatiently waiting out at the curb when Taryn got there. Stone's daughter couldn't wait to get outside to use her cell phone while she waited. Going without her cell phone all day had to be torture.

Taryn snorted softly. If she had acted like that at ten, she'd have that phone permanently welded to her fingers by sixteen.

She still wasn't thrilled that Sunny had a cell phone at her age, but when it came down to it, it really wasn't her place to say much about it. That was between Stone and Sheena.

If she had to guess, Taryn doubted Sheena gave a shit. She was probably glad the phone kept Sunny occupied and out of her hair.

A book would do the same.

Her heart swelled as she saw Wren squeeze between two fellow students, then run to where Taryn was parked.

When he reached the Honda, he jerked open the back door, slipped his backpack from his shoulders, and flung it inside before climbing into his booster seat.

"Hey, kiddo! How was your day at school?" Taryn watched him over her shoulder to make sure he buckled up.

"It was really, really, *really* good!" he spouted loudly as he strapped himself in.

"Wow. What made it really, really, *really* good?"

"Someone came from the Hershey Zoo and brought a bunch of snakes! I got to hold one!"

Yuck. "You did? How exciting! Do you mean ZooAmerica in Hershey?" She had taken him there while at Hershey Park last summer.

"Yes. I want a snake, Mommy. And I wanna go to the zoo again."

He would not be getting a snake while they shared the same roof. "Okay, I'll take you and Sunny soon. I'm sure she'll enjoy it, too. Speaking of...where is she? She's not out here waiting like she normally is."

Wren shrugged. "Dunno."

She glanced back toward the school, ignoring the honks and nasty looks from the other parents picking up their children. Taryn didn't care. She wasn't moving until both kids were in the car.

Five minutes later with still no sign of her, Taryn texted

Sunny, asking where she was. Her heart began to pound when she didn't get an immediate answer.

But that also didn't surprise Taryn. While Stone's daughter was slowly softening around the edges when it came to her and Wren, she still had plenty of bristly moments.

Today could be one of them. Or it could simply be that her battery died.

With a sigh, she reluctantly moved out of the pickup line and parked where she could still see the school's doors.

After another five minutes and no sign of her, the fine hairs on the back of Taryn's neck began to stand.

Something had to be wrong.

Either that or Stone forgot to tell her that his daughter was being picked up by someone else for whatever reason.

Or she could be stuck in detention. At ten. Because why not follow in her father's footsteps and get started early with being detained for acting out?

She rolled her eyes at her own ridiculous doom and gloom.

She should get out, head into the school, and speak to the staff. Someone had to know where she was.

But before she went in there looking like a clueless idiot, she texted Stone. Maybe Sunny had contacted her father and he forgot to pass on the info to Taryn.

Do you know where Sunny is?

School, came his answer. Apparently, he didn't have a clue either.

"Shit," she whispered and quickly texted back: *I'm at the school. She never came out.*

She glanced in the rearview mirror to see Wren's nose already tucked in a comic book. "Did you see Sunny at all today? In the hallways? At lunch?"

He didn't even bother to look up. "Last time I saw her was when Stone dropped us off."

Her heart began thumping in her throat and her stomach churned.

Sunny always came out on time, even if Taryn was picking her up, because she hated school. She didn't want to spend more time there than she had to.

Ghost-like fingers walked down her spine.

She didn't like this. Something was off.

Would someone from the Kings pick her up without telling her father?

Before she rushed into the school and looked like a paranoid fool, she called Stone.

The first thing in her ear was, "You find her?"

"No. I'm still waiting out in front of the school. Wren said he hasn't seen her since you dropped them off this morning."

"Fuck," he grumbled. "No idea what got up her ass to pull this shit."

"Can you try calling her? She might answer for you. Maybe today was a hate Taryn day."

"Already tried. Only got her voicemail. Left her a message to call me ASAP. Told her if she don't, her phone's gonna be confiscated again. That usually gets her to respond fast."

"Did Sheena get out?"

"Not that I'm aware of."

"Think she'd run away?"

"She only knows how to run her mouth. She ain't runnin' anywhere. Her bitchin' is all for show since she knows she got it good with me. With us."

With us.

Like Taryn was a permanent fixture in their life.

"What do you want me to do? I can go into the school and ask around."

"Yeah, do that. Lemme know if you find out anythin'. Gonna head home to check for her there. Wouldn't put it past my damn nut nugget to thumb it home."

The thought of a ten-year-old girl hitchhiking scared the crap out of Taryn. As it should. "Okay, you do the same if you find her or hear from her."

Chapter Thirty

Taryn ran up the steps looking for Stone. His Harley was parked by the house, but he wasn't downstairs.

Unfortunately, no one at the school had any damn clue where Sunny went. That discovery made the blood in her veins turn to ice.

Before she left the school, Taryn tried calling Stone to report in but he didn't answer. So she sent him a quick text telling him she was headed home with Wren and asked if he could send a prospect to sit at the school in case she showed up.

Taryn had a weird feeling that Sheena got out of prison early and took her daughter back. The same scenario as what she feared would happen with Vic and Wren. It was why they never let the kids take the bus to or from school.

She had told Wren to finish reading his comic book in the living room while she searched for Stone.

When she reached the upstairs landing, she called out Stone's name.

She found his bedroom empty, but before heading back

downstairs to check the garage next, she noticed Sunny's door was slightly ajar but the room was completely dark. Maybe she had gotten home somehow and was taking a nap.

She pushed the door open wider and stepped inside.

She didn't find Sunny, but almost jumped out of her skin when she spotted a shadowy figure sitting on the bottom bunk.

Holy shit.

Stone had something clutched within his fingers. As soon as her eyes adjusted to the dark, she saw what it was...

A cell phone.

"Stone, why didn't you answer—"

"Get out," he growled.

What? What was going on? "Did you—"

"Get the fuck out!" he roared, causing her to wince at both the volume and angry tone. "Don't make me put my hands on you and force you the fuck out."

Her heart got jammed in her throat and every nerve ending prickled.

While the man could be dangerous, she was damn sure he would never hurt her. Unlike Vic. *Good lord*, she hoped she wasn't wrong. "Stone..."

When he surged to his feet, she stumbled backward a step. She quickly recovered and forced herself to hold her ground. Why was he lashing out at her?

"What fuckin' part of get the fuck out didn't you hear? Are you goddamn deaf?"

She was so confused about what was going on and, screw him, she wasn't leaving the room until she knew what that was. If he was angry at her, she deserved to know why. "I only want to know what's going on. If you haven't found Sunny, I want to help."

"Coulda helped by not interferrin' with what I wanted to

do in the first fuckin' place, Taryn. Now that motherfucker has Sunny."

Holy shit. What?

"If one fuckin' hair on my baby girl is out of place..." Stone shook his head. "Don't fuckin' matter. He's gonna get the endin' he deserves, no matter fuckin' what."

She stared at him as that information sank into her brain. Then panic began to rise. She had to find her breath to ask, "Why would Vic take Sunny?"

How would Vic know about Sunny in the first place? And how did he tie Sunny to Taryn and Wren? Did he have someone spying on her, like a private investigator? And if so, why would he take Sunny instead of Wren?

None of this made any sense.

"I never would've thought he'd take Sunny instead. How would he know she even existed?"

"The motherfucker's fuckin' unhinged. He's gonna use any tool he fuckin' can to get to you." His jaw shifted. "Or get back at me."

Her already ice-cold blood turned frigid and her pulse began to pound in her ears. "Get back at you for what?" For beating the crap out of him over a year and a half ago?

He shook his head and didn't answer. Even in the dark room she could see his jaw popping. And if she looked hard enough she was sure he was white-knuckling that cell phone.

"Get back at you for what, Stone? How would Vic know about Sunny? How did he even tie the two of us together?" She wanted answers. And if Vic really had Sunny, they were wasting time hashing this out.

She went over to the drawn curtains and threw them open. He was hiding something and she needed to see his face clearly.

"*You* wanted me to spare him so gave him a warnin',

instead," Stone finally answered, his tone losing some of that grumble.

"What do you mean? When?" Why was this the first she was hearing about this?

He pulled in a deep breath and told her about waiting for Vic out in front of SCI Dallas.

"Oh my God," she breathed when he was done with his story. She was damn sure he omitted some details, if not most, but she heard enough to know that what Stone did to Vic had poked the nasty bear.

And the bear snapped back.

"Never shoulda left the motherfucker breathin'. Knew it was a mistake. And was proven right."

"You're blaming what you did to him on me?"

"You talked me outta doin' what needed to be done. Shoulda just done it and not told you, then we wouldn't be in this goddamn mess."

"Do you have proof he has her?" Maybe this was all a big misunderstanding and all this drama and anger was for nothing.

She could only hope.

"You wanna know how?" he growled, stepping up to her and shoving the cell phone in her face.

The picture on the screen caused her heart to skip a beat and a gasp to slip from her.

Duct tape was wrapped tightly around Sunny's ankles, securing them to the legs of the chair and her wrists were taped to the chair's arms. More silver tape covered her mouth. Her cheeks were streaked with tears, her nose and eyes red from crying.

No wonder Stone was pissed. That image would be burned in Taryn's memory for a long time, if not forever.

She hoped it was Photoshopped but deep down she knew

it wasn't. Taryn found out the hard way that Vic was a vindictive asshole.

If Stone "taught him a lesson," her ex would want to return it two-fold.

Kidnapping a child would cut any decent parent down at the knees. However, kidnapping the child of your enemy was a deadly mistake.

Stone wouldn't leave one stone unturned to find his daughter. And when he did find her...

Taryn wouldn't tell Stone to spare his life again.

Her ex would reap what he sowed.

She prayed that Sunny was found unharmed. The girl would be traumatized, but they could deal with that.

Stone began to pace the short length of the room like a caged tiger.

Taryn could hardly hear her own questions over her pounding heart. "Did he give you a location? Is he demanding anything in exchange for her?"

He paused, stabbed at his phone, then turned it again to show her. The text simply read: *My boy for your girl.*

Taryn slapped a hand over her mouth. Her temples throbbed and she met Stone's eyes. Would he sacrifice her son for his daughter?

Stone shook his head and continued to wear a path in the floor. "He ain't gettin' Baby Bird. No fuckin' way. My job's to protect him. Failed my girl, ain't failin' him."

Taryn closed her eyes in relief for a second, but it was short lived. Vic still had Sunny. She had no idea what lengths her ex would go to get back at her. To get back at Stone. "Did he give you an address for the exchange? Maybe I can go and try to convince him—"

He spun on her and roared, "The fuck you will!" He closed his eyes and pulled in a breath. When he opened them again, he said in a more reasonable tone, "Still waitin' for the fucker to text me where to meet, but you're not fuckin' gonna be anywhere near there. This time we're gonna handle this shit the right way. The only heart that's gonna be bleedin' this time is gonna be his when I rip it out of his fuckin' chest."

Was he calling her a bleeding heart because she asked him to spare Vic's life? Wait...

We're?

As if on cue, she heard the loud rumble of Harleys. She went back over to the window to glance outside. *Of course.* That was why Stone wasn't out there searching. He was waiting for his army of bikers to show up. She estimated that almost every member of the Kings filled his driveway. She turned. "The calvary has arrived."

With a shake of his head, he left the room.

Taryn chewed on her bottom lip and her heart thumped as heavily as his boots rushing down the steps.

This was a disaster. She had no idea how to stop it. Or even if she wanted to.

Vic would end up dead.

Stone might end up in prison.

Sunny could end up without either parent.

Wren would be devastated about losing his father.

All because of her.

No.

Vic started down this careening path by going off the deep end and taking his anger about their custody fight out on her. *He* was the reason.

What he did to Taryn was wrong.

Kidnapping Stone's daughter and using her as a pawn was even worse.

It was unforgivable.

Stone was right.

And she'd been wrong to simply try to do the right thing.

That threat needed to be removed from their lives once and for all.

✦

STONE GLANCED at the dumb motherfucker's most recent text.

Did Gentry really think Stone would show up with only Wren? Exactly what he was demanding?

The fucking insane part was Gentry thought he was in a position to make demands. He was going to quickly find out he wasn't.

The Kings were in charge.

Taryn's ex would soon learn that nobody fucked with the Kings.

He didn't learn the first time in the Shoppes at Susquehanna's parking lot.

He didn't learn the second time from Stone's face-to-face warning.

The third time would be the last time.

Gentry's time had run out. No more lessons, no more warnings.

Making sure he stayed out of view, Stone sent a text to his daughter's phone: *Here w/ ur kid. Send out my girl & I'll send him in.*

Stone doubted the asshole would fall for that trap, but it would give his brothers enough time for a sneak attack.

The place Asshole wanted to meet was nowhere near other humans. Great for Stone, stupid on Gentry's part.

Of course, Stone assumed Sunny's kidnapper was alone.

Gentry assumed that Stone was alone, too, since that was one of his demands.

While Taryn's ex was a lone soldier, he would soon find out that Stone had an army at his back. They only needed to get to Sunny before Gentry figured that out and hurt her.

Half of his brothers stayed nearby but out of sight. The other half quietly moved around to the back of the abandoned hunting cabin.

It wouldn't be hard to get in since all the windows were broken out and the doors hung crookedly on their hinges.

The abandoned cabin wasn't secure at all.

Again, a benefit for Stone and his brothers, but not for Gentry.

Stand where I can see you, came the next text. *You better have my son.*

Stone had his son all right, just not with him. Gentry was never getting Baby Bird back. In fact, Stone would make sure he never saw his son again.

Bones worked his way closer and mumbled under his breath, "Gonna go pound on the door. While that fucker's distracted, Ogre and the rest are gonna rush in from the rear. Gonna do a little shock and fuckin' awe maneuver. Catch the fucker off guard."

"Yeah."

"Ogre told us to send two prospects in the front door to shield us, just in case the motherfucker's packin'."

"Good idea."

"Ogre's pretty fuckin' smart sometimes. Other times, not so much."

Stone wasn't in the fucking mood to joke. He'd laugh about that shit later. Right now he needed to concentrate on his daughter and the *soon-to-be-dead* asshole.

Chapter Thirty-One

Stone could see nothing but his daughter restrained in that fucking chair. Nothing else.

"Cut her loose!" he roared. "Now!"

While his brothers rushed to free his baby girl, he turned to find Ogre standing over Gentry. The man was on his knees with one side of his face already swelling and blood trickling out of his right ear.

Goddamn shame. But that was only a taste of the payback he'd be getting.

Stone growled. He wanted to cut off the motherfucker's dick and stuff it in his mouth, then rip his head off with his bare hands and shit down his throat.

He wanted to shove a pike up the man's asshole and post him out in front of The Castle.

A clear statement that would tell everyone: *Nobody fucks with the Kings.*

No-fucking-body.

He waited until Ransom finished taping Gentry's wrists and ankles together and slapping another long piece over the man's mouth. Gentry's wide eyes tracked Stone as he took his time approaching. He hoped his asshole was puckering tighter with each step closer he took.

When he got to where Gentry was forced to kneel, he grabbed the fucker's neck and squeezed, holding back only enough pressure to avoid crushing the fucker's windpipe. Gentry didn't deserve a death that was quick or easy.

Fuck no. The bastard needed to suffer.

Stone leaned down and got in his face. "Gonna deal with you shortly. First, gonna check on my girl."

"Dad!"

He turned to see Sunny's arms now free and her pinning both across her stomach. Grim quickly hacked away at the tape on one ankle while Patch worked on the other.

Despite that, his girl's red-rimmed eyes remained locked on him. And for every tear that spilled over, it ratcheted up his anger another level.

When she was finally free, another "Dad!" came out on a sob and Stone rushed over to pull her out of the chair and into his arms.

"Jesus fuckin' Christ." His nostrils flared in an attempt not to spin out of control.

Stone took a moment to hold her away from him, just far enough to quickly assess her visually. No blood. No bruises. No torn clothing.

Squeezing her tightly again, he rested his cheek against the top of her hair, taking a second to breathe.

Taking a second to be thankful she hadn't been violated or seriously injured.

Thank fuckin' fuck.

It didn't matter that she wasn't physically hurt, the rat bastard touched what was Stone's.

The fuck if he would touch anything again after today.

"You're okay," he assured her when she wrapped her arms around his waist and smashed her damp face between the flaps of his cut and against his gut. He stroked her hair, pushing it out of her face. "Gonna take you home, yeah?"

She hiccup-sobbed but nodded.

Her phone appeared in front of his face. He took it from Bones and tucked it into his cut. He didn't want to give it back to Sunny until he scrubbed the fucking thing clean of the texts going back and forth between him and Gentry.

He glanced over at Ogre, still standing over Gentry. "Take him to the garage. Takin' Sunny home, then gonna meet you there."

The sergeant at arms gave him a chin lift and his lips tilted upward.

That particular smirk would make most men shit their pants.

But it wasn't Ogre the bound asshole had to worry about.

⚜

STONE REALLY DIDN'T WANT to let his daughter out of his sight, but he needed to get to the garage. He had three important roles to step into.

Judge, jury, and executioner.

If he stayed with her and let his brothers handle it, he wouldn't be any good to Sunny, anyway. He'd be distracted and restless until he knew Gentry had taken his last goddamn breath.

As soon as he pulled into the driveway, the rear screen door was shoved open so hard it slammed against the house's siding. Taryn raced down the deck steps, through the gate, and over to his sled.

Questions filled her face and concern was visible in her

eyes, but he didn't have time to explain shit. He needed to get shit done so he could return as quickly as possible to help Sunny deal with the aftermath of her goddamn kidnapping.

He helped his kid off his Harley. "You good?"

"Dad, who was he and why did he do that?"

It killed him that her voice still trembled. Hearing that along with seeing her face ravaged from all the crying raised his rage to epic fucking levels. He forced himself to swallow it back down. He'd save it for Vic the Dick. "Gonna talk about it later, yeah? Go with Taryn for now. She's gonna take care of you 'til I get back."

"I don't want you to go!" she cried out, snapping his black fucking heart in two.

"I know, baby girl." When he held out his hand to her, she took it and he pulled her closer, pressing a kiss to her forehead while murmuring. "Promise to be back soon."

He lifted his gaze over her head to Taryn, waiting just a few feet away, wringing her hands and looking anxious. After he gave her a stiff chin lift, she rushed over, gathered Sunny in her arms and held her tight while rocking her back and forth. "I've got you, baby." He didn't miss that her eyes held a sheen and her voice was thick when she assured him, "I have her."

He gave her a single nod. "Gotta go take care of fuckin' business." He reached over and tucked his finger beneath Sunny's trembling chin and lifted it. "Be back soon. You listen to Taryn, you hear?"

Sunny, her red eyes and nose swollen and running, nodded. Her voice cracked when she said, "Okay, Dad."

Thank fuck she wasn't being her normal obstinate self today. She didn't even pull away from Taryn. Instead, she snuggled closer.

Damn.

The anger he had directed at Taryn earlier was now focused on the man waiting for him at the chop shop.

Seconds later, he was racing off. His fingers itched as he twisted the throttle. His fury rose even higher with every rotation of his sled's wheels.

One thing was on his mind...

The asshole who beat the fuck out of Taryn.

The asshole who gave his own son nightmares by beating his son's mother in front of him.

The asshole who fucking *dared* to touch Stone's daughter.

He arrived at the Kings' garage hidden in the woods in record time. No surprise that Ogre's sled with an empty side car was parked out front next to several other bikes.

As soon as he cut his sled's engine, he was off it and heading inside.

What he saw waiting for him made him proud of his brothers. They kept the fucker alive just for him. He wanted the opportunity to have a few words with Asshole before the man closed his eyes for the very last time.

In one of the garage bays, his daughter's kidnapper hung suspended by his arms, using the chain from a ceiling-mounted engine hoist.

Wasn't that a beautiful fucking sight?

He gave a chin lift to Ransom and one to Ogre as he strode toward where Gentry hung like a side of spoiled beef. Thor sat by the sergeant at arms' side, his eyes not shifting once from their guest of honor.

They might not have knocked the fucker out, but they certainly knocked him around.

In fact, the man was hard to recognize. His pants were torn in several places, exposing ugly-looking canine bites.

Good boy, Thor.

When Stone stopped in front of Gentry, he lifted one corner of the duct tape covering the motherfucker's mouth and held it in one hand while spinning the man with the other.

"Fuck!" Gentry yelled when the tape was ripped free.

"You think that hurts? Just wait."

Once Stone had him spun completely around to face him again, Gentry snarled, "You took my kid so I took yours. That's only fair, right?"

Every muscle on Stone locked solid. "Ain't no fair when it comes to love and war."

"Damn right! You told me to stay away from my wife and kid. Your stupid ass never mentioned your own."

For fuck's sake.

One side of Stone's upper lip pulled up as he leaned in closer to make sure Gentry heard every word he uttered next. "Just wanna let you know, I fuck your ex at least twice a day. Fuck her like she's never been fucked before. She said you sucked in bed. Bet you couldn't make her squirt or even come, you selfish motherfucker. You should also know that I plan on raisin' your kid like he's my own." He emphasized his words by digging his finger into one of the punctures in his thigh.

Gentry's body jerked like a fish caught on a hook. Between gritted teeth he said, "You can have the bitch and that money-sucking leech."

That money-sucking leech? That was what he was calling his own damn son?

What a motherfucker.

Death would be too good for this asshole. "Don't worry, about to guarantee that you ain't ever goin' near that bitch and your money-sucking leech again. Gonna help you achieve financial freedom." Like a goddamn infomercial.

After slipping his knife free from the sheath on his hip,

Stone kept his eyes on the blade as he slowly scraped dirt out from under his nails. "Three to zero, motherfucker."

"Speak English, you uneducated animal."

A smile slowly spread across Stone's face. "Means you got your ass beaten three times versus my big fat fuckin' goose egg. Guess you only like beatin' women, you cocksuckin' coward." He drove a finger into one of the other dog bites and wiggled it around.

Gentry grimaced. "Fuck you."

"Nah. I'm about to fuck you. Just not with my dick."

After taking about fifteen strides away, Stone spun on his boot heel to face the woman beater.

He pursed his lips as he considered his target. So many good bullseyes.

With a flick of his wrist, the knife left his hand and appeared in Gentry's right shoulder.

"Jesus fucking Christ! This is barbaric! Let me go or you'll regret it!"

"Barbaric? Like kidnapping a child? Like abusin' the mother of your child. I mean, *money-suckin' leech?*" Stone went over and yanked out the knife. Of course, that was after wiggling it a little to loosen it from the bone. "Damn. Looks like I need to practice my aim some more. I really fuckin' suck at this." As he headed back to the spot where he'd previously stood, he ordered Shit Stain, "Tape his mouth shut. Don't wanna hear any more of this whiny fuckin' bitch. Nothin' he says is gonna change his fate."

The prospect quickly disappeared from his peripheral view and when Stone turned to face Gentry again, Shit Stain had already returned with a roll of duct tape.

"No! Don't—"

Shit Stain tore off a long piece and slammed it over Gentry's mouth.

Finally. Blessed fuckin' silence.

The wide, silver tape over his mouth began to puff in and out rapidly. Maybe someone was having a panic attack.

Damn shame.

"Stay there," he told Shit Stain. He addressed the prospects standing off to the side. "All of you, stand by Shit for Brains. You're gonna retrieve my knife so I don't gotta tire myself out by walkin' back and forth."

Ogre snorted and Ransom chuckled.

Nut Sack appeared worried as he moved into place. "Just don't miss and hit us."

"Why you think I'm usin' prospects 'stead of my brothers? If I miss, I fuckin' miss." Stone shrugged. "Now, do what you're fuckin' told 'less you wanna give up your fuckin' cut."

They fell into line with wide eyes, clenched hands, and tense muscles. Little did those pussies know that Stone had damn good aim. Maybe he should pretend he sucked and land one directly between Nut Sack's eyes.

It would be no loss since they had plenty more potential recruits wanting to take his spot.

Throw after throw, the knife landed exactly where he aimed. Right shoulder, left shoulder, right thigh, left thigh; all easy targets. None of them fatal.

All of them painful.

The prospects kept retrieving the knife and bringing it back to Stone.

Only, he was now getting fucking bored. And extremely dissatisfied.

He needed to up his game.

It certainly wasn't by doing more knife throwing.

He ordered Squid, "Go clean my knife good. Don't wanna see a speck of this asshole's blood on it when you hand it back to me." He then snapped his fingers at Shit Stain. "Grab me one of those reciprocatin' saws."

The prospect jerked into motion, rushed over to the area where they kept the tools for chopping up stolen vehicles, and brought it over.

Instead of taking it, Stone stared at the dumbass. "What fuckin' good is it if it ain't plugged in?"

His fellow Kings' low chuckles rose around them as Shit Stain scrambled to find an extension cord.

Since Gentry was still conscious, Stone had no doubt he'd be a whiter shade of pale if his face wasn't already shades of purple and blue from the bruises gifted to him from Stone's brothers.

"Thinkin' you had enough. Gonna cut you down," Stone announced calmly, as if he was ordering a beer. Shit Stain handed him the now plugged-in saw.

Stone powered it up and watched the blade's back-and-forth motion for a few seconds before giving Gentry a huge smile and raising it above the asshole's head. But instead of putting the blade to the chain, he placed it at Gentry's wrists. Cutting through flesh and bone would be a lot easier and faster than steel.

The second Gentry realized what was happening, Stone heard a muffled shriek coming from under the duct tape.

The saw sliced through his forearms like butter. It was quick, but messy, and Stone doubted it was painless.

Damn fuckin' shame.

Gentry dropped hard to the ground while both partial limbs remained dangling from the chain above them. Reduced to a heap at Stone's feet, Taryn's ex would eventually bleed out from the stubs where his hands used to be.

Stone held out the bloody reciprocal saw and a prospect

rushed over to take it from him. He tilted his head and sucked his teeth, studying the damage.

It still wasn't enough.

Lifting his boot, he jammed the heel into Gentry's still taped mouth. The fucker would have no use for those teeth, anyway. Stone then unzipped his jeans, pulled out his dick and pissed all over the unconscious man's face.

Only, it was no longer fun now that Gentry wasn't aware of what was happening.

With an eyebrow cocked, Ogre sidled up to him and stared at the bloody heap on the floor. "Want me to finish the fucker off?"

"Fuck no. Let him continue to suffer 'til his last fuckin' breath." Gentry wouldn't be breathing long. Not at the rate the blood was pooling from his severed arms.

"Think he suffered enough?"

Stone's nostrils flared. "Fuck no. No sufferin' would be enough," he answered the sergeant at arms. "Do what you want with him. Just don't end it too quickly. Headin' home to check on my baby girl."

Chapter Thirty-Two

Stone quietly opened the door and stepped into Sunny's dark room. He was relieved to hear her steady breathing instead of sobbing.

His baby girl was wrapped up in her blanket like a burrito. That was a good sign, too, since that was how she liked to sleep.

He squatted down next to the bottom bunk and stared at his daughter as he lightly stroked her dark brown hair. If Gentry had hurt her, Stone would've burned the fucking world to the ground.

He had never wanted a kid, but now that he had one, he would die to protect her.

He closed his eyes and pulled a long breath in through his flared nostrils.

He'd failed her.

He fucking failed.

With Sheena in prison, he was all Sunny had. His girl relied on him to keep her happy, healthy, and safe.

No, he was wrong.

He considered the woman he had ignored downstairs because he only had one thing on his mind when he walked through the back door.

Sunny.

She had been his priority. But now that he saw with his own two fucking eyes his girl was in one piece, he needed to deal with the other female in the house.

He was still pissed at Taryn, but he should really be pissed at himself for letting her influence his decision about sparing Gentry.

That was *his* mistake. Not hers.

Not once in his adult fucking life had he ever let a woman tell him what to do. Not fucking once.

Why the fuck did he let her get to him?

It wasn't because he was trying to be a better person. Fuck that. It was because he was trying to make Taryn happy.

Or at least not upset her.

Or make her look at him differently. Prove to her he wasn't just a bad person, that he had good moments, too.

Though, with what he just did to her ex-husband, he might be past that point.

With one last glance at Sunny out cold—no doubt mentally and emotionally exhausted from that ordeal—he closed the door softly behind him and headed back downstairs.

Taryn sat on the couch with her arm around her son, keeping him pinned to her side. The TV volume was down low and only Baby Bird was concentrating on whatever movie was on the screen.

Taryn's eyes remained glued on him as he approached. He jerked his chin toward the back door.

She whispered something to Wren, who nodded, then

she rose from the couch and followed him outside. He didn't stop until he was far enough away that the kids wouldn't overhear the conversation.

"What happened?"

"Ask me no questions, won't tell you no lies."

She shook her head. "So basically, if I ask, you're going to lie about what happened."

"Just said I ain't, if you don't ask."

"You do know that double negatives makes a positive, right?"

He scowled. "He ain't gonna be a threat no more." *For fuck's sake.* He just said the opposite of what he meant because of his use of double fucking negatives. "He was eighty-sixed."

Her eyebrows pinched together. "Eighty-sixed? I have to assume that your version isn't anything like mine."

Yeah, the meanings weren't even close. Once again proving how different the two of them were. "Your version sounds borin'. For us it means taking someone eight miles out and burying them six feet fuckin' under."

Her mouth dropped open. "Mine might be boring but yours sounds illegal. "

Stone cocked an eyebrow. "Ain't illegal if it never happened."

Her lips flattened out. "I'm sure the person being eighty-sixed would beg to differ."

"By that time, the beggin's over."

She pulled in an audible breath as she scrubbed her palm across her forehead. Her gaze sliced from him back to the house. To where her son was.

Stone got it. Her son just lost his father and would be upset when he found out. Even though Baby Bird didn't know all the truth about what a piece of shit his sperm donor had been.

The remains of his anger washed away. Everyone who belonged to him was now back together and safe. He needed to make sure it stayed that way.

"You don't look upset," he murmured.

Her blue eyes landed back on him. "Believe it not, I don't feel anything. What Vic did to Sunny was unforgivable. I'm sorry I told you to spare him in the first place. That was my mistake because I was trying to be the better person. Just like I hoped he would've learned his lesson in prison. Again, my mistake. His downward spiral was never going to reverse direction." She sighed. "Now my concern is with Wren and figuring out how to explain why he'll never see his father again. I'm going to have to lie about it."

No shit.

"Sure you'll come up with somethin'. Thinkin' you didn't tell him it was his father who took Sunny."

Taryn shook her head. "No. If possible, I never want him to know that. Maybe you can ask Sunny not to tell him, either."

"Doubt she put two and two together to figure out who he was. If she did, after she wakes up, gonna ask her to keep his name to herself. Can't guarantee she won't slip or he won't figure it the fuck out."

Her expression turned grim. "I'll deal with it if that happens." She placed her hands on her hips and glanced around. Like she was trying to avoid meeting his eyes. "In the meantime, it looks like my problem has been solved."

He wasn't liking how she said that. "This one, yeah."

"That means Wren and I will no longer need protection."

He definitely wasn't liking the direction this conversation

was headed. They had already discussed her staying so she could save more money. "From your ex, no."

"I can go back to living my life as it should be. I can find a new place and a new school for Wren."

Yeah, fuck that. She might still be bent about him being pissed earlier, but he'd had a damn good reason. "Nothin' wrong with the school he's in now."

"I would have to remain in the district for him to stay in that school."

"No point in movin' him, then. He likes it there." Wren also loved having a "sister." And Sunny was starting to enjoy having a "brother." She might try to hide it, but Stone could see right through his girl.

Taryn continued as if he hadn't said shit. "I'm not sure where I want to settle yet. Now that the cooking channel is going strong and my online classes are bringing in a decent amount of money, I can move my business anywhere."

For fuck's sake!

Almost everything he suggested or did for her made it possible for her to leave.

Taking care of her threat. His suggestion about doing the online classes...

He'd cut his own damn throat. A throat that was getting tighter by the second with her talk of leaving. "No."

She pulled in a breath and set her jaw. "Look—" She raised her palm to stop his next *no*, then finished with, "I appreciate everything you've done, but—"

"Fuck that shit. No buts."

Again, she continued like he hadn't even spoken. "I need to give my son a stable home and living with the VP of an outlaw motorcycle club isn't it. He's seen enough violence already and I don't want him exposed to more."

"Taryn," he growled.

"This was supposed to be temporary, remember?"

"Fuckin' know what we agreed to. You're supposed to help me with Sunny."

"Are you saying that you only want me to stay because of Sunny?"

Holy fuck, she just expertly backed him into a corner.

She outsmarted him.

She was trying to get him to admit *he* wanted her to stay. That their "arrangement" was no longer that. It was a relationship.

Jesus. He could kill a man and not miss a second of sleep, but the idea of being in a committed relationship made him fucking sweat. His heart was racing and his palms were getting clammy.

What the actual fuck?

"You only want me here to help with Sunny?" she asked again.

"Want you here..."

"For Sunny," she finished.

He squeezed his eyes shut. He should let her leave whenever she was ready. He didn't need a ball and chain. He didn't need to be tied down to one woman. A woman who would expect one hundred percent loyalty.

A soft "Got it" had him opening his eyes.

As she turned to head back to the house, he grabbed her arm and swung her back to face him. "No."

Her eyebrows jumped to her hairline. "No? No what?"

"Don't want you to go."

"You'll be able to find someone for—"

"For fuck's sake, Taryn! Don't want you to go."

"Because of Sunny."

He closed his eyes, and when he finally opened them again, he admitted, "'Cause of me."

. . .

"That had to hurt to admit."

"A little bit."

"So, you want to be with me? Or do you only want this to continue like I'm a house mouse with benefits?"

His jaw tightened. "You ain't a house mouse."

"When I heard what a house mouse was, it sounded exactly like this situation."

"Ain't a house mouse," he repeated.

"What am I, then?" She waited. One heartbeat. Two.

Ten.

Twenty.

She could see the man struggling. He had never been in any type of real relationship before. The only females in his life long-term had been his mother and his daughter.

He probably didn't recognize it for what it was despite the fact they'd been living as a family. Two parents. Two children. All they needed yet was a dog.

Taryn mentally rolled her eyes. They were far from a typical family. But so far, what they had created worked. In fact, it was working better than most families. Despite the fact he was an outlaw biker, their home life was less dysfunctional than most.

Less being the key word. But then, what family was completely normal?

Despite that, Taryn didn't hate it here. She actually liked it and it now felt like home. She had liked their arrangement. She liked both going to bed and waking up next to Stone. The sex was the best.

She loved how good he was with Wren.

She had a soft spot for Sunny, despite her taking so long to come around. They could continue to work on their relationship at the same time working through the trauma of what Vic did to her.

But if she stayed, she would need to do it for the right reasons. Because she and Stone had a deep connection. Not for only the kids or because the sex between them was great.

They would also need to figure out what to do about the bedroom situation. Sunny and Wren really needed their own rooms.

She knew Stone was capable of being loyal if he wanted to be. She saw how loyal he was to his club, to his brothers. But what she would not do was be in a relationship with someone who cheated.

Been there. Done that. Had the divorce to prove it.

She did not want to go through that again. Not ever.

She met his eyes and whispered, "What am I to you, Stone, if not a house mouse?"

She jumped when he suddenly went from frozen in place to jerking her hard against him. He dipped his head and took her mouth, sweeping his tongue through it.

Normally when he kissed her like that, she melted against him. But not today. She pulled free. "Don't try to avoid the question."

"Ain't avoidin' the question. Answerin' it."

"I refuse to make assumptions from a kiss." She needed to hear how he felt loud and clear. She did not want to make another disastrous decision.

He grabbed her shoulders firmly and kept his head tipped down to hers. "You wanna hear it? Fine, gonna say it. Don't want you to leave. Not 'cause of Sunny, 'cause of me. Want you here. Want you in my bed. Want you in my life. You're fuckin' mine, woman. No one else's. That's who you are. Mine."

Her lips parted and a soft puff of air escaped. *Holy shit.*

As much as she wanted all of that, wanted to throw caution to the wind, she also had to face reality and be completely honest with him about her reservations. "Stone, I'm not sure if this is the best situation for Wren and I."

"Only problem we had came from your motherfuckin' ex."

Maybe. But no relationship or situation was problem-free. Plus, they needed to consider the fact that Sheena wouldn't be in prison forever.

They might be dealing with this same scenario all over again once she was free. "Are you also going to eighty-six Sheena when she gets out?" She'd never think of that culinary term in the same way again.

"If she's a threat to me and mine, fuck yeah."

She blinked. Could she really love someone who had no issue with killing someone?

"She leaves us the fuck alone and realizes Sunny's better off with us, then no. You acted more like a mother to Sunny in the past few months than that bitch has been for the last ten years."

If so, that was sad. "Sunny deserves a good start in life."

"Yeah," he said softly, his grip on her shoulders loosening a bit. "And you'll help with that."

"So does Wren."

"Will do my best to give him that, too."

She believed him. It didn't take long for Wren to love Stone. She could argue it didn't take long for her, either. "Tell me what this all means."

"Means I want you to be my ol' lady."

Holy shit.

She was aware that being claimed by a King as an ol' lady was as good as a proposal. They were similar to wives but without the legal paperwork.

Did he really want to spend the rest of his life with her?

Wait. Did she really want to spend the rest of her life with him?

Taryn stared at the man that, with zero guilt, "eighty-sixed" her ex-husband probably not even an hour ago.

The sexy one with long, messy hair.

The one covered in tattoos.

The one wearing a leather cut that told the world he was an outlaw and didn't give a flying fuck what anyone thought about it. Including law enforcement.

The one who didn't even flinch when it came to snuffing out someone's life.

The one who'd never be fake or pretentious. What she saw was what she'd get.

If she accepted him, she'd have to accept the good, the bad, and the ugly.

And be able to live with herself.

Could she do that?

Did she love him enough to accept all facets of his lifestyle?

An invisible two-by-four smacked her across the forehead.

Holy shit, she did.

Chapter Thirty-Three

"Gonna say somethin'?"

"I'm processing it," she murmured.

Stone closed his eyes and shook his head. "Not a lot of processin' required. Just gotta answer yes or no."

"It wasn't a question but a statement."

He released a little growl. "Woman, want you to stay and be my ol' lady. But what I ain't gonna do is fuckin' beg. Want you to want it."

"I mean, can I get a minute to think about it? This would be a major change to my life."

His dark eyes flicked to the house before landing back on her. "Before you decide, need you to know somethin' else. Somethin' I don't wanna talk about in fronta the kids."

With him, it could be anything. But with his grim expression, whatever it was couldn't be good. She forced herself to swallow. "Okay."

"Told you about my brother, but there's other shit you need to know before you decide to become my ol' lady."

Why did she feel the need to brace herself?

He pulled a cigarette from inside his cut, plugged it between his lips, then dug around again until he pulled out a lighter. After lighting it, he blew the smoke up and away from them.

She hated that he smoked but that was minor compared to everything else the man did.

"Killed my own father."

With fingers pressed to her lips, she whispered, "What?" *Holy shit.* She didn't know what to expect but it certainly hadn't been that.

He frowned. "Ain't repeatin' it."

A rock dropped into her gut. "So then, why even bring it up?" She could've easily gone her whole life without knowing that.

"Want you to be one fuckin' hundred percent sure 'bout bein' my ol' lady. Don't want you sayin' yes, then realize you made a mistake down the fuckin' road and can no longer stand to even look at me."

Someone who murdered others without any remorse certainly didn't make the perfect significant other. Despite that, she was willing to hear him out. It wasn't like he was going out killing people because he was a psychopath and enjoyed it. He had a good reason. Or at least a reason he thought was good.

Whether others would see it that way was a different story.

She agreed that Vic reaped what he'd sown after taking Stone's daughter. She would've wanted to kill Vic herself if he had done the same thing with Wren.

But unlike Stone, could she go through with it?

How was any of this real life?

"Are you just going to drop that bomb and not explain?"

"Gonna tell you this once and once only. Fucker had

been drinkin' all night, his favorite hobby. Problem was, he was a nasty fuckin' drunk. Got pissed easily and even over shit that never happened. Broke my arm twice. Fucked up my older brother too many times to fuckin' count. My mother constantly lived in fear. For us and for herself. But she was trapped. She couldn't stay. She also couldn't leave. Fuckin' trapped," he repeated, his jaw working. "He told her if she left him, he'd track her down, kill my brother and me as punishment while makin' her watch. So, she stayed and took the brunt of his anger. To protect her own sons, she continued to be his punchin' bag."

After taking another long drag on his cigarette, Stone blew the smoke away from Taryn and continued. "Grew up thinkin' that kinda shit was normal. All fathers, husbands, were like that. A man was supposed to be the head of the household. Rule the roost. As I got older, I realized my mother had no friends, wasn't allowed to communicate with her family. He kept her isolated and under his fuckin' thumb." He took another pull on his cigarette. His head jerked to the right before saying, "Got home after school one day to find her unconscious, naked from the waist down, blood smeared on her inner thighs, face unrecognizable. He done a fuckin' number on her. Worst I ever saw."

She struggled to breathe as the memory of what Vic had done flooded her. It was bad enough for her to be hospitalized, and he was saying what happened to his mother was worse than that.

His Adam's apple rose, stuck there for a second, then dropped like a rock. "Found the fucker passed out in his recliner with a vodka bottle in one hand and a baseball game on the tube." He paused to take another pull on his cigarette, but once he exhaled a long stream of smoke, he simply stopped talking.

She waited anxiously to hear the rest. When it didn't come, she prodded, "And?" That couldn't be it.

"That's where this story ends."

She pulled in a breath. *Bullshit.* "You mean that's where *his* story ends."

"Yeah. Don't need to hear the fuckin' details. Just like I ain't gonna share what happened to your ex. Just know they both got what was comin' to 'em." He dropped the remainder of the still-smoking cigarette to the driveway and ground it out with his boot. "Shoulda figured this out by now but got a thing about motherfuckers puttin' their hands on females. I see that problem, gonna solve it."

"Obviously. You solved it that day in the parking lot. You also solved it today." She shouldn't be relieved that Wren's father was dead, but truthfully, she was. Was she a bad person for thinking that way?

At this point, she didn't care if she was. Vic got what was coming to him, which was a generous helping of karma.

"Need to know if you're gonna be able to deal with that kinda shit."

She considered him. If she wanted to be with Stone, she needed to completely accept him for who he was and his life-style for what it was. If she couldn't deal with the way he handled problems, she needed to leave. This was not a half in, half out situation. That wouldn't be fair to Stone, or even the kids.

She also needed to remember the man spent over a year in prison for her without expecting anything in return. If she hadn't tracked him down, he never would've searched her out to collect. He would've simply done his time and moved on.

Who else would've stopped Vic that day?

So many other people witnessed what happened at the popular shopping center and not one other person stepped in.

Not one.

Stone wasn't a white knight.

He was a dark King.

And, *holy shit*, she loved him for who he was. For stepping in to help a woman he didn't know. For how much he loved his daughter, despite them butting heads. For how much he cared about a six-year-old boy who wasn't his blood.

He didn't have to open his house to her and Wren, but he did. He took on that burden without complaint.

Her heart ached simply at the thought of leaving him and Sunny. Of breaking up their unlikely family.

Of never waking up next to Stone again.

Of never feeling his mouth on her. Of never feeling his hand spread possessively pressed to the small of her back. Or his heated eyes raking over her, causing every part of her to tingle.

Or his elusive smile pointed her way, making her heart swell.

"Do I have a choice?"

One side of his mouth pulled up. "Not if you wanna be my ol' lady. Gonna come with the territory."

"Then I guess I'll deal."

Both sides of his mouth were now hiked up. "Good choice."

She hoped so. Time would tell.

What a crazy last few months. She'd gone from a personal chef and single mother, trying to make ends meet, to running successful online cooking tutorials and soon, to becoming a biker's ol' lady.

"Will I get to wear a Property of Stone cut?"

He snorted softly. "Damn right you will. Gotta tell every other motherfucker out there you belong to me."

"How do I tell the world that you belong to me?"

He gifted her with one of those heart-stopping smiles. "By wearin' that fuckin' cut."

At first she thought the cuts the women wore were oppressive. Now she couldn't wait to put his on. Would she wear it all of the time? Of course not. But like his brothers' ol' ladies, she'd be fine with wearing it on the club runs. And maybe around The Castle to remind the other women that Stone was off the market.

He was hers.

All hers.

And unlike Vic, Stone would do whatever was needed to keep her and Wren safe. Even if that meant going back to prison. Not that she wanted that.

The kids needed him.

So did she.

She tipped her head toward the house. "We should check on the kids."

And once Sunny woke up, encourage her to join Taryn and Wren in the kitchen. She could try to distract Sunny—at least for a little while—by maybe teaching Stone's daughter to make cookies. It would be a simple, but fun, bonding activity for all of them. Taryn hoped it would lead to Sunny eventually feeling comfortable enough to talk to her about anything. Even what Vic did to her.

"Yeah." When he offered her his hand, she took it, interlocking their fingers. But instead of immediately heading toward the house, he once again yanked her into him, pressing their chests together and giving her another thorough kiss. He squeezed her ass firmly, murmuring against her lips, "That's mine."

"That's yours," she agreed, then leaned back enough to see his face. "You need to promise me something."

"What?"

"No sweet butts." She did not want a repeat of what had happened with Vic. Not today, not tomorrow. Not ever.

"Woman, ain't fucked a sweet butt since the day you were brave enough to walk into The Castle, surprisin' the shit outta me. After that, had no eyes for anybody but you."

Holy shit.

She hadn't expected that confession. But... "Having an ol' lady hasn't stopped some of your brothers from doing the same." With all the time spent at The Castle, she had witnessed quite a few of them cheat time and time again. And they didn't care who saw it.

She also saw some of the ol' ladies fight with the sweet butts over it. Taryn did not want to deal with that drama.

In fact, she refused to.

"See this?" He pointed to his name patch with a long, tattooed finger. "What's that say?"

"Stone."

"Right. Ain't my bothers. Know what Vic the Dick did to you. Ain't gonna do the same."

"You swear?" Could he really stick to one woman? "I don't think I could deal with being betrayed again, Stone."

"Babe, I fuck up, gonna hand you my knife and gonna let you cut off my fuckin' dick, yeah?"

She shouldn't laugh at that, but she couldn't help it. "Yeah."

"Just don't cut it off 'cause of some stupid misunderstandin'. Kinda would like to keep it attached. Can't fuck you without it."

She elbowed him. "Then don't get caught in a situation that might be misunderstood."

"But if you ever want one to join us..."

"Stone!" She tried to pull her hand from his, but he clutched it tighter.

On a chuckle, he said, "Always an option." He tugged on her hand. "C'mon, let's go."

As they walked down the driveway, she asked, "By the way, how'd you get rid of the body?" He had mentioned he was in school at the time. That meant he had to be pretty young when it happened. How would a kid know what to do afterward?

"Which body?"

She had to lengthen her stride to keep up with his. "Your father's."

"Not sure what you mean. Far as I know, my sperm donor went out for milk and never came home. Guess he didn't want the responsibility of a family no more."

"Oh. I—"

"Don't ask that shit again," he said softly. "About my father or Baby Bird's. Ain't anythin' you need to know. Same as club business. If there's somethin' you need to know, gonna tell you. You don't, I won't. Better to be clueless in case shit ever goes down with the pigs."

She nodded. "Got it."

Good lord, she was really going to live the biker life.

Willingly.

It wasn't a life she would've ever chosen, but it just happened to be tied to the man she did choose.

Some might tell her this would be a big mistake. Hopefully, she'd made enough of them to know that this time it wouldn't be.

It seemed different this time.

The idea of spending the rest of her life with this man settled her soul.

Fate had led Stone to her in that parking lot. Fate had led Taryn to find him at The Castle.

She had to trust in fate.

Epilogue

When The Stone Stops Rolling

"ALL RIGHT. I'm heading over to The Castle to shoot some new tutorials and catch up on a couple of meal prep orders. I also have a private dinner scheduled at five. Can you run the kids to and from school today?"

Stone's eyes tracked her as she talked and walked at the same time. Without stopping, she disappeared out the bedroom door.

What the fuck?

"Yo!"

She peeked her blonde head back around the door. Her blue eyes were wide. "What?"

This better be a fucking joke. "Forget somethin'?" he grumbled and pulled himself up into a seated position against the headboard.

Her brow furrowed. "No?"

"Sure?"

"I guess not." One eyebrow rose. "Is it important?"

Was she fucking serious? "Fuck yeah, it is."

She came around the door with a confused expression. "What did I forget?"

Apparently, a reminder was needed. "What do I own?"

"A Harley? An old truck?" She shot him a bright smile that woke up his dick. "My heart?"

He liked hearing that last one but it wasn't the answer he was looking for. He curled his index finger in a *come here* motion. "Mouth."

She came over, leaned in and did a light lip touch.

"Woman," he growled, grabbing her hips and pulling her off balance and on top of him.

He smothered her squeal with a much more dick-hardening kiss. One that made her cling to him and fill his mouth with her moan.

Fuck yeah.

He should try to convince her to stay in bed all day with him, but that would be a failed mission. The woman was determined that they pay off the addition and the improvements they did to his mother's house. Now theirs, of course. The kids each had their own rooms now, along with a new family room to avoid arguments on who was watching what on TV.

The house still wasn't huge but it worked for them.

When he released her mouth, he put his lips to her ear. "Know what else I own?" He grabbed a tit and squeezed. "These." He cupped her cunt over her pants. "This pussy. And..." He smacked her ass next. "Workin' on buyin' that ass."

Her giggle made him smile. "It isn't for sale."

He cocked an eyebrow at her. Challenge accepted. "Sure 'bout that?"

She rolled her eyes. "You bikers sure do expect women to fall to their knees at your feet."

"Nope. Just you. And when you're down there, expect you to be suckin' my dick."

He drove his fingers into her hair on both sides of her head and forcefully yanked her head back. He dropped his and their gazes locked. "'Bout that heart thing..."

She told him she loved him too many times to count. But he could never hear it enough.

He never thought he'd find a woman he'd want to hand his heart to. But with Taryn, he had ripped it out of his chest and offered it to her on a silver fucking platter.

"What about it?"

"Ain't just a piece of meat to you?"

She tapped his cheek. "You've never only been a piece of meat to me. But I do like your meat." She wiggled her eyebrows and squeezed his sheet-covered hard-on.

"You haven't had breakfast yet," he reminded her. "How 'bout a breakfast sausage?"

"I'll eat something at The Castle. I have a long list of things to do today. That also means you need to make sure the kids get breakfast."

"Woman, I need to eat, too." He could go for chowing down on a piece of pussy pie.

He rolled her over and pinned her on her back, settling between her legs, his favorite spot, but it would be better if she was naked. Fuck it, he'd take what he could get.

He'd fucked plenty of holes in his lifetime and none had developed into any kind of attachment. He rarely spent more than the time it took to bust a nut. Even Sheena was only supposed to be a quick fuck. Unfortunately, that backfired.

But what he had with Taryn was so damn different. The unexpected connection had grabbed him by the balls and had never let go.

Over a year after she hunted him down, he still couldn't

get enough of her. He never thought the day he witnessed her ass getting beaten would eventually change his outlook on getting an ol' lady.

But here he was.

Hell, here *they* were.

Both of them pretty damn happy, as well as content.

Even better, he didn't feel like he was being tripped up by a ball and chain.

"About that heart thing..." He slowly unbuttoned her chef's jacket so he could get to eating *his* breakfast.

"What about it?"

"Did I break it?"

A smile flirted with her lips. "No."

"Then, what about it?"

"You already know."

Stone tapped his ear. "Nope. Need to hear it."

She dragged her thumb across his lips. "You make my heart whole."

"Not sure how I do that."

"Simply by being you."

"You mean a badass biker?" he teased.

"I have to admit, that part's kind of sexy. But no. Despite you being rough and gruff, you're a great father."

He was hardly a great father but he did his fucking best.

"And a supportive ol' man," she added.

Ol' man. He liked the sound of that.

He swore every time she slipped on her Property of Stone cut, he got an instant hard-on. Her wearing it was sexy as fuck.

Especially when she was naked. In their bedroom, of fucking course.

"You're a great mom. 'Cause of you, Sunny now smiles

and laughs instead of being a fuckin' grumpy, argumentative nut nugget."

His ol' lady had gone above and beyond to bond with his stubborn girl. It was a slow, bumpy path, but her persistence finally paid off.

Thankfully, every time Sheena raised her nasty head, Stone only had to toss some scratch her way and she quickly hid back under her damn rock and left them alone.

Sheena didn't want to raise their kid. Feeding her addiction was her priority.

Crazy how some parents thought scratch was more important than their own damn kids. Luckily, Taryn wasn't one of them.

And he loved her for that.

She whispered, "I wish you'd stop calling them nut nuggets."

He grinned. "Ain't gonna happen."

She sighed.

"Want one with you."

Her blue eyes went wide. She breathed, "Stone..."

"Don't want another?"

"You do?"

"Yeah. This time I get to pick my kid's mother."

Her smile was gone and she stared up at him. "And you choose me."

"Damn right I do. Yeah?"

"I don't know. Can I process it first?"

"You and your fuckin' processin'. Can we practice while you process?"

"Meh. I guess so."

"Don't act like it's a sacrifice. Know you love my dick."

"I love the man attached to it, too."

"Not sure why."

"Me either."

He huffed out a laugh. "Smart asses get spanked."

"No one said I'm smart."

"Hooked up with me. I'd call that smart."

"I'd call that desperate."

With a playful growl, he finished opening her chef's coat and shoved up the tank top she wore under it, nipping at her tits.

She wiggled and giggled underneath him.

He loved that fucking sound. Just like he loved hearing his daughter laughing while learning to cook in the kitchen with Taryn or playing a game with Baby Bird.

Or all of them sitting together watching some dumb, but funny, movie.

His girl now had a good future.

Hell, they all did.

It was mind-blowing how quickly his life had changed.

They'd gone from temporarily sharing a bed and roof to sharing a life together. They'd created a family.

A real fucking family.

One he'd never take for granted.

And would die to protect.

Because nobody—absolutely nobody—fucked with the Kings.

※

Sign up for Jeanne's newsletter to learn about her upcoming releases, sales and more! https:// www.authorjeannestjames.com/

※

Despite spilled blood and broken bones, Blood Fury will rise from the cold ashes left behind...

Trip, son of the former president of the Blood Fury MC, is determined to resurrect his dead father's destroyed club. It'll be a long, difficult road as the new president attempts to rebuild the club from the cold ashes left behind.

Bad blood and bitter memories are only some of the obstacles Trip has to overcome. The local police department, Manning Grove PD, is another, since they don't want to see their small town once again overrun by outlaw bikers.

Then there's Stella, a local bar owner and a major distraction Trip doesn't need, but can't resist, even though she gives him every reason to. She's tough, she's broken, and the last thing she wants in her life is a man like him.

In the end, Trip has to decide if the war is worth fighting. And if Stella is the warrior he needs battling by his side.

**Turn the page to read the prologue of
Blood & Bones: Trip (Blood Fury MC, book 1)**

Blood & Bones: Trip
Blood Fury MC, Book 1

*"Sometimes you have to burn yourself to the ground
before you can rise like a phoenix from the ashes." ~ Jens
Lekman*

Prologue
Turn the key

Trip stood in the middle of the deserted building, shaking
his head, wondering if it was worth the fucking hassle to start
the club back up. To reclaim its territory.

But what other fucking choice did he have?

He'd already had it set in his mind, not only to do it, but
to do it right this time.

He wouldn't let his father's club, which died a violent
death, just remain a memory. And a bad one at that.

But now that he had done his time in the Marines, done
his time in prison, he needed something.

Because he had nothing.

Except his granddaddy's run-down farm, a barn full of

farm equipment he had no clue how to use and didn't want to, and the abandoned warehouse he was currently standing in on the outskirts of town.

While he was in prison, his lawyer had shown up and read him his granddaddy's will.

Yeah. He got everything.

Sig got nothing.

Trip was sure his brother wasn't happy about that, if he even knew.

But most likely Granddaddy had made up the will when Trip was still doing time in the service and not doing it behind bars. Unlike Sig who had been in and out of county jail, or the state pen, off and on since he turned eighteen.

But now here he stood. In an empty building, feeling fucking overwhelmed. But still, it was something.

And something was better than nothing.

He also had new ink on his back and an old cut in his hand.

The leather was worn, the rockers and patches on it dirty. All except one.

One rectangular patch on the front had been torn off by his own fingers after using the point of his buck knife to loosen the threads. The patch that used to say "Buck" was now replaced with one that said "Trip." But above it, the patch that had deemed Buck as president remained. That now belonged to Trip.

He'd also used that same knife to remove the 1% diamond patch off the back. He wouldn't need that one anymore.

The club used to be outlaw. But Trip was determined to keep it above board. For the most part.

He'd spent many a night down in Shadow Valley talking with the members of the Dirty Angels MC, soaking up everything their prez named Z told him. Learning how to rebuild

Blood Fury stronger than ever. How to keep the money flowing into the club's coffers.

One way to do that was to keep the members out of prison and, even better, keep them breathing.

Dead or incarcerated members weren't any good to a club.

And there had been too many of those in the Blood Fury MC in the past. It had been its downfall.

Trip didn't want that mistake to happen again.

So, they had to play the game. Keep shit on the up and up as best as they could. Become a powerful force, strong enough to withstand the occasional bump in the road.

He had no fucking clue how he was going to pull it off, but he would take the advice he was given and do his fucking best.

He scrubbed a hand through his long hair before tucking it up under his baseball cap, blowing out a loud breath and shrugging on his cut.

His cut.

It wasn't his father's any longer.

This club was no longer his father's, either.

This world, even as broken as it was, now belonged to Trip.

It was his and he wouldn't let anyone destroy it again.

The Fury was about to rise once more. This time stronger and smarter.

Get Trip and Stella's story here:
https://buy.bookfunnel.com/figo5glb5o

If You Enjoyed This Book

Thank you for reading Property of Stone. If you enjoyed Stone and Taryn's story, please consider leaving a review at your favorite retailer and/or Goodreads to let other readers know. Reviews are always appreciated and just a few words can help an independent author like me tremendously!

Want to read a sample of my work? Download a sampler book here: BookHip.com/MTQQKK

Also by Jeanne St. James

Find my complete reading order here:

https://www.jeannestjames.com/reading-order

Buy direct from the author here: https:// jeannestjamesauthor.com

<u>Standalone Books:</u>

<u>Made Maleen: A Modern Twist on a Fairy Tale</u>

<u>Damaged</u>

<u>Rip Cord: The Complete Trilogy</u>

Everything About You (A Second Chance Gay Romance)

Reigniting Chase (An M/M Standalone)

Property of Stone (Kings of Anarchy MC: Pennsylvania)

<u>Brothers in Blue Series</u>

A four-book series based around three brothers who are small-town cops and former Marines

<u>The Dare Ménage Series</u>

A six-book MMF, interracial ménage series

<u>The Obsessed Novellas</u>

A collection of five standalone BDSM novellas

<u>Down & Dirty: Dirty Angels MC®</u>

A ten-book motorcycle club series

<u>Guts & Glory: In the Shadows Security</u>

A six-book former special forces series

(A spin-off of the Dirty Angels MC)

Blood & Bones: Blood Fury MC®

A twelve-book motorcycle club series

Motorcycle Club Crossovers:

Crossing the Line: A DAMC/Blue Avengers MC Crossover

Magnum: A Dark Knights MC/Dirty Angels MC Crossover

Crash: A Dirty Angels MC/Blood Fury MC Crossover

Romeo: A Dark Knights MC/Blood Fury MC Crossover

Beyond the Badge: Blue Avengers MC™

A six-book law enforcement/motorcycle club series

Double D Ranch

A six-book MMF ménage series

COMING SOON!

Dirty Angels MC®: The Next Generation

WRITING AS J.J. MASTERS:

The Royal Alpha Series

A five-book gay mpreg shifter series

About the Author

JEANNE ST. JAMES is a USA Today, Amazon and international bestselling romance author who loves writing about strong women and alpha males. She was only thirteen when she first started writing and her first published piece was an erotic short story in Playgirl magazine. She then went on to publish her first romance novel in 2009. She is now an author of almost 70 contemporary romances. She writes M/F, M/M, and M/M/F ménages, including interracial romance. She also writes M/M paranormal romance under the name: J.J. Masters.

Want to read a sample of her work? Download a sampler book here: BookHip.com/MTQQKK

Buy ebooks and audiobooks directly from the author here: https://jeannestjamesauthor.com

www.jeannestjames.com

Newsletter: https://www.authorjeannestjames.com/
Jeanne's Down & Dirty Book Crew: https://www.facebook.com/groups/JeannesReviewCrew/

facebook.com/JeanneStJamesAuthor

instagram.com/JeanneStJames

bookbub.com/authors/jeanne-st-james

goodreads.com/JeanneStJames